MURDER IN MERMAID CITY

WILLIAM O. HARRIS III

Copyright © 2013 William O. Harris III

ISBN: **0989703800**

ISBN-13: **978-0989703802**

AUTHOR'S NOTE

The book is a work of fiction set in Norfolk, Virginia (Mermaid City) using quoted articles from The Virginian-Pilot archives to support a September-October, 2006 timeline. As background characters **I've fictitiously used the 'given names' of**: Virginia Zoo animals and a few zoo employees; several local businesses and some of their employees; plus many friends who helped shape the story and encourage my effort… However the main characters; their names, viewpoints, description, dialogue and action; are all taken from my imagination and any of their resemblance to actual people or events is entirely coincidental. The story was conceived and written while I volunteered at The Virginia Zoo as both an Education Docent and a Keeper's Aide.

DEDICATION

This book is dedicated to **John Raymond Brandon and Andres Rene Bacuzzi,** two dear friends and long-time advisors to my wife Amy and my self. **John** and **Andy** are sadly missed by their wives and families, their many friends and business associates, and their former compatriots-in-arms during their honorable service to The United States of America. May GOD bless you both and may HE now forever enjoy the friendship, dedication of service and generosity of spirit you both brought into our lives.

ADDITIONAL RECOGNITION

My thoughts and prayers are with **Monica and Keana**, two Virginia Zoo animals featured in the story that passed away before the book's completion.

PROLOGUE

SEPTEMBER 11, 2001

09:18 EST, NORTHEAST AIR DEFENSE SECTOR

The Deputy Director rose from his desk to confront his boss as he hurried into the Central Control Room. "Boss, we've got to get our birds in the air, this thing's turning bad! We don't know what's happening yet, but we need eyes in the sky now!"

"We go through the military for that, you know they have the Attack Authority," The Director began, but his deputy interrupted,

"That's wrong Boss!" He stated as he slammed his NEADS OPERATIONS MANUAL down on his desk, "I've checked it out, The National Command Authority is responsible for giving the 'Shoot-Down Order', that can come later, but we need OUR birds up RIGHT NOW!"

The Director reached for the manual to check his deputy's assessment, but thought better of causing further delay and said, "OK, you're right, call Otis and Langley, tell them to LAUNCH!"

09:28 EST, LANGLEY AIR FORCE BASE

As two USAF F-16s fast-taxied to the active runway as Langley's Tower Operator transmitted, "Fury 41 Flight cleared immediate takeoff Runway 09 - Maintain heading - Cleared unrestricted climb to Flight Level Two Five Zero - Contact Langley Departure on Channel 7 when airborne."

"Roger Langley, this drill an Exercise?" Fury 41's flight leader transmitted,

"Negative 41 - I repeat, NEGATIVE - Langley OUT."

The NEADS Alert Klaxon that scrambled the two alert-pilots eleven minutes ago still echoed in the second pilot, Fury 42's head, forcing her to yawn and stretch her jaw muscles as she tried to clear the resonant rattle from her inner ear canal. Now taking the runway, 42 lined up on her leader's right wing and heard him broadcast,

"Fury 41 AB now - Rolling at three zero Langley – 42, go Channel 7 airborne."

"Roger," 42 acknowledged watching her lead's afterburner section plume an instantaneous flame, then she felt her own AB ignite and heard the welcomed *WHOOMP* noise from her jet's own raw fuel ignition. Immediately the vibration impact surrounded her senses and brought back the welcomed 'kick to her butt' as her bird accelerated down the active runway.

Airborne, landing gear up and airspeed increasing through 300 Knots, 42 switched her radio to Channel 7. Thirty seconds later the flight leveled at 25,000 feet and 400 Knots and 42 moved her bird into a loose look-out formation as she began to visually clear the surrounding area. First she concentrated her protective scan eastward, above the vast Atlantic Ocean, where enemy attacks had been forecast to originate. Now comfortably in position 42's eyes momentarily focused downward to an inbound container ship's image as it appeared under the pointed edge of her aircraft's nose then slid rearward along her canopy rail as she heard through the radio,

"Fury 41 Flight, Departure Control - Turn left to three four zero and Contact Washington Center this frequency."

"Roger, Departure -" Fury 41 replied before he broadcast, "41 Flight coming left to 340 - Steep turn 42 - GO WEAPONS GREEN,", followed immediately by "Washington Center, Fury 41, flight of two F-16's out of Langley at Flight Level Two Five Zero, heading three four zero and 400 Knots - OUR WEAPONS ARE HOT."

When 42 heard her leader warn a 'steep turn' and direct 'WEAPONS GREEN', she selected WEAPONS SYSTEM ON and rolled her F-16 into a 90 degree bank-left, added full-power and backpressure to her side-mounted control stick as she crossed rapidly behind the leader's aircraft. While turning, 42 thought, what the hell can be happening?

Once 42 steadied her bird and focused her visual concentration northward toward Washington DC and her eyes began to search the crystal clear September morning sky, Ray Bradbury's story, "Something Wicked This Way Comes", spiked her memory causing her jumbled thoughts to add; there's something bad out there and I'd better get ready for it...

10:30 PM LOCAL, BEIJING, CHINA

The General Secretary of the Chinese Communist Party instructed his committee members as he waited for expected news, "We must proceed carefully in all we now attempt. We must cross new-rivers of opportunity with caution, treading on available stones; one stone at a time..." He paused reflectively then added, "But our footing must be assured and we must remain vigilant for each new path of opportunity to arrive on the distant shore of our success."

The General Secretary's speech was interrupted when an assistant passed a folded message to him. After scanning the expected message contents the General Secretary relayed the information to his committee and announced,

"The City of New York has just been attacked by terrorists."

Hearing the General Secretary's announcement, his Special Operations Director removed the printed Execution Order for 'Operation Deep Dragon' and showed it to the General Secretary. The General Secretary clearly recalled the secret program's specifics and nodded his head in approval.

CHAPTER ONE

NORFOLK, VIRGINIA

SATURDAY MORNING SEPTEMBER 23, 2006

Staring at his blank computer screen, Wilber Harrington was anxious for the pages of his new book to come together as chapters before smoothly uniting to tell his story. Wilber visualized his new book, 'Pacific Secret', to be an art gallery filled with exciting story-pictures he'd create and display for future visitors... But so far this morning, that wasn't happening. In his earlier book Wilber had been more fortunate; once his story characters were defined and released into his peculiar plot; they had performed independently and produced sustainable action... But now, while his muddled mind and tired eyes watched the pulsating cursor at the top of a blank page 167, he reluctantly admitted there was no story-picture developing here. Wilber forced the throat-choking clutch of 'writer's block' from his mind and tried his coffee. Sadly, both story and coffee had gone cold.

Wilber had been methodically reviewing his chapter outline and lengthy research notes while trying to structure his twelfth chapter, but his efforts had produced very little success. As an unschooled writer he was often forced to edit numerous drafts by measuring his words with an internal micrometer, marking excessive words for deletion with his broad-pointed chalk, then removing his redacted words by swinging a blunt-bladed editorial ax... Now stymied Wilber admitted aloud,

"It's been a Ready, Fire, Aim process..." His declaration was interrupted by his wife Sally's grandfather clock and he counted the ten *GONGS* of mid-morning before deciding to take a much needed coffee break. Rising up from the antique desk, Sally had also inherited from her parents, Wilber stretched his back and headed to the kitchen barefoot and wearing the dark blue navy sweatpants and khaki Virginia Zoo Volunteer T-shirt, he had slept in. "I definitely need better planning... But right now I need some hot, mind focusing caffeine."

Ideas are easy, Wilber's thoughts persisted as he shuffled toward the kitchen, but fleshing-in around the idea-bones; to give the book a real life; seems to be my problem... Maybe swinging my editorial ax so aggressively has cut out too much character background, "I'll check on that," He announced as he paused in the den to observe his vast water-view to the north of their Lakewood property. Focusing a pair of binoculars on a small boat and fisherman tending crab-pots on the eastern branch of Norfolk's Lafayette River, Wilber recalled how in 1890 this section of the river existed solely as a tidal-marsh, often used by enterprising locals to hide bootlegged contraband. Later in 1896, the newly designated City of Norfolk, Virginia, chose to curtail their 'citizen-bootlegging' and dredged the marsh to create the now tidally-navigable river-extension. As he watched the fisherman; a short heavyset man in a fish-stained t-shirt, bib overalls and high-top rubber boots; the crabber moved his boat from one crab-pot marker to another, stopping only to pull up a connecting line and raise the crab trap for inspection. Wilber could see the few crabs exposed in the wire mesh cages were not moving; probably dead from contamination at the bottom of the river... A river long polluted by the lawn fertilized and nitrogen infused storm water run-off from Lakewood's many homes. The crab traps had become death traps, "Definitely a burial at sea", Wilber muttered to himself, commenting on crab deaths and his own curtailed career in the US Navy. Discarding his disappointments, observed and experienced, Wilber resumed his travel to the kitchen where his thoughts of poor crabbing, a shortened navy career and a stagnant storyline, needed to be put-on-hold. Pouring himself a fresh hot cup of the strong coffee his wife Sally had purchased in Germany last week, he sat at their counter island and gathered in the Saturday morning newspaper. Wilber opened the Hampton Roads Section of The Virginian-Pilot and read how:

Two Sheriff's Deputies, in nearby Portsmouth, Virginia were forced to resign for using inmate labor for personal chores...

Wilber took a second sip of coffee and thought of his wife Sally's older brother, Stephen Irons, who had also been forced to retire from the Norfolk Sheriff's Department, "But, under far different circumstances." Wilber corrected his thoughts that were quickly *JANGLED* away by the kitchen phone ringing. He checked the ID read-out that indicated Sally was calling from her cell phone and tapped the ANSWER button to activate the SPEAKER function, "Hi, Sally, how's the trip going?"

"It's great Will, we're at the Beer Factory in Mainz, better send me more Euros!" Sally's joking reply came back through the speaker. In the background noise Wilber heard chattering Germans and one laughing American voice he recognized,

"Check's in the mail, Sally. Is that Maribeth leading you astray again?"

"Yeah Will, she and Margo traded a Paris run to fly on my Frankfurt trip. It's been an old-home-week-reunion for us." Sally said.

As Wilber listened he remembered Sally flying with Maribeth and Margo when they all lived in San Diego, California, before he and Sally moved to Norfolk four years ago. The three 'Beach Bitches', as they had labeled themselves, bid to fly their trips each month from San Diego to Hawaii to enjoy Honolulu's white sandy beaches. Now they all flew international together, but out of DFW in Dallas, Texas, where American Airlines' largest permanent home base was located. Wilber specifically recalled Margo, the sexy raven-haired friend of Sally's that had 'hit on him' just after he and Sally became engaged. Wilber was certain Margo's half- effort had been a loyalty-test to see if he was worthy of marrying her friend Sally and he had passed that test. Margo and Maribeth still lived in San Diego and commuted to fly their trips out of DFW, just as Sally now commuted from Norfolk to Dallas.

Wilber's memory shot forward to a July trip when he accompanied the three flight attendants on another Frankfurt trip. During that flight Margo noticed him working on his book ideas and insisted he use her lap top computer to transfer all his hand written book notes,

Discarding both memories Wilber said "Hey Sally isn't it hard for three 'California Beach Bitches' to get any real recognition in Germany?"

"Don't think so Will, Margo has the bartender wrapped around her little finger, I'm sure we'll get a plane load of 'recognition' when she's through with him. Hey, how's your 'Pacific' book coming? Have you killed-off all your characters?"

Wilber chuckled at Sally's idea of his developing storyline. But, unlike several of his other book-projects, he had chosen to keep this one very secret, sharing details only with his new Literary Representative in San Diego by providing the book's premise, plot and storyline along with a complete chapter outline and his ten earliest chapters. Wilber hoped his new agent, Mr. Cecil Li, would get a publisher interested in the book so he replied,

"Not yet, Sally, I'm waiting for feed-back from a publisher before I murder more than half the cast. My agent said I should receive something soon," Wilber stopped speaking as a UPS truck pulled into their circular driveway, "Hold on Sally, the book info may be here now."

"That's great Will, but I've got to go, the bartender's pouring more beer. See you Sunday night. Love you Will." Sally added closing the connection and prompting Wilber to tap the OFF button as *THUMP, THUMP, THUMP* resounded from the side kitchen door.

"Be right there," Wilber yelled as his heart raced and a shot of adrenaline hit him reminding him of his last submarine cruise, "That was a ball-buster", Wilber mumbled as he saw the UPS guy standing by the door. The guy's physical appearance; 6'2", about 220 pounds, broad shoulders, big, gloved hands and a craggy Asian-like face had eyes hidden behind dark, reflective sunglasses. He could become a minor character-villain in the book, Wilber thought as he opened the door.

In his right hand the delivery guy carried a large plastic bucket, holding it by its long metal-handle. Wilber could see the bucket was heavy, the handle deep cut into the surface of the guy's leather glove. In his left hand the guy held a receipt book and a manila envelope. "Good morning, what's in the bucket?" Wilber joked.

"I have a delivery for Mr. Wilber Harrington, the bucket goes next door." The UPS man said as presented the envelope to Wilber.

"I'm Wilber Harrington," Wilber announced, reaching for the envelope.

You must sign first," the guy said then added, "Oh, sorry, forgot my pen,"

"I've got one," Wilber prompted and turned to go back in the kitchen. The delivery guy followed into the house as he removed a silenced 22 caliber revolver from his right cargo pant's pocket. He placed the envelope and receipt book on a nearby counter before catching Wilber by the right shoulder, forcing him to turn.

The assassin quickly pushed the silenced gun-barrel to the right side of Wilber's head and fired one shot, *CRACK,* the weapon made a slight noise, like a small, dry twig breaking.

Wilber's eyes first looked stunned then they rolled back in his head as he lamented, "No, no, not now," then, his left hand grabbed at the killer's uniform shirt before he collapsed dead on his kitchen floor.

CHAPTER TWO

THE BEER FACTORY, MAINZ, GERMANY

SEPTEMBER 23, 6:00PM LOCAL

"Will says hi," Sally announced as she approached the bar and sat down next to Maribeth. Sally looked around for Margo as she began to tie her long red hair into a loose pony tail. Sally fixed her bright hazel eyes on Maribeth and added, "He's working on a new book and hopes to hear from a publisher soon,"

"What's the new book about?" Maribeth asked as they both sipped the restaurant's dark German lager.

Sally smiled, brushed a small amount of lace-like foam from her upper lip and said, "Not sure 'MB' a foreign mystery, maybe the CIA... Will's fascinated with that kind of intrigue now. But, he hasn't shared that much with me. I guess he's still 'freaked out' about his first book's publisher going bankrupt so he had to self-published. I guess he could have talked with my brother, they've gotten close since Stephen got out of the hospital,"

"Hospital, oh yeah, from getting shot, right?" Maribeth interjected then she began looking around for the bartender Margo had been talking to, but he was gone too. A young German girl was working behind the bar and Maribeth turned her attention to the girl, "Hey, Fraulein, where's your bartender?"

"Gone with your friend, they go for dinner, maybe more." The girl said then she laughed, rolled her eyes and dramatically flipped her long twisted braid of palomino-hair as she performed a military snap-turn and marched to the other end of the bar.

"Can you beat that? Margo just left us." Maribeth said to Sally, who began rocking her head from side to side mocking the female bartender by swinging her own pony tail back and forth. Maribeth laughed at the mockery and added, "That's funny, Sally. You want to eat here, or go back to the hotel?"

"Let's stay here, the hotel's 'Cave Restaurant' will be crowded with flight-crews and I love the schnitzel here too, Margo can take care of herself." Sally added, as they walked to a nearby table and looked for a waiter. "You wanted to know about Stephen right?" Sally said as they both sat down.

"Eh, yeah, when was he shot?" Maribeth asked.

"Six months ago 'MB', he stayed in the hospital for a month or so but he's out now. The Sheriff medically retired him in May, so now he's bored just doing nothing. Will and I got him involved with exercise-walking at The Virginia Zoo,"

"The zoo, what does Stephen know about a zoo? He was in the navy, then, a sheriff's deputy, right?" Maribeth interrupted then she turned to the approaching waiter and demanded, "Hey, Mien Herr, we need some cold white wine, your beer's too heavy!"

The waiter looked surprised, but responded, "Our beer is zee best, Madam!" Then he turned to a nearby wine cooler and withdrew a locally labeled bottle of German Riesling, returned to the table and in a remarkable presentation extracted the cork and twisted the plastic cap-covering back around the cork, re-affixed the cork to the top of the bottle and smiled as he poured the thick, icy wine into two chilled glasses adding, "And for zee dinner please,"

"We'll both have Pork Schnitzel," Maribeth said, then added, "my treat, Sally, you paid last time."

During dinner Sally and Maribeth talked about their careers as Flight Attendants for American Airlines and their great times in California with many exciting trips to Japan, Hawaii and Australia. When they finished the meal they both complimented the waiter, who finally, seemed appreciative. It was almost time to head back to their hotel but Margo hadn't returned so Sally asked,

"Do you think Margo is alright? Now I'm worried going back to the hotel without her being here."

"Oh, don't worry about Margo she's probably already at the hotel. If not, she certainly knows her way around Mainz and all the German men. Actually, I don't know any man's ever gotten the better of Margo." Maribeth stated with a bit of Riesling laughter rolling around in her voice.

I know she likes being single, MB, but you sound like she's been out with every man you know, including your husband Rick." Sally offered her joking response with a little white-wine giggle on her own tongue.

"That's what I'm talking about," Maribeth asserted, "Margo's HAS been out with everyman I know. She dated Rick before I met him, but, I like to say, 'when I came into the picture I swept Rick off his feet and stole him from Margo'. I like to say that for my own ego, but they were over each other long before Rick and I met," Sally was becoming aggravated with Maribeth's cavalier attitude about

Margo's life-style and interrupted with,

"Well, you know my husband Will, so Margo hasn't been with every man you know,"

"Oh yes she has." Maribeth giggled before she could stop herself then she quickly added, "Oh, shit, I'm sorry Sally, I didn't mean to say that."

"Bullshit Maribeth, Margo didn't know Will before I met him! I was the one that introduced them. Admit it you're just jerking-my-chain!"

Maribeth recalled how Margo had bragged about 'setting her cap to get Old Wilber in the sack' soon after Wilber and Sally became engaged. Then, a month later Margo announced, 'I've bagged Old Wilber'. Maribeth remembered those had been Margo's exact words and she had no reason to doubt them.

The waiter returned with the check and poured more Riesling into Maribeth's glass. Sally placed her hand firmly over her glass rejecting more wine. Maribeth was happy for the distraction and said,

"Here, I'll pay," and removed the Euros she needed plus a small tip and placed the money on the table. Maribeth's eyes misted and she tried to continue, "Sally, you know I love you, you and Wilber both. I know you've got a great life together but the thing with Wilber was just a challenge for Margo, it was long before your wedding,"

"Wait a damn minute!" Sally interrupted, her wide eyes narrowing to focus her anger as she stood, "Margo didn't even know Will until after our engagement, now you tell me he cheated on me with Margo and you didn't say anything? I don't believe it! You're supposed to be my friend MB, I'm leaving now!"

"Sally wait, we need to talk, please don't go like this," Maribeth began but Sally was up and gone from the small table, immediately through the bar area and out the restaurant's door and into the street.

Hurrying uphill toward the Dorint Hotel Sally's eyes began to fill with tears of anger, disappointment and resentment as she walked away from The Beer Factory. She paused approaching 'The Second Century Roman-Wall Exhibit' as she neared the hotel, it was starting to rain and she wanted to call Will back to confront him about Maribeth's disclosure.

Sally had never known Will to lie to her and he'd never given her any cause to doubt his loyalty. Will knew how she hated lying and deceit. When the rain began to intensify, Sally decided she was too upset and confused to confront Will right now. No, now isn't the right time to call him back, she decided and hastened her travel to lessen her rain exposure time.

Arriving at the hotel her disturbing thoughts persisted. This is so unlike Will, he's always been so mature, so loyal, so dependable and honest. He couldn't have done this to me. "Maybe I should call Stephen," Sally voiced her new solution as she entered the hotel lobby. She needed her brother to help with her new resolve and she repeated her decision more emphatically,

"Yes, I'll call and talk to Stephen," before she hurried to her room.

CHAPTER THREE

THE VIRGINIA ZOO, SATURDAY, 4:30PM, EST

"STEPHEN IRONS"

I'm sitting on one of the many benches surrounding the large entry area into The Virginia Zoo. This area's called 'The Compass Rose' because the four Cardinal Points of the compass are 'Metallically Bronzed' and embedded into the area's large concrete circumference. I'm sitting near the large 'E', facing west and looking at the afternoon sun, still high enough in the sky to sustain unseasonably warm temperatures for late September in Norfolk, Virginia. I'm starting to relax as I watch heavy streams of water erupt vertically from the eight surface fountains ringing the large granite sculpture of our world positioned in the center of the entry area. The zoo's massive earth depiction, almost twenty thousand pounds of sculpted granite, is supported by more water being forced up from below its spherical surface, causing the globe to continuously roll as it literally floats on the manufactured water-flow. Several young children are running in and out of the spraying fountains, excited about their wet adventure, as they attempt to cool off from the heat. A few teenage boys are gathered near the rolling globe itself. These twenty first century teens are typically, attired in dark clothing worn loosely about their slender bodies with pants draped low on their narrow hips. As each young boy tries to apply enough force to stop the globe's rolling movement, I can recall other teens acting together that were able to stop the zoo's world from turning. But these kids have rejected cooperation and no single kid can apply enough force to halt the zoo's rolling world.

How like my own life, I begin to think, what I wouldn't give to stop my world and go back in time. I'd definitely take that opportunity to change the direction of my life. I smiled thinking of Superman in his first movie, you know, when he slowed, then stopped and reversed the rotation of the earth, pushing the movie's time-frame back enough to save Lois Lane from her earlier film-death.

Well, like Superman in the movie, I wished for a seven month reversal of time to prevent myself from being wounded so badly that my life changed dramatically for the worse. I could feel the corners of my mouth turn down and a spurt of bile rise from my gut as I recalled my earlier meeting with Norfolk's new Sheriff,

"Deputy Irons," Penny, my boss' secretary said as she rose to greet me, "welcome back. I'm so

happy you're doing better. Sheriff Wayne will see you now, please go on in."

"Thanks Penny," I replied as I took up my crutches and begin working my way to the Sheriff's door. The journey was short but growingly-familiar-pain began to throb in my left leg and lower abdomen and I paused to catch my breath. As I reached for the door handle, the Sheriff Wayne's door jerked open and he appeared, looming to fill the full doorway,

"Stephen good to see you up and moving around, come on in Boy." Sheriff Wayne offered as he hit my right shoulder with a SLAP from his large left hand. I wasn't sure if his physical contact was a stability check, but his 'Boy' reference pissed me off. I caught my breath and managed to remain standing while I resumed crutching my way into his office and the Sheriff went on, "I've just read your hospital report, its good the doctors believe you could eventually make a full recovery."

"Thank you," I answered, trying to smile through my discomfort and negative attitude. I was upset with his use of the word, 'could', but I knew my doctors thought it 'would' be a long battle for me to totally recover. I sat down to rest and gain some composure while the Sheriff continued,

"We're all proud of your sacrifice Stephen, it brought great credit to MY department, but your health issues remain a concern to me..."

"Sir," I interrupted, biting my tongue against a stronger response, I wanted to change the direction the conversation, "as you can see, I can get around okay now, I know it'll take some time, but I should be back to one hundred percent in a couple of months..."

Sheriff Wayne interrupted me, "Yes, Stephen, you'll probably be better in a few months, but your doctors feel your progress is slower than desired and I'm not sure they think you'll ever be back to one hundred percent. They're concerned about the pace of your recovery, both physical and emotional. So, their concern prompts me to offer you an administrative position for the next year while we all watch your progress... How's that sound?"

"Irons, damn it, you've got to get past all that crap!" My buddy David Thornton said to me as he stopped the begrudging memory of my earlier visit with the Sheriff and brought me back to reality, "This is what you went through before you quit the navy and came home to help your mom."

Thornton was lounging near me on an unoccupied bench. He looked worn out, you know, like he was exhausted from one of our extended patrols. But, I knew it couldn't be from our 'zoo-walking' that'd only taken us an hour or so.

Thornton was dressed in Shore Patrol CAMOS, as he always is, wearing his large SP arm-band and carrying his night-stick-persuader at the ever-ready position. He had his favorite black SP ball-cap on his head, masking his golden curls and he was acting typical, you know casual-like and smiling, but, I could tell he was disappointed in me again. I looked around the zoo to see if his tirade had startled anyone, but no one else seemed to have noticed him. When I looked back Thornton stood up, shook his head, showing more yellow curls, then, he transferred his 'night-stick' from left hand to right, swung it around twice and drifted away.

I wanted to respond to Thornton's comment, you know, have a clarifying conversation about the recent changes in my life and how I now regretted my poor attitude when I rejecting the Sheriff's 'administrative offer'. But Thornton had distanced himself, his fading CAMO clad image melted away watering-down his affect on me. I forced myself to breath more deeply, attempting to calm as I began to feel the pain in my leg subside as the watery memory of Thornton's retreating cap, CAMOS and night stick flowed from my mind and washed in among the muted clothing colors of real zoo patrons.

To be totally honest with you now, I don't agree with my doctors, or Sheriff Wayne. I don't really feel bad keeping my recovery slow by limiting my physical exercise to walking around the Virginia Zoo every day. I know I could be doing more to speed-up my recovery and I hate to admit it, but my attitude toward life has definitely changed since I was shot. Now, during my prolonged recovery, I seemed to have lost a lot of my will to challenge life. I no longer have the desire to push my body harder each day to get better as soon as possible. I hate the loss of self-confidence and initiative that I gained from the twelve years of military service before my reassignment and deployment to Afghanistan to help with the 'hunt for Osama Bin Laden' just after the US suffered through 9-11.

Actually, with all my Navy jobs I had pushed to achieve, pushed to be respected by peers and superiors and pushed to complete each directed assignment. I did experience some close calls while serving in Afghanistan just before I was allowed to resign from the navy; the most traumatic being when my partner Thornton was killed in a cluster-screw-up of an Afghani-initiated insurgency-ambush. Then, a week later, during the Navy's investigation into Thornton's death and my ultimate rescue, my father died and my mother was so distraught she contacted the Red Cross and requested my immediate return home. Sadly, as traumatic as that time was it was nothing like getting shot three times in a Norfolk courtroom and two months later Norfolk's Sheriff forcing me to medically retire. After that, my desire to strive for a full recovery took a nosedive and the following weeks were plagued by a steady physical decline. I now felt the whole experience caused me to be broken down from solid rock into small pebbles then slowly crushed into a pile of pulverized sand.

After another month of emotional relapse, while I exerted almost no effort toward my own physical recovery, my sister Sally and her husband Wilber Harrington, both Volunteer Education Docents here at the Virginia Zoo, encouraged me to at least exercise by walking the zoo-grounds every day. I agreed to give their suggestion a try and now I'm happy to report that in my second month of this program, my strength is definitely coming back. Admittedly I'm not the 28 year old 'NAVY HUNK' I once was, but this limited effort toward physical improvement has been a big positive for me. This effort is something I can finally take pride in and place the old picture of me as the 28 year old SP back on my refrigerator knowing that now, as a recovering 38 year old Navy drop-out and medically retired Norfolk Deputy Sheriff, I finally know where I'm headed.

The persistent ache in my leg lessened more as I massaged my left thigh and watched the grungy teenagers; with one now directing a combined effort; finally begin to slow the zoo's rolling world. I smiled at their approaching success as I sighted, coming around the left side of the rolling globe, marching steadily between running kids and spraying fountains, the unmistakable figure of the Norfolk Sheriff's Department's, Master Deputy Sheriff, Jimmy Osborne, as he walked purposefully toward me.

Sheriff Osborne often referred to as 'Sheriff Os' by other law enforcement types in Hampton Roads, is also known as 'the wizard' by friends and enemies alike. Os; like me, a life-long Norfolk resident; dropped out of William and Mary to become a hard-assed deputy-sheriff the same time I graduated high school and volunteered to serve in the navy. Much later, when Os became a Master Deputy and I resigned from the navy, he was instrumental in my recruitment into the Norfolk Sheriffs' Department after both my father and mother had passed away. I tried to smile as I greeted my old friend,

"Os, you old bull, funny to see you at the zoo in civvies." I said as he approached wearing a light blue, short sleeve pull over with open collar, blue jeans, and black tennis shoes, sans socks, unless his socks were jet-black like the rest of Os. "Careful, Os, the zoo might put you in a cage! Without your uniform, you're definitely on someone's endangered species list." I joked as 250 pounds of ebony skin, hard bone and muscle, exhibited a broad smile on his dark face that towered over me from a 6'-5" perspective,

"Don't give me any grief, 'Scrap'. You look like a red headed stepchild hiding from the big bad world. I'm surprised someone hasn't called in a CODE ADAM to come rescue you." Os joked back about the CODE ADAM alert called when a zoo visitor's child goes missing. Os was right, I felt lost myself.

Hearing no caustic reply from me, Os smiled, shook his head and planted his 250 pounds down next to my now frail 165 and I asked, "How'd you find me, Os?"

"Your new landlady told me you were here, Scrap." He said as he settled onto my bench and sent my mind traveling back to happier times,

I remembered being given several nicknames in the navy; 'Red', 'Freckles' and 'Asshole' came immediately to my mind, but the one that stuck with me was coined by Thornton during an

Advanced Physical-Combat Re-fresher in Norfolk just before we were both recalled to a directed-duty-assignment in Afghanistan. Thornton called me 'Rusty Irons' and at that time my red hair; and Thornton pushing me to 'get stronger and keep trying harder' became the motivating spirit I needed to stick the special-training out just before 9-11hit us all. My red hair and 185 pounds of iron-like muscles made the nickname work for me. Rusty' had also been my dad's nick name, he and I were never close, but I liked Thornton's timely choice and I wanted to encourage its use again when I quit the navy and applied for the deputy sheriffs' job. When I did join The Sheriff's Department and had to work hard to complete their program, Sheriff Os said, "Stephen, you fought hard to build a new you from a 'rusty old pile of navy junk', so, to us you'll always be 'Scrap Irons'."

I came back to the present with Os towering beside me, "Scrap, I've got some bad news, the Norfolk Fire Department found your brother-in-law, Wilber, dead from a gun shot, late this morning. They called the Police and put the small kitchen fire out before it did any major damage to your sister's home,"

"Jesus Christ, Os, does Sally know about this?" I almost shouted as I stood and interrupted his information. Os sat as he pushed down on my forearm reseating me,

"No, Scrap the detective in charge hasn't located Sally. Do you know where she is?"

"Not sure, maybe Germany, I missed a phone call from her earlier, but she left a message, 'just to say hello'. I might have a copy of her schedule somewhere. Sally emails me so I can get together with Wilber when she's gone." Saying Wilber's name and the shock of his loss immediately made me think of Thornton and I looked around for my buddy's image but he was AWOL.

"You okay Scrap? I know this is a shock to you." Os said bringing me back to reality,

"Wilber and I were getting close, Os, he's older and a bit secretive, but he was starting to open up with me. We had different navy backgrounds but we both love Sally and that was bringing us closer," I was attempting to compose myself when I heard the zoo's PA system,

"The Virginia Zoo will close in 5 minutes thank you for visiting your zoo today." Before Os added,

"Come on Scrap, the Police haven't cleared 'the scene' at your sister's house but CRACKERS is opening up now and I can fill you in over a martini, I know I could use one, this hasn't been easy for either of us."

Os paused and placed a large arm around my shoulders. I was looking for anything to take my mind off Wilber's death and I began to focus on

CRACKERS, a small Bistro serving 'Spanish tapas type-food', you know, 'small-meals with big-flavors', something like appetizers. Anyway, the restaurant had been a hang-out for sheriffs' deputy trainees and now, because I live in a West Ghent apartment complex near the restaurant, I still go there a lot. Os knew that and went on,

"Can you drive, Scrap, or do you want to go with me in my Sheriff's Cruiser? The old smell of 'convicts and cocaine' might bring back some better memories."

"No Os, I'll drive. I need the time to think about Wilber's death and how I've got to help Sally. It'll take me a few minutes to get my focus back on the real world. All I've thought about lately is my own problems." I concluded as Master Deputy Sheriff Jimmy Osborne shook my hand, turned and marched back through all the departing zoo patrons.

When I got up to leave I saw the teenage boys gathered together, probably discussing the possibility of a more interesting Saturday evening. I envied their youth and optimism about far better circumstances that were destined to come into their lives, but most of all I envied their apparent attitude of 'not giving a shit about anyone but themselves'. Those kind-of-thoughts for me had been shattered by my own physical problems and now the death of my brother-in-law. But, my problems would have to wait, Sally and I lost both parents just before she and Wilber moved to Norfolk and she was just coming to terms with that loss. Now she had lost her husband too. I had to be there for Sally.

Poor Wilber; I thought as I headed out of the zoo; a twenty year career in the navy, a second marriage to my sister five years ago, then navy retirement and a new job with a local shipping company. And just recently, the exciting possibility of getting his new book published. Who had shot Wilber? Who started the fire? Why would someone kill him? They live in Norfolk's Lakewood Area, not really a place for violent crime. Suddenly I remembered how Os had said,

"The Fire Department and Police haven't cleared 'the scene',"

'The scene', I thought. Why not 'crime scene'? Why not 'arson scene'? All of a sudden I was motivated to move faster and as I passed through the zoo's exit area my pain evaporated and my damaged left leg responded well carrying me toward the zoo's crowded parking lot.

CHAPTER FOUR

VIRGINIA ZOO

"STEPHEN IRONS"

I opened my Volvo convertible's door and slid in behind the leather covered steering wheel. Seated, I began to slow my breathing, hoping to gain some control over the mounting tide of stress that threatened to overwhelm me. Insidiously another loss, the memory and guilt surrounding David Thornton's death, began to return,

As a two- man scout-team Thornton and I were sent out near Kabul's northern perimeter to check a recent Naval Intelligence Summary that reported Afghani supporters of al Qaeda operating in our region. As recently qualified SP Special Ops, deployed on temporary duty (TDY), we were tasked only to 'Recce and Report'.

"Jesus Christ Thornton," I whispered crouching behind some heavy bushes, "don't you hear the zipper noise? They're a much larger group; they've got a bunch of suppressed weapons." There was no answer from my bud, he just kept moving toward the noise and signaled me to stay low and cover his movement.

"Thornton, Thornton, we're 'Recce', we need to report back and get help, there's too damn many," I whispered toward the sound of his movement. Still no answer, but I heard Thornton ratchet his AR4 as he slid below my sight line and immediately my worst suspicion was confirmed, Thornton was going to engage the assholes.

The suppressed weapon noise intensified, getting closer to my hidden position and dozens of spraying rounds rattled through the sparse greenery and rotting trees, before bouncing off the rock outcroppings that covered my position. Carefully I inched higher looking for Thornton and I heard his weapon fire three sustained burst. Another chorus of zippers filled the surrounding area, followed by a disjointed mumble of Afghani shouting, Thornton's weapon had gone quiet.

I shook off the terrible memory and reached up to remove the state of Virginia handicap tag that hung from the rear view mirror's support-arm. I took in a deep breath, wiped my eyes clear of moisture and tried to focus past the hanging plastic to a distant statue that guards one of the secure side gates into the Virginia Zoo. The statue is a tiger-mermaid with a small cat-like face gazing out below intermingled strands of black and gold tresses that cascade over her rounded shoulders, her upper body and onto her scale covered hips, before spreading out and forming an ebony-satin fan covering the top edge of her tail-fluke. Mermaid statues are the city of Norfolk's chosen symbol to market its nautical history and legendary significance and you can find the statues located throughout the city with site-appropriate depictions of aquatic sirens striving to bring success and good fortune to their chosen locations; like the tiger-mermaid now watching over the Virginia Zoo.

Again, groping for some distraction, or mental comfort, my mind went to my earliest foreign travel in the navy when I saw the world's most famous mermaid statue, the one recognized as being the symbol of good luck and security for the location she guards. I'm speaking of Hans Christian Anderson's 'Little Mermaid' located near the entrance to the port of Copenhagen, Denmark. This mermaid's promise of 'security, good luck and great fortune' was evident when I first observed her gazing wistfully out across the peaceful Danish harbor. Her implied promise had made a lot of sense to me then when as a horny eighteen year old sailor, turned loose in the blonde haired, blue-eyed city of Copenhagen, Denmark, I had truly 'gotten lucky' several times. But, now regretfully, I knew that wishing for a Lucky Mermaid to save Wilber was like asking Superman to take me back to a time before I was shot, neither wish had a 'Chinaman's Chance' of being granted.

Driving away from the zoo, I crossed through the Granby Street intersection and turned left where fifty yards later I angled right to continue south on Granby. Approaching 27th Street I could see a long train of coal-cars moving east to west, literally blocking Granby Street and my route of travel. The train was pulling 100 or more rail-cars full of coal heading to the Lamberts Point Docks for transfer onto cargo ships and seaborne travel to some foreign-shore. The slow train blocked my intended progress so I took an immediate right on 27th and headed west toward Colley Avenue where a left turn would get me to a train-track-underpass and access to 21st Street and my destination, CRACKERS Little Bar Bistro.

Cruising west on 27th I began to notice a lot of single family homes and apartment complexes going through an extensive restoration process. Presently, the City of Norfolk; isolated by the Chesapeake Bay, the Elizabeth River and Norfolk's bordering cities of Portsmouth, Chesapeake and Virginia Beach; encourages older urban neighborhoods to improve their existing property by granting substantial tax and financial incentives toward neighborhood restoration. I could see the results on 27th Street, certainly a positive example of what those incentives could accomplish with: new roofs, new siding, new paint, resurfaced driveways and recently poured sidewalks everywhere. While observing the new construction I mistakenly let the Volvo's front tire and rim *BANG* into one of the larger pot-holes on 27th Street. "DAMN," I voiced to Norfolk's City Government, "the city should be giving incentives to fix pot-holes!"

Smiling at my own joke, I winced, recovered and continued to serpentine my way westward toward Colley where I turned south until I cleared the railroad underpass then turned right onto 21st Street. Continuing, I passed a brown Norfolk Sheriff's car parked in front of CRACKERS and pulled left into an almost empty side parking lot where I parked and headed to the little bistro to meet Sheriff Os.

Entering CRACKERS I saw their bartender, like me named Steve, wearing one of his boldly printed shirts that always announce, 'Hey, I'm Steve and you're not', definitely his own private trademark. Steve waved 'hello' and continued to set-up for an expected Saturday night crowd as I watched his shirt's large floral prints move back and forth while he polished bar-glasses and rearranged a lot of liquor bottles. A pretty, young waitress I hadn't seen before was prepping the few small tables in front of the bar. I returned Steve's wave and focused on one of the tables against the back wall now occupied by two large CRACKERS' martinis and one extra-large Sheriff Os, who immediately offered,

"You took your time Scrap. Did you wait for the train? You should know how to deal with that kind of Norfolk delay. Come sit down and have a drink, it'll be good for you."

"No, Os, I didn't get caught by a 'frigging train' I took longer at the zoo to replay some of your info." I blurted all this out as I sat down and we both took a large gulp of martini. The thermal characteristic of the ice cold gin changed immediately going hot in my throat. As I waited for the welcomed burn to subside I added in a gin influenced whisper, "You got some shit to straighten out Os, you said 'the scene' not 'crime scene', or 'arson scene', what gives with that?"

"Glad you picked up on that, Scrap, makes it easier," Os gave me a few seconds to calm but while I felt my face flush red against the amber lighting of the small restaurant the young waitress I noticed earlier arrived and said,

"Can I get you another order, Sheriff?" Either she'd seen this large black customer pull up driving a Norfolk Sheriff's vehicle, or like so many others in our area she knew who Os was. "I'm Cora and I'll be your server." She informed us as we downed the last of our martinis with one swallow.

Seeking more distraction I began to concentrate on Cora, focusing on her short wavy black hair, her burnt umber eyes and the provocative wire-rimmed glasses that rested on her small nose and subtle cheekbones. She was definitely a small, sultry beauty and if she'd been shoeless I could have mistaken her for Ava Gardner in 'The Barefoot Contessa' movie. Cora was shapely 'eye candy' and a welcomed boost of confidence hit me as a subdued hint of physical desire returned... But, as I anxiously waited, NO sign of arousal followed my returning desire. It saddens me to tell you now that since the lower abdominal surgery my lack of physical arousal is becoming a concern to me. I placed the current blame on my brother-in-law's death and handed Cora my empty glass.

"Two more please, Cora." Os said. This was unlike the Os I was familiar with, he seemed to be going out of his way to be pleasant, probably responding to the anxiety he knew I was experiencing. As I watched closely Cora tray carried the glasses and took the two short steps she needed to transport her small shapely body from our most distant table in the restaurant to our bartender Steve still working behind the 'L' shaped bar that serves CRACKERS ' customers. Following Cora's travel I gazed up at the display of the 'higher-priced, high-shelf-booze offerings' that are mounted over the front portion of the bar. That trail of expensive booze drew my eyes to the hanging sign that proudly proclaims this small bistro's well-earned reputation in Norfolk's Ghent Area. The sign, awarded by some local food critic, emphatically stated:

CRACKERS ? THIS PLACE IS SO SMALL IT OUGHT TO BE CALLED CRUMBS!

"Stephen," Os now said, setting me back on edge, he never calls me anything but 'Scrap', "the police believe Wilber's death was a Suicide."

"Jesus Christ Os!" I stood and shouted loud enough for all to hear. Immediately Jeremy, one of CRACKERS' chefs, came into the restaurant area, probably expecting trouble. But, he seemed to reassess the situation and go back to the kitchen when he saw Cora and Steve ignoring my outburst and a very large black customer easily restraining the frail looking red-headed guy at the only occupied table in the place. So, I went on,

"You can't be serious Os Wilber had everything going for him. Why would the cops think it was suicide? And, who started the damn fire?" Os stood and eased me back to a seated position before he replied,

"Scrap, along with the gun found in Wilber's hand and the Gun Powder Residue found ON his hand, the cops have a crumpled-up publisher's rejection letter and a short suicide note printed out from his computer. They believe Wilber trashed his computer and some of the house then set the fire before he killed himself."

"Damn, Wilber wasn't like that Os, he was 'a loner' but he loved Sally and had a great career on subs before retiring. He's got to have been through enough shit and survived to put suicide way out of his thought process," Os interrupted me as he sat back down,

"Sometimes those are the ones to do it, Scrap. You know how you military guys get bored with the civilian world not going the way you expect it to. I'm just repeating what the Police are focusing on." Os' comments hit home as I reflected back on my own military career and my mounting depression after being shot. Then Os asked, "Do you know anything about the book Wilber was working on?"

"Uh, no not specifically, he did say he'd let me look at it soon."

"His first book was Science Fiction, right?" Os asked, confusing me further.

"Well, Wilber called it a Sci-Fi Medical-Thriller because he researched a lot of medical information on old people before creating an injected drug to punish criminals by aging them as punishment for their crimes. You know, so the U.S. could get rid of prisons."

"Scrap, do you think his new book could be Science Fiction? When I talked to the detective in charge, Detective Knowles," Immediately I cut him off,

"Knowles, Damn Os, she's the cop that got me shot!" I bellowed standing again as I recalled the pain in my gut when three bullets slammed into me and I collapsed near death.

"Hold it, sit back down, Scrap, you know that's bullshit, YOU got YOU shot! YOU took three bullets meant for Judge Knutson and Knowles. You chose to do your duty. You were the one that got you shot." Os stood again and placed one restraining hand on my shoulder and easily pushed me back down into my chair, "You've got to get a grip on yourself Scrap, I was proud when your selfless response saved the Judge's life and brought a lot of pride to our department, we were all grateful for your sacrifice."

I was on the verge of losing it now, the possibility that Wilber could have taken his own life and set fire to Sally's home was just too damn much for me to deal with. Cora returned with two new martinis, removed them from her small tray and set them down carefully. I watched as the ice crystals on the high-stem glasses reacted to warmth and gravity as they melted and slid slowly downward,

"Is it okay, Sheriff Os?" Cora said as she looked directly at Os not glancing at me. I wasn't surprised at that, but I'd been right, she definitely knew who Os was.

"Thanks Cora, please leave us for a bit." Os stated and Cora smiled and hurried off to speak with Steve, probably about not bothering the Sheriff and his sad friend.

After another martini and a long silence at the table I got control of my emotions and asked Os, "Will the Police let me look at Wilber's body and Sally's house?"

"Sure, Knowles is concerned how all this will hit you, Scrap. She'll meet us at the house tomorrow." Os said.

"Okay, I'll try to locate Sally's schedule, then, I'll call Knowles." I said as I drank the last bit of my martini and set the empty glass on the table.

"Knowles is working out of Police Ops on Virginia Beach Boulevard…" Os began as I rose and reached into my pocket, "Don't bother, Scrap, I've got all this."

"Oh, I was reaching for my keys Os, sorry, I owe you for the drinks. Thanks for telling me personally, I'll see you tomorrow at Sally's house. Ten okay?"

"Ten's good. I'll let Knowles know. We can check Wilber's body out later. Sorry for your loss, Stephen." Damn he did it again, he called me Stephen. I turned and worked my way past several people at the bar and a few others now sitting at the four other small tables making up CRACKERS ' limited dining area.

Exiting the restaurant I saw two local produce suppliers, Dave and Dee, unloading and passing their home-grown mushrooms to Jeremy. I forced a smile and waved at the three of them as I got in my car still slightly embarrassed about the earlier outburst that brought Chef Jeremy into the dinning area.

As I drove away I could see Os through a smoked glass window, he was standing and talking with Cora, probably settling the check. 'The wizard', I thought is definitely still taking care of everything.

"Sorry for your loss, Rusty, are you going to be okay?" Thornton asked me as we drove away.

"Yeah, bud, I'll be okay, someday," I responded honestly, but I couldn't force myself to look at Thornton. Tears were forming in my eyes for Sally and Wilber and Thornton's image would just be another sad watery reminder of my past errors.

CHAPTER FIVE

NORFOLK POLICE OPERATIONS

Norfolk Police Detective Linda Knowles sat at her desk with a small amount of paperwork piled in front of her. A second pile was on the floor and a third spread out on a small table nearby. On her crowded desk a green-shaded accountant-light produced a lime-like glow that made her assorted papers appear more organized. Knowles' accumulating papers were the initial draft-reports concerning the death of Wilber Harrington sixteen hours ago. Knowles held a fourth sheath of papers that included several interviews and statements from Harrington's neighbors and a few of his co-workers at NISCO, (Norfolk International Shipping Company). Knowles was thinking about the pressure she was under, her Chief of Detectives, Andy Beck, had insisted she close the case soon during their Saturday afternoon meeting,

"Knowles, I'll give you a few days to close this up, looks open and shut to me. You know we're short staffed so get moving on whatever's bugging you about the suicide, but get it resolved soon," Chief Beck began,

"Okay Chief, but I think it could be a 'dog and pony show' set up to look like suicide. The fibers under Harrington's fingernails could be from his own shirt, forensics is doing spec-analysis on that, but can't you give me another cop and a little more time?" Knowles asked attempting to stretch her Chief's 'few days,' into a full week with more help.

"Damn, Knowles you're not hearing me. Okay, okay, maybe I can get you Bradshaw from Vice, but unless you show me a definite 'homicide' soon, I want this 'suicide' closed by the end of the week."

Knowles had been pleased to get the promise of extra help and the additional time, now she was determined to gather as much evidence as possible before her next scheduled meeting with Chief Beck. Waiting on forensic reports Knowles had split her small group up, assigning individual investigators to get as many interviews as possible in their first 48 hours... But so far no one interviewed believed Wilber Harrington had taken his own life. Harrington's immediate boss, James Carlson and one of Harrington's co-workers, a Margarete Kroger, said they knew him well and thought he was working on a book he hoped to get published soon, but neither had any idea what the book was about. Both had guessed submarines or some aspect of the US Navy. Or, possibly, as Knowles read her notes,

"Because he works for NISCO the book could involve some aspect of our international shipping business. You know something Wilber would know about,"

The extracted quote was part of Carlson's interview. Knowles sighed as she placed a portion of the papers back on her desk, still holding the first report she'd received from Sergeant Morris Bradshaw, the new officer on loan from Vice. Bradshaw was working with her lead investigator, Detective Sam Millers who assigned Bradshaw to interview Harrington's neighbors and the three kids who were practicing soccer in Lakewood Park Saturday morning. Knowles reread the oldest kid's initial offering,

"We stopped kicking the ball and saw some smoke from the Harrington house so I got a neighbor to call nine-one-one…"

A nagging aspect of the investigation sliced into Knowles' thoughts and she responded with, "Millers have you reached American Airlines yet?" She voiced into the darkness surrounding her office space hoping Detective Millers could give her a positive answer to soften her knife-edged concern for the widow, Sally Harrington.

"Millers' still out Detective Knowles, he's looking for Sally Harrington's brother." An unfamiliar voice drifted over from the other end of the hall.

"Who's there?" Knowles answered, confused by her exhaustive efforts and the late hour's unidentified response.

"Sergeant Bradshaw, Ma'am, I'm working with Detective Millers collecting the information on Wilber Harrington,"

"Oh yeah, I've gotten some of your info, when can I have the complete report?" Knowles asked rising from her desk and walking toward Bradshaw's voice. As she moved along the hallway her height became apparent. Knowles stood 6'1" in her stocking feet, but walking now, in low heeled work shoes, she was at least 6'2".

Bradshaw listened to her approach and remembered a co-workers saying, *"Detective Knowles is all legs, but you better be careful or she'll run you down with 'em,"* Looking up Bradshaw focused on Knowles' medium length blonde hair, cut in a page-boy style with heavy bangs. As she neared, Bradshaw saw her flaxen hair bounce lightly above a very pretty, but sensible face. He focused on a sculptured nose, thin-lined mouth and blue-gray eyes as she approached him, eyes that had been described to him as *'bright and inquiring'*, but, as she neared, he saw her eyes were showing the strain and pupil edged fatigue from her last sixteen hours on the job.

Arriving, Knowles' features hardened under the fluorescent lighting that washed over Bradshaw's desk and he discarded thoughts about her long legs and focused on the 140 pounds of determination that stood before him as he rose to greet his new boss. Bradshaw extended his right hand presenting his final draft on Wilber Harrington and said, "This is what I've put together so far, Boss."

You're working full-time with Millers on the case, full-time for me?"

"Yes, Ma'am, Chief Beck assigned me 'til you determine the cause of Harrington's death. Is that okay, Ma'am?" Bradshaw said.

"Of course," Knowles replied as she took the report with her left hand and extended her right hand down to shake Bradshaw's now empty palm, "I need all the help I can get and I do like being called 'Boss'."

Bradshaw smiled up at her remark and took her hand a little more firmly than he intended. Knowles was okay with that from men, especially the ones she towered over. She returned a firm but non-challenging response as she gazed down on Bradshaw's 5' 6" statue. Bradshaw quickly withdrew his hand, sat down at his desk as he began to recall another co-worker's remark, this one from his new partner Detective Sam Millers. The remark was one of Millers' observations about their mutual boss, *"Knowles is less intimidating when you're sitting down staring at her belly button. Don't get me wrong, Bradshaw, I haven't had the pleasure of seeing her real belly button, not yet anyway."*

Bradshaw smiled remembering Millers' remark and focused his eyes on Knowles' mid-section, just to test Millers' advice. Knowles scanned his report, and said, "I'll take this back to my desk Sergeant Bradshaw, but give me a quick summary."

"Yes Ma'am, Harrington was a local area boy, 46 years old. He went to high school in Franklin, Virginia, did a year at Old Dominion then the Naval Academy and twenty years in the navy, mostly on submarines. He came back to Norfolk for his last navy assignment in January 2002, then, retirement in late 2003 and the NISCO job. He first married June '83, right out of the Naval Academy, got a divorce two years later and stayed a bachelor 'til he met his present wife, Sally. They married in San Diego right after the 9-11 attack. She's a Norfolk native with a little more than ten years working for American Airlines."

Bradshaw was reeling off the facts from his small green note book, Knowles liked his presentation but she was tiring from a long day and finally sat down. Bradshaw watched as her imagined bellybutton disappeared into her lap, then, he continued, "Sally's 30 now and they lived in San Diego for a year before Harrington was reassigned to The Joint Forces Staff College on Hampton Boulevard. He did a year and a half as an Instructor before retiring in '03, that's when he got the job with NISCO,"

"What about Sally?" Knowles interrupted with her growing concern for a wife who had just lost her husband, "You said she worked in San Diego for American before they married, did she move here with Harrington in 2002?"

"Yes Ma'am, she started with American in 1996, her first basing was San Diego where she met Harrington in April 2001. He was 41 and Sally was 25. They dated for six months then married in October where they continued to live 'til Harrington was reassigned to Norfolk. They were on-base at the Staff College for a year, then, bought their home in Lakewood just before Harrington retired. Sally changed her airline basing from San Diego to Dallas when they moved here and she fly's her international trips out of DFW. She commutes from Norfolk to Dallas for her trips, usually one trip a week,"

"You found out a lot about American Airlines, why haven't you gotten them to reach Sally Harrington?" Knowles asked with her growing edge of concern for Sally Harrington infecting her voice,

"All this info came from Sally's neighbors, a doctor and his wife that socialize with Sally and Wilber. Sally shared a lot of her history with the wife, Mrs. Connie Hall. Detective Millers is still trying with American, but he hasn't had much luck, I think that's why he's out looking for Sally's brother."

"Did you talk to Harrington's neighbors in person?"

"First I phoned but Mrs. Hall had so much information I went over and had a little 'chat' for an hour or so. She likes the couple, thinks of Sally 'like a daughter'. Mrs. Hall's devastated by Harrington's death, but mostly she's worried about Sally."

"What about Harrington's first wife, do they have any kids?"

"Eh, Mrs. Hall doesn't know a lot about the first wife, presumably Sally doesn't either, since all Mrs. Hall's info comes from Sally," Bradshaw paused when his desk phone rang. Knowles nodded and Bradshaw stood to answer the call,

"Homicide, Sergeant Bradshaw. Yeah, wait a minute Millers she's right here, I'll put you on SPEAKER - It's Millers," Bradshaw, said to Knowles as he tapped the phone's SPEAKER button. Knowles stood, reached across the desk, disconnected the SPEAKER function and took the phone from Bradshaw who immediately appeared crestfallen at being denied the conversation.

"Millers, its Knowles, tell me what you've found out." Knowles listened for about 30 seconds then she motioned to Bradshaw for a pen and pad, took a few notes then asked,

"How are they going to do that?" Knowles listened again, writing for a full minute,

"Okay, I've got all that, call me if you get more. You can head home now but come in early Monday we've got a lot to do." Knowles handed the phone back to Bradshaw, noted his saddened expression and realized she'd been rude not allowing him to hear Millers' information. Here it was 3 AM on Sunday, and Bradshaw was still here helping her out, she needed to cut him some slack.

"Sorry about the phone," Knowles whispered to Bradshaw, "but Sally's brother, Stephen Irons, is standing by my desk and I didn't want him to hear anything before I knew what the call was about. I'll check back with you later."

As Knowles departed, Bradshaw took the opportunity and leaned out to get a better look at Stephen Irons. In the distance, Irons appeared frail, a thin, rumpled red headed statue of dejection with slumping shoulders now standing in the shaded lighting from Knowles' desk lamp. Hardly the picture of the former deputy-sheriff-hero Bradshaw heard about six months ago.

CHAPTER SIX

NORFOLK POLICE OPERATIONS

"STEPHEN IRONS"

I felt physically exhausted and emotionally drained while I stood watching Detective Knowles talk with another policeman. It wasn't exactly gentlemanly of me but I remained standing by her desk while she took the time to answer a phone call. It had been a very long afternoon and evening for me before I finally decided bring the police some contact information I found on Sally's employment with American Airlines. I'm still standing and watching as Knowles replaced the phone and talked a bit more to her cohort in blue then she began to walk toward me.

As Knowles neared I realized I've never been this close to her. The first time I saw her was when she testified in court the day I was shot. I remembered hearing the bailiff call her to the witness stand and I half listened to her testimony until I saw the defendant's wife stand and point a gun toward Knowles and Judge Knutson. My mind reluctantly went back to that day,

I was standing to the far left side of Judge Knutson's bench. Opposite my position, on the judge's right side, was the court clerk's small table and between myself and the judge was the witness box, now occupied by Detective Knowles. I remained standing guard as I heard the prosecutor say, "Detective Knowles please tell the court the circumstances that led to the arrest of the defendant,"

"Of course," As Knowles began her response I saw a large black woman rise up in the second-row of the court room. The woman stood over 6'tall and weighed at least 200 pounds. Those assessments flashed through my mind as she pulled a small revolver from her handbag and began to point it toward the judge.

"Stop," I yelled as I moved to place my body between the woman's position and Judge Knutson, "Drop the gun and put your hands in the air!" I shouted as I moved in front of the woman and attempted to un-holster my weapon as she began to fire. The noise was deafening CRACK, CRACK, CRACK was all I heard as I felt the impact of three hammer-like blows that stopped my movement and SLAMMED me back into the witness box. My last memory was the odor of burnt cordite, then, my world went totally black and I collapsed.

Now, as I watch Detective Knowles near, her height and beauty had another impact on me. Once again my desire hurdle was cleared, but sadly, no hint of arousal followed.

"Stephen, I'm very sorry for your loss. How are you doing now?" Knowles said.

"I've been better, Detective Knowles." I replied as I looked slightly higher to gauge her eyes while I shook her hand. Her eyes looked tired but warmly reflective, probably encouraging dismissal of my own stress and anxiety. Her initial grip was soft and I got the feeling she thought I might break if she squeezed normally.

"Stephen, please call me Linda. I want to thank you for your courtroom response six months ago, I'm certain Judge Knutson and I owe you our lives." Knowles offered her statements quietly and with genuine respect. Then, she added, "What can I do for you?"

"I've been up all night looking for information on Sally's trip, I didn't find that, but I have her supervisor's name and phone number in Dallas, so I thought I'd bring it over and give it to the Duty Officer. He told me you were still here and encouraged me to bring it back. I think Sally's in Germany, probably getting ready to come back to Dallas, but no one answered when I tried her supervisor." I paused and sat down.

"Sorry I kept you standing, I'm sure you're still in recovery and yesterday couldn't have been an easy day. Did Sheriff Osborne inform you of your brother-in-law's death?" Knowles asked as she sat down behind her desk.

"Yes, he found me at the zoo, I'd been exercising to get my strength back,"

"Our zoo has an exercise room?" Knowles' question interrupted me, then, she added, "I've been there with my eight-year-old daughter, Ella. She loves the zoo."

"No, sorry," I began, feeling a small smile slide onto my face for the first time in weeks. I knew Knowles was a widow but I didn't know she had a young child. "Actually I walk around the zoo every day, its good physical exercise for me and watching the animals is emotionally relaxing, Sally and Wilber got me started. They're both Education Docents with the zoo," I paused after saying Wilber's name, "Sorry, Wilber WAS a zoo docent." I added as my voice weakened to a whisper and I felt my earlier smile morph back into a growingly familiar pained expression. Knowles reached for my hand again,

"Are you and Sally close?"

"We've gotten much closer since Sally moved back to Norfolk," I began thinking her question a bit odd, "we were never very close as kids, we're eight years apart. Growing up, she was my mom's favorite, being the little girl my mom said she always wanted."

"What about your mother and father?" Knowles asked.

"Well, my parents married late in life, my mom was forty when I was born, forty eight with Sally, probably her last chance for a little girl. Our parents both passed away four years ago, our dad first, then mom 6 months after. I actually resigned from the Navy to come home and help my mom when our dad died. But six months later our mom passed just before Sally moved back here with Wilber," I paused for a second, catching my breath. Thornton came in and sat his ass down on the edge of Knowles' desk. I was certain he was going to comment on my resignation from the navy, but he only pointed toward Knowles and fluffed his own blonde curls. Thankfully he had the good sense not to speak, so I just ignored his image and tried to look back at Knowles to complete my response,

"As you might guess from my leaving the Navy and coming home to help my mom, growing up I was very close to her, but my dad and I were never close. He was a big guy, very athletic, played and coached football at William and Mary," I caught myself wondering why I was rambling on about my life, then, I recalled the reason for my visit, "Have you been able to reach Sally through American? You don't seem very interested in my information."

"Sorry, I should have told you before, yes we've reached American and as you guessed Sally's on her flight back from Germany. She took off about 30 minutes ago from Frankfurt… But, because of American's 'death notification policy' they'll wait until Sally lands in Dallas to inform her in person about her husband's death. Their records have you listed as a Secondary Emergency Contact so they want to offer you a flight to Dallas to be with Sally when they tell her. Would you like to be there when Sally arrives in Dallas?" Knowles paused for my answer but I must have seemed hesitant, so she added, "Stephen, are you well enough to fly to Dallas and back with Sally?"

"Yes, I'd like to do that." I said and Knowles continued reading from her notes,

"Okay, American's Flight from Norfolk leaves this morning at 7:15, arriving at 9:15 Dallas' time. Sally's flight isn't scheduled to land until 10:20 at DFW. American's rep will meet your plane and brief you on their notification procedures while you both wait to meet Sally. I've got some info for you with flight numbers and times and I'll tell American's ticket counter that you'll be going on the flight."

"Thank you. Can you let Sheriff Osborne know where I've gone? We were going to meet you later this morning to look at Sally's house."

"Sure, I'll tell him. Did Sally leave her car at the airport?"

"Eh, I'm sure Wilber took her, he always does." I replied, remembering how Sally always bragged about being an American Airlines' Executive that was chauffeured to and from her work place, "I can drive my own car, but do you think Sally will be able to go back to her house?"

"Oh, not sure yet, the kitchen and den are a mess, but the rest of the house seems okay. Are you really up to this, Stephen? I can have a car take you home and to the airport, then we can pick you both up when you return."

"No, no, I'm okay Detective Knowles. Do you think Wilber really killed him self?" I finally asked preparing myself for the worst.

"It looked that way at first, but it could be a homicide, staged to appear a suicide. To be honest that's my gut feeling right now. I'll have more for you when you return. You can tell Sally we don't know yet, it could be either way. I'm not sure that'll be a comfort, but it might help."

"Okay, I'll talk with you when we return. Is the book Wilber was working on important?" I asked. Knowles rose from her desk, took my hand again and said,

"I guess what's in the book could be important, especially if Wilber's death is judged to be a homicide. I'll be happy to share more when you return."

"That would be good. This whole thing seems weird to me, it's not like the Wilber I know." I offered as I slid my hand from the comfort of hers and tried to smile.

I departed wondering why I hadn't already tried to return Sally's call to tell her about Wilber's death myself. Thornton caught up with me at the car and offered,

"Don't worry Rusty, now you'll be there to tell her, better for both of you."

CHAPTER SEVEN

BEIJING, CHINA, SEPTEMBER 24

Cheng Tieren, or Iron Man Cheng as his father Dr. Cheng Ji affectionately called him, sat at his desk contemplating his scheduled briefing for China's Science Director Dr. Niam Wang, now a Special Assistant to the President of China. Director Wang was the Chief Scientific Advisor to the two leaders wielding the power in China, the President/General Secretary and the Premier. Both rulers had placed heavy responsibilities on Director Wang and in turn Director Wang depended on Iron Man Cheng. As Cheng worked on the briefing he began to feel the full pressure of his responsibilities. He knew his father's influence helped secure his assignment as the Operations Officer for Deep Dragon, the secret program conceived in 1996 and activated on September 11, 2001 and he began to remember his father's words, *"Most Honored Son, China's decreasing lack of Nationalism is our nation's greatest shortcoming,"*

In 1996 China's economic growth and growing demand for increased nationalism, coupled with scientific strides in nuclear fusion research, gave birth to the concept of Deep Dragon, the idea that China could gain an advantage over other nations by manipulating global weather. This revolutionary program brought about the development of a two stage nuclear device to be placed deep in the Pacific Ocean. Once operational, the device would provide a continuous stream of high temperature seawater into the deepest levels of the ocean in an attempt to influence weather throughout the world. Cheng's membership in China's Tenth Directorate of their Secret Service Organization precipitated his assignment as Deep Dragon's Operational Commander and on October 6, 2001, in the Pacific Ocean just north of the Tropic of Cancer, a Chinese nuclear fission reactor was coupled to a nuclear fusion device and submerged to the Pacific Ocean's floor. Once activated the fission portion of the device would superheat ambient seawater to the high temperatures required to initiate the fusion process and the fusion section would generate higher seawater temperatures for direct expulsion of the 2000 degree water back into the Pacific Ocean. China's scientists believed this constant stream of super-heated seawater would act as an ever-present El Nino causing unpredictable weather changes for the northwest part of the Continental United States, Hawaii, Canada, the Philippines, Korea, Japan and other Pacific Rim Nations.

As Iron Man Cheng looked over the scientific data from one of China's deep sea probes, and the follow-on evaluations of his staff, he confirmed that all systems were operating effectively. Cheng decided his briefing should not dwell on only the projects' past five years' individual successes, but stress that the total number of recorded hurricanes had doubled when compared to the previous five-year period. These comparisons were impressive alone, but when added to the statistic that the number of severe hurricanes, Categories 3, 4 and 5, for the same period, had also doubled, he believed this data proved that Deep Dragon's five year success was undeniable. In addition, Cheng reasoned that several Tsunamis recorded during the same period could have been influenced by his program. The constant increase in the deep-water temperatures of the Pacific could have influenced the plate movement beneath the ocean floor and brought on the wave generations that rapidly gained size and speed until they crashed on distant shores as a mature Tsunami.

His hard work and the confidence his father had shown in him had finally been justified and he believed his report would be pivotal concerning how China should continue striving for even greater world influence. Cheng knew Deep Dragon Two was on the drawing board and he speculated the second attempt for an even greater influence on global weather would be the submerged duplicate of the original Deep Dragon somewhere in the Atlantic Ocean's Gulf Stream. The design and installation of Deep Dragon Two depended on this five year report since China's new President had stated, "*Additional stones to cross each new river of opportunity are always welcome,*"

Cheng's private phone sounded, interrupting his reflections. He rose from his small desk, closed the outer-door to his office and moved back to the desk to remove the hidden phone. "Cheng Tieren, please speak," Cheng touched the Amplification Audio's Scrambler Function and after ten seconds the scrambler's GREEN light illuminated and the Audio volume increased clarifying the call from a distant asset. Cheng listened for 30 seconds more then replied,

"Yes, very good, does this complete our necessary action?" Cheng listened this time for a full minute, writing only one name on his yellow pad of paper. 'Stephen Irons'. Interesting, Cheng thought, one Iron Man set against another. "This person, how is he a threat?"

Cheng listened for 20 more seconds then he interrupted his caller, "Yes, more action IS necessary, remove that problem also, but there must be NO connective link to your primary mission." Cheng directed, then he disconnected and folded the paper showing Stephen Irons' name and ran it through a small desk top shredder. Cheng's shredder machine *WHIRRED* loudly before expelling several thin strips into a burn-bag near his desk.

Cheng returned to his briefing paper and began listing the all major storms he believed were influenced by Deep Dragon. His briefing could slant to suggest a connection to some of the earthquake activity in Japan.

CHAPTER EIGHT

NORFOLK, VIRGINIA, SUNDAY, 5:30AM

Eric Chin, masking his face with dark reflective sunglasses, drove east on Norview Avenue toward the Norfolk International Airport. After crossing Military Highway he was forced to stop for a red light at the intersection with Azalea Garden Road. He glanced over his left shoulder to the sign welcoming air travelers to the Norfolk area. The sign pictured a mermaid and the City of Norfolk's optimistic greeting:

WELCOME TO NORFOLK - LIFE CELEBRATED DAILY

Norfolk, Virginia surrounded by water with heavy navy and commercial-ship traffic, Eric mused, Similar, but not as good as San Diego, he concluded as the light changed and he passed across the small bridge leading to the airport.

Continuing to the northernmost entrance of the parking garage he acquired a ticket and proceeded up succeeding ramps until the uppermost level where he parked in an open construction area that afforded a look around the presently empty level. Moving to the back of the car Eric opened the trunk, removed a large fiberglass guitar-case and carried it to the western end of the vacant level for an unobstructed view of approaching traffic. Positioned in the dark shadows of a large concrete support pillar he was pleased to be able to see both ticketing entrances to the garage, one directly west and the other to the north where he had entered. No cars were approaching and Eric considered the possibility that Stephen Irons would use one of the more convenient outside parking lots. But that area was exposed to the weather and heavy rain was forecast from Sunday afternoon through Monday evening, when Irons was thought to be returning. Eric gambled on Irons' concern for the weather so the covered parking area seemed his best option. He moved to the outer edge of the open level positioning him self to watch for Irons. Eric checked for the possibility of a shot from this vantage point but both the western and northern ticketing gates were obscured by the late September leafing of surrounding trees precluding a one hundred percent assured shot.

His reasoning paid off as Eric spotted Irons' small convertible enter the northern access area and stop at the ticket gate. He had been right there was no way he could take this shot. He hoisted the guitar case and headed down the stairs to the second level to be ready for Irons' eventual arrival. LEVEL TWO opened up directly into the airport terminal and he had seen several available spaces and was sure that level would be Irons' choice for parking.

Exiting the stairway onto LEVEL TWO Eric crouched in the shadows behind a broad support structure well away from the drive-up ramp. Quietly he opened the case and slid the modified Chinese QBZ - 95 Sniper Rifle from under the Classic Guitar he carried. Quickly he assembled the short foldable stock onto the long sleek barrel section of the weapon. Assembly complete he withdrew the adjustable 2X16 Starlight Scope from its small pouch. The aroma of lens solvent wafted his nostrils and an adrenaline spike brought a familiar feeling of muted excitement as approaching headlights from a moving vehicle reflected off the garage's interior supports.

Eric completed the scope installation and noted no other traffic, vehicular or pedestrian. So far he was a go. When he began to sight toward Irons' vehicle, another pair of head lights followed closely behind Irons' car, "Damn, another traveler," Eric voiced bitterly to himself, but decided to wait to see the result of their parking, possibly he could still get a shot. Now concerned of more people and a gun-fire disturbance Eric retrieved the weapon's noise suppressor and clamped the modified accessory onto the barrel. It would still be much better here than traveling to Dallas to do the job, as he had been instructed if this airport option failed. There was a risk of discovery in Norfolk, but with existing local support, that risk, Eric had been assured was minimal.

Norfolk was not to be Eric concluded as he watched Irons' Volvo, now followed closely by a Dodge Caravan, come around the row in front of him and park side-by-side with the van closer, totally blocking his view of Irons' car. Eric waited as Irons got out and began to lock his car. Still hoping for a clear shot he watched as a pregnant woman in her thirties exited the van and filled his sight line. As the woman struggled with her luggage, Irons appeared to move over to help, then, disappeared again. Irons then partially reappeared to pull one of the family's bags as the small group of travelers moved toward the airport with Irons leading their movement, effectively blocking Eric's option for the shot.

Eric disassembled his weapon and stored it back under the guitar. Then he carefully removed the large base string from the classic instrument, closed the case and hurried back up the stairs to his own car. After placing the guitar-case in his trunk, he drove down to LEVEL TWO and found a convenient spot a few spaces from Irons' car. He retrieved a folded sports coat, donned the jacket and pocketed the coiled guitar string inside his coat assuring his ticket and the strong nylon wrapped string were both accessible.

Confident of his preparation Eric began to walk toward the airport entrance to travel to Dallas with Irons. After a few steps Eric heard the automatic access door leading into the airport *HISS* open and he watched as Stephen Irons walked through the doorway and back into the LEVEL TWO parking area.

CHAPTER NINE

NORFOLK INTERNATIONAL AIRPORT

"STEPHEN IRONS"

I used the key activation device to open the Volvo trunk and get my carry-on bag out for the trip. I'd been distracted by a traveling family and forgot my own luggage. Too damn much on my mind I guess. I closed the trunk and checked my watch. Just past 6AM American knew I was coming so I should still be okay on time. I began to think of Sally and her shock when she was finally told of Wilber's death. I was pleased American Airlines had offered to fly me out to be with her, not sure I could have worked those travel arrangements out on my own. As I walked toward the airport entrance again, my last conversation with Wilber reformed in my mind,

"Do you want to meet for Sunday Brunch?" I remembered asking Wilber late Friday afternoon when we were sitting down after an hours walk through the Virginia Zoo.

"That's a great idea Stephen I've got a lot of work to do on my book Saturday, but I should finish early Sunday. How about AW Shucks at 11:30, you know, before the after-church crowd arrives?"

"Sounds good Wilber, can I see some of the new book then?" I asked.

"Well, I'm not quite ready for 'show-and-tell' Stephen, I've completed the first few chapters but right now I'm hung-up on an important transitional area, maybe in a week or so after I hear from a publisher. Okay?"

"Someone's agreed to publish the book?"

"Well, I've got a California agent that has a foreign publisher interested. If everything goes okay, they'll give me some money to finish the book…."

"That sounds great, I remember the problems you said you had with your first publisher, I'm sure you don't want to go that way again."

"You're right Stephen publishing that book was a mess… But, I didn't have Sally then, so it's all going much better for me this time."

I smiled recalling our conversation but my smile faded as I continued to walk back toward the terminal building thinking how sorry I was about Wilber's death. He had always looked forward to Sally returning home from a trip, but the events during this trip would be almost as devastating for Sally as they had been for Wilber.

Walking by a parked SUV I heard the sound of sliding feet *SCRAPE* on the concrete behind me and I turned to see a tall man hurrying toward me in a threatening manner. My self-defense training came back in a flood, disjointed and unstructured, but demanding my immediate reaction. I dropped the carry-on bag and rotated my body prepared to protect my damaged leg from a frontal assault. As the tall man continued to approach I could see the thick cord hanging down loosely between his two gloved hands and I realized this is serious, this guy wants to strangle me!

The attacker moved closer and karate kicked out toward my left leg and my head pounded demanding I do something now! The pain from my slow reaction spiked in my brain like an ice cream headache and I stopped thinking and went totally with muscle memory, twisting away to avoid his first leg thrust.

I was pleased to feel the responding adrenaline surge when my damaged leg reacted without apparent pain and my heart beat galloped with the rush of heated blood that coursed through my body. The old acetylene torch of fear had flamed my cardio-vascular system again and I embraced the feelings' return, got cocky and challenged my attacker, "What's your problem jerk, you think a little guy like me can't hurt you. You'd be wrong, asshole!" I shouted, positioning myself for an offensive strike after fending off his first leg thrust.

As my attacker twisted away to create a returning momentum I could see his face, it was dark and rough, he actually looked Asian to me. While I processed that physical information the guy lunged with his right knuckled fist and I felt the nearness of his thrust. Fortunately his punch was restricted by the lengthy cord he had wrapped around his hands and as I rotated my head he missed direct contact with my jaw.

Excited now, I twisted my body and leaned back on my damaged leg to shoot out my own attack with a strong right leg kick. I was pleased when the guy seemed startled as I connected a foot *SLAM* into his left knee. The impact was partial, not severe enough to cripple the man but effective enough to knock him down. As I rebalanced for a follow-up attack my peripheral vision picked up a Norfolk Airport Security Guard entering the parking area. The tall guard saw our scuffle, about a hundred feet from his position, and responded by running toward us shouting,

"Stop, what's going on?" he yelled as he drew his weapon and continued to run toward us. When I heard the guard yell, I backed up slightly, making it impossible to take full advantage of my earlier strike but I felt better about my returning ability to defend myself.

Noting my momentary retreat, my attacker was up and gone toward the exit ramp and down a nearby stairway before the guard got within twenty feet of our position.

"Jesus Christ, what was that?" I uttered as I felt my left leg and was reassured that no damage had been done. The guard arrived and was now on his radio calling for help as he described the exit area my attacker had used.

"You okay, sir? What happened here?" he asked.

"The guy attacked me! He was hidden behind an SUV then he jumped out and attacked..."

"Did he threaten you? Demand your wallet, or money?"

"No, no, he wanted to kill me! He had a garrote stretched between his hands." I replied, winded from exertion and becoming upset with the security guard's questions.

"Are you sure?"

"Of course I'm sure!" I almost shouted, getting really upset with this rent-a-cop, "I've been trained to know when someone's trying to kill me."

"Can I see some ID please?" The guard asked, lowering his view from my eyes to my empty hands. He seemed reassured of my legitimacy and placed his weapon back in his holster. I showed him my Virginia Driver's License and my retired Sheriff's ID, then, I explained my pre-arranged trip to meet Sally in Dallas and he responded,

"Okay, can we keep talking on the way to American's ticket counter?"

"Sure that would be helpful," I replied.

As we walked away the guard's radio replied concerning the fleeing attacker, but the caller had failed to find anyone near the lower garage level. I was both confounded by the aggression toward me and encouraged by my ability to produce enough response to have thwarted the attack.

Thornton caught up with us and said, "I'm proud of you Rusty you're definitely on the road back."

"Thanks bud," I turned to reply to Thornton, but he was gone. The Airport Security Guard seemed confused at my comment and said,

"Hey, my name's Joel! Who're you calling a bub?"

CHAPTER TEN

POLICE OPERATIONS, MONDAY, 7:30AM

Detective Knowles approached her desk carrying her leather briefcase and a small 'Sponge Bob' lunch box. Ella had forgotten her lunch when Linda dropped her off at grandmother, Shirley Knowles, house for Montessori School pick up. "I'll have the PB&J myself." Linda mused out loud as she reached for her desk phone and punched #9 for an outside line. She tapped in Shirley's number and waited two rings, then, touched SPEAKER ON as Shirley answered,

"Hello, Linda, I know, I know, you forgot my granddaughter's lunch, what do you want Ella to take? I've got left-over chicken and some carrots. Or, I can make a cheese sandwich with lettuce and tomato. Which sounds best?"

"Thanks Shirley, the chicken will be fine." Linda responded mildly upset that Shirley guessed who and why she was calling, probably the 'City of Norfolk' showed-up on Shirley's phone ID read out,

"You're welcome, Linda, Ella seems unsettled this morning; I'll read her some stories after school. You should read to Ella every night Linda," Knowles interrupted her mother-in-law's comments,

"I'll try to read more WITH Ella, Shirley." Linda wanted Shirley to know that she was totally involved with helping her eight year old improve her reading skills, "See you around six. Thanks again." Linda disconnected before Shirley could reply.

Linda wanted to call Shirley 'mom' as she had when Dwight was alive, but now, with Dwight gone almost three years, she couldn't seem to bring herself to use the 'mom' term for her mother-in-law. Linda had used Dwight's life insurance to buy a Norfolk condo and she had his small monthly pension to help with Ella's education. It wasn't a lot of money, but it allowed Ella to attend a Montessori School near Shirley's home and also put some funds away for Ella's follow-on education. Linda was sure she and Ella would be okay, as she pushed the phone away from her work space and turned when she heard Millers and Bradshaw enter the Operations building's side entrance,

"Morning Chief," Detective Sam Millers offered, "Be back after we get some coffee, you want some?"

"We'll meet here Sam. Bring what you've got back with you." Knowles replied.

"You need a refill, Boss?" Bradshaw asked, if Knowles missed Millers' offer.

"No, I'll get some later." Knowles said as she placed Ella's lunch box in a lower drawer pushing her back-up weapon, a holstered 10 shot GLOCK 26, farther back into the drawer to make room for Sponge Bob and Ella's PB&J sandwich.

Knowles rose up showing that her Police 38 S&W remained snug against the turn of her left hip, positioned for a quick right hand pull. She fingered her hair and smiled toward her door-mirror reflection. Her black pant suit, with just a hint of light gray vertical striping, was definitely thinning for her figure. At 6'1" Knowles had no problem carrying 140 pounds attractively, but any slimming was always good for a tall gal's ego. She hung her jacket on her chair-back and turned to watch as just over six-foot, craggy faced, rumple suited Detective Sam Millers and five six, thin, fashionably dressed Sergeant Morris Bradshaw returned with their coffees. Linda pushed her phone back more to accommodate their papers and coffee as she greeted her crew, "I haven't heard from Stephen Irons," Knowles began as Millers and Bradshaw sat down. "They must have stayed in Dallas. It can't be easy for either of them,"

"There's more to it," Millers interrupted as Knowles sat back down, "I picked up an Airport Incident Sheet last night, Irons was attacked early Sunday morning in the airport's main parking-garage, he was certain the guy was trying to kill him."

"Is Stephen okay?" Knowles interrupted and Millers suspected Knowles' past association with Irons had brought on the first name familiarity. Millers took out his small notebook and answered,

"I think so, he reported the guy carried a garrote, but Irons said 'he was able to dodge the attack and actually placed a strong kick to the guy's left knee before some Airport Security guy named Joel intervened and the attacker fled'."

"Did this Joel give us a description?"

"Actually Irons gave a detailed one, his formal training I guess. Here it is Irons said *'the guy was tall, six two and over two hundred pounds, dark Asian face, with eyes hidden behind dark, reflective sunglasses'*," Millers flipped to the next page and continued, "He said, *'the guy had black hair, mid to late thirties and was dressed for travel in a light weight tan jacket, dark slacks and open collared dark brown shirt'*, hmm, that's hardly like the I'm planning to attack you and choke you to death, criminal's choice of attire," Millers jokingly offered as tucked his notebook away and passed the airport sheet to Knowles. "You can see in the report Irons thought the guy was a professional, Irons said, *'the guy seemed trained, focused and agile'*, but Irons added, *'he was careless, restricting his fist thrust by holding both ends of the garrote'*. Maybe, he thought Irons was going to be easy, like he knew about Irons' prior injuries. What do you think Chief?"

Knowles ignored Millers' speculation and said, "Did you talk to the Security guy?"

"Eh, not yet, but I plan on going out later with Bradshaw, I want to talk to the soccer kids too. You know the ones Bradshaw interviewed earlier. Hey, this could connect with the Harrington case, you know, Irons being part of that family." Millers thought a second and added, "Maybe since he gave such a good description, Irons could work with a sketch-artist when he comes back?" Millers waited but got no response concerning his question about the attacker's prior knowledge, or the sketch possibility because Bradshaw intervened,

"The kids didn't have a lot to say," Bradshaw said, momentarily taken-back by Millers second-guessing his interview with the soccer kids.

"Yeah, I understand, but the kids may have seen something you didn't ask about. I want to feel them out just to make sure. You have names don't you?"

"Of course, two ten year olds and a twelve, kicking a soccer-ball around in Lakewood Park, one of the tens and the twelve are brothers, the other ten year old lives close-by." Bradshaw offered quickly, then, tried to think of everything he might have asked the kids but remembered only how they said, *"We were kicking the soccer-ball between the trees for practice before we saw the fire."*

"I'd like Bradshaw to go with me Chief. He's met the kids, might help put them at ease." Millers now said trying to calm Bradshaw's obvious concern.

"Good idea Sam, do it when we've finished here, get the kids before you go to the airport for the Security guard, Lakewood's right on the way." Knowles said then added, "The sketch is a good idea too, I'm not sure there could be a connection but I'll ask Stephen to help when he returns."

"Okay," Millers replied without telling Knowles he'd go to the airport first because the kids would still be in school.

As Knowles stood to summarize the report she carried, Millers and Bradshaw caught each other glancing beyond the report to her hidden belly button. They both smiled conspiringly as she began, "From the preliminary reports here are my thoughts." Millers relaxed further and leaned-back in his chair, Knowles was center stage now he'd just finish his coffee and listen. Bradshaw saw Millers' body language adjustment and followed the lead as Knowles went on,

"The gun found in Harrington's hand was the weapon used to kill him. Only one set of prints, Harrington's. Fresh scrape marks on the barrel, where a slide-on silencer could have been attached." Knowles paused and rechecked her notes, then, "Looks like Harrington handled the gun once, no smears or overlaps almost a perfect set. His right hand did test GPR positive for firing the weapon and some of his skull fragment spray was on the gun's trigger guard that matched the star pattern bullet wound residue from his head. Funny, skull fragments on the trigger guard but no residue from on Harrington's hand or the gun barrel. Whoa, that's damn odd,"

"Huh, you think the gun could have been silenced, fired, cleaned, then, shoved in Harrington's hand and fired again? Millers said almost laughingly.

"Well, it could be a suicide as Chief Beck believes, but I think it's possible someone killed Harrington, put the weapon in his hand and fired it again to get a positive GPR."

"They found another slug?" Bradshaw asked,

"No, the body was found in the den where Harrington was working but they found sand grains dispersed around the kitchen floor and leading into the den. Some were on Harrington's back too, so I think someone could have killed Harrington in the kitchen with a silenced weapon, placed the gun in Harrington's dead hand and fired it into some kind of sand filled container. After that the killer replaced one of the empty shells with a live round and removed the silencer before dragging Harrington's body into the den. That, would leave everything the way we found it. Like Harrington did-himself-in where he was working," Knowles paused for comments, got none so she checked her report and continued.

"Fibers under his fingernails weren't from Harrington's shirt. They could be from the killer's clothing or some other fabric in Harrington's house. We're still checking for that possibility. Basically I'm leaning toward a Homicide, what do you think?" Knowles asked.

"Might be a stretch without prints on the shell casings or positive fiber evidence," Bradshaw offered, wanting to participate, "And if it was Homicide, how come no one saw the killer before or after? There was Pee Wee, football in Lakewood Park but no one saw anything until the fire trucks arrived, then the police cars,"

"Maybe the kids saw something else," Millers interrupted, "the football people were farther away watching the games until the fire trucks showed up making a lot of noise. But Morris, did you actually ask the kids if they saw anyone coming or going to the Harrington house while they kicked the soccer-ball around?"

"No, I didn't ask specifically, the kids just said," Bradshaw's face turned slightly red as he paused to retrieve his own small notebook from his shirt pocket. He opened the green pad to the fourth page where he found the referenced interview and quoted notes, *"We stopped kicking the ball for a minute, looked up, and that's when we seen the smoke. I ran to the closest house to call the fire people,"* Bradshaw closed his notebook and continued, "That quote was the twelve year old, Bobby Foster, the other two kids mostly parroted his remarks."

"Well, I still believe it could be a suicide, but here's my point," Millers said, "the kids are having fun kicking the soccer-ball around the trees, why did they stop for that minute and look up before they saw the fire? What made them look up? It may be nothing but maybe they saw something else. It's just a thought. Or, if there was a killer, he could have come in by water and no one would have seen him… "

"Okay, check with the kids first. If nothing, then chase down the water-traffic, seems to me there's still crabbing in the river and a local girls-school rowing team practicing on Saturday mornings, you can check on the rowers too," Knowles instructed.

"Sure," Millers answered then asked, "any other prelims from the lab?"

"Two more concerns, I think. One, debris from the computer was on top of Harrington's body, hard to achieve unless he was already on the floor, dead, when the computer got smashed and scattered broken bits around. Two, no fingerprints on the suicide note or the letter from his agent rejecting Harrington's book idea 'Pacific Secret'. The rejection paper was crumpled up and thrown on the desk like it was the final straw that broke his back. He could have let the suicide note print out without touching it, but it's hard for him to read the agent's letter, crumple and toss it without leaving at least a partial." The phone on Knowles' desk, rang and she picked it up,

"Knowles," she replied to the operator, "Sure, put him through, it's Stephen Irons." she offered Millers and Bradshaw, then to the phone, "Stephen, are you alright? I've heard about the airport attack." Knowles listened for about 20 seconds, reached for a pen, flipped over one of her earlier reports and began to write on the back. Then she asked,

"How's Sally doing?" she listened for another 30 seconds,

"Okay, when will you return to Norfolk?" another 20 seconds,

"I've got all that, call me when you get back, we'll get together and bring you up to speed. Were getting more evidence in now and Sally's house is okay for her return. We're finished there but I'll need to talk to both of you about Wilber. We don't know if there's a connection, but maybe you can help us with a composite sketch of your airport attacker." Knowles listened to Irons' answer then closed,

"Thanks for calling, tell Sally how sorry we are for her loss and we're working hard to find a lead if there is a killer." Knowles replaced the phone and seemed to be thinking of something more. Millers and Bradshaw kept quiet and waited. "Okay, nothing Stephen said changed my thinking about the case. Check with Airport Security, the soccer kids and if needed the water traffic possibility. Bradshaw, you and Millers might also try the neighbors Dr. and Mrs. Hall one more time, if it is a Homicide the key could be this 'Pacific Secret' book, maybe they know something about it. I'll check with forensics for fiber results then call our accounting people they're working on Harrington's financials, any questions or comments?"

"I hope you're right Chief, but it seems to me, you're jumping to a Homicide too quick." Millers offered and waited but Knowles didn't respond, so he added, "Okay, we'll head out, did Irons add anything that wasn't in the airport report?"

"Not really, just that he was certain the guy was a professional and out to kill him. He said he'd been lucky the security guard came along when he did. Get back to me when you've got more info." Knowles said as Millers and Bradshaw departed.

After Millers and Bradshaw had gathered their information and communication devices they left the building headed for Millers' car. When they drove off in the unmarked Ford Crown Victoria, Millers asked, "Didn't you think that was a little weird, not letting us hear Irons' information on the speaker? I think three heads listening would be better than one."

"Yeah, she didn't use the speaker when you called in Sunday morning. I guess she wants to evaluate everything before asking our opinion." Bradshaw stated as they drove north on Chesapeake Boulevard headed toward to the airport. Millers thought for a minute about Knowles, then, he replied,

"Well, Chief Beck's got her under some pressure, but she's definitely been secretive and in a big hurry to prove herself since her husband was killed. I guess it could be a protected turf thing, you know, she and her daughter Ella are 'alone and against the world' now." Millers said as he began to ease the car through the Five-Points Intersection turning onto Norview Avenue headed to the Airport. Passing Alexander Street, on their left, they could see a lengthy string of Crime Scene Tape cordoning off a large area and a police officer patrolling the street with a shotgun. WAVY- TV10 News was starting to set-up outside the Crime Scene Tape.

"What's that all that about Millers, have you heard?" Bradshaw asked pointing toward the growing commotion near the crime scene tape.

"No, but that's Alexander Street, one of the roughest areas in Norfolk and it is on 'our turf', so we'll know about it soon enough."

CHAPTER ELEVEN

DFW, AIRPORT, MONDAY 10:15AM

"STEPHEN IRONS"

Sally and I are seated in First Class on American Airlines' non-stop flight to Norfolk, she's by the window and I'm on the aisle. Last night was tough for Sally, but several of her friends learned of Wilber's death and stayed with her before going home to their own families. They were very helpful since most of her friends knew Sally's emotional needs far better than I did. I promised myself to do something to change that. We were quiet now as the aircraft taxied toward the runway and I heard through the PA system,

"Ladies and gentlemen, good morning, I'm Karen. We've been cleared for an immediate takeoff once we reach the active runway - All cell phones and computers should be turned OFF at this time - Thank you." After Karen made her announcement she came over to where Sally and I are sitting. She knelt down in the aisle and leaned across me and said,

"Sally we're all so sorry for your loss, please let me know if there's anything I can do for you, or your brother, during the flight." Karen smiled up at me then looked back to Sally. Consciously I breathed in her fragrance and looked at her young profile. Karen has rich, auburn hair, shorter, curlier and much darker than my sister's long red tresses. I smiled looking at her young facial features; her subtle cheek bones, clear skin and calming hazel-green eyes. Sally responded,

"Thank you Karen and please thank everyone for their kindness." Karen smiled, touched Sally's arm then she went to speak with other passengers. I continued to watch as Karen rose-up, turned and moved away. Then, once she was well away and my olfactory sense had cleared of her memory, I came back to reality and asked Sally,

"Do you know all American's Flight Attendants? I thought you said there're over twenty thousand of you,"

"About twenty three thousand Stephen, but I don't really know more than a couple hundred... It's just that the word," Sally's eyes glistened with tears and she wiped them with a tissue before she continued, "You know the word about such a loss to one of us gets around quickly and the crew knows what happened to Will and want me know how sorry they are."

"I'm sorry too Sally, maybe we shouldn't talk about it." I offered as I noticed her eyes filling with tears and Karen made another announcement interrupting our conversation,

"Ladies and gentlemen, thank you for choosing American Airlines, please fasten your seat-belts and stow your tray tables - Flight Attendants please take your seats for an immediate takeoff." Karen instructed from her jump seat position near the cockpit door.

Thirty minutes later our aircraft leveled at cruising altitude and several of the flight attendants began to move about the First Class Cabin preparing to serve the passengers. Our conversation had been quiet during the climb-out and I again listened as Karen returned to speak to Sally, "I know it's early, Sally, but can I get you something to eat or drink?"

"No, Karen, we had breakfast, but maybe Stephen?" Sally said.

"No, no, I'm fine." I responded looking directly into Karen's eyes as she smiled, touched Sally's arm again and departed. I continued to watch my little sister as she stared through the window looking at contrails from some other aircraft headed back toward Dallas or farther toward the west coast. Finally I broke the silence and asked,

"Sally, you said you need to talk about Wilber's death, do you really?"

"Yes, I want to know everything you know. I want to hear what the police thought initially and what they believe now. I know you told me last night but last night's a horrible blur. I'm much stronger today, and I want to know." Sally's eyes began to tear again and I quickly offered,

"Sally maybe it's just too soon,"

"No, no, it's not that," she interrupted, "when Will and I traveled on vacations, we always shared Mimosas on early flights, I want to have one now, for Will, okay?"

"Sure, I'll have one for Wilber too." I looked around for Karen but she was in the rear of our cabin so I reached up toward the Flight Attendant call-button located on the overhead compartment. Sally saw my effort and lightly clasped my forearm to stop me,

"No, Stephen, someone will be back, please don't bother them with the call-bell."

"Sorry," I replied and brought my arm down.

"It's okay, it's just that the 'call-bell' is so over-used, we sometimes tell kids that use it all the time, that, 'it's only for important stuff, like death'" Sally heard herself make the familiar joke then her eyes re-flooded, "God, I need that drink."

Another flight attendant, name-tagged Chris, arrived and I asked for two Mimosas. She was a tall blonde gal that could have just stepped off a 'fashion runway' to help us. Chris touched Sally's arm with comfort and did an about-face and marched off on her assignment.

After Chris delivered our drinks, another thirty minutes went by as we cruised allowing time for Mimosas in uninterrupted calmness. As we sipped I continued to watch Sally remembering her as a child with big freckles and bright red hair carrying a small Raggedy Ann Doll when she followed me everywhere. I was flattered at first, then annoyed, and finally down-right pissed that every time I wanted to go with my friends, my mom wanted me to take four year old Sally with me. Pretty soon all my friends began to call her 'Tagalong', then, they shortened it to 'Tag' and the nick-name stuck until five years later when Sally was in the fourth grade and she just refused to answer anyone unless they called her 'Sally'. I smiled remembering,

"You're smiling Stephen, what are you thinking about?" Sally asked.

"You and me when we were kids, you know the 'Tagalong' name you had and how stubborn you were once you decided you were tired of the name. It just occurred to me how concerned mom was for your safety." I paused with emotion building in my chest threatening to restrict my breathing. I fought off the discomfort and went on, "It was like all my training in the Navy that pushed one rule, 'Never leave a buddy, always stay and protect your partner'." I could feel my face flush with shame and embarrassment about what the Navy's investigation finally labeled as 'gross inattention to duty' for my not forcing my self to respond and try to protect my own partner. I looked around for Thornton and his reaction to my thoughts but he must have missed the flight. So I smiled at Sally and tried to continue,

"Our Mom must have known that 'navy rule' when she tried to tell me my job was to protect my little sister. I guess I was too young and selfish to understand then." My voice faded again, I had just agreed with the navy's findings judging my own lack of response to Thornton's decision to confront the Afghani insurgents. Damn, I was still having loyalty issues. I took a deep breath wanting to talk to Sally about when Thornton was killed and I was rescued. I wanted to talk about our dad dying and the investigation into Thornton's loss that was postponed initially due to that loss. I wanted to talk about the navy's final verdict's reprimand and my mandated duty- and grief-counseling. I truly regretted the events of the war and the resulting erosion of my self-confidence and physical health. But talking about my personal issues was self-serving, focusing on my own problems not Sally's. So, I fought the temptation and tried to stay focused on my little sister, adding only,

"I hope I've been able to be there for you Sally."

"Of course you have, Stephen. When I was ten and you were graduating from high school we were close, but you were changing. I'd never seen you so defiant of dad when you enlisted in the Navy and started off on your new life. I'm sure that's when we began to drift apart, you know, you going in the Navy and growing-up on your own." Sally was beginning to tear-up, so I took her hand and said,

"Sally what I loved most about you marrying Wilber was that he brought you and I close together again. Not just geographically, when you moved back to Norfolk, but as a real family, you know, brother and sister," I was reluctant as I offered this observation and expected Sally to start crying again. Instead she smiled squeezed my hand and said,

"I know it was sad that I didn't see you much when you were in the Navy, then after 9-11 you were deployed and missed our wedding. I was so upset,"

"Upsetting for me too, Sally, you know, my little sister getting married and me not being there to see how beautiful and happy you were."

"I felt happy and beautiful Stephen, Will made me feel that way. After the wedding, when mom and dad went home, Will and I talked about you and me and our sibling relationship. Will told me as an only child he'd grown-up selfish, introverted and secretive, but he'd always wanted a brother or sister so he could have opened up more and learned to share his thoughts and feelings with someone close, someone in his own family he could trust. It's one of the reasons I fell in love with Will. Maybe he was an 'older father-figure' like some friends thought, but I think it was more about his consideration, his experiences in life, both the good and the bad. Will helped me with all my problems, even with 9-11 and continuing to fly after the loss of so many friends to that horrible tragedy. Then, after you deployed to Afghanistan and later when we lost dad and mom, Will was always there for me. Even now, after the loss of Will himself, just remembering his past kindness and caring can help me get through all of this." Sally smiled holding on to my hand as she added, "Sorry I carried on so, please, tell me again what you know so far."

I felt like crying myself after Sally's disclosures but I got control and talked non-stop for forty minutes about what I had been told initially by Sheriff Os, then by Detective Knowles. I covered everything I could remember, only leaving out the attack I had experienced at the Norfolk airport. Sally remained attentive and undisturbed until I said, "The police think it could be important to know what the book Wilber was working on is about. Do you have any idea?"

"Not really, we joked but he hadn't shared much about the 'Pacific' book with me. Will did say it was futuristic and a bit scientific, like his first book… Don't the police have any hope of gathering the information from his destroyed computer?"

"I'm not sure, Sally, I don't know much about computers, but didn't Wilber have copies of his ideas on other papers, or maybe another computer disc…"

"Oh my god, Margo's computer," Sally said, then, she began to cry again,

"Who's Margo?" I asked. Sally kept crying but between her sobs she offered,

"She's a flight attendant friend. On an earlier trip when Will traveled to Frankfurt with me, Margo loaned him her laptop so he could transfer all his hand-written notes. She made him a copy of the information on a computer disc to take home. I guess that's gone, but the original's probably on Margo's computer."

"Sally, that information could be a big help to the police, what's upsetting you?"

"Another flight-attendant friend, Maribeth, told me Will and Margo had an affair right after we got engaged. She told me Saturday night in Germany. I had just talked to Will on the phone, it was the last time I heard his voice. I didn't know what to do I was too upset to call Will back so I tried to call you. I just needed to talk to someone."

Chris saw Sally crying and came over and asked me to move to an empty seat, then, she sat down and tried to comfort Sally. I had no idea how to handle Sally's concern about Wilber and Margo, but, whatever Margo might have on her computer could be a big help to Detective Knowles. I moved to the rear of the cabin and sat down in an empty row. Thornton hadn't missed our flight and I watched his image enter through the business section's curtain, then he moved forward and sat down next to me and said,

"You should have returned Sally's phone call Rusty maybe you could have saved her some heartache. Now she's got Wilber's death and possible betrayal piled on top of your lack of consideration. You've got a real mess here bud."

CHAPTER TWELVE

TIEN CHING, CHINA

Director Niam Wang's penthouse office overlooked Po Hai Bay to the east. Farther east, through the growing smog that drifted in from the industrialized west, Dr. Wang was certain he could make out the Yellow Sea, the large body of water that separated China from the Korean Peninsula. As he moved slowly around his elevated office he watched the start of the construction in Beijing for the 2008 Olympics. The towering cranes in the distance resembled an uncoordinated concert, like a large orchestra during 'tune up' prior to the opening overture. Now, with China's designation as the Olympic Site for the year 2008, Director Wang remembered the great optimism his new leaders had shown initiating China's economic revival. But he also recalled the opposition they faced from right-wing critics concerning China's rapidly growing population's deteriorating sanitary conditions and lack of flexibility when dealing with Socio-Economic issues. Dr. Wang recalled the leaders stating,

"The people want the Rulers of China to finally show the 'iron fist' that has been so carefully hidden in China's diplomatically gloved hand."

That 'iron fist' comment gave Wang the opportunity to brief the new rulers on Deep Dragon and its Operational Commander, Cheng Tieren, the oldest son of Dr. Cheng Ji, China's well known and respected voice for the people demanding China's revived focus on nationalism. Seizing the opportunity, Wang had been able to convince the new leaders that Deep Dragon could be the hidden 'Fist' China needed to gain respect from the rest of the world. A soft knock sounded at the door, "Yes, Sun Jing," Dr. Wang responded,

"Your, telephone Director, the President calls," Dr. Wang's secretary answered and closed the door behind her departure. Wang removed the phone from its cradle, activated several switches to secure the conversation and spoke into the instrument,

"Yes, my President, how can I serve you most honored sir?" Director Wang listened for 30 seconds, took several notes on the pad, then,

"Yes, Cheng has just departed and his briefing was excellent. Deep Dragon remains operational at full capacity. His points were as expected, plus several others designed to foster even greater nationalism. He was very professional and highlighted the program's many successes." A minute passed listening and taking several more notes,

"Thank you sir, my only desire is to serve you and our great Nation." 20 seconds listening,

"Yes, Cheng believes totally in Deep Dragon, he is fully committed and has initiated several actions to protect its operational secrecy." Two minutes more, following with several notes taken in BOLD characters,

"You are correct Sir we have highly trained assets already in-place and Cheng is frequently in protected contact with our primary asset now controlling a second operative on temporary assignment. Cheng assures me they have worked together and he has every confidence in their ultimate success." Two more minutes of intense listening, note taking and major point characters overprinted to emphasize their importance,

"Yes sir, I too have seen the beginnings of Olympic construction and I now fully understand your concern and your ultimate desire. I will have Cheng speak with our primary and I will personally contact our guarded American associates with your assurances." Ten seconds more listening while underlining one final note,

"Thank you, sir. Yes, you have my most humble word on the issue." Dr. Wang replaced the telephone receiver, reached to his safe and extracted his monthly security listings and coded ciphers. He must act immediately he had just given his word to the President of China.

CHAPTER THIRTEEN

THE VIRGINIA ZOO

THE ELEPHANT BARN

Eric Chin, now wearing an elastic support brace on his left knee, felt his leg strain as he pulled the large water hose across the fourth elephant stall and opened the flow nozzle to direct heavy spray against the etched concrete floor. This Monday morning's clean-up had been strenuous because the elephant stalls were exceptionally filthy due to a heavy wind-laden rainstorm on Sunday that kept the zoo's three elephants restricted to the barn. While Eric hosed down the last elephant stall, Ursula Volk, the Virginia Zoo's Elephant Manager, was outside coordinating with a Norfolk Sheriff supervising several local convicts performing physical labor for the city owned zoo.

Eric picked up the pace of his effort knowing Ursula would return soon to bring the three elephants back inside the barn. After that she and a second keeper would bathe and feed them before the zoo opened and the three large animals were released into their exercise yard for visitors to view. Eric continued to work inside the large vertical bars installed to contain the elephants. The anodized steel bars were massive, 8" in diameter and spaced 2 feet apart allowing human travel between the bars but restricting the elephants' massive heads and gigantic bodies. Each separate stall had large electrically controlled and hydraulically operated gates that required coded-key-access to activate them open or closed. The stalls and gates kept the elephants separated, or allowed them controlled travel from one secure space to another. The Virginia Zoo's three African Elephants, Monica, Lisa and Cita, weighing approximately nine thousand, ten thousand and eight thousand pounds, respectively, were three of the zoo's showcase animals on display daily. Like many other AZA (Association of Zoos and Aquariums) members, the Virginia Zoo had responded positively to earlier studies recommending the use of 'protected contact' when elephant keepers interacted with their elephants. As a result the zoo's elephant keepers strived to have containment bars between themselves and their elephants at all times.

As he directed the heavy spray onto the highest side of the final enclosure Eric was reminded of his introduction to forced-water torture-training in the Chinese Special Agency Program. Exhaustive training that employed the practice of water-boarding and lengthy confinement in extremely small enclosures. Eric discarded his thoughts as Ursula Volk reentered the barn and he heard, "Eric, are you finished?"

"Almost, must clean and flush the drains, then, finished." Eric replied.

"Do it quickly, Eric, Dennis will be back soon to help bathe the 'girls' then you and I will truck the 'animal waste' to the dumpster." Ursula Volk instructed.

When Dennis returned, he and Ursula brought the three elephants into the barn and positioned them for bathing in separated stalls. The elephants were bathed individually by the two keepers then fed a mixture of compressed grains, food supplements, antibiotics, salt, vegetables and fruits. During their bathing each elephant were asked to respond to the many commands given by the controlling keeper to position and reposition them throughout the process. Commands and food rewards were used to reinforce each elephant's willingness to follow directions and remain under the keeper's control. As the two keepers finished Ursula said to Eric,

"Outside are some long stalks of green bamboo piled by the road, drag a dozen stalks in the barn and we'll feed the girls a treat before we go to the dumpster."

Eric went outside the barn, located and counted out twelve of the bamboo stalks that had been grown at the zoo for the elephants. When he returned with the bamboo Ursula positioned four stalks near each elephant stall and said, "Dennis, we're going now, finish with the giraffes and when I get back we'll move everybody out."

As they departed the barn, with Eric walking well to the left of the red restricting line, assuring no elephant conflict, he turned to watch the dominant elephant, Monica, pull a green bamboo stalks into her stall. She held the stalk with her trunk, stepped on it with a gigantic forefoot then twisted it, splintering the long green bamboo, making it easier to devour. While Monica ate the bamboo she watched Eric with her right eye tracking his every movement, *CRACK, CRACK, CRACK,* the rapid sound of green bamboo splintering in three separate stalls echoed in the barn causing Eric to flinch from the piercing sound that brought another memory, the memory of initial weapons training after joining China's Ministry of State Security, when he first learned to fire a hand-held, semi automatic pistol. The acoustics of the elephant barn were similar to the Ministry's indoor range and the resultant excitement of repetitive, rapid-fire noise brought a spurt of adrenaline to Eric's system as he exited the barn and climbed in the large lift-back truck.

When Eric closed the truck door, Ursula spoke to him, bringing him abruptly back to the present, "Eric, we need to talk, I'm concerned that your mission failed,"

"No opportunity with rifle," Eric offered but Ursula cut him off,

"You were to travel to Dallas to complete the mission. Why didn't you go?"

"Irons came back to his car and I chose to attempt in Norfolk what I planned in Dallas." Eric answered quickly looking for understanding but only hearing,

"A suppressed rifle protected you, but a physical confrontation here was risky, I'm concerned with your carelessness Eric." Ursula paused as the truck stopped near one of the front service gates to the zoo grounds. Eric began to answer but Ursula pointed toward the gate so Eric got out with the key to unlock and slide the large gate open and let the truck move out of the secured area.

As he waited for Ursula to drive the truck clear of the gate, Eric's mind looked for comfort from her inquisition and he focused his thoughts on the mermaid statue near the sliding gate. The statue depicted a tiger-mermaid with cascading hair. Her image brought back his childhood memories of the Little Mermaid statue in the harbor of Copenhagen, Denmark. More memories tried to return, but his nostalgia was interrupted as Ursula called,

"Eric, hurry up. Close and lock the gate now."

When Eric reentered the truck cab, he tried to explain Sunday's mission failure, "You said Irons was recovering from earlier wounds and would be an easy target in Dallas, I assumed he would be 'easy' in Norfolk, so I made the attempt. But I found Irons in good health. He is well-trained and defended against my attack. This was a surprise,"

"Yes, I received bad information," Ursula allowed as she stopped the truck again. They were now at the back entrance gate to the zoo and needed to open a second gate to access the fenced-in dumpster area. Eric left the truck again, opened the second gate then closed and relocked it once the truck passed through. He returned to the truck cab and Ursula continued to drive toward the large garbage dumpster adding, "Your assignment is OFF until we have more information on Irons' condition and knowledge of the book information you destroyed,"

"Very well," Eric replied, pleased with him self for keeping three of the computer discs he had removed from the Harrington house. The discs could prove to be his safety net.

As Eric and Ursula climbed into the back of the truck and began to dump the four large wheelbarrows into the Norfolk city dumpster, Ursula became concerned again and said, "Eric, did you personally destroy all the Harrington information?"

"Yes, of course, all destroyed." Eric replied confidently.

When they finished dumping all the waste material and got back in the truck to begin to back-track their earlier route Ursula asked, "Can you work at the zoo next Sunday?"

"Yes, Ursula. Here at 7 AM?"

"No, we have night work. I'll meet you at 10 PM, Sunday night. Okay?"

"Yes, I will be here." Eric replied believing his initial failure would be soon forgotten and he would be given another opportunity to deal with Stephen Irons.

CHAPTER FOURTEEN

CIA HEADQUARTERS, 9AM

FBI, Deputy Director, Russell Rollins had been sent to meet with a senior level representative of the CIA. Rollins was ushered into the office of the CIA's Deputy Director's for Far Eastern Operations, Dr. William Kale. After introductions Dr. Kale and Rollins moved to a small conference room where Dr. Kale asked an assistant, Craig Cooper, to brief Rollins on some newly acquired information. Cooper began,

"Please direct your attention to the charted area in the Pacific Ocean," Cooper instructed as a large screen presentation showed a vast area of the Pacific Ocean with a small circled section near the Tropic of Cancer. The area was centered at 58N and 157E and was labeled - 350 NAUTICAL MILES NORTH OF WAKE ISLAND – Cooper went on, "We have recently gained confirmation concerning the installation of a Chinese nuclear device on the ocean floor at this location, approximately 25,000' below the surface." Cooper used a laser pointer to indicate the exact spot.

"The Chinese device is a combination Fission/Fusion Reactor designed, built and deployed to dramatically increase the deep-water temperature through the expulsion of superheated seawater. Currently the device's exhaust temperatures are in excess of 2000 degrees Fahrenheit," Cooper paused to emphasis the fact that the CIA was capable of obtaining this technical data then he went on,

"The device was activated on October 6, 2001, in an attempt to influence weather patterns throughout the Pacific area, to include Hawaii, California, Washington, Oregon and Alaska. Further investigation revealed China waited to deploy the device immediately after the September 11 terrorist attack on New York," Cooper stopped abruptly noting Rollins was attempting to write information in a small notebook. In a strong voice Cooper said,

"Mr. Rollins, this briefing is TOP SECRET- DIRECTOR LEVEL SEVEN - EYES ONLY. The information has been provided under separate cover to your director. Please push your notebook to the center of the table, now. After 'Sanitation' your notebook will be returned."

Rollins did as he was told, diverting direct eye contact with Cooper and his host. Cooper nodded and continued, "Thank you. Further information, confirms the secret project was initiated primarily to assuage aggressive nationalistic factions throughout China…"

The presentation screen changed showing Mainland China and a number of Chinese Provinces highlighted in a pale yellow. Cooper's laser pointed to several provinces with labels indicating the location of nationalistic factions and their relative strengths before he clicked a small device and the presentation change back to the Pacific Ocean. Cooper turned a page in his briefing guide and went on, "Hurricanes, typhoons, earthquakes and tsunamis, have all been on the rise in the past five years. However, reliable scientific data now indicates the increases were predominantly cyclical in nature, and not overly influenced by the installation of the Chinese device. This verification is born out by the very low incidence of such weather phenomena in 2006. Recent studies confirm that global weather patterns are far more influenced by the sea temperatures near the 'Cromwell Currents' of the Pacific Ocean, rather than the deep water temperatures affected by the Chinese device." Cooper paused to see if Dr. Kale wanted him to explain the Cromwell Current but Kale supplied a 'move on with the briefing' indication and Cooper resumed,

"The Chinese believe their program has served its purpose and will probably be terminated soon. We are presently focusing on the need to monitor the termination of this operation. Are there any comments or questions?"

Rollins started to speak, to ask about the Cromwell Current but Dr. Kale cut that discussion off, "Thank you, Cooper, you're excused for the time being." Cooper closed the viewing screen and departed the room as Dr. Kale turned to Rollins, "Mr. Rollins, I'm certain you may have other questions, but our Director has personally briefed the FBI Director and any additional information for you will be disseminated by his office." After removing three pages from Rollins' notebook Dr. Kale handed it back to Rollins. "This briefing and our conversation remains TOP SECRET and should be treated as such."

Rollins was ushered from Dr. Kale's office and he hustled to keep pace with Cooper through an increasing number of hallways and stairways. When they entered an elevator and the door slid closed for their travel to the parking basement, Rollins reached over and grabbed Cooper's jacket sleeve to gain his attention. Cooper's mind was far away in Afghanistan and he reacted immediately, twisting toward Rollins, seizing Rollins' arms and forcing them behind his back as he dropped Rollins' butt to the floor of the elevator with a heavy *THUD,*

"Sorry, Director Rollins," Cooper offered immediately realizing his mistake as he helped Rollins back up, "Some muscle memories are far more responsive than a lulling brain, my fault entirely. No disrespect intended, please accept my apology, sir."

"Apology accepted." Rollins replied attempting to recover some resemblance of dignity as the elevator door slid open, they exited the carriage and cleared the final check point. Arriving in the Visitor's Parking Section in the CIA basement Cooper led Rollins to his waiting automobile now parked near a convenient Exit. Rollins smiled that the CIA had surreptitiously moved his car and he now decided Cooper owed him, for that and the physical affront. Rollins asked,

"Could you give me a quick brief on the Cromwell Current?"

Cooper remained embarrassed about their elevator incident and offered, "I can tell you that the Current is a much shallower body of water flowing in the Pacific for 3500 miles along the equator. It has a width of almost 250 miles. Sorry, Director Rollins but I've got to hurry back now… You can find more information on line, sir." With that, Cooper closed Rollins' car door and turned on his heel to depart.

CHAPTER FIFTEEN

CIA

Dr. Kale turned toward the door as Cooper returned and said, "Rollins' headed out Boss. I've got an update on 'Snoop One', when you're ready…"

"What happened in the elevator Cooper? Security just called." Dr. Kale said.

"My reflex response to Rollins' grabbing me, sorry, Boss."

"You're NOT on assignment Cooper you're home now. Get a better grip while you're in a more civilized environment. How far along is the sub?" Dr. Kale asked as he dismissed Cooper's earlier reaction, turned away and thumbed through his day planner looking for an opportunity to brief the DCI later in the afternoon.

"The subs in Honolulu sir, her Captain will be in Admiral Bennett's office receiving briefings and mission orders within the hour. Travel time should be four days, arriving, Tuesday, 3 October, late Tuesday their time early hours for us. At that time Admiral Bennett should get a direct message concerning the actual expulsion temperatures of the device, indicating Chinese compliance or non compliance," Dr. Kale interrupted Cooper,

"I want a Point Paper this afternoon, Cooper, give me three outcomes and recommendations for the DCI. First, the most logical two, list the most likely as the kick off, then, go worst case for the second, after that close the paper with something questionable, something for the Director to puzzle out. Who's the sub's commander?"

"Captain Benson B. Bordeaux, like the wine, sir, he's been in Nuke Subs almost his entire career. He's a deep draft promotion a year ago. Probably make Rear Admiral, lower-half, next year. He's been recognized for superior performance lately,"

"Lately, Cooper? What else should I know?" Dr. Kale asked,

"Nothing really sir," Cooper paused weighing whether he should mention the connection between Bordeaux and Commander Wilber Harrington in February 2001 when their sub ran aground, but Cooper decided against it. "Captain Bordeaux is well qualified for this mission, sir. He had a normal career progression until serving on the White House Staff during the President's first term, then, he got a promotion boost and went back to subs as CO of the Hampton Roads. Now, he's commanding the Chattanooga, perfect for the mission."

"His timing seems good, late 2001 at the White House must have been challenging." Dr. Kale pondered, then, added, "You ever sorry about coming with 'the company' Cooper, you know, not continuing your navy career?"

"No Boss, I'm fortunate working for you, you've given me plenty of chances to serve my country and do my own thing. I appreciate it. Is that all sir?"

"Be careful 'doing your own thing' especially here at home Cooper, that's important." Dr. Kale offered, then, "Get on the paper, I'll need it by three this afternoon. I'm setting up with the Director at 3:45. I want you available in case he has questions."

For two hours Cooper looked at all the pertinent information in the CIA Research Facility that dealt with the Chinese and their growing attempt to make inroads into recognition as a world power. Cooper read through China's association with other countries and their interventions to deny the U.S. access to their theater of operations. During his research Cooper came across two unfamiliar references, 'assassin's mace' and 'trump card', Cooper began to read from a detailed report:

"…developing of 'assassin mace' weapons is not a new concept in China. However, since 1999 the term has appeared more frequently in Chinese professional journals, particularly in the context of fighting the United States in a Taiwan conflict. What actually classifies as an 'assassin's mace' weapon remains unclear. However, the concept appears to include a range of weapon systems and technologies…"

Cooper thought the Chinese Fission-Fusion Device was applicable and smiled planning how this could work for his point paper. Next he changed his attention to 'trump card',

"…the Chinese concept of 'trump card' weapons extends beyond specific systems or technologies to include non tangibles such as 'people's war' as a deterrent to a land invasion of China or 'economic and trade diplomacy' as increasing China's competitiveness with the United States in an Asia-Pacific region…"

Cooper smiled and began to draft his point paper, he had all the information he needed to address the 'most likely' and the 'worst case'. With a little more thought he could have an intriguing puzzler for the DCI.

CHAPTER SIXTEEN

FBI HEADQUARTERS

FBI Special Agent Clayton Davis entered the outer office of his boss Russell Rollins, the Deputy Director for The Department of Organizational Liaison, (DOL). The DOL is a spin-off Section created to do what the FBI called C3 work, an acronym for Coordinate, Communicate and Collaborate. The DOL handled the FBI's dealings with the CIA, NSA, DIA, Congress and Homeland Security. Clayton was transferred to the DOL in January and now believed he was working in one of many bureaucratic shells designed to insulate the FBI from aggressive congressional scrutiny. Clayton's only assignment so far had been to act as full time liaison and bodyguard for Senator Allen Folds Jr., a newly appointed senator and his young wife Irene. After the death of Senator Alan Folds Senior, his son, then a State Senate Representative, was appointed by the state's Governor to fulfill his father's remaining term. In response to his appointment, the new senator had received what the FBI called, 'a red-neck death threat'. Clayton recalled the recorded message the FBI had received,

"If Folds junya don' change his polotiks to somethn more 'coserv'ative, he's gonna' never be sworn inta' office an his wife'll be wearing her li'l ole black dress 'n mornin'."

As a freshman senator, Allen Folds Jr. spent a large amount of time in the Senate Office Building, a building staffed with enough security to make Special Agent Clayton Davis' protective job redundant for sixty percent of his time. During that time, when Senator Folds Jr. was covered by Senate Office Security and senate liaison staffers, Clayton spent his time covering Senator Folds' young wife Irene, mostly minus her 'little black' dress. Irene was young, beautiful, rich and sexually insatiable, all qualities Clayton admired.

While he waited for Director Rollins, Clayton gazed out the sixth floor window onto Pennsylvania Avenue admiring his own reflection as he pretended to look down onto the hustle and bustle of Washington DC. At 6' 3" Clayton's reflection showed a striking figure in his new charcoal gray Armani, a gift from Irene. After the gigantic ego boost of his on-going affair with Irene, Clayton thought he just might be, as Irene had often said, 'irresistible'. Maybe, Clayton now thought, my good looks and seductive talents are being wasted just doing 'gopher-work' for the FBI.

"Agent Davis," Rollins' secretary interrupted Clayton's self-serving-analysis,

"Director Rollins will see you now."

"Thank you Sharon." Davis then, he entered Rollins' office, "Good Afternoon sir."

"Not, much good about it Davis," Rollins said as he motioned Clayton to sit, "you know you're through with the Folds' business, don't, you?"

"Yes Sir, I received your memo."

"Something more important has come up, you've, been to Norfolk, Virginia, haven't you?" Rollins asked.

"Twice, actually sir, once during an exercise from Quantico then a second time during surveillance training at Camp Peary," Clayton answered, remembering an FBI Academy exercise then a later program at the CIA's rural Virginia training facility near Williamsburg, Virginia, a facility both insiders and outsiders fondly referred to as 'the farm'.

"Good, we've received new information from the CIA that's sending you to back to Norfolk. There's been a Homicide with 'National Security' implications for the FBI and for Homeland Security. It started in the CIA's ballpark but it's a natural spillover into ours. Read the information and get with Agent Lance in Norfolk. Take him this sealed envelope." Rollins instructed as he handed Clayton a large sealed packet. "Lance has you set up with a hotel and he'll brief you on the assignment." Clayton made a motion to interrupt with a question but Rollins waved him off and continued,

"Familiarize yourself with the information in your packet it'll probably take two or three weeks. Work through Lance until you're finished then call for instructions. Good Luck Agent Davis." Rollins finalized, stood, shook Clayton's hand and opened the door for him to leave, "Sharon set Agent Davis up with all the Norfolk information then get the Director on the phone for me."

"Yes sir, right away," then to Clayton Sharon offered, "Here's you information Agent Davis, have an excellent trip, Norfolk's very nice this time of the year. Do you want me to let Senator Folds and Mrs. Folds know about your new assignment?"

"Thank you for offering, but no Sharon, I'll handle all that myself." Clayton directed as he left the office.

"I'm sure you will." Sharon offered quietly toward the closing door, "I'm sure you will Special Agent Davis."

CHAPTER SEVENTEEN

NORFOLK, THURSDAY, 2:45PM

On Monday Detective Sam Millers and Sergeant Morris Bradshaw went to the Norfolk Airport to interview Joel, the Security guard that responded to the attack on Stephen Irons. Millers remembered Joel had only added that,

'Irons' seemed to have a bit of a mean streak in him. He's got a short-guy-complex, you know, he's a feisty little bantam rooster that enjoys a little confrontation. Maybe he needed a chance to prove himself…"

When Millers called Knowles to report the interview she informed him that he and Bradshaw were reassigned temporarily to help gather information on the shooting of a Virginia Beach man on Alexander Street in Norfolk. Now, after two exhaustive days of lengthy interviews, their help had filled in some supporting evidence but failed to solve the seemingly drug-related crime.

This morning they were released back to Knowles and after their assignment debriefing Knowles sent them for two delayed interviews concerning the Harrington case. Arriving to talk with Mrs. Connie Hall, after Bradshaw re-introduced him self, then, he introduced Millers. Mrs. Hall invited them into her kitchen and offered cookies,

"I'm Sorry Dr. Hall is working at De Paul today, but please sit at the counter and I'll make some hot chocolate to go with my oatmeal cookies,"

"Thank you Mrs. Hall but we've just had lunch." Millers replied quickly, "If we could just ask a few questions about Wilber Harrington, it should only take a few minutes."

"Oh my I've got nothing but time today detective I don't do 'Meals on Wheels' for DePaul until tomorrow. How can I help you?"

"Did you or your husband ever talk with Wilber Harrington about his books? We're interested in a book called 'Pacific Secret' but any book information could prove helpful."

"Dr. Hall is very busy as the new Medical Director of De Paul Hospital, he knew Wilber of course, but he's not a reader, other than medical books. Is the 'Pacific' book medical?"

"I don't think so but," Millers started to respond but Mrs. Hall interrupted,

"Well, Wilber, god bless his heart, did give me a personal copy of his first book, you know, the 'Too Old to Die' book," Mrs. Hall reached into a nearby book shelf and held up the white book with wide red striped cover picturing a hypodermic syringe and needle under its bold title. Mrs. Hall opened the book to the inside cover page and pointed to Wilber Harrington's signature, then she continued, "Wilber signed it for me. I was flattered, of course, he knew I read a lot, but, what he didn't know is I don't read fiction. I never turned a page past his signature," Millers interrupted, anxious to regain some control,

"Mrs. Hall, are you sure you didn't hear Mr. Wilber Harrington or Mrs. Sally Harrington ever speak of the 'Pacific' book?" Connie Hall began to laugh and responded,

"Mrs. Hall? Mr. Wilber Harrington? Mrs. Sally Harrington? Well, la-de-dah, you must be a Yankee, son," Millers let the opportunity to say he was from Portsmouth, Virginia slide-by without comment and Mrs. Hall went on, "No detective, Wilber, or Will as Sally liked to call him, never spoke about his books to me. I'd see him going to work, or puttering in the yard, we'd wave some, but we didn't talk much. I'm sure if Sally had known about the 'Pacific' book, I'd have heard about it from her. We do talk a lot. You know she lost her parents a few years ago, and she's been like a daughter to me since then. Sure you don't want some hot chocolate to go with the cookies?"

Millers graciously declined again, offered his gratitude and departed for their second interview with the soccer kids from Lakewood Park.

Millers and Bradshaw waited in Mrs. Fosters' living room while she was on the phone asking her neighbor to send Rick over to talk to the Police, "No, Mildred, it should only take a few minutes, the detectives are here now, I'm sure Rick can make his 5 o'clock game." Mrs. Foster said and Millers glanced at his watch, it was ten after three, the kid had plenty of time. Mrs. Foster returned her attention to her guests,

"Mildred's sending Rick over to help with your questions detective."

A few minutes later, Rick knocked on the front door and Mrs. Foster let him in. "Do you remember Rick?" Mrs. Foster asked as she ushered him into the living room.

"Yes ma'am, I remember him." Then to Rick, "Please sit over by Bobby and Ben," Bradshaw paused to assure the boys were comfortable and attentive, then, "I spoke with my partner, Detective Millers after I talked to you boys," Bradshaw indicated Millers sitting across the room near Mrs. Foster then he went on, "I told Detective Millers everything you boys told me about your soccer-ball practice around the trees and seeing the smoke from the Harrington house before asking a neighbor to call the fire department. I'm sure you know we found Mr. Harrington's body in his house so the investigation has become much more important. Please think back to the Saturday morning when you were practicing soccer. Detective Millers, would you like to talk with the boys?"

"Yes, thank you Morris. Bobby, I know from reading Sergeant Bradshaw's report you did most of the answering, is that correct?" Millers asked the oldest. Bobby nodded and smiled, so Millers went on, "Okay, now, since there was a 'death' associated with the fire." Millers let the 'death word' settle in to see if the kids would get spooked, then, he started to resume, but he was cut off by Bobby,

"We all seen the same, we looked up from practice, then we seen,"

"Bobby, you all 'saw the same' you looked up and saw," Mrs. Foster interjected, then, "Oh, sorry Detective."

"That's alright Mrs. Foster, Bobby, what did you see?"

"Okay, we looked up from the practice and saw some smoke, not a lot, just some white, string-like stuff coming up from the house," Bobby began,

"That's good, Bobby, before we didn't know the first smoke was 'thin like a string and white' that will help the fire investigation, anything else?" Millers encouraged,

"The guy didn't wave back," Ben now interrupted and both Bradshaw and Millers turned toward Bobby's younger brother, Ben,

"What guy, Ben?" Millers asked quietly,

"Yeah, the 'ups' guy," Bobby now added, not allowing Ben to continue, "Ben's right, an 'ups' guy drove away before we saw the smoke."

"Ups, guy? You mean UPS, a delivery truck driver, brown uniform, brown truck?" Millers asked.

"Yeah," Rick now got involved, "we saw the truck come from the Harrington house, we stopped and waved, but the guy drove off, he didn't wave back."

"So you've seen a lot of these delivery trucks in Lakewood?" Millers asked.

"We see 'em all the time, big brown trucks, big yellow UPS on 'em," Bobby chimed back in, "mostly they're friendly, waving and yelling 'Hi', this guy just drove off. Sorry I forgot 'bout him 'til Ben said something."

"That's okay I can understand you might forget the truck driver with the excitement of the fire. Did anyone get a good look at the driver?"

"Eh, Ben was closest," Bobby answered reluctant to allow his brother back into the spotlight, "He just looked like a regular guy to me."

"Okay, Ben did you see the driver well enough to give us some kind of a description?" Millers said.

"Tall, guy, sat way up in the seat, looked like Tom Cruise, in 'Top Dog'," Ben added, then as the other boys laughed, Ben corrected him self, "No, no I mean 'Top Gun.'"

Millers' was adding to his notes now and asked, "Was the driver a white guy, Ben?"

Kinda', you know dark in the face, maybe foreign, but not a real black guy, not real black skin, oh, yeah, he had on big gloves too," Ben added.

"That's great Ben, but you said the guy was tall, sat up in the seat, Tom Cruise is short, why Tom Cruise?" Bradshaw now asked.

"Pilot glasses," The three boys chimed in together, then, Bobby explained, "He wore pilot glasses like from 'Top Gun', you can't see in 'em, you know black mirror glasses."

"This is great, boys, this is a big help. Now, let me see if I've got all this." Millers made a show of leafing through his notebook, scanning it then reading it back to the boys. "Okay, just before you saw the white string-like smoke from the fire, you noticed a UPS truck and driver come out of the Harrington's driveway. His face was dark, maybe he was foreign and he looked tall, sat way up in the seat. He was wearing a pair of big gloves and pilot sunglasses. Is that it?"

"He didn't wave," Ben added, "I tol' you he didn't wave."

"Oh yes, I forgot, he didn't wave," Millers wrote the omission into his notes, "that could be important too. Boys, Mrs. Foster, thank you, I'm sure your information will help us. Millers smiled and he and Bradshaw shook hands with Mrs. Foster and the three boys. Millers patted Ben on the head for remembering the guy that didn't wave.

Driving to Police Operations, Bradshaw offered, "You were right, Sam, there was a lot the kids knew that I didn't ask about, I'm glad you insisted on coming back.

Guess I'm still learning. I think the Alexander Street business distracted me. Does that kind of reassignment happen often in Homicide?"

"Homicide is no different than Vice, Morris, no matter what you're doing there's always something comes up that you, or one of your bosses, thinks is more important, so, you change priorities or you get reassigned, like when you came to work with us to help take care of a new 'Homicide fire-drill'. Anyway, Alexander Street is just another example. I'm sure Knowles was directed by Chief Beck to reassign us to show Norfolk's determination to help solve the shooting of a Virginia Beach man on Alexander Street," Millers paused, made sure Bradshaw was listening then he got back to original question and the subject at hand. "It was just my guess there could be more to learn from the kids, but, it was an opportunity for to be more proactive and keep things moving in the investigation. Not just to make sure all our bases are covered, but actually revisit those bases again and again looking for more information. Murder investigations have a life of their own, it's not a spectator sport, you've got to get involved, you've got to look for a way to push the envelope, test all the options, you know, over-participate."

Bradshaw reddened a little and sunk lower in the seat responding to Millers' pointed lecture but he promised himself he'd take the lesson to heart. Millers' cell phone rang. He pulled it from his coat pocket and flipped the cover open,

"Millers," he said into the cell, then, "it's Knowles" he offered to Bradshaw then he listened for a long time and added,

"Okay, we'll be there soon, but unlike YOU Chief, we've got some good news." Millers closed-up his cell phone and added, "Shit, the frigging FBI."

CHAPTER EIGHTEEN

FBI OFFICE, FEDERAL BUILDING

NORFOLK, VIRGINIA, 7PM

Special Agent Layton Lance was in his office waiting for a phone call from Clayton Davis, the FBI's Special Agent coming to Norfolk to assist in a local Homicide investigation. Lance picked up the FBI's file on Wilber Harrington and began to reorganize his thoughts about the crime:

First, Commander Wilber A. Harrington was approaching a twenty year career in the Navy, mostly on nuclear submarines when he was restricted to 'shore duty' and assigned to The Naval Amphibious Warfare School in San Diego, California.

Second, Harrington's follow-on assignment closed his twenty year career at the Joint Forces Staff College in Norfolk, Virginia, his last duty station in the US Navy.

Third, after Navy retirement Harrington worked for NISCO, before he died. The more Lance thought about the case the more he saw the probability of Harrington being involved in some aspect of espionage or terrorism that Deputy Director Rollins was focusing on. Rollins had said,

"Davis will bring some illuminating information about Harrington and a sealed packet for you with guidance concerning Davis' FBI history and the depth of FBI involvement I'm looking for in the Harrington case."

Lance had been warned that 'the highest level of the Justice Department was monitoring this case and he should keep a tight reign on Davis' activities'. This was not just a test for Lance this was also a test for the newly formed communication's initiative between the CIA, FBI, NSA, DIA and Homeland Security. As Lance scanned the coroner's report on Wilber Harrington's death, his desk phone *BUZZED,*

"Sspecial Agent Lansse," he answered with a lisping sibilance. Then he listened for 10 seconds,

"Yesss, good, to hear from you too, are you at the hotel now?" 20 seconds more,

"Did you bring casual clothes, something non-agency?" 10 seconds,

"Good, we should meet tonight, on the ground floor of your hotel, near the front entrance, is a small bistro called EMPIRE, clean up and change-into something that won't spotlight us. See you in forty minutes, I'll be sitting at the bar wearing a beige jacket." Lance said before he closed the conversation.

Clayton Davis hung up the phone, laughed to himself and thought, Agent Lance sounds gay, who else would hiss words and brag about wearing a 'beige jacket'? Clayton opened his hanging bag and took out khaki trousers and a print silk shirt, one Irene had given him, a shirt she said would bring out the sharp color of his green eyes. After looking at the shirt Clayton decided it could be a 'spotlight' or, even a 'gay- magnet', so he went for a dull-green pull-over with a turtle-neck and long sleeves. "Yep, that's 'Butch' enough", he snickered and headed for the shower.

Norfolk, Virginia, Clayton thought as he rummaged about the bathroom setting up his grooming articles, not much of a place, hope I'm not stuck here for the full three weeks I might start missing Irene. Possibly, he now mused, Linda Knowles could be interesting, or I could 'hook up' with someone else right here at the hotel.

Clayton watched himself in the mirror as he lathered and shaved. He wanted to be presentable for this 'casual meeting' this assignment could be a career opportunity for him. After reading about the CIA's involvement, the possible Chinese Secret Service connection and the need to keep his boss Rollins informed on the progress of the case, it seemed to Clayton that Lance was being put on the spot. Maybe Rollins wanted Lance evaluated? No matter, it was better than babysitting a freshman senator he concluded as he stepped into the shower and placed the water on full COLD to revive his lulling senses.

Clayton exited the shower, toweled off and spent extra time drying and brushing his hair. He dressed, locked his room and entered the elevator to travel to the ground floor. As he stepped from the elevator and walked toward the hotel desk, he heard, "Good evening Mr. Davis, I'm Becky, can I help you with something?" The pretty auburn haired receptionist asked with a big smile as Clayton approached her desk.

"Yes, thank you Becky, is the Tazewell Hotel the owner of EMPIRE?"

"We have a 'business relationship' with the restaurant, is there something I can arrange for you?" Clayton took 'something I can arrange for you' as encouragement,

"Yes, can you page me at EMPIRE if I get a phone call?"

"Of course, I know Robert, he's one of the owners and he's the bartender tonight. I can call him, if you want."

"Yes, thanks, but if there's no call for me, please page me at 9:30. Will you do that Becky?" Clayton asked as he slid a twenty-dollar bill toward her.

"My pleasure," Becky stated as she folded the money into her own hand. "Enjoy your meal, talk with you later Mr. Davis."

"Yes, maybe later, what time do you get off Becky?" Clayton asked, continuing to follow his instincts,

"My shift goes 'til 2AM Mr. Davis, maybe some other time. Thanks for asking."

Clayton smiled his acknowledgement, turned and waved as he walked the short hallway toward the Tazewell Hotel's Granby Street entrance. He stopped two steps before the hotel's front door and turned right into the side door of EMPIRE, noting the Little Bar Bistro emblem that decorated the glass portion of the entrance door. Clayton pushed the door open and stepped down into the restaurant.

EMPIRE was bubbly with chatter from an eclectic group enjoying a Thursday night- out. The small restaurant had a total of five, four-top tables, four lined-up against the wall across from the longest portion of the bar and one more near the front entrance. All the four-tops were full so Clayton watched as the bartender moved back and forth behind the lengthy bar filling requests. A pretty, blonde waitress welcomed him,

"Hi, I'm Kristin welcome to EMPIRE. Let me know if I can help you with something." Clayton nodded hello and speculated about 'the something' as he watched the trim, fashion-model blonde, move seductively away from him.

Near the ceiling, large fan blades that resembled feathered palm tree leaves, slowly turned like helicopter blades above the restaurant's activity and memories of the movie "Casablanca" impacted Clayton's thoughts and drew him into EMPIRE'S nostalgic atmosphere. The lengthy bar had 20 or so seats with only four seats presently occupied. Sitting near several empty seats, on Clayton's far right with his back to Clayton, was Agent Lance wearing his beige jacket as he talked and gestured dramatically to the bartender. Clayton smiled confirming his earlier speculation about Agent Lances' sexual-orientation and continued to watch as the bartender poured an assortment of liquors and mixes into a gigantic cocktail shaker half-filled with ice. The concoction turned several different colors while shaken, then, settled on a dark tangerine hue before being poured into four large martini glasses. The bartender fussed with fruit decorations on the four chilled glasses then he arranged and moved them, using a large 'martini carry apparatus', to the opposite end of the bar, away from Agent Lance. Clayton's eyes followed the bartender's movement as he stopped and placed four drinks in front of one empty bar-seat and three very attractive young women seated at the other end of the bar,

"Sex on the Beach' for the ladies…" the bartender announced as he carefully delivered the four decorative drinks.

The three ladies smiled and replied in unison, "Thanks for all the 'Sex', Robert." They giggled as the bartender waved and took the empty carrier back to the center.

Clayton instinctively moved toward the three young women noting the one empty bar-stool with the unclaimed drink and said as he stood behind the empty seat pointing to the extra drink, "Excuse me ladies, is this 'Sex' taken?"

At the sound of his voice the three women turned toward him. The one sitting nearest Clayton, a gorgeous red head, smiled up at Clayton's six-three presence and replied, "Well, that SEAT is taken by Denise, she's in the john, but sharing 'Sex' is definitely open for discussion. Hi, I'm Gay and this is Aubry and Patti," the red head explained indicating the other two young women, then, "What's your name big guy?"

"I'm Clayton nice to meet 'you-all'. I'll just stand and wait for Denise I wouldn't want her to miss anything." As the girls giggled again and joked among them selves, Clayton turned to the bartender and added, "Robert, these gorgeous ladies will certainly need more Sex real soon, and I could use some myself. Five more please."

"Five more 'Sex on the Beach' headed your way." Robert replied and got busy concocting another even larger offering of the tangerine colored mixture.

By now Agent Lance had heard enough and began to get up from his seat to walk toward Clayton. But, as Lance took his first steps to intervene, Denise returned and heard Clayton's bar order. She slid by Clayton onto her vacant chair, offered her hand in greeting and said,

"Hi, I'm Denise, I'm the Parole Officer for these three hussies and I'm required, by law to inform you that buying 'Sex', for parolees in Norfolk…"

Special Agent Lance arrived at this moment, smiled and interrupted the frivolity, "Excuse me ladies, my sincere apologies for the untimely interruption, but your new friend has some serious business elsewhere." Lance added directly to Clayton,

"Leave a fifty on the bar Davis, we need to adjourn, now." Lance's statement was emphatic and Clayton took it that way, 'Hooking up' would have to wait, once again.

"Clayton, you know you can be penalized for an early withdrawal." Gay said and the girls all laughed together and raised their glasses toward Clayton's reluctant departure. Gay smiled at Clayton and added, "Think some more about 'sharing sex' big guy."

"Sorry ladies, some other time." Clayton replied as he slid a fifty on the bar and turned to follow Agent Lance. Then he turned back and added, "Gay go ahead and enjoy your 'Sex' without me this time, but don't make a habit of it. Thanks Robert, see you again."

"Cheers, come back soon, 'Eat, Drink and Repeat'." Robert responded with the Little Bar Bistro's marketing slogan.

Lance and Davis departed EMPIRE and walked down the hallway of the Tazewell Hotel. "Clayton," Lance began as they rode in the elevator, "you definitely live up to your bio, its good to meet you I'm Layton Lance." Lance offered as Davis led them to his room. Clayton opened the door with his computerized pass-key and stepped in with Lance following.

"How about we use Davis and Lance? This business with Clayton and Layton's going to throw me off." Lance nodded his affirmation and Davis went on, "Okay, what's up Lance?" He asked as they entered the room.

"I'll get right to it, Agent Davis. You're here to help control an ongoing investigation into a local Homicide. The Detective in Charge, Detective Linda Knowles, is a tall, very pretty widow with an eight-year-old daughter. Your boss, and mine, wants you to help her with the Harrington investigation. Get it concluded quickly but steer it away from unnecessary embarrassment to the Chinese. I'm sure that's in your packet,"

"Yes, but…"

"No butts Davis, you're the sspecial agent assigned to help the Norfolk Police with their Homicide investigation because the victim's untimely death has 'National Security implications'. The FBI has information for you to make available to Detective Knowles to keep the murder from incorrectly embarrassing the Chinese. Clear enough?"

"Are the Chinese actually involved in the murder Agent Lance?"

"That's not the question Davis, your real question is, 'how do I achieve the results Deputy Director Rollins, and the Justice Department, desire?" Clayton, was confused,

"Okay, what you said the question should be, now, how do I do THAT?"

"You answered your own question in the bar, that's how you do it. You're here to help the pretty widow solve the Homicide and get a lot of credit for herself but not at the expense of US relations with China. Watching you interact with the young ladies in the bar tells me your well documented qualifications in that arena are genuine, so, I see little problem in you accomplishing the mission. Just use your looks, charm and abundant testosterone," Clayton shook his head as he interrupted,

"That's it? That's the guidance you're giving me?"

"You're obviously a lot slower than Director Rollins thinks you are, Agent Davis! Of course that's your guidance. Now, where's MY packet?" Clayton remained frustrated but he turned away, moved to his dresser, got the sealed packet and handed it to Lance.

"What's in your packet, Agent Lance?"

"Incriminating evidence concerning you and Irene Folds, just in case I have a problem with you completing your mission as directed." Lance smiled, waited for a response but noted that Clayton seemed shocked by the packet's contents, so Lance went on,

"Just keep me informed with a verbal report every other day and get in touch immediately if something important happens. Do the job you were sent here to do Agent Davis, nothing more. Just use the 'talent, tenacity and testosterone' you've used so well in the past." Lance offered as he stepped into the hallway and was gone after closing Clayton's door.

CHAPTER NINETEEN

LAKEWOOD, SUNDAY, OCTOBER 1

The Memorial Service for Commander Wilber A. Harrington, USN Retired, had been a comfort Sally reasoned as she reentered her home. But she couldn't keep her mind from returning to Thursday at the funeral home. Stephen had gone with her for support but she declined his offer to help identify Wilber's body prior to his scheduled cremation and it all came back to her,

I'm very sorry Mrs. Harrington, but the state of Virginia requires final identification of the deceased prior to cremation. I'll just move away and leave you for a moment with Commander Harrington, please take your time,

Oh, my god Sally thought as she approached the open casket, this is so hard I'm still devastated by his loss but anxious and unsure of Will's fidelity. I should have let Stephen come with me for this, Sally paused as she approached the casket glanced at the funeral director who had stepped away. Finally Sally summoned her courage and moved forward to within a foot of her husband's body and looked directly into the open casket. Will looks so peaceful, so patriotic and honorable in his uniform, Sally thought, rejecting her misgivings of Will's possible infidelity. But how could this violence have happened? Who would want to harm him? Sally wanted to touch Will, to assure her self this was reality and not just a horrible dream. She paused reluctant to place her fingers to his cheek, fearful with a foreboding of unfathomable desecration against Will's lifeless body. Finally her need for closure won out and she placed the backs of her fingers gently against Will's cheek and began to weep as the coldness of his sallow, lifeless complexion overwhelmed her hand and numbed her spirit. Sally fought her tears and offered quietly, to no living soul,

"I'm so sorry Will I should have called you back." Sally turned, embarrassed for her now regretful admission to her dead husband. Sally nodded her positive identification to the funeral director and left the room.

Commander Harrington's body had been cremated on Friday and the blue and gold urn that contained his remains was entrusted to the skipper of the SSN Hampton Roads for prominent display during the memorial ceremony that would honor Commander Harrington's military service and his life. Sally's tears began again as she sat in her new kitchen remembering the afternoon sunlight that filtered in through stain-glass windows, washing the Naval Chapel with warmth and compassion. Sally's memory of the background strains of 'Eternal Father, Strong to Save' that drifted through the chapel as the skipper of the SSN

Hampton Roads, Captain Ford Westerly, one of Wilber's 1983 Naval Academy Classmates, delivered the eulogy returned. Captain Westerly gratefully accepted the honor of fulfilling Wilber's request to have his ashes distributed in the Atlantic Ocean, where his first naval cruise from Norfolk began in the summer of 1980 and had promised,

"Our Final Ceremony at Sea' will honor Commander Harrington's distinguished career and his devotion to his country throughout his twenty five years of military service, the first year in the Naval ROTC program at ODU, then four years as a Midshipman at the United States Naval Academy, followed by twenty years of active duty in the United States Navy..."

Sally's mind drifted forward to her personal conversation with Captain Westerly,

"Sally, thank you for sharing Wilber's desire for a 'Final At Sea Ceremony', it's a great honor for myself and the crew. Please accept this 'memorial plaque' from the Hampton Roads and all of her crew." Sally took the small plaque with Submarine Service Dolphins ensconced above the emblem of the SSN Hampton Roads and said,

"Thank you Captain Westerly, I'll place the plaque in our den, I know Will would be pleased, it was his favorite room."

"Sally, please call me Ford and you're very welcome, it's my pleasure and honor. And if there's anything further," Sally interrupted Captain Westerly kindness,

"Ford, I know you served with Will many times during his career, could you please tell me why he was restricted to shore duty in San Diego just before I met him? Will told me he had been restricted, but he never told me why."

"Unofficially I can tell you what I know, Sally, Wilber was the Chief Navigator aboard the SSN Greenwood during a deployment on February 2, 2001 and while entering the port in Saipan, during their deployment, the boat ran aground. Wilber was off-duty due to illness, but some miscalculations by his Assistant Navigator were judged to have caused the incident. The Greenwood's underside, the rudder and secondary propulsion motor, suffered minor damage requiring dry docking and extensive delay to their deployment. After the incident's initial inquiry the sub's Captain was reassigned to Washington DC and Wilber, as Chief Navigator, and his Assistant, who was actually on duty at the time of the incident, were also removed from the ship's crew and reassigned. During the 'Incident Hearing', naval authorities decided that Wilber and his assistant should be restricted to 'shore duty' for the remainder their careers and at that time the Navy assigned Wilber as the Submarine Service's Liaison Representative to the Naval Amphibious Warfare School in San Diego, that's where you met Wilber isn't it?"

"Yes we met in April, 2001," Sally replied, *"but Ford, if Will was sick, why would the Navy punish him for something that happened when he wasn't even there?"*

"Sally, it's probably difficult to understand from your perspective, but the Navy looks very carefully at this type of incident. They saw Wilber's involvement as the training and supervision of

his assistant, so they judged Wilber shared in the responsibility that precipitated the incident. A second factor influencing the Navy's findings, probably in Wilber's favor, was that the USS Greenville had a much more tragic incident a week later on February 9. The Greenville's incident involved a collision with a Japanese Training Ship. That incident caused the deaths of nine Japanese sailors, do you remember that Sally?" Sally nodded her affirmative and Fred went on,

'Well, the Greenville's much more serious incident may have lessened the punishment of the Greenwood's Captain and of Wilber as the ship's Navigator. But, Wilber's assistant navigator continued to argue strongly against the conclusion of the proceedings and took the punishment very hard. He actually resigned from the Navy immediately. The former Captain of the Greenwood has now been returned to sea duty and is the CO of a submarine operating out of Hawaii. Sorry that's just information and not important to you, but, Sally, I do think what is important for YOU is to remember that Wilber told me personally , that meeting you, falling in love with you then marrying you during his assignment in San Diego, changed his life. He said 'it was the best thing to ever happen to him'. I think you can see that the incident investigation was not that bitter to Wilber after meeting you in San Diego."

"Thank you Ford, Will not telling me was confusing,"

" Wilber was trained as a Nuclear Submariner, consequently he was probably very secretive with you about the operational aspects of his military career, but as I said, he did tell me he loved you very much."

Sally returned to the present, thinking about the many guests in attendance at the Naval Chapel, her neighbors Dr. and Mrs. Hall, several flight attendant friends, including Margo from San Diego and a few others from the surrounding area, Will's immediate boss, James Carlson and his senior boss at NISCO, Mr. Charles Taylor were all in attendance. Master Deputy Sheriff Osborne, Stephen's friend and former boss was present and several of Will's NISCO co-workers also attended. Sally tried to thank all of the military participants and every attendee personally. She knew most of the people, except for a few that now stood out in her memory. One, a man named Adams from Will's home town, Franklin, Virginia, said he was a friend that read about the service and wanted to pay his respects. Sitting with Adams was a woman and a young man, probably Adams' family. Adams actually seemed familiar to Sally and she regretted not taking the time to ask how he had known Will.

With Sally's permission, Stephen had asked Detective Knowles to attend the service, it had been over a week since Will's death and Sally had undergone several days of questioning by Detective Knowles and her staff. Stephen felt it would be comforting for Sally to have Linda Knowles attend in a more supportive capacity. Stephen, now living with Sally, had been right Sally had enjoyed meeting Knowles' daughter at the service and now felt a lot more comfortable around Detective Knowles herself. Stephen was taking Detective Knowles and her daughter home and should be back soon.

Sally poured herself a glass of wine and toasted Will's memory as she waited for her friend, Margo to deliver her lap top computer. Sally was still concerned how this meeting was going to go but the wine finally relaxed her as she held the small plaque and thought of the pleasure Will would have gotten from the respectful ceremony and the honorary gift. She relaxed and began to think more positively now, focusing on how Stephen's health was showing some improvement, his exercise program was working and possibly, a budding interest in Linda Knowles might be another reason. Sally's thoughts were interrupted by a soft KNOCK on the side kitchen door. Sally looked up and saw Margo standing at the door with her computer in hand. Sally fought tears and apprehension and moved to open the door,

"Margo, please come in, thank you for coming to the service and bringing your computer, Detective Knowles promised to have it back late tomorrow afternoon, if that's okay." Sally offered as she opened the door. Margo was crying as she stood in the doorway, reluctant to enter Sally's home,

"Sally, I'm so sorry about what happened to Wilber and the stupid stuff I made up to boost my own ego and impress Maribeth." Margo blurted out through her tears.

"You didn't have an affair with Will?" Sally said,

"No, Sally, honestly I was concerned about you marrying such an older guy and I gave it a half-hearted try just to test Wilber, but he only laughed and turned me down. He never told you about me hitting on him?"

"No, but, I'm sure he was flattered." Sally replied, hugging Margo now that the burden of Will's infidelity with her friend had been lifted.

"Thank you for saying that, Sally. It was a lovely service, I'd like to stay longer but I'm flying back to San Diego tonight. American's afternoon flight from Norfolk has open seats, so I've got to go. My taxi's waiting, so please tell Detective Knowles she can keep the computer as long as she needs it. You have my address she can send it when she's through. I've never looked at Wilber's notes, but I'm sure they're still there." Margo offered then paused and apologized again, "I'm so sorry about what I said to Maribeth. Please forgive me Sally, it was all so stupid."

"It's okay Margo, I think I understand. Thanks again for coming and telling me personally, and please say hello to Maribeth when you see her." The waiting taxi HONKED interrupting the conversation and Sally added quickly,

"I know you've got to go, but I'd like to talk more, please tell your taxi driver I'll run you to the airport, okay?" Margo hugged Sally and smiled through her tears as she headed to the taxi to get her travel bag. Sally watched Margo through the glass panels of the back door and began to reminisce about the many shared times she had enjoyed with Margo and Maribeth. She fought off her tears, she needed this closure time with Margo and she penciled a quick note to Stephen before she headed to get her purse and car keys.

CHAPTER TWENTY

NORFOLK, GHENT GARDEN CONDOMINIUMS

"STEPHEN IRONS"

I've just driven Linda Knowles and her eight year old daughter Ella home from Wilber's Memorial Service and I'm sitting with Ella while Linda checks in with Police Operations. Their home is located with a lot of other condos near a large that park used twice a year for 'The Stockley Gardens Art Festival'. I can see another small park area behind their home with benches, cobblestone walkways and children-friendly areas boasting swing sets, sand boxes, kiddy slides and monkey bars. The living room has a picture window, hardwood floors, a gas burning fireplace and a couple of mid size sofas covered in a tan or beige canvas-like fabric. The sofas have reddish and orange pillows spread around to coordinate the seating area with a large oriental carpet that covers most of the living room floor.

The kitchen and breakfast area, where Ella and I are seated, has a small table with four chairs next to a wrap around counter that presently holds several appliances, including one very large Kitchen Aide mixer that gleams shiny black on their stone-gray Fieldstone countertop. Ella and I are enjoying home-made cookies and conversation. She's still wearing her church clothes and looks stunning in a light blue dress with her long blonde tresses bundled-up with a dress-matching pony-tail ribbon that 'pops' the color of her clear blue eyes. Eyes she turns to me as she asks,

"Stephen, do you like the cookies? I helped mom make them." She bragged while pointing at the large mixer.

"The cookies are great Ella. I love the cranberry stuff, was that your idea?"

"Yes, those are like 'Craizins', you know cranberries and raisins all mixed-up together. They make cookies the best." Ella announced full of pride, then, she looked directly at me and her blue eyes flashed a liquid-like transparency. I immediately thought of Sally's watery eyes since Wilber's death and I was certain Ella was going to cry. But, she quickly regained her eight year old composure and pressed-on with her information, "I lost my daddy when I was five, Stephen, I miss him a lot. Do you miss your brother Wilber?"

Her question hit me hard as her eyes peered into my soul. I smiled and tried to be as brave as she was, "Wilber was my brother-in-law, Ella. You know my sister Sally's husband… But, yes, I miss him a lot. We were both in the Navy and both love Sally very much. Wilber and I did a lot of things together, every week we went to the Virginia Zoo and your mom told me you've been to the zoo too, did you like it?" I asked hoping to redirect the conversation away from her s and my sad memories.

"Yes, I love the zoo my daddy took me a lot before I lost him." She paused, ran into the living room and retrieved a framed photo of herself and her father taken in front of the Virginia Zoo's big rotating world. In the photo Ella was pointing toward some distant area of the zoo and trying to pull her father in that direction. "This is me and my dad when I was five Stephen, just before I lost him."

"I'm so sorry Ella I know it was sad for you and your mom, but you must have great memories of your dad and your trips to the zoo." Pondering my statement and our conversation, she smiled up at me then hurried to return the picture to the living room. She came back and took my hand and I felt a warming relief begin to calm my concerns and I relaxed a little too. But, it seemed the subject of her daddy wasn't going away. Ella responded after our quiet moment by offering brightly,

"WE can go to the zoo, Stephen you know like help each other. You can help me when I miss my dad and I can help you when you miss Wilber."

I continued to hold Ella's hand fighting against my own tears, "That would be great, Ella, I have a lot of time-off now, so when you're not in school we could go." I responded as Linda came into the kitchen.

"Go where?" Linda said.

"Stephen loves the zoo, mom, we want to go next weekend. Can I?" Linda smiled,

"You're definitely learning the way to Ella's heart." Linda stated, and Ella smiled at her mom. I smiled too as I stood and said,

"Well, it's only fair Ella won my heart with her 'crazy cookies'."

"Craizin cookies Stephen, I like told you that." Ella offered laughing at my attempted humor. Smiling more now, I sat back down and bit into another large cookie. Linda shook her head, gave up and reverted to her mom job.

"Please get changed, Ella, you can put your church clothes away and set your school clothes out for tomorrow. You're going early to see your Grandmother Shirley before your ride to school." Linda instructed. Ella responded by going to the counter to finish her milk, then she came over to where I was sitting, beamed a smile at me, eye to eye, and gave me a small hug around my neck as she offered,

"Thanks for taking us Stephen, I like Sally, she's very pretty."

"You're welcome Ella, I'm sure Sally liked meeting you too... Maybe she'll go with us to the zoo. She volunteers there, showing some of the zoo's animals." I said as I rose-up again and began to move toward one of the couches in the adjacent living room.

"Wow, maybe we can help show-off her animals." Ella said.

"Enough zoo-talk, you two," Linda interjected, "Ella, go get changed now, please." Ella immediately made a funny, 'zip up her lip' gesture and ran off down the hall. "What a child, actually you're both acting like a couple of kids," Linda said with a broad smile, then she went serious, "Please thank Sally, I know it wasn't easy for her, seeing me so soon after I've been questioning her all week. She was very gracious to invite us."

I nodded and shifted to serious also, "This is tough for Sally, I'm sure they loved each other very much, do you think you'll be able to find Wilber's killer?"

"The cause of Wilber's death hasn't been determined officially, but I'm sure it will be ruled a Homicide. Hopefully the computer information from Sally's friend can help find the motive and the killer. We're also getting some help from the FBI with fiber forensics and weapon history, so I think we'll have a better chance to solve the mystery. The FBI believes the case may have some espionage or terrorism implications because of Wilber's Navy career and his employment at NISCO."

"Thanks for sharing that Linda, but I think Wilber was kind of a 'boy scout', I'm not sure he could have been involved in anything illegal, especially something against his country." I was taken back by Linda's disclosure but I tried to remain open to whatever could help solve the mystery. "I'm sure Sally will appreciate the FBI's help,"

God, I thought as I looked at Linda's beautiful features, standing very close to me, if only I could get past this desire phase and revive an arousal response, I'm certain I'd be on the way to a full emotional recovery. I've got to check with my doctors, something's still weird about my lack of physical response to sexual thoughts. As if reading my mind, Linda sat down next to me on the sofa and moved very close. She took my hand and I felt her thigh push-up against mine causing a slight pulse in my groin, more like a twinge resulting from some of my blood flow resuming an old journey through long dormant body parts. I was immediately conflicted with excitement at the beginning of physical arousal and I looked around to see if Thornton was witnessing my excited discomfort, fortunately Thornton seemed to have gone AWOL. As my 'embarrassment' grew

I remembered a 'Monty Python, Search for The Holy Grail' quote and opted to, 'Run Away, Run Away'... Not much like the solid 'HUNK' I wanted to rebuild from pulverized rock, but, I offered defensively,

"I've got to go Linda I'm staying with Sally now while she decides what to do with her house. I'm sure she could use my company it's been a difficult day for her. Sorry to leave so abruptly but this has been hard," I caught myself feeling more redness splash over my face after I confirmed Dr. Freud's subliminal response theory that caused me to use the word 'hard', "Will you see Sally tomorrow about the computer information?" I asked as I rose and turned sideways to hide the arrival of my welcomed embarrassment.

"Yes, if everything works out with our Computer Tech, we'll come by tomorrow about ten, if that's okay?" Linda replied, looking puzzled at my contorted body language,

"Sure, ten's good. I'll see you then but I need to go home and check on Sally now. I hope you'll let Ella visit the zoo with me." My words sounded a bit feeble, even to my ears so I left quickly and closed the door behind my ungraceful departure.

As I drove away from Linda's Condo I was torn between my new feelings for her, which could prove to be a physical and emotional catalyst for my full-recovery, and the obvious insecurity that sent me 'running away'. Thornton was sitting with me now and offered,

"Wake up Rusty, I know you want your body protected by sleeping with a cop, but Sally's hurting, get yourself focused on your little sister, you've got to be there for her, bud." I chose not to respond to Thornton's 'sleeping with a cop joke' and put my 'growing interest' in Linda aside and drove home.

After a ten minute drive I pulled into the circular driveway fronting Sally's house, parked my car and entered the side kitchen door. Looking around the empty kitchen I found a note on the kitchen table from Sally,

Stephen, I've taken Margo to the airport for her flight. Beer's in the fridge, gin's in the freezer and there's some open wine on the counter. Be back soon. Love you, thanks for coming to live with me. Sally had signed the note, *Tag*

Sally was out on her airport mission, so I got a beer and started toward the TV and a lead-up game to the World Series. As I turned toward the den I saw a brown, Norfolk Sheriff's Cruiser, pull into Sally's driveway and park behind my Volvo. I continued to watch as the super-sized frame of Master Deputy Sheriff Jimmy Osborne exited his car and headed toward Sally's side kitchen door. In full uniform, Os gave me the feeling that no matter what my troubles were, he was here to help. I smiled to myself and got another cold beer from the fridge as I waited for 'the wizard's' arrival.

CHAPTER TWENTY ONE

LAKEWOOD

"STEPHEN IRONS"

Sally returned from her airport mission with a small kitten and after twenty minutes of explanation she prepared a small bowl of milk and some canned tuna for the kitten before she headed upstairs. Sally had driven by the SPCA on her way home and stopped in to look at the many recently trans-planted Hurricane Katrina animal-orphans from Mississippi and Louisiana that had barely survived last years storm. Sally had picked a kitten out to help the Norfolk SPCA and was very excited about her choice, a small black and white Manx kitten with a stub for a tail. Sally had explained to Os and me in an excited, child-like voice,

"I met the SPCA Vet, her name's Dr. Carol. She was a flight attendant, just like me, but she got hurt on the job and went to Vet School. How cool is that! She showed me this kitten, he's from Louisiana and he's called Willy-nilly because he won't sit still, he just runs around everywhere. Anyway, I fell in love with the little guy because he's cute and named Willy." Tears slid down Sally's cheek as she went on about her adventure with the career-connected SPCA Vet and how the small kitten had survived last year's horrible storm. Os and I both drank our beers while Sally talked and rummaged around the kitchen looking for cat-appropriate food. Finally, after she had prepared a bowl with milk and another one with canned tuna, she was satisfied the kitten wouldn't go hungry she excused herself and took 'Willy-nilly' upstairs in a small cardboard box with newspaper for kitty-litter.

Released from Sally's late afternoon adventure tale I headed to the fridge for a second bee, but Os' voice interrupted my journey, "Don't you have something stronger Scrap? That kitten story requires more serious medicine."

I laughed at Os' rare display of humor and said, "Sally has some red wine open and we've got Bombay Sapphire in the freezer, how about an icy 'bomb on the rocks'?"

"Just what the doctor ordered, how'd you know that?"

"Not too difficult Os, but what's really on your mind. No disrespect, but I can't remember you as a friendly-visit, small-talk-guy." I offered this observation as I poured Bombay's icy-smooth liquid into two large tumblers and added a few cubes of ice to legitimize the 'on the rocks' offer. Os pulled out one of the tall bar stools and gathered in his new drink. I waited as he ingested a sampling of 'bomb' before he said, "I'm worried about you Scrap, you're coming around physically with your zoo-walking', but emotionally you've still got a problem dealing with Sheriff Wayne medically-retiring you. And now, you've got a handful of new responsibilities with Sally. I know you feel confident the Norfolk cops can chase down Wilber's murderer, if it was a murder, but Knowles is new in this business and Norfolk cops are full of a lot of 'red tape' and 'be-no-more-of-that' type regulations, so they'll never solve the case quick enough."

I smiled at Os' logic, sat down and finally said, "You offering me my old job back, Os?" I was half joking, but I knew Os was familiar with a lot of city politicians and their politics. He knew where a lot of Norfolk's political skeletons were hidden and just how most people would react when approached on almost any subject. He did smile at my comment, so I added, "But, I don't think you've got enough 'street-cred' to pull off my reinstatement,"

"Nothing like that Scrap, just sip your gin and hear me out, okay?" Os interjected as I tried more 'bomb' and he went on, "Wilber's senior boss, Charles Taylor, is the Executive Director of NISCO and he's a close friend of mine. He and I played football for your dad at William and Mary. Did you know that?"

"Not about Taylor, no, I wasn't much into my dad's football career,"

"Yeah, I know, Scrap, sometimes you can be a jerk!" Os quipped half joking, but his interruption made his point and he went on, "Charles, shares my concern about the Norfolk Police getting the job done, and about their commitment to keep him informed with police progress. At Wilber's Memorial Service Charles asked me for a suggestion on how he could help the police effort and insure he was kept informed. Did you meet Charles at the service?" Os paused here waiting for me to answer. I shook my head NO and remained quiet. He gave me a funny look but he went on,

"Charles' respect for the outstanding job Wilber did for NISCO makes him anxious to find Wilber's killer, if there is a killer. Charles wants the case solved and if it turns out to be a suicide, like the police initially believed, then, he wants to know why one of his employees caved-in to such depression," Os paused again, expecting a reaction from me, but I was still listening. "I've thought about it Scrap and I think you and NISCO would be a good fit. Your background working for the Shore Patrol was the reason I wanted you as a Sheriff's deputy when you left the Navy. And, like me, you're a 'Norfolk native', you know, you're familiar with our people and our way of life. To me your biggest plus is your closeness to Sally and Wilber. All that and your available time tell me you should get more involved, the synergism's a natural. What do you think Scrap?" Os drained his glass and proffered the empty tumbler toward me.

After I got over his reference to my dad, I was taken-back by his reasoning, certainly flattered but still a bit skeptical. I poured more Bombay into our glasses as I tried to form my response. "I'm flattered you think so highly of me, Os, but, time-wise I've got a full plate with my physical recovery and moving-in here to help Sally get through all this."

I waited for a quick retort as I handed Os his new drink, but he seemed willing to hear me out. "I've had no up-to-date training as an investigator Os, no organization would hire me to look into Wilber's death,"

Os lost his patience and jumped back in, "That's wrong, Scrap, your present lack of authoritative status is one of the reasons Charles would consider hiring you. You working as a 'civilian NISCO consultant' wouldn't raise any red flags to the employees while you nosed around their internal business. You know, yourself, it would be in everyone's best interest. Sally will bounce back soon, she's sharp and she'll refocus on her career, but YOU can help find out if what Charles believes is true. He thinks someone at NISCO could be responsible for Wilber's death. Bottom line, whatever you can do to set both Charles' and Sally's minds at ease about Wilber's death, would be a big plus for you too, don't you think?"

I started to answer, but Os wasn't through, he held up a big flat palm toward me, took a large gulp of his new drink and resumed, "As for your medical situation, I've talked with your doctors and I know you're on the mend physically. Their biggest concern is your emotional welfare," Shit, that really pissed me off. I jumped up and cut Os' explanation off.

I stabbed my finger across the counter toward his direction and said, "Damn Os, what gave you the right to talk to my doctors?" I shouted coming around the counter toward him.

"Easy, Scrap, easy." Os said as he stood up and placed a large black hand flat against my chest, keeping me at least three feet away. "Your father was my coach and my friend, he's gone now but I'm YOUR friend and that gives me the right. I was the one that assigned you to Judge Knutson's court room six months ago and I feel responsible for putting you in a situation that almost took your life. I just want to help you now." I backed off slightly, reached for my own drink and sat back down. I took a large swallow and emptied my glass, got up and headed to the freezer for more alcohol. Os' size and his solutions were getting to be too much for me. He recognized my pause and went on, "I know about the concern your doctors have about you being able to father a child, I know that's a lot for a guy like you to carry around," Os was actually voicing things I'd held inside far too long, so I let him go on, "Now that Wilber's not here, you really need a friend Scrap, and I'm not applying for that job, I'm just taking it!"

I recalled after meeting with my doctors how I had experienced increasing emotional distress and a lot of interpersonal difficulties but I rejected more counseling about my issues and what had happened to Thornton. All that plus the loss of my mom and dad had become too traumatic for me. Then, after I was shot and began to 'zoo walk' I had actually decided to talk to Wilber about my problems. But as Os pointed out, Wilber was gone, so Os was here offering to help me handle my 'emotional baggage'. Maybe my physical reaction to Linda's influence could be a positive sign for my 'returning manhood', maybe time would help and maybe talking with a close friend could help too. I fought back tears as I replied,

"Os, I want to thank you. Yes, it upset me that you talked to my doctors behind my back but I do understand that you just want to help. But right now NISCO might be too much for me. I'll sleep on it and get back to you tomorrow. I'll call you in the morning. Okay?"

"Sure Scrap," Os offered as he rose, extended his hand, then thought better of the gesture and came around the corner of the counter top and gave me a bear-hug. "You think about it, I know Charles will want to talk with you one way or the other. So, let me know when to set up the meeting." Os released me, finished his drink and turned and walked out the kitchen door, his mission completed.

Thornton was sitting at Sally's small kitchen table. There were tears in his eyes. He looked up at me with his golden curls highlighted under the small light over Sally's kitchen table, but for once he withheld any judgmental comment. He just shook his head slightly and lowered his eyes in sympathy. I was surprised that Thornton hadn't known about ALL my problems.

CHAPTER TWENTY TWO

VIRGINIA EASTERN RAIL CORPORATION

RICHMOND, VIRGINIA

Morgan Folds looked out his 11th floor office window watching the traffic flow around downtown Richmond. Cars and trucks heading north on Interstate 95 were splitting near Richmond, either turning east on 64 toward Williamsburg or continuing north on 95 toward Fredericksburg and Washington DC. Morgan watched the streams of red tail lights separate into divergent pathways around Richmond as his private line buzzed. Morgan tapped SPEAKER ON and offered, "Folds here,"

"Sir, I'm fetching Mr. Zimchi at your jet, then, I'll head to the office, any change to your wants?" Conrad Holmes said.

"No change Conrad, have Myers hangar the plane, it needs an inspection before I use it again. I'll expect you back here in twenty minutes."

"Yes sir, call if you adjust plans," Morgan heard before he touched the OFF button mid-sentence and raised his binoculars to look directly toward Richard E. Byrd Airport. Moving the large pair of binoculars he identified the executive area north of the main airport facility and began to watch for the powerful halogen lights on his stretch-limo. Byrd's rotating tower beacon presented an alternating split white beam followed by the green-light indication of airport operation as he finally located the large limo and began to follow its progress away from the airport. As he watched, Morgan began to recall ten years ago in Kenya, when this developing partnership began,

One hundred miles south of Nairobi, during the winter of 1996, Morgan Folds contemplated the day's activities, "Sonchi, that's a beautiful trophy you bagged, you brought that gigantic beast down with one terrific jolt."

The lodge was cold, only a small fire burned against the winter wind that carried sporadic snow from Mount Kilimanjaro, twenty kilometers to the south on Kenya's border with Tanzania. Morgan thought they should have gone with the 80 bearers that lugged the huge elephant carcass back to their main camp. A camp more comfortably located in the warmer open plains, much nearer Nairobi where the chilling influence of Kilimanjaro was less threatening.

Gunter Wilhelms, their host-guide and companion-hunter responded in broken English to

Morgan's congratulatory offering, "Sonchi's shot vas 'ser good', but I vas zee one who track zee beast."

"Sure you tracked him, but I killed the bastard and I'll take the trophy home with me to Norfolk." Sonchi replied, then to end the conversation he finalized, "You actually had me shoot the Bull Elephant in Tanzania, Gunter, and I'm certain your permit stops at Kenya's border. No wonder you were in such a hurry to get the carcass moved 40 miles north, away from the shadow of Kilimanjaro."

"I can't wait to see your presentation in Norfolk," Morgan replied then joked, "But, he's going to cost big bucks, even for you, Sonchi, maybe we need to consider some augmentation to our present income sources, what do you think?"

"You should do like my friend," Gunter quickly interrupted, seeing a money opportunity, "My friend does the printing of 'phony-money' in Brazil, makes big bucks. Gerd is 'premier engraver', zee very best, very much artistic talent, and Brazil paper is poor, so no problem for her. She makes much money and can even pay for my visit next year. Great visit for me, Gerd is beautiful. She is actual Gerda von Richter,"

Morgan's attention came back to the present, as he heard the Executive Elevator function and knew Conrad Holmes and Sonchi Zimchi were on the way up. The elevator noise stopped and the solid brass safety gate parted as the mahogany elevator doors slid open to reveal Conrad and Sonchi stepping from the elevator's carriage.

After an hour Morgan and Sonchi had discussed and dictated their decisions while Conrad placed each offering on a large chalk board. The cluttered blackboard now showed the detailed breakdown of their plan to add hundreds of millions of dollars to the vast sum the two billionaires already controlled. The new scheme had been titled: 'BUCK':

Engraving – Gerda Von Richter - BRAZIL

Printing and Rail – Morgan Folds– UNITED STATES

Paper and Shipping – Sonchi Zimchi - CHINA

Marketing and Distribution – Gunter Wilhelms – KENYA

(Morgan and Sonchi had also considered chemical gemstones', specifically diamonds. Conrad's research showed lab grown diamonds could be forged from graphite subjected to temperatures as high as 2,500 degrees Fahrenheit and pressures 50,000 times the earth's atmosphere. While this option had been interesting they put it aside due to the present undeveloped state of the industry, now only producing smaller diamond chips for high-end cutting tools and cosmetic skin defoliants).

After lengthy discussion Morgan and Sonchi decided on Gerda's offer to engrave plates for twenty pound notes from four separate issuing locations in Great Britain. Conrad, as overall Security Consultant, had researched the paper production through the Loughton Banknote Printing Facility and Sonchi had found China suppliers for identical paper for all four separately issued notes. Chemists had tested and examined the Chinese paper and were certain the one million sheets would pass easily through the distribution centers being set up throughout Africa and Europe by Gunter Wilhelms. Morgan had succeeded in acquiring similar inks for the printing of over 8 billion US dollars worth of the British currency in Twenty Pound notes to be printed in the US. The ink had been trucked from Tennessee and was waiting in a large warehouse in Fredericksburg, Virginia where Morgan had acquired the computer printing technology for the operation. Completion was expected a little over a year from now, in December 2007. The paper was in the process of being land and water transferred to Hong Kong, then through Zimchi Shipping to The Port of Hampton Roads for off-loading and eventual transfer as packing material. All foreign shipping would arrive and transfer through NISCO facilities at the Norfolk International Terminals.

Mr. Charles Taylor, the CEO of NISCO was involved through his association with Zimchi Shipping and Virginia Eastern Rails, but Taylor was a pawn participating only in the lucrative business of shipping, he was not a partner with any knowledge of 'BUCK'.

The four major partners, and Conrad Holmes acting as overall Security for 'BUCK', expected to net a total of 800 million dollars US after the estimated up-front cost of 50 million dollars from Morgan and Sonchi who were funding of the start-up cost of the operation. "Conrad, I believe we've gotten it all done, some Champagne please." Morgan requested.

"Yes, Conrad," Sonchi added, "I do believe we can let the planning rest for the evening, some Champagne is certainly in order."

Conrad retrieved a bottle of champagne from the refrigerator and poured saying, "Here's to BUCK gentlemen, I'm eager for the fray," To Conrad 60 million US was well worth his efforts. Morgan and Sonchi quickly agreed, 200 million each for them was also an exciting prize.

CHAPTER TWENTY THREE

NORFOLK, SUNDAY, 9:30PM

Eric Chin downed the last of his beer as he examined the three computer discs he'd taken from the Harrington house. He wasn't sure what information they held, but he knew he'd killed for them. They had to be valuable, a good insurance policy against being left without necessary funds. His mind drifted back to Saturday, three weeks ago, when he had murdered Wilber Harrington.

Eric had been told eliminating Harrington and destroying all the information concerning Harrington's novel, 'Pacific Secret', was the reason he was in Norfolk. Ursula had provided his instructions and Saturday morning seemed the perfect time,

There was a lot going on in Lakewood Park, Pee Wee Football games were on several fields and he was sure they would help divert attention from his mission. Eric carried the large UPS envelope with the publisher's rejection letter for Wilber Harrington as he followed Harrington into the house removed his silenced 22 and immediately fired one fatal shot into the right side of Harrington's head. That had been the easy part, then, some problems began to threaten his mission.

Wearing surgical gloves Eric searched Harrington's computer files deleting all relevant data on the hard drive. Then he had gone through Harrington's desk until he found several computer discs, including his target, 'Pacific Secret'. He found two more, 'Honorable Service' and 'The Devil on Angel Flight', with hand written titles on their covers, so he pocketed all three discs and discarded everything else into a large trash bag for destruction later. After wiping all prints from the weapon and placing it in Harrington's right hand he pushed the gun's barrel into the half filled bucket of sand and fired the second shot pressing Harrington's dead fingers hard against the handle and trigger. Eric removed and pocketed the weapon's silencer and one of the spent shell-casings from the cylinder, replacing it with another live round he carried.

After dragging Harrington's body into the office area Eric typed and printed a short, bold faced suicide note on the computer then he raised the computer processor above his head and smashed it onto the floor. Eric was forced to step on pieces of glass, plastic and bright shinny metal fragments that were spread throughout the room as he gathered up the bucket and the trash bag and prepared to go. As he was leaving Eric spotted the unopened rejection letter and was forced to stop and tear it open before he could crumple the letter and throw it on the desk. Wanting to destroy more evidence, he set a fire using decorative window curtains he placed against the heating plate of an operating coffee maker. He could feel the plate was hot but he was in a hurry and decided to

light the curtains with a match. He watched the small, thin, column of smoke begin to rise from
the kitchen as he gathered evidence and pulled his heavy gloves on over the surgical gloves. Finally
satisfied, Eric started the truck and drove away.

Eric smiled and closed the drawer containing the three discs, picked up a lightweight jacket, wallet, keys and sunglasses, then locked his apartment door. He lived only a mile from the zoo and thought the walk could help clear his head before work.

Leaving the apartment building he headed down Waverly Street pausing on Granby to check-out the building project presently underway next to the Granby Street Bridge. A massive construction project was beginning and the nearby billboard called the project, the River View Condominiums. The construction bordered on the Lafayette River, and Eric dreamed of living near similar water when he returned to San Diego where he had been trained to work for Ursula Volk.

Eric continued south on Granby past a gift shop, an old movie theater and the 7 – 11 before turning left on La Vallette Street next to Lafayette Park. Picking up his pace he headed across the open field toward the Animal Care Building at the Virginia Zoo. He could see the building's Halogen Security Lighting in the distance and noted Ursula's dark BMW was the only car parked in the employee lot. Ursula was no where in sight, so Eric leaned against the stockade fence bordering the parking area and waited.

After five-minutes Eric spotted Ursula opening the front door of the building, she waved to him and he headed her way. No wonder she can handle those elephants so easily, Eric thought, she's an Amazon, at least my height of 6'-2" and about 190 pounds, only 30 pounds less than me. Be careful around her, Eric concluded, she's highly trained and experienced. Ursula opened the door and said, "Thanks for coming Eric. I've got the truck keys we'll drive the back way to the elephant barn."

"No problem Ursula, I walked over." Eric responded as he followed her into the admin building. "Do you want me to sign the volunteer time-sheet?"

"No, do that later." Ursula answered as they exited the back of the building and headed to the one of the zoo's large lift-back trucks. Ursula entered the truck and unlocked the passenger door for Eric to enter.

"Can I leave my jacket in the truck?"

"Sure," Ursula said as they drove around the Siberian Tiger exhibit, past the back of the African Village Restaurant and down the access road leading behind the Red River Hog and Mandrill exhibits to the elephant barn. When they arrived, Ursula said, "I've opened the barn, Eric, two of the 'girls' are outside in the holding yard, but Monica's in the end stall. You can clean the first two stalls but keep an empty stall between you and Monica. I've got to get something in the office, then I'll be back to check on you."

This was different from their normal routine, it was late and he was being left alone and unsupervised, so Eric asked, "Why are we cleaning at night, Ursula?"

"I'm expecting a major donor early for Monica to do an elephant painting so I want the first two stalls presentable." Eric knew the zoo always needed donations and he was familiar with Monica's ability to use her trunk to do water based swirl-like paintings on a flat canvas for major donations, so Ursula's explanation was accepted without further concern.

Eric worked alone, cleaning the first two stalls, checking Monica in the distance from time to time. Monica continued to stand, watching Eric intently, as she always did. It took only 40 minutes to clean the two stalls, then, Eric moved the loaded wheel-barrow needed to remove the elephant matter from the stalls and began to wash down the concrete floors of the first two stalls. Ursula was still in her office as Eric remembered his 'insurance policy' hidden in his apartment. The three computer discs from the Harrington house could be his ticket to get away from having to take orders from Ursula Volk or shovel elephant shit ever again.

While Eric continued to direct the heavy spray from the fire hose against the etched squares on the first stall's concrete floor, Ursula returned and shouted, "Eric, I'm going to check on the Grants gazelle, I'll be right back," as she exited the far end of the barn heading toward the back area stalls where the gazelle was kept.

Ursula closed the large hallway doors connecting the giraffe and elephant area to the separated confinement areas for several Bongos two large Ostriches and the Grant's gazelle. She stopped down the hallway remembering her earlier conversation with Iron Man Cheng and orders to, *'Destroy all possible connection between the primary mission and failed elimination of Stephen Irons,'* Ursula had personally guaranteed no further problem would occur. She had too many years invested to allow Eric's failure to threaten her primary mission. She was anxious to get past this temporary job concerning Harrington's book idea and back to her original assignment to establish a local information network for the Chinese that would rival Russia's earlier successes with the Walker family.

Pausing at a small refrigerator Ursula withdrew her medical kit and removed two small syringes and three glass vials. She carefully extracted 10ccs of Sodium Thiopental into one syringe, withdrew a second vial and added 20ccs of Versed. Ursula watched closely noting the combining of the two liquids, she needed the truth and she needed a strong drug with a rapid onset of dreamy helplessness. The mixture would bring-on an immediate anesthetic reaction allowing a quick interrogation immediately followed by total muscular collapse. Ursula completed her preparation by drawing 20ccs of SECONAL into the second syringe then she capped both syringes before pocketing them and walking back toward the elephant stalls. Approaching the closed hallway door she took out her cell phone and called Zoo Security and waited for the call to connect, she heard, "Security, Lawson,"

"Tom, it's Ursula, I'm in the elephant barn prepping for a painting tomorrow morning, just thought I'd let you know. Where are you, Tom?"

"Other side of the zoo Ursula, near the Education Trailer, you need help? I've got to finish rounds here but I'll be in your area in about 40 minutes." Lawson replied.

No, thanks Tom, my volunteer didn't show, but I'm almost done. I'll be through in 20 minutes so you can keep to your schedule. See you tomorrow Tom." Ursula closed and pocketed her cell-phone and headed back to where Eric was working. She had time to act.

Ursula pushed open the large connecting doors and walked down the wide hallway separating the elephant and giraffe stalls. She took the first syringe from her breast pocket, removed the cap and called out as she approached the small rolling-cart used to transport hay bales into the barn, "Eric, shut the water off and give me a hand with these hay bales," then she watched Eric close the nozzle before he headed toward her.

When Eric arrived and bent down to help Ursula raise a bale of hay, he slipped on the wet floor and nearly lost his balance. Ursula saw her opportunity and quickly moved toward him ordering, "Hold the bale Eric, I'll come around and help you,"

"Okay," Eric responded as Ursula approached behind him and quickly wrapped her left arm around Eric's neck and thrust the 30cc syringe's needle into the area at the base of his skull, pushing the contents rapidly into his system. Eric tried to break away and tipped the rolling-cart, slamming it against the concrete floor. *BANG* the cart noise resounded in the barn and Monica raised her head and trunk toward the distant activity.

Eric continued to struggle but Ursula balanced herself and applied more pressure as she bent her knees to lower her center of gravity for better stability. Eric's physical effort faded and he released his grip on the hay bale and slumped to the concrete floor. "Are you okay Eric?" Ursula whispered.

"Woozy, head hurt... breeth... bad... hard to tall-k.., wha' hap?"

"You lost balance, Eric," Ursulah said believing the drug was taking affect, "Eric, what did you do with the computer discs from the Harrington house?"

"Eh, destroy mos, keep som, in...sur...ance." Eric hesitated at first then answered.

"That's good, Eric, where are the ones you kept?"

"Apar..men, dress'..r, feel bad Ursula. Sorry Irons' mis..ion, can do bedar... " Eric smiled as he slipped gently into a deepening coma. Ursula brushed the back of her hand lightly over Eric's eyelashes, no reaction. She spoke softly into his right ear,

"Eric can you hear me?" Still no response, Ursula left Eric propped up against the tipped cart recapped and put the empty syringe in her side pocket as she moved into the elephant stall to retrieve the hose and finish the cleaning. Ursula spoke to Monica in quiet tones as the large elephant continued to stare at Eric, now lying motionless on the concrete floor. Ursula turned toward the far elephant stall and said,

"Alright Monica, go back to your food, Eric's resting now."

CHAPTER TWENTY FOUR

VIRGINIA ZOO, MIDNIGHT

It took Ursula Volk twenty minutes to finish in the elephant barn and place Eric's comatose body in an oversized plastic coroner's bag normally used to remove large dead animals from zoo property. She hefted the bag containing Eric's 220 pounds and carried him outside the barn in a large orange wheel barrow. She hid the wheel barrow behind a small storage shed, locked the barn and drove the truck back to the Animal Care Building where she removed Eric's jacket and personal affects before carrying them through the building headed to her own car. Ursula drove to the zoo's rear service entrance, unlocked the gate and drove along the back service road to the elephant barn. She loaded Eric into the BMW's trunk and drove her car back through the rear gate. When she relocked the gate she could see the lights from a small security vehicle making its rounds near the Africa Restaurant. Lawson was at least 300 yards away, Ursula was certain she was safe now as she drove toward a new construction site near Eric's apartment building.

Arriving near the Granby Street Bridge construction area, Ursula parked her car deep in the shadows off Waverly Street Circle, half way between the construction site and Eric's apartment building. She removed Eric from the trunk, carried him through heavy weeds to the water's-edge portion of the site. She slid the large coroner's bag under the temporary construction site's gate and carried it down to the temporary pier that ran under the bridge. Hiding in a darkened area, Ursula unzipped the bag and placed Eric on the pier. Kneeling down she removed the second syringe and injected 20ccs of SECONAL directly into Eric's arm leaving yet another drug related needle mark for the authorities to discover. She recapped the syringe and tossed it into the Coroner's bag with the first syringe and three small vials from her pocket. Finally she folded the large bag up and shoved it into a smaller draw string trash bag before she tightened and knotted the cinching handles to enclose and the coroner's bag.

Ursula dragged Eric further under the bridge, squeezed his fingers around a gin bottle for prints then forced him to gulp down several swallows. Eric coughed with a gag reflex and his eyes fluttered spasmodically but he showed no other physical sign of muscular response. Rolling Eric over she checked his pulse; it was vacillating between rapid and almost non-existent. The powerful mixture was beginning to cause ventricular tachycardia before sporadic arrhythmia set in and gave way to Eric's death. Ursula watched as Eric slipped slowly into the Lafayette River where he floated about two minutes with no movement then settled deep into the river's rising tide. Eric was unable to move but the last of his shallow breathing would ingest enough river water to provide confirmation of an accidental drowning. She removed Eric's keys from his jacket, tossed the jacket and the empty gin bottle on the pier then carried the garbage bag to a large trash dumpster for disposal. Eric had been useful but failure to complete his assignment with Stephen Irons threatened to expose her primary mission and her orders were specific, *"Protect your primary mission,"*

After entering Eric's apartment, Ursula found the three computer discs and the Chinese sniper rifle hidden in Eric's guitar case. She gathered everything together and departed leaving Eric's keys on a small desk. She wanted to get rid of the rifle but she pocketed the discs planning to hide them in the elephant barn, in an area where only she had access. Leaving the apartment Ursula carried the guitar case and walked outside toward her car. As she passed under a street light she heard sounds behind her and turned to see two teenagers on bikes coming quickly toward her. The closest was a small black kid pumping hard to speed-up and catch her. The second kid, a much larger teen, was lagging behind. The big kid looked to be her height but weighed well over 300 pounds and carried a baseball bat in one fat hand. Ursula continued to walk away as the smaller black kid sped past her and laid his bike down on the street in front of her. The kid jumped off with a large revolver drawn and pointed in her direction. Ursula placed the guitar case on the ground and looked closely toward the kid's weapon, a Colt 22, she thought. The black kid moved within her reach and pointed the weapon directly at her face,

"Git on th gron Ho! Wha's ina git-case?" The kid yelled as he thrust the weapon until it almost touched her nose then he began to turn the gun sideways, like he was in some joke of a cop movie. Dumb, Ursula thought as she noticed the front sight had been filed off to accept a silencer. The black kid continued to move the gun back and forth and Ursula laughed,

"You stupid, kid!"

"Wats yo takin 'bout, bitch?" The kid exclaimed as Ursula grabbed the kid's wrist and twisted, *CRACK,* his wrist bones fractured. She let the gun clatter to the street and jerked the kid's broken arm toward her. "Oooww," the kid's outcry was sharp and piercing like a razor's cut, then, the sound folded into a soft, hoarse, moan as Ursula kicked the kid in the testicles and silence collapsed his throat. Ursula released the kid's arm and as he fell unconscious on the street and she turned to see the black kid's buddy, with bat in hand, lumbering slowly up behind her.

The fat kid arrived, out of breath and swung the bat hard. Ursula turned her shoulder, avoiding the bat and instantly slammed her knuckled fist into the big kid's right arm. A second *CRACK* echoed out as the kid's forearm bones shatter under Ursula's knuckles forcing him to release the bat to the ground. Ursula kicked the 22 revolver away and turned the fat kid's body around, placing her right forearm tightly around his neck and squeezing on his carotid artery. She joined her left elbow under and around her right wrist and began to tighten, pulling up hard, denying blood flow to the kid's brain. "You're big like an elephant, kid, but you got the brain of an ostrich," Ursula uttered in the kid's ear as she increased pressure until the big kid lost consciousness, very near death. Ursula dropped the body, retrieved the weapon and Eric's guitar case and kicked the bat away,

"Three strikes, you're out kid!"

CHAPTER TWENTY FIVE

NORFOLK INTERNATIONAL TERMINAL (NIT)

"STEPHEN IRONS"

Sally didn't hear from Detective Knowles on Monday so I called Sheriff Os to arrange an appointment with Charles Taylor for this morning at 10:30. Now at 10:15 I'm in the long line of traffic heading north on Hampton Boulevard waiting to turn left into the NIT complex. During my Navy career I had been assigned to the nearby Norfolk Naval Operating Base but this was the first time I would enter the adjacent NIT area. The last ten years of shipping growth in Norfolk has had a dramatic impact throughout Hampton Roads and I was anxious to see the NIT influence personally. I turned left off Hampton Boulevard, lining up behind several trucks waiting for clearance to enter NIT. Now stalled in the long line I glanced to my right toward the Joint Forces Staff College (JFSC), Wilber's last assignment before he retired from the navy. JFSC is a large military campus with academic instructors from all the services and the support staff needed to train over 200 mid-career level officers from the US and several Allied countries. The six-month course focuses on the 'Application of Joint Service Operations' worldwide. Waiting in line I began to recall Sally and I watching Wilber play softball with his new seminar-group just after they returned to Norfolk,

"Sally, does Wilber like it here at the staff college?" I asked as we both watched Wilber step into the batter's box and wait for the opposing seminar's slow-pitch delivery.

"Hit it Will!" Sally yelled loudly, encouraging Wilber to get a hit, then she turned to me, "I think so Stphen, he loves being around the younger students, he said most of them have only been in their service about twelve years, maybe their mid thirties, much younger than Will, you know more like my age."

"So, they're Majors or Lieutenant Commanders in their respective services…but Sally, you said Wilber thinks it's really good for the Navy, doesn't he think the program's good for all the services?"

"Probably, but Will says 'the Navy needs it more because they're slow to jump in the Joint Arena', then he added 'the Navy's never happy sharing military responsibility or congressional appropriations with the other services'. He's so concerned he signed up to take a correspondence course on inter-service cooperation."

"You're joking aren't you? All the Special Forces people like Army RANGERS and

Navy SEALS, depend on the Joint Arena to gather intelligence and provide combat support."

"Run Will, run!" Sally yelled as Wilber hit the ball through the infield and headed to first base with a single, "You should talk to Will, Stephen, I'm sure he'd enjoy talking with you. Maybe you can find out why the Navy put him on restricted duty in San Diego, he's never told me. He's actually very secretive about a lot of his service experiences."

"Sally, Wilber was on nuclear submarines most of his career, he's always had to deal with classified material. He's been involved with a lot of secret stuff." I offered,

"Oh well, its no big deal, he's getting out in a few months anyway." Sally replied.

I was pleased that Sally had finally learned at least one of Wilber's secrets from CAPT Westerly, who had explained why Wilber had been placed on 'restricted shore duty' and I re-focused on the traffic going into NIT and looked farther west at four huge cranes clearly visible against the horizon. A large truck in front of me began to move forward and two more cranes came into view to my right. All six cranes were identical, rising up over 200 feet in the air separated by 300 feet or more between each grouping of two. The northern most set was now actively servicing a large container ship, by my estimation at least 1000 feet in length, virtually as long as an old battleship or one of our newest aircraft carriers. While I watched the crane reached onto the docked ship and plucked containers from the ship's deck transporting them onto the nearby dock. The crane operation reminded me of kids trying to beat an arcade's 'Claw Machine', you know, paying a quarter for one try at picking up a soft toy when the 'released claw' drops down and 'grabs at' one of many toys, but usually coming up with thin air. A very loud *BLAST* from a truck's horn behind me let me know it was time for me to move up in line. I shifted the Volvo into DRIVE and pulled up alongside the large entrance gate.

"Good morning," the guard said as he leaned into my open convertible and glanced quickly at my briefcase on the passenger seat, "how can I help you, sir?"

"My name's Stephen Irons. I'm here to see Mr. Charles Taylor at NISCO, he told me to ask for Fred at the gate."

"I'm Fred, Mr. Irons," Fred replied tapping his name tag, confirming his honesty and my lapse in observation. "May I see your Drivers' License please?" I smiled acknowledging my error, opened my brief case, took out my wallet and handed Fred, my Virginia Drivers' License and my Retired Sheriff's ID. Fred glanced at the Virginia ID and spent a little more time on the Sheriff's plastic, then he smiled and handed my cards back. "Wait here a minute Sheriff Irons I'll get you a pass and a facility diagram."

Thirty seconds later Fred was back, "Here's your pass, sir, just hang the chain around your neck until you come back through the gate." The pass had a large VIP stenciled across it in Bold Red Letters. I hung the pass around my neck and Fred went on, "Go straight ahead for a hundred yards then take a right at the intersection. Drive across the tracks for another 100 yards or so and the NISCO Operations Building will be the four story structure on your left. Mr. Taylor's office is on the third floor."

"Thanks Fred, eh, for the record, I'm retired from the Norfolk Sheriff's Department. By the way, what's Mr. Taylor's office number?"

"Sorry, 1 misspoke," Fred replied with a small laugh, "Mr. Taylor's office, IS the third floor Sheriff Irons. Have a nice day." Then Fred added, "Hey, sir, you've got a great car, retirement can't be all that bad." Fred was definitely one up on me.

CHAPTER TWENTY SIX

NISCO @ NIT

"STEPHEN IRONS"

The entrance lobby walls were a bland battle-ship gray and there was an unmanned reception desk to my left with gray vinyl flooring everywhere. I gave up on the vacant desk and memories of battleship-gray shipboard experiences and started toward the distant elevator.

I got no more than a step when I heard a movement from behind and turned back to see a beautiful young woman, probably Sally's age, walking quickly toward the back of the reception desk. The blonde beauty stopped behind the desk, smiled and waved to me. She was my height, 5'-10" or so, with a long twisted braid of golden hair and striking cobalt blue eyes. She was dressed in a pale blue outfit that resembled a fighter pilot's 'flight-suit', probably a set of some 'designer coveralls' that fit her like semi-gloss skin.

"Hi, are you Sheriff Irons?" the blonde inquired with a big white toothed smile that lit her blue eyes up provocatively.

"Yes, but I'm retired now, my name's Stephen," I offered, holding my VIP badge up with my left hand and reaching anxiously to take her hand in greeting with my right. She continued to smile brightly but declined my touch. I blinked with regret, then, surprisingly she dropped down behind the reception desk. I assumed she was after another brochure and moved closer to assist. But as I started forward, she popped back up smiled and said,

"You can go up to the third floor Sheriff Irons, Mr. Taylor's on the phone but he'll join you soon. Welcome to NISCO, I'm Margarete Kroger, one of Mr. Taylor's Personal Assistants. I hope we'll be seeing much more of you, Stephen." Margarete finalized, then, smiled again and finally, to my great pleasure, she shook my offered hand vigorously before she turned to depart.

"Thank you, Margarete," I said as I stepped back from the desk and watched with pleasure as her flowing pony tail and skin-tight, blue coveralls exhibited a smooth rolling gate that moved her body seductively out the automated side door. I continued to look past the reception desk trying to catch one last glimpse of her departure and thought I heard a faint giggle, but I glanced around and saw nothing. When I looked back toward the door, the coveralls that contained

Margarete's hypnotic 'fan-tail' had vanished.

The elevator ride was short. As the door slid open on the third floor all my earlier impressions of the NISCO 'bland, navy-like surroundings' took an immediate leap to the bazaar. If you can remember ever seeing the movie, 'The Snows of Kilimanjaro', or maybe 'Mogambo,' you might believe, as I did now, that you'd been transported to one of the movie's jungle sets. Thoughts of 'Mogambo' triggered my memory of Clark Gabel and Ava Gardner in Africa. Thoughts of Ava Gardner brought my mind back to Cora, the young CRACKERS ' waitress I'd met earlier with Os. I smiled to myself and decided I needed another encounter with Cora, just to see if I could now jump from desire to arousal without Norfolk Police involvement.

Concentrating on the third floor surroundings I found the entire area filled with lush green jungle plants in large pots that rested on wall to wall, thatched sisal carpeting extending up each wall to at least a ten foot level. Above that level, the walls took on the dark jungle green color of the plants before reaching a glass paneled, 1940's factory type ceiling made up of hundreds of glass windows framed and mounted in a bow-shaped, dome-truss, type structure that covered the large room. As if the jungle plants weren't enough, dispersed throughout the high walls leading up to the glass ceiling structure were the stuffed and mounted heads of every large mammal known to inhabit the African Continent. Except, there was no elephant, giraffe or rhinoceros head mounted on the walls. Actually, those three animals were on full display in their gigantic physical entirety. The giraffe stood erect with its large head and upright ears reaching up over sixteen feet. The large stuffed rhino was to the left of the giraffe and farther left, stood an elephant, possibly a large bull because of the awesome size of the beast but I was unable to tell its gender due to the tall artificial grass surrounding the elephant's body. The displayed rhino was the size of a small Hum-V and the elephant was much taller, at least ten feet at the shoulders. The rhino's single horn was about three feet in length and the tusks on the elephant were much longer curving-up and out six feet or so.

No sign yet of my host, so I began to wander around and look more closely at the wall displayed animal heads. After ten minutes I had seen Reedbucks, Red Roan Antelopes, Southern Kudus, White Tailed Gnus, Red Bucks, two Southern Impalas, a Blesbok, several large Yellow Duikers, a Wart Hog and finally the head of a gigantic African Cape Buffalo. Shaking my head in amazement I returned to the open hallway and now saw, striding in the middle of what I believed was the most impressive room I had ever seen, a tall, light complexioned black man as he moved toward me. Certainly this was my host coming to greet me. He was at least 6'1" and about 210 pounds and looked exactly like what he was, a college football player from 15 years ago, still in great shape with broad shoulders and narrow hips. Os' statement about he, and Charles Taylor playing for my dad at William and Mary came immediately to my mind. I was pleased to see Mr. Taylor was wearing a charcoal gray suit, not the full jungle attire of some 'Animal Hunter' that I might have expected. Accenting his gray suit he wore a green silk shirt with a dark green tie. He was color coordinated to stalk-about in this jungle room.

"Sheriff Irons, sorry I'm late, I'm Charles Taylor, please call me Charles," He offered as he grasp my much smaller hand between his two large palms and gave me one firm, almost intimidating pump, then, he continued before I could respond, "Os has told me a lot about you. I see you're a little overwhelmed by my office, I can certainly understand, I'm just getting use to it myself. This is only my second month in the building owned by the Zimchi Shipping Company of Beijing, and Shanghai. The Zimchi family built this jungle office in the 1990's and their Director of Foreign Investments at that time, Mr. Sonchi Zimchi, used the office exclusively until he was recalled to China earlier this year. Zimchi Shipping is our major foreign shipper and my landlord, in addition to being a very good friend of Mr. Morgan Folds, the President and CEO of Virginia Eastern Rails, the rail company that carries seventy percent of our interstate transfer business. Morgan and Sonchi hunted together in Africa for many years prior to the present restrictions and quarantines imposed on big game hunting. The animal trophies you see are from their hunts."

Charles Taylor moved slightly to our left and pointed toward the large elephant I had noticed earlier. I decided to continue being a quiet student as Taylor went on,

"Behind the bull elephant you can see the picture of Morgan and Sonchi with their African guide, Gunter Wilhelms. The picture shows Sonchi's elephant kill in 1996. It's the only photograph allowed in the office. Pictures of my family, my wife Millie and other memorabilia, like old pictures of me and Os when we played football for your dad at William and Mary, those are kept in my downtown office."

"Please call me Stephen, sir," I answered when Taylor paused to breathe and allow me a response, "I'll bet PETA's upset about this place." I joked, referring to the organization, People for the Ethical Treatment of Animals, who maintain their corporate offices in downtown Norfolk. I was trying to lighten the atmosphere, getting a little tired of Charles' lengthy lecture format.

"You might be inclined to assume that Stephen, but I'm not at liberty to comment on your speculation." Charles replied without the trace of a smile, then, he went on, "I wanted to meet you here so you could view the entire NIT complex as we talk about your employment opportunity with NISCO. Is that acceptable?"

"Yes sir, that's fine," I replied as Taylor turned away and led me past the big elephant toward a wrought iron staircase spiraling up another level to a small elevated room. "When you and Os played for my dad at William and Mary you must have had a great team, how'd you do that year?" I asked as we climbed up the spiral. Charles glanced back down at me and smiled for the first time, but as he implied earlier, he wasn't going to comment on any of my speculations, so we just continued to climb-up toward the elevated room and what I assumed would be 'a step-up to a higher education'.

Arriving, a little winded and in possession of an aching left leg I could see the small room had large glass windows from waist-high to roof-top. Charles positioned his self in the center of the room and it was obvious his lengthy dissertation was going to continue. Charles was like every instructor I had endured in the US Navy, he was here to impart information and I was required to listen and learn. I resigned myself to my fate and stepped onto the observation deck dragging my bad leg and mounting skepticism behind me.

Spreading out above me was a small domed ceiling made of thick glass covering a room that looked like an airport control tower with communication devices ranging from land-line to hard-wire or wireless interfaced computer technology everywhere. A large flat paneled screen presently showed a schematic diagram that matched the hand-out Fred provided me earlier. Four sets of binoculars were spaced throughout the room to amplify views around the complex and four small microphones were suspended with stretch cords that extended down from the elaborate metallic structure holding the expansive domed ceiling in place. As I looked around waiting for more information, I harkened back to my navy training and remained quiet, looking straight ahead, you know 'eyes in the boat', paying direct attention to my instructor. Charles resumed,

"This is not the actual Control Center for NISCO, that space is below ground, but this area connects me to the center and to the NISCO vehicles, operating machinery and employed personnel presently on shift. This area provides me with what I like to call a 'God's Eye View'," Charles paused for a blink of his god's eye, maybe a second, or so, then he went on, "And from this advantage I have the responsibility of assuring all is well in my NISCO world." I couldn't wait anymore, so, to keep from laughing at his pompous presentation, I jumped into the conversation,

"You said you have a family and an office downtown, I'm certain this is a 24 hour operation here, when do you have time to check on what's going on in the rest of your NISCO world?"

"Yes," Charles laughed quietly, finally agreeing to answer one of my questions, "we are an around the clock operation, but I have two very capable assistants. It's their expertise and support that gives me time away from my responsibilities here," Immediately recalling my encounter with the blonde I got excited and shoved my way back into the conversation,

"I think I met one of your assistants, Margarete Kroger, is that right?" I asked, fondly remembering the retreating pony tail and light blue coveralls that enclosed the rear end of her earlier exit.

"You probably met both of them, they're identical twins and they enjoy confusing people when they first meet them. I believe they're descendents of the Krog family in Denmark but they Americanized their name to Kroger. Arnold Krog, probably their great-great-great grandfather, invented the process used to produce white under glazed porcelain in the late 19th Century. Did the Margarete you met, show up, disappear then reappear?"

"Yes she did, she approached the reception desk, ducked down behind it then came right back up. Was that the two of them?"

"Most likely," Charles replied, "here let's take a look." Charles picked up a large remote-controller device, pointed it at the large flat screen showing the facility diagram and pressed several buttons. There, before my eyes, was a view of the reception desk taken from behind my back soon after I entered the facility. I could easily make out the back of my red head and the downward slope of my presently out of shape shoulders. As my ego and I attempted to square my actual shoulders, here in real time, my recorded image turned toward the desk and began to observe the person I'd met as Margarete Kroger as she approach rapidly through the doorway. My film image extended its hand in a greeting attempt and the girl disappeared momentarily, then, reappeared slightly to the right of her earlier vanishing point. I started to laugh as the scene played out before us in living color, right up to the point when I turned my head and began walking toward the elevator. Then as my film shoulders turned and I watched my image depart, I could see in the background the first, or second Margarete, pop back up from behind the desk, smile and wave at the camera before she followed her twin sister's departure.

"Why would they go to all that trouble? Is it a joke?" I asked.

"Yes, initially a joke, but it keeps my other employees on their toes. The Kroger Twins, the one you believe you first met as Margarete has a sister named Elizabeth, probably one of them hid below the desk until they switched on you. They both worked for Zimchi Shipping, in San Diego, then here in Norfolk before I was fortunate enough to hire them when Zimchi's headquarters moved back to China. They're invaluable to me, providing me time to manage the company without always having to be here on-site."

I shook my head slightly, tried to muster a small laugh to keep from betraying the fascination I was having with the two beautiful blondes I had encountered. Quickly my mind joined the Kroger twins with my present fascination with another blonde, Detective Linda Knowles, and I knew my life was improving rapidly.

Charles and I moved out of the control area, back down the spiral stairs, past the large elephant and walked into an adjoining area I suspected was his private office. This room was large, 20 by 20 with very few furnishings. It followed the 'jungle motif' with several large potted plants surrounding the black, onyx like, glass topped desk. But, in contrast to the earlier dark green upper walls and sisal flooring of the operations area, the battleship gray of the entrance lobby had been muted and softened in tone to continue above a matching soft gray wall to wall wool carpet beneath our feet. In the center of the surrounding walls was one large 'palace size' oriental carpet under-laying the onyx desk and two extra chairs. Charles seated himself behind the glass topped desk and motioned me to sit opposite. As I sat down, I asked, "Charles, could you give me a quick summary of why you're interested in me coming on board?" He looked at me a bit differently and I hoped he'd finally get to the point.

"Basically I need some one to go through my organization to find out why Wilber Harrington had to die." Charles paused like he wanted me to say, 'well that's certainly quick enough', but I wasn't falling in that elephant trap, I waited for more, so he continued, "Stephen, I actually need some one to look at the NISCO operation, using my authority of course, to ascertain the reason Wilber was fatally removed. Right now I believe he died because he worked for me. I could be wrong, but somehow it all seems connected to his working here. Wilber learned something, or became involved in something, that got him killed. I need you to find out who in my organization benefited from Wilber's death and who should be prosecuted for his death. I don't have the time to do this myself, but it's very important to me. I need someone as motivated as I am to find these answers. Os tells me you might be that person. Is that straight-forward enough?"

Charles paused, waiting for my reply. I wanted to reply 'Charles, you might assume that was the case, but I couldn't honestly speculate'. But I was too interested in the job, so I just answered, "Yes, Charles, that's simple enough and, I'm definitely interested, please continue." As soon as I finished my statement, Charles' cell-phone sounded, he excused himself for the interruption, picked up and activated the phone,

"Charles Taylor" he responded, then waited about 10 seconds and added, "No, Judge that will not suffice you must revisit my guidelines and carry my instructions out to the letter."

Charles stood and turned away from my seated position with his hand held phone shielded from my view. Although I couldn't see the expression on his face, it was clear he was disappointed in the 'Judge', whoever that was. Charles waited another 10 seconds then answered,

"Yes, please call again when you're certain my instructions have been followed correctly. I'm very busy now Judge, check with Os if you have other questions." Charles disconnected the call with the Judge, who was obviously some associate or friend of his and Os' then Charles returned to his seat. I was curious about the Judge and Os' connection to Charles but I decided now wasn't the time to ask.

Charles replaced the phone and apologized. "Sorry for the interruption Stephen, lets get back to our business. I have a couple of formalities we require before going further." Charles passed several sheets of business stationary across the desk toward me and offered, "This is a non-disclosure document concerning anything you may see or hear during your visit here today."

After looking over the initial paper about confidentiality, I took the pen Charles offered and signed. A second sheet stated that my sole responsibility and accountability would be to Charles and the job was described as: 'Special Assistant to the Executive Director of NISCO', created to assist the Director, and other Authorized Investigative Authorities, in the on-going investigation into the death of Wilber Harrington. The salary was shown as $10,000 per month plus expenses, with the non retractable first and last month's compensation payable upon my acceptance of the offer.' I could feel my eyes widen and I asked,

"Working directly for you Charles?"

"Yes, of course." Charles answered, "Will the salary and terms be acceptable to you, Stephen?"

CHAPTER TWENTY SEVEN

POLICE OPERATIONS, TUESDAY, 2:30PM

Detective Linda Knowles returned to her office with two copies of the extracted data from Margo's lap-top computer. Knowles left a third copy behind for Sally and Stephen to check-out and comment on. One of Norfolk's Police Computer Technicians was reorganizing one of the copies as Linda focused on the original and Sergeant Bradshaw entered the office, "Afternoon Boss, how'd the computer business go? Any help for the case?"

"Not sure Morris, our tech's creating some better organized copies so we can discuss them this afternoon. I'm not sure any of it will prove Harrington's death was a Homicide, but it should clear-up what he was writing about in the 'Pacific' book."

"Great." Bradshaw replied thinking how things were changing now for the better. After working a couple of weeks with Knowles she was more relaxed around him which was a big change from how she operated earlier when Bradshaw felt he was being ostracized as a height challenged, over-dressed Catholic neophyte investigator from Boston, Massachusetts. Bradshaw was taking Millers' comments to heart and hoped this change for the better would last. "Boss, there's something on the Police Sheets this morning, it's about a drowning victim found near the Granby Street Bridge." He added as he handed Knowles the report, Knowles quickly scanned the report and said,

"Why are you interested in this Morris? Looks like an accident at a construction site, the guy had too much to drink and fell in the Lafayette River and drowned."

"The construction boss said they found some articles on the pier yesterday, then, the body floated up under the bridge today. The cops told him the wallet in the jacket indicated the dead guy was probably Eric Chin. They thought he could have fallen in and drowned, or maybe he was pushed in the river and the other guy ran off."

"So, YOU think this might be a Homicide, instead of two guys goofing off with the one still alive and too scared to come forward and talk to us?"

"Well, could be either way, but check the bottom of the third section for articles found on the pier Monday, that's what got my attention."

"Okay, empty gin bottle with Chin's prints, tan jacket, wallet and a pair of sun glasses. So?" Knowles asked. Bradshaw opened his notebook and read, "When the rescue people pulled Chin out of the river, the construction boss added, 'He was a tall, dark complexioned Asian guy and his wallet and sunglasses were found in his jacket. The glasses were pilot glasses with big reflective lenses so an observer can't see the person's eyes,' Those were his words,"

"You're right Morris this could be something for us. I'll call the Medical Examiner's office and have Dr. Ski expedite the exam. She can do a complete drug and alcohol screen too. You head over to talk with her, take the duty photographer with you. Get a photo of the guy's face, with and without the glasses. This is good work we may have caught a break."

"Okay, I'm on the way." Morris smiled now believing he was starting to respond to Millers' challenge to be more thorough and proactive in their investigation.

———————

Sergeant Bradshaw drove downtown and entered the coroner's building carrying a large camera; the duty photographer had been rushed to another crime scene with the police digital so Bradshaw would be his own picture-taker with an old Polaroid. As he moved toward the coroners' section of the basement he looked forward to seeing the Medical Examiner again. Dr. Katherine Kowalski, or Dr. Ski as Detective Knowles had referred to her, was short, 5' 2" and exceptionally pretty. She and Bradshaw hit it off when they met in April during the Police Department's Spring Orientation. Looking basically eye to eye, with Dr. Ski in heels, Morris and Katherine had been well below the visual level of the average Police Department employee and had spotted each other across what seemed to them to be a crowded basketball court, full of their taller teammates.

As Bradshaw approached the reception desk, he felt the resident chill that permeated this area of the building. A tall guy in a scrub suit, was leaning over the desk munching french-fries and swigging on a coke, "Hi, I'm Dr. Kent Clark," the tall guy mouthed through his fries, "no jokes about a backward Superman, please. I'm Dr. Ski's assistant, you must be Bradshaw." The guy said as he stood fully and extended his hand down toward Bradshaw and added,

"I can see why she likes you, you both being down there on a lower level."

"Yeah, thanks, I'm Sergeant Bradshaw, can I go in?" Morris was encouraged with Dr. Clark's comment about Dr. Ski liking him for whatever reason.

"Sure, but I'll warn you, this one's messy, you want some french-fries and catsup?" Dr. Clark laughed as he sat down and took another swig of coke. Bradshaw shook off the 'morgue humor' and pushed through the large double doors entering Katherine Kowalski's domain.

Bradshaw entered a room filled with the sounds of running water and the sights of eight stainless steel tables, each with a porcelain sink, chrome and glass storage cases, plastic tubes, small electric saws and several razor sharp implements spread out near each table. The tables were arranged throughout the room, but with no logical order that Bradshaw could discern. All the tables were presently unoccupied, save one, in the far back area where on one of the tables in the room was what Bradshaw assumed to be the body of Eric Chin. The room was physically cold and depressing with exposed piping and ceiling hung electrical conduits throughout the concreted enclosure. It resembled what Bradshaw thought fit his idea of a nineteen fifties bomb shelter, without the stocked-supply of bottled water or canned food provisions for survival.

Bradshaw stopped and stared at a large doorway walled off with thick vertical strips of heavy six inch hanging plastic. As the strips parted and CLATTERED their icy contact with adjacent strands echoing their forced separation and Bradshaw smiled. Through the clattering strands marched Dr. Katherine Kowalski with her scalpel raised in a makeshift salute. "Hi, Morris welcome to my world." Katherine offered as she headed toward the occupied table and motioned Bradshaw to follow. Even attired in bloody scrubs, with a surgical mask hanging loosely below her full lips, seeing Katherine again gave Morris a jolt of pleasure. "Sorry about the odor, you might try a mask, but some Vicks under your nose should help more. Jar's on my desk." She pointed to her desk area just beyond the large table that held Eric Chin's body.

"Good to see you again, Morris, I've missed you since our last get together at the Chrysler. We should try, 'all that jazz', again", Katherine joked, "maybe a week from tomorrow, if that works for you."

Bradshaw was having trouble keeping up with Katherine's information but he remembered getting the courage to ask her for a date a month ago when she suggested the Wednesday night 'Free Jazz Concert at the Chrysler Museum' and he agreed. They met at the museum and talked while they listened to 'Grace Street', a local Jazz group that performed for an hour or so. Jazz wasn't Bradshaw's musical choice, but he'd been pleased with the evening, the group, their music and especially Katherine's company. He thought the date had been an exciting beginning, so he replied,

"I've missed seeing you too, Katherine, a week from tomorrow would be great."

"Morris, call me Kat or Dr. Ski, your choice, but I'd prefer Kat from you."

"Kat it is then," Bradshaw answered, "how's it going with the guy Chin?"

Dr Ski raised a large clip-board and began in practiced voice, "Eric Chin; ID from his California Driver's License, died at the age of 35 probably late Sunday or early Monday morning. Most likely a drowning verdict, but there's some facial muscle trauma indicating his death was a bit more prolonged. There is a small amount of water in his lungs which wants to confirm the drowning, but other indications show he suffered some mounting stress prior to his death, so there should be a lot more water in his lungs. His body's been in the water a couple of days, there's crab and fish feeding and he was recovered wearing a large elastic support sleeve on his left knee, indicating some physical problem he was dealing with. But, there's some other weirdness I'm still working on."

Bradshaw caught the phrasing and asked, "Weirdness, Kat? How so? And, you said, 'facial trauma', what's with that?"

"Well, Morris, telling the difference between an accidental drowning and a Homicidal suffocation death in water is tricky. Chin's blood remained in the blood vessels around his heart indicating his brain failed first, yet as I said, there was only a small amount of water in his lungs. The water tested from the Lafayette River so accidental drowning is a possibility, but right now it's a lot more complicated than I thought it would be. There were no small hemorrhages over the surface of his heart or lungs so I'm still leaning toward the drowning but with added stress and heavy drug involvement,"

Bradshaw was listening, but becoming confused, so he moved on to his own mission, "Kat, sorry to interrupt but do you mind if I get a picture of Chin's face with and without the sunglasses they found nearby?"

Dr. Ski was a bit thrown by the interruption, but still receptive to Morris' question so she smiled and said, "Sure, I'll call Dr. Clark to help you prop Chin up for the photo shoot."

Dr. Clark arrived and helped Bradshaw position Chin's body for the pictures. Chin's face was now a motley gray, ashen in color and his neck and chin had the dullness of picked over spoiled meat resulting from local marine-life feedings. As the oversized flash from Bradshaw's Polaroid lit up the room, the *POP* of the flash gave the already present odors a big boost. The formaldehyde, bleach and alcohol present, when Bradshaw first entered the room, joined the Lafayette River stench from Chin's body, the Vicks under Bradshaw's nose and the sulfur like smell from the functioning flash-bulb. Bradshaw took one more shot with sunglasses, then, he began to lose focus. Dr. Ski said,

"You Okay, Morris?" then, to Dr. Clark, "Quick, help me catch him Kent, he's woozing on us!" After a slow recovery in the hallway and confirming another rendezvous at the Chrysler next week, Bradshaw carried two prints of Chin's face, one with and one without sunglasses. He also held a makeshift report, dictated by Dr. Ski into some kind of Electronic Blackberry gadget that took her voice input and printed out the recorded information onto a cash-register like tickertape. Dr. Ski had offered as her closing comment, "The complete report will come out in a couple of days, I'll forward that to Knowles, but everything she asked for is in the print-out." Dr. Ski finalized.

Driving away Bradshaw placed the car's AC on full blast, checked his watch and turned north onto Monticello headed for Virginia Beach Boulevard. After a quick call to Police Ops, Bradshaw was told his group had been rescheduled to meet tomorrow morning. Good, he thought, at least I'll have the night for my stomach to recover. Morris changed directions and turned left on Virginia Beach Boulevard headed for his West Ghent apartment and some recovery time. He was certain Dr. Ski wouldn't betray his earlier display of physical weakness but he wasn't too sure about her assistant, the 'backward Superman', Dr. Kent Clark.

CHAPTER TWENTY EIGHT

PACIFIC OCEAN, NORTH OF WAKE ISLAND

The brightly colored device resembled a large orange football sinking through the depths of the Pacific Ocean. The device, a Remote Diagnostic Probe, (RDP), was programmed to record its descending progress as it transmitted salinity levels and migratory phytoplankton saturation. The RDP was the primary piece of scientific equipment carried by the USS Chattanooga for the study of ocean plant, mineral and animal ecological relationships. As the ocean's salinity levels began to increase, starting near the surface at approximately 33 parts per thousand, they were expected to build to a reading of 36ppt when the probe arrived at its destination depth of 25,000, feet where the Chinese Nuclear Device was located. Passing 12,000 feet, brightly colored fish, attracted to the color of the device, quickly darted away from the unexpected light that signaled the new predator's intent on having them for dinner. As the probe continued deeper, the main source of food began to change from recognized plant and animal life to what's normally referred to as 'Pacific Snow' or the flaking of dead animal remains. The RDP presently was recording little or no sunlight causing its light source to split into several new outputs. Outputs that would adjust automatically to allow both the wider search mode and the brighter pin-point accuracy required for precise monitoring the Chinese Device's operation. The probes' widest spread illumination highlighted a small group of deep sea squid that responsively ejected clouds of opaque ink toward the new intruder while changing direction and propelling themselves away from this new and unrecognized threat.

———————

Aboard the USS CHATTANOOGA the RDP transmitted a depth of 23,000 feet, a salinity level of 36ppt with an ambient temperature of one degree Centigrade as the probe's laser-light locked focus on the Chinese Device. The RDP was being maneuvered to approach the discharge outlet of the Chinese device and CAPT Benson B. Bordeaux, USN, the Commanding Officer of the Chattanooga watched the operation over the shoulder of his Chief Sonar Operator, SN1C Ronald 'Ears' Washington. Ears was focused on monitoring the ship's Electronic Situational Display and concentrating on the visual and aural feed-back through the presentation shown on the ship's flat screen display as he attempted to listen through his Audio Monitoring System. Ears' concentration was so focused he failed to realize CAPT Bordeaux was observing the operation perched within touching distance of his left shoulder. Ears spoke softly into his microphone, asking for cooperation from his shipmates,

"Come on Dillon get your guys to knock the chatter off, if I don't get this info for B-cube he'll be on my ass,"

"Look around Ears, B-cube's already on your ass." Dillon responded quietly.

"Oh Shit, sorry Captain, no disrespect intended." Ears offered with a slight head turn to acknowledge his CO's presence.

"None taken Ears, what's the status of the probe?"

"I've got the probe locked up and holding in the exhaust area of the device." Ears answered now controlling the RDP at an indicated depth of 23,943 feet below the surface of the Pacific Ocean. Evaluating the data internally Ears was confused by the probes readings compared to the data he been briefed to expect and he attempted to explain his confusion, "Right now I'm not seeing the 2000 degree temp we had an hour ago, Captain, but there's still a significant reading of 230 degrees near the exhaust port, it's a lot hotter than I expected. I guess it t could be residual from shut-down, or, the device is programmed to go-off in stages and we won't see a 1 to 2 degree temp for awhile, I'm just not sure, sir."

"How's positional control going to be if we ease the boat up enough for the Long Range Antenna to transmit?" Captain Bordeaux inquired wanting to establish a communication link with Admiral Bennett, his Pacific Fleet boss.

"If you take her up slow, Captain, I can handle the probe."

"Roger that," The CO replied then turned to the Officer on Duty, and said, "Mac take the Boat up slow to a hundred and extend the LRA. Call me in cabin when we're stabilized and ready to transmit." Commander Mac Murphy, replied,

"Aye Captain - Two degree up bubble, Helmsman, give us a slow-go to a hundred."

Captain Bordeaux moved aft down the passageway toward his cabin and on the way he stuck his head into the Communications Center, and asked, "Sparks any traffic?"

"Negative Captain, all's quiet from Admiral Bennett, but we're still too deep," "Thanks Sparks, we're on the way up to a hundred, keep me informed in quarters."

The Captain crossed the passageway and opened his cabin door. His small, compact stateroom was as he left it, he had ordered NO ENTRY upon arrival in the 'target area' and all indications were that his order had been respected. He sat down and opened his bedside document safe removing Admiral Bennett's mission-message from its storage folder.

*TOP SECRET 09290300Z*****8700231*

PACFLT DIRECTIVE CO USSCHATTANOOGA, MESSAGE FOLLOWS

PROCEED VICINITY 18-10N/15710E, DEPLOY GENDW-70 FOR OBSERVANCE OF OPERATIONAL TERMINATION OF CHI NUC DEVICE, LOCATED PACIFIC FLOOR (APPX 26,000' BELOW SURFACE) 0900Z 102306. REPORT DATA BEGINNING @ 0730Z/100406 (OR EARLIER) UPON ARRIVAL ON STATION. UPON ARRIVAL – MONITOR AND CONFIRM TERMINATION OF CHI OPERATION @ PLUS 8H AND MONITOR AS REQ. SIGNAL SIGNIFICANT, OUT OF NORM OBSERVATIONS AND CONSIDERATIONS.

09290300Z, BREAK-BREAK-BREAK

Captain Bordeaux replaced the message and tried the hour old coffee knowing the results would be less than desirable. Assessment confirmed he activated his COMM switch, and announce "Galley, Captain here, bring me a new cup in quarters."

"Aye, aye Captain," The expected reply sounded through the intercom and Captain Bordeaux activated the stop watch feature. Two minutes and 14 seconds later the knock on his stateroom door announced the Steward's arrival.

"Enter," the Captain offered, then, "You're late MacDonald." The CO stated as Seaman First Class MacDonald entered the stateroom with a hot cup of coffee.

"Sorry, Captain I didn't see you leave COMMO, I was helping Commander Mac Murphy train a new guy. I got distracted and was not thoroughly prepared for your call…"

"Wise up MacDonald, I know you don't have a lot going on in the galley right now but that's where your primary responsibility is. You need to focus on your own job, not try to help everyone else do theirs. You need higher motivation on your primary responsibility. Make sure everything's ready at your own work station and stay prepared to do your own job!" The CO instructed, then, he thought better of his over-reaction during the encounter and quietly added,

"Your coffee's late but it is excellent, you're dismissed MacDonald." Captain

Bordeaux watched his state-room hatch close slowly and he began to draft a message for Admiral Bennett. He had been briefed to expect the exhaust temperatures to decrease to ambient seawater temp almost immediately. The decrease from 2000 degrees Fahrenheit to 230 was significant but it definitely was NOT an indication of total shut-down. Contemplating the message, Bordeaux shook his head at his over reaction to late coffee delivery and his mind began to focus on his first command as CO of the SSN Greenwood in December of 2000. His smiling recollection turned sour as his memory slid forward to February 2001 and he was catapulted into the murky morass of another over-reaction, one that had threatened to destroy his career,

February 2, 2001, the SSN Greenwood arrived just after daybreak and the glaring sunrise was hampering port arrival. The OD had just surfaced the ship for arrival into the port of Saipan, 10 miles northwest of Tinian Island. These were historic waters and Commander Bordeaux wanted to take it all in as they approached the arrival port. Bordeaux joined his XO looking out from the Greenwood's sail tower as the vast amount of trapped water from the boat's surfacing maneuver continued to slosh over the submarines decking, vacating water from all the open spaces covering the outer surface of the boat.

"You're relieved Jim, I have the con, Check with Harrington at 'PLOT', make sure we're headed clear of the shallows between Saipan and Tinian.

"Wilber's sick in quarters, skipper, he looked terrible when I got up this morning. He decided to stay in the rack, Coleman's on duty and we're on a track of 070 at 8 knots." The XO reported to Commander Bordeaux.

"What's the matter with Wilber?" the CO asked knowing the XO would be reporting Harrington's illness first hand, they bunked in a shared cabin.

"Three of the crew are sick with food poisoning, Captain, Wilber's one of 'em. The others are Dawson, and the new cook, Seaman Holt. Holt fixed pork fried rice for all three of 'em last night when Dawson and Harrington came OFF DUTY at midnight. Holt thinks the eggs may have gone bad."

"Okay, check with Coleman, make sure we're staying clear of the shallows, I thought 060 was the prescribed entry track," Bordeaux voiced, then, he added, "Jim, send Coleman up." as the XO retreated down the sail ladder to confer with Coleman.

Remaining on the Submarine's Sail, Bordeaux looked directly into the rising sun and slewed the binoculars further south, toward the island of Tinian, momentarily his thoughts focused on August 6, 1945 when the Enola Gay lifted off Tinian for America's first use of the atomic bomb against the Japanese city of Hiroshima. Commander Bordeaux lowered his binoculars and decided to go with his first instinct, "Helm, come right to 085 intercept an inbound track of 060."

Coleman arrived on the bridge as Commander Bordeaux ordered the change of heading

and he spoke up, "Captain, I'm certain we're correct for port entry on the track of 070, you should reconsider the 'change of heading', the shallows are starboard we're in the middle of the desired course…" Commander Bordeaux interrupted, "Did you bring the chart Coleman?"

"No sir, but I'll go down to 'PLOT' and bring it right up. Set and drift show minimal sir," Coleman didn't know what else to say, so he turned to go below to get the chart,

"You sure about that course Coleman?" Bordeaux's words were drowned out by a scraping noise that erupted on the starboard side. "Easy Left, Helmsman!" the Captain shouted into the intercom system and the grinding noise subsided.

Captain Bordeaux came back to the present facing the fact that up to that point in his career he had lived by what he believed were true moral codes, high human values and uncompromising ethical standards, but his stressed over-reaction had helped cause that incident and set him adrift in a muddle of uncomfortable behavior. He had compromised his past beliefs and settled on blame-transfer to ensure his own future and he was still pushing toward over-reaction. No wonder he had responded so abruptly with the galley steward.

Now disgusted with parallels of his past and present behavior Bordeaux attempted to shake off the horrible memory and determined to return his life to a correct moral compass. His stateroom intercom CRACKELED and announced,

"Captain, COM here, we're stabilized at 100, LRA deployed."

CHAPTER TWENTY NINE

NORFOLK

"STEPHEN IRONS"

Sally is working in a small upstairs bedroom Wilber converted into office space for her. She uses a COX Telephone and Internet hook-up for her monthly American Airlines trip-bidding, commute-scheduling and tracking of her employee responsibilities. Her HP computer system was printing Wilber's book information as I arrived with two coffees and trailed by her new kitten, Willy-nilly. I offered, "Sally, I brought us some coffee while we try to sort all this information. Have you changed the small pest's name to something more cat-like?"

"No Stephen, I like Willy-nilly, he still runs around a lot and it comforts me to say the Willy part, you know, like I did with Will. I'm sure that's nutty, people will think I'm crazy doing it." Sally said as the small kitten rubbed his butt up against her leg, then, he remembered his name and dashed out of the room.

"I think Wilber would be pleased, and you're right the cat's still chaotic... But I'm sure he was sent to you by a much 'higher authority' than the SPCA's Dr. Carol, so, Willy-nilly, is the PURR-FECT name," I purred and Sally laughed, so I went further trying to comfort my little sister,

"Wilber told me you actually saved his life by falling in love with him and marrying him, so I think he's looking down and trying to thank you with this kitten."

Sally smiled and began to cry, just small tearing before she said, "Captain Westerly told me Will said the same thing to him, so it must be true! Okay, we stay with Willy-nilly!" The kitten ran back in the room and jumped up into Sally's arms. I gave Sally and Willy-nilly a small hug then I began to look over the three book outlines printed out from her friend Margo's computer. Sally placed the kitten on the floor and began thumbing through a lot of photos in her desk drawer.

"What's that stuff Sally?" I asked,

"Some photos I haven't put in a scrapbook yet," She announced misty eyed as she passed me some recent pictures of she and Wilber working with some of the Virginia Zoo's Education Animals. I glanced at one that showed Sally and Wilber holding a big black and white llama by a red lead and halter and I said,

"You guys worked a llama at the zoo?"

"Sure, we checked out together. His name's Apollo and he's a hand-full. It took both of us to show him off. Will held his lead, and I controlled the kids coming up to pet him. Kids love the big guy and Apollo likes putting on a show for everybody, unless someone scares him…"

"What happens then?"

"Usually he throws his head back and spits at whatever scares him." Sally responded laughing at some memory, "He did it once when a big guy ran up to take his picture… Hit the guy right in the camera. The guy wasn't hurt, just embarrassed."

"Is that a bow tie around his neck?" I asked, still looking at the photo.

"Yes, last year's July the fourth, the zoo had a Military Appreciation Day and we dressed Apollo up," Sally stopped in mid-sentence, turning over another small photo in her hands, "I remember this one." She offered as she handed me the photo of Wilber coming away from some woodsy area waving a large bunch of wild flowers toward the camera. "This one's funny. Let me see if I can recall what Will said when I took the picture."

"Is this the zoo?" I asked,

"No, no, The Norfolk Botanical Garden a year ago, we went there a lot when they let you bring your bikes to ride around all the gardens. Will told me he went there every week, even when I was away on trips. He said he made it a part of his exercise program,"

"I didn't know you could pick the flowers there." I said as I looked at the photo of Wilber in a short sleeved pull-over shirt waving the big bunch of yellow flowers back toward Sally. He looked really happy.

"You can't but Will was acting nutty, he picked the flowers and had me take this photo. I'd forgotten about this one."

"That was dumb wasn't it? Couldn't you guys have gotten in trouble picking those flowers in a Norfolk park?"

"Yeah, but the nutty thing was what he said when I took the photo, 'Show the picture to Stephen. When he figures it out, he'll be proud of me.' That's what he said."

"You mean because I was a Deputy Sheriff he wanted me to see a picture of him breaking the law and getting away with it? Why would that make me proud of him?" I asked as I looked again at the photo of Wilber waving wild flowers toward the camera.

"No idea, but you keep the photo." Sally said, shaking her head and putting the other photos back in her desk drawer, then, she smiled at me and changed the subject, "How'd your meeting with Charles Taylor go?"

I had told Sally about Os' recommending that I talk with the Executive Director of NISCO, but I didn't explain the real essence of the job to her. I placed the small photo of Wilber in my pocket and replied, "Taylor was Okay, he spoke highly of Wilber's efforts for NISCO and how much of a loss Wilber's death is to him. Taylor's a bit pompous, acts like he could be a big jerk. Did Wilber ever talk about Charles Taylor?"

"Once, after he was hired. Will was impressed with Mr. Taylor, said he was a little stuffy and all business, I actually met him at a combined USO and Armed Services YMCA Event for some of our local servicemen. What kind of job is Taylor talking about?"

"Some security work," I replied, "Os bragged about my dedication as a Deputy Sheriff and my SP time in the navy, so I'm sure their friendship got me the interview... But nothing's definite, we're still talking."

"How do Os and Taylor know each other?"

"Eh, they played football for our dad, but that's all Taylor said." I stopped abruptly, not wanting to talk any more about our dad. "So, how about we get into some of our own investigative work, Sally?"

"Wow, that's something, the two of them playing football for dad, maybe this job is a good omen for you Stephen." Sally offered, smiling a little, remembering our mom and dad, then, she said, "Okay, let's check out the book ideas. You looked over the original printout, what do you think, so far?"

"Doesn't seem like a lot of information to me, I'm not sure how much help the Police will get from any of this, even with our help." I offered as I reviewed the information that had been separated into three pages with book ideas titled and broken down in an outline format. Wilber's three book ideas were: 'Honorable Service', 'Pacific Secret' and the last one, 'The Devil on Angel Flight', which he had annotated as NON-FICTION. We knew Wilber was working on 'Pacific Secret' when he was killed but Linda thought any of his book ideas could have led to his death. She hoped Sally and I would be able to remember something about each one.

"Detective Knowles thought it was confusing too, but maybe we can help. Let's take this one first," Sally said as she picked up Wilber's book idea titled, 'Honorable Service', "I'm most familiar with this one, I remember Will talking a lot about it in San Diego. He said he had written quite a bit on this one, but I guess all that work was stolen or destroyed," Sally was tearing again as she handed me a print out,

HONORABLE SERVICE

GRANDDAUGHTER OF DISHONORED CIA AGENT

AGENT KILLED - GD TAKES ON PROVING AGENT'S INNOCENCE

GRANDMOTHER / CIA DEPUTY INVOLVED IN FRAME AND COVER UP

WATCH DOG, JAPAN HOSTAGE – ATOMIC WEAPON

SECRETS – PENEMUNDE, ME-163, MANHATTEN PROJ., KIATANS

JAPAN, HOSTAGE TIE IN – BAGHDAD - ATOMIC WEAPON

DC DETECTIVE HELPS GD PROVE GRANDFATHER'S INNOCENCE

GRANDFATHER EXHONORATED – DETECTIVE + GD TOGETHER

"Funny", I said after reading the page, "I remember Wilber talking about this too, he asked me if I was familiar with the World War II secret programs he was writing about. I knew about the Manhattan Project and the German V2 Rocket development but I'd never heard of the ME-163 or Kiatans…"

"Will said Kaitans were Japanese Suicide Torpedoes," Sally responded, "when Kamikaze planes were almost gone the Japanese built manned torpedoes to launch against the Allies. Those suicide pilots were called a Kiatans. Will said they actually sank a couple of US ships in World War II and he was going to fictionalize a Kiatan attack against the USS Indianapolis when it was sunk returning home after delivering the atomic bombs,"

"Okay, that's interesting, but what's the ME-163?" I asked.

"Not sure, some kind of German rocket plane, I think." Sally added as she continued to read the outline, before she said, "I'm not sure something in this book could have gotten him killed, except, Will said the most controversial part involved a mission to put a third nuclear bomb near the Japanese Emperor's Palace and threaten to detonate it if the Japanese didn't live-up to their end of the surrender treaty. He said he'd write this fictional part as something instigated by the head of the newly formed CIA and a high ranking staff officer working for General Douglas Mac Arthur. Later, in the book, Will said he wanted to plot the same type of weapon-hostage program against Saddam Hussein in Iraq, you know, when the first President Bush sent our troops to defended Kuwait, then, ended the campaign in the early 1990's..."

"Wow," I interrupted, "that would have brought the story up to date. Putting an atomic weapon near Baghdad as a threat against Saddam Hussein,"

"Well, The Mac Arthur Museum's in Norfolk, so I guess his idea could have upset a lot of people there, even if it was fiction."

"You're right Sally and if Wilber's 'Baghdad Bomb' ended up being the WMD we started looking for in 2004. Then, his story could upset a lot of Washington DC people. I think we've worked pretty well to come up with something on this one for Linda." I replied and Sally smiled at me mentioning Detective Knowles, but referring to her as 'Linda'. I decided to avert that subject and added, "Let's take a break, you do some of the 'thank-you' correspondence you mentioned and I'll take a walk, I've got some thinking to do about the job offer,"

Sally interrupted me, "You had a job offer?" Sally stopped crying and looked straight at me, "You said you were still talking, Stephen. What's the real answer?"

"Well, Taylor did make me an offer, very generous too, but I'm still thinking about it. We're scheduled to talk again soon."

"Okay, but please be honest with me and let me know, OK?" Sally said and turned away to begin her thank-you notes.

Downstairs, I gathered up a light jacket and saw Thornton waiting outside. As I headed out for my walk, Thornton said, "Rusty, you've' got to be a lot more up-front with Sally, she's going through a tough time with Wilber's death, and all this job-offer crap you're hiding from her. Let me see that photo of Wilber." I held the photo up so Thornton could see it as we began walking.

"Damn," Thornton said, "he's carrying a big bunch of yellow flowers... Wilber was nuttier than we ever thought he was." I couldn't disagree, so I placed the photo back in my pocket as we headed down Huntington Place toward Lakewood Park.

CHAPTER THIRTY

WEDNESDAY, POLICE OPERATIONS

Detective Knowles reread the printed information from Wilber Harrington's book ideas, but no matter how hard she looked, it didn't make a lot of sense to her. If she was searching for the 'smoking gun' concerning why Harrington had to die, she didn't see it. The Police Computer Technician had separated the three book ideas and Knowles' frustration grew as she spread the three sheets out on the table before her and once again looked over the printouts. First,

HONORABLE SERVICE

GRANDDAUGHTER OF DISHONORED CIA AGENT

AGENT IS KILLED, GD TAKES ON PROVING AGENT'S INNOCENCE

GRANDMOTHER/CIA DEPUTY INVOLVED IN COVER UP

WATCH DOG, JAPAN HOSTAGE – ATOMIC WEAPON

SECRETS, PENEMUNDE, ME-163, MANHATTEN PROJ., KIATANS

JAPAN, HOSTAGE TIE IN TO PRESENT – BAGHDAD ATOMIC WEAPON

DC DETECTIVE HELPS GD PROVE GRANDFATHER'S INNOCENCE

Second,

THE DEVIL ON ANGEL FLIGHT – NON FICTION

INTERNET INFO ON PAT ROBERTSON

LOCAL CHRISTIAN UNIVERSITY

GLOBAL HUMANITARIAN EFFORT

OPERATION BLESSING, FLYING HOSPITAL

GOVT. RELATIONSHIP – CHURCH-STATE VIOLATIONS

RIGHT WING, GOLD & DIAMOND MINES

CAYMAN ISLANDS – MONEY

LIBERIA + GOSPEL + GREED

INFORMATION SOURCE - ZOO DOCENT FRIEND, RICHARD MILLIGAN

OPERATION BLESSING PILOT WORKING FOR PAT ROBERTSON

Linda pushed the two outlines across the table and picked up the last one, the book Harrington was working on when he died,

PACIFIC SECRET

PROLOGUE, 9-11-2001

RETIRED NAVY PROTAGONIST

JAPAN – ECONOMIC OPPORTUNITIES

JAPANESE RIGHT WING NATIONALISTIC PRESSURES

PACIFIC SECRET DEVELOPMENT – FISSION/FUSION DEVICE

CIA DISCOVERY, SUBMARINE INVESTIGATION

WEATHER DEVISTATION 2002 - 2005

MOUNTING PRESSURE TO DESTROY SECRET

CIA / JAPANESE SECRET SERVICE COOPERATION

PROGRAM HALT

CIA ULTIMATE RECOGNITION OF PROTAGONIST

Linda shook her head as Detective Sam Millers entered the room, she was frustrated and rattled off several questions without waiting for answers, "Sam, have you seen these outlines? They don't make a lot of sense to me, just thoughts Harrington had. We've got to talk to Stephen and Sally they must know more than we have here. There's some Navy guy listed as a main character in the 'Pacific' book, maybe Stephen knows more about that. I'm sure the 'Devil' book's an expose' about Pat Robertson, at least there's some zoo docent guy listed as a reference. Here it is, a guy named Richard Milligan, we need to chase him down. Have you called the agency that sent the rejection notice to Harrington?"

"Well, I spoke to a Mr. Li in California, he'd gotten the same information we have on the 'Pacific' book. He was sorry to hear about Harrington's death, but he'd only received this very same outline." Sam looked at his small notebook for confirmation and went on, "He rechecked his records for me and in August he said he phoned Harrington asking him to expand on this original outline to provide more on the book. Li said he, 'Asked for a chapter outline, character profiles, motivations and a sample chapter,' Harrington told Li he'd send the updates, but Li never heard from him again. So Li sent the rejection letter to wake Harrington up. Phone records show he and Li did talk late August,"

Knowles interrupted, "Okay, have we heard from Bradshaw about Chin?"

"Bradshaw might be a little late, chief. Dr. Clark called and said Morris got woozy and fainted on them before he left the morgue," Millers paused as Bradshaw entered the room, and said, "Morris, how's it to be among the living?"

Knowles spoke up, "That's enough Sam, I'm sure Morris has had it with morgue humor." Then to Bradshaw, "We haven't gotten much from Harrington's computer info, let's see your medical print-out on Chin, You okay, Morris?"

"I'm better today boss, sorry about yesterday, Dr. Ski had places to go so I didn't get more than the print-out and a couple of Polaroid shots of Chin."

"It's alright I'm just frustrated with the computer business. Let's see the print-out, I've seen them before."

PRELIM EXMN:

ASIAN/ POS CHINESE MALE 35

COD – PRL AC-DN

INTL TOX:

ALC – TRC

DRG – SIG / VERSED / SECONAL / SOD TRIPEN

ADDL: INJ-KNEE

TOD – 11P + - 2 --- DR SKI

"I've got to check on the VERSED reference and the knee injury, but the rest I'm okay with." Knowles said, finally happy to be sure of something. "Preliminary Examination of: Asian Male, most likely Chinese - That fits the name on the Driver's License, Eric Chin." Knowles interjected, then, "Age 35 - That specific's from the California license - Preliminary Cause of death - accidental drowning, Initial toxicology screen - alcohol trace - I guess that rules-out a stupid alcohol induced mistake. But there WAS a significant amount of, VERSED, SECONOL and SODIUM TRIPENTAL in his system - Could be a drug problem I guess. Damn," Knowles paused rechecked some of her notes and continued, "SODIUM TRIPENTAL is presently used for the Lethal Injection Protocol in California. They're holding a 'Protocol Revue' right now to examine the drugs used in their death penalty procedure, but, I don't think SECONAL or VERSED are part of that same study. I think those two are muscle relaxants, or surgical anesthetics. I'll ask about the knee injury too, he probably had a scar from earlier surgery,"

Bradshaw interrupted, "No boss, Dr. Ski found a large elastic support sleeve on Chin's left knee, like he'd hurt it recently. Whoa, didn't Irons say he kicked his airport attacker in the left knee?"

"You're right Morris get your photos together for Stephen and the Lakewood kids to look at. Sam, has Irons helped with a sketch?"

"No, our sketcher's been tied up,"

"Okay we'll try another approach. Morris, just use your photos with Stephen and the kids. I'll call Dr. Ski and get confirmation on the drugs and any other thoughts she has, but my guess is this guy had a drug related death. Check with Sally Harrington about any information she and Stephen have put together on Harrington's books. Maybe they can stop by and help with this mess. I'll need it for Chief Beck and the FBI Agent later this week."

"Sure, I'll check with Irons and the kids and ask Irons and his sister to visit."

"Apologize for the inconvenience, but we need help if we're going to make something out of this outline mess. Press Irons about the Navy guy referenced in the 'Pacific' book, maybe Harrington said something that slipped Stephen's mind."

"Okay Boss, funny thing about those books, the fiction ones anyway, both of them list the CIA, that's curious, don't you think?" Bradshaw said.

"Harrington was just keeping things interesting. You know the CIA's always a good target for attention in a book. On a positive note we have gotten some information back from the FBI tracing the weapon that killed Harrington." Knowles said as she retrieved her reference sheet from the FBI and continued, "Here it is, manufactured in 2000 and shipped to a Norfolk gun shop on Granby. Sale was recorded in 2001, bought by a sailor named Brooks in April of 2001. Brooks reported it stolen in 2002. The gun's history was inactive until it showed up with Harrington, not really proving anything other than it was a stolen weapon. So far we haven't turned up any of Harrington's clothes matching the fibers under his nails. His zoo shirt matched the color but that's all. Sally's looked all over their house but so far nothing. She's gathering up all his old clothes for donation, so I'll give her a couple more days then talk to her when they come in to see us later this week but we need the kids and Stephen to look at your photos now."

CHAPTER THIRTY ONE

NORFOLK CHIEF OF DETECTIVES, FRIDAY

Linda Knowles approached Chief Andy Beck's Conference room as Janet, the Chief's Administrative Assistant, came out of the room with an empty tray. "Good morning Linda you're the first, welcome to downtown Norfolk. There's coffee and donuts inside, you know the chocolate covered ones, Chief Andy's favorite,"

"Morning, Janet, who's coming to the meeting?" Linda asked,

"Well, you, Chief Andy, the FBI Special Agent from DC and Sheriff Osborne… Wait 'til you meet Special Agent Davis Linda, he's a 'tall blonde hunk of a guy'." Janet said.

"Do you know why Sheriff Os will be here?" Linda asked,

"Not sure, he wasn't on my original listing, the chief just added him. How's Ella doing?"

"She's great, her grandmother's taking her to The Norfolk Botanical Garden this afternoon, she's bound to come back full of 'flower-power'." Linda replied.

"Ella's trip might not go, they're forecasting heavy winds and rain later today, maybe you'll have to wait for her horticulture education. Oh, good morning Sheriff Os, there's coffee and donuts in the conference room, please enjoy."

"Thanks Janet, the rain's just started, I guess WAVY TV's weather guesser got one right again. I'll just have coffee. Morning Linda, how are you?" Os said.

"I'm good Os. To what do we owe the pleasure of your company?"

"I've got some info for your investigation and Chief Beck wanted the Sheriff's Office to meet the FBI Agent," Os replied then, "Sugar, no cream right?"

"Yes, thanks. Good morning Chief," Linda announced as Chief Beck entered the room with a definite 'hunk' in tow. Davis looked 6' 3" to Linda, blonde, green eyes, good looking and dressed to the nines in some designer suit. That'll be a mess, Linda mused, if the nor'easter' continues.

Chief Beck brought sat down at the conference table and brought the meeting to order, "Good morning all, this is FBI Special Agent Clayton Davis, he's here to offer information and assistance on the Harrington case. Please get some coffee everyone and pass the donuts this way," Chief Beck paused for a donut then continued, "Clayton, this is Linda Knowles, the Detective in charge of the Harrington Case, and the very big gentleman is Master Deputy Sheriff, Jimmy Osborne, who kindly allows us to call him Os. Os, thanks for coming on short notice."

"You're welcome Chief. The Sheriff sends his apologies and gratitude for allowing me to attend in his place. Agent Davis, welcome, we're all glad to have the help." Os paused and turned to Linda, "Now, if I may, Linda, let me offer some possible assistance from the Sheriff's Department. I've come by to let you know that one of our deputies was assigned to escort several of the Sheriff's 'downtown guests' in the Lakewood Park area the morning of Harrington's death,"

Linda interrupted, "This is the first I've heard of that Os, why has it taken you so long to let us know?"

"Who are the Sheriff's 'downtown guests'?" Agent Davis interrupted,

"It's Sheriff's slang for residents of the city jail," Knowles began then she returned her attention to Os, "Os, just when was your deputy in the park?"

"Deputy Belton took the workers to Lakewood Park to clean up the area before and after Pee Wee Football. He arrived around eight thirty and departed at four..."

"Just where in the park did Belton work his crew?" Knowles asked and Sheriff Os checked his notebook,

"All over, Linda they started on Willow Wood across from the Lafayette Branch Library, worked their way toward Huntington Place then back to the football fields. They stayed there a couple hours before their lunch break, then, after lunch they finished cleaning up around the ball fields and the tennis courts before going back to the lock up." Os watched as Linda's expression showed her concern about this late revelation, so he added, "I was in the office Linda, remember? You called about Harrington's death and asked me to help you find Stephen Irons. Your information probably caused me to forget about Belton's proximity, sorry."

"Well," Chief Beck interrupted as he stood carrying a chocolate donut and several napkins, "I've got another meeting, Linda, call Janet if you need anything else. Agent Davis, enjoy your stay and thanks for the offer of help. Os, my gratitude to the Sheriff and thanks for your information," Andy Beck smiled, waved at the group and departed without additional comment.

CHAPTER THIRTY TWO

DOWNTOWN NORFOLK

"Go ahead Linda sorry about the confusion," Os began, "I wanted to come here because I thought Deputy Belton's crew might have seen something that could help your investigation."

"When the crew was near Huntington Place, Os, what time was that?"

"Ten, maybe a bit later, Deputy Belton took his workers to clean up around the games before their lunch break, maybe for an hour or so,"

"Did any of them see a UPS truck enter or exit the Lakewood area while they were working?"

"That's one of the reasons I'm here, Linda, Deputy Belton said he didn't see anything, but when I asked one of his workers, an inmate called 'Bull', he said he saw a UPS delivery truck come in around eleven with 'a brother driving',"

"Did he say anything more than, just 'a brother driving'?"

"No, but I could set it up for your people to talk with Deputy Belton and Bull. Bull's a little vague on the ID with me. I can understand his reluctance, he's not sure what he's getting into, or what's in it for him. Is this important?" Os asked.

"Could be, we're still running down a few leads right now. Do you know how, many were in the crew?"

"Five total, Deputy Belton, Bull and three others."

"Did Deputy Belton or anyone else from his group see the fire trucks arrive?" Knowles asked.

"I don't think so, they were at the games probably too far away to see Huntington Place itself, but maybe they heard them arrive. You should talk with Bull he seems to be the only one that saw anything of interest. Sorry for the delay, Linda, I've been in Richmond a couple of days, then, when I returned, I saw Belton and remembered his assignment that day. Have you determined whether Commander Harrington's death was a Homicide yet?"

"Not officially, but all indications point that way. Chief Beck's given me another week to decide. I'll have Sergeant Bradshaw call Deputy Belton. What's Bull's real name?"

"Carter Moore, Linda. Tell Stephen hello when you see him. Hope he's doing okay, I'm still worried about his health. Do you know if he took the job with NISCO?" Os asked,

"A job at NISCO? I didn't know he was considering going to work again." Linda replied, then, she became quiet. Os ignored her remark and said,

"Nice to meet you Agent Davis, let me know if the Sheriff's Office can be of further assistance. Linda I'll talk to you soon." Os finalized and stood to leave. Knowles said, "Sergeant Bradshaw will call for the meetings and I'll check back with you if I think of anything else." Os smiled stood, shook Davis' hand and departed. Linda's face showed her frustration with this new information, and she began making a note in her folder. Agent Davis noted her show of anxiety, smiled and said,

"Detective Knowles, you and the Sheriff mentioned Stephen Irons, is that correct?"

"Stephen Irons, yes, Sally Harrington's brother, he's medically retired from the Norfolk Sheriffs Department. Is the FBI going to take over the Harrington case?" Knowles asked now responding to Davis' interruption of her note taking.

"Well no, we don't normally do local murders. I'm here in an assisting capacity,"

"Good, I'm glad to hear that." Linda interrupted, "Thanks for the gun info and I'll be happy to get more on fiber analysis. And, if there's any other efforts you or the FBI can make to help us find answers, I'm all for it. But, having said that, until I'm told otherwise, this is MY case! Anything needs done, warrants, subpoenas, press communication, goes through my office. So if you or other feds up your food-chain have a problem with that, then, you better drop the bomb on them now. Clear, Agent Davis?"

"Yes, very clear." Davis said, then, added, "Sorry, but I think we may have gotten off on the wrong foot, possibly, my foot was unintentionally put in my own mouth, but, I'm only here to help with the information we've compiled on Wilber Harrington, his wife and some of their associates. So, with your permission, I'd like to try a new start. Please call me Clayton and here's the FBI print-out, background information and speculation, some yet to be verified concerning Wilber Harrington, his wife Sally, and Stephen Irons."

"The FBI is looking at Sally Harrington and Stephen Irons as possible suspects?" Linda asked, "Don't you think that's a waste of effort?"

"We try to be very thorough in our investigations, Stephen Irons was in the Shore Patrol and Navy Special Forces before he resigned and came home to become a Sheriff's Deputy... So he definitely knows police investigative procedures, probably well aware of their pluses and minuses," Linda interrupted,

"I'm not sure I understand how that fact could make him a suspect?"

"Please give me a minute, Linda, you'll have to read the entire report, but Stephen Irons has been protective of his sister most of her life, especially after their parents died. If Irons found out about some of the things we suspect Wilber Harrington was involved in, he could have seen Harrington's actions as a direct threat to his sister and he could have acted on that threat." Davis paused as Knowles scanned the report.

Linda thought about sharing Harrington's book information, especially the Navy guy mentioned in 'Pacific Secret' but she decided to wait and let Davis go on with his information, "Again, you should read the entire report, but summarizing; we know Harrington carried a lot of debt and we believe he was actively looking for a foreign contact to help fund him out of the debt. We've followed up with most of the contacts he gained while he was an Instructor at the Naval Amphibious School in Coronado, then later at the Joint Forces Staff College here in Norfolk. We traced his dealings with Israelis, Jordanians, Iraqis, Syrians, Chinese, Japanese and Pakistani,"

"Both those schools are 'Joint Service with Allied participation, they've got all sorts of students parading around their campuses." Knowles responded,

"Yes, that's true, but if you factor in the Navy punishing Harrington by removing him from their 'Sea Duty List', and the fact that his wife is an International Flight Attendant for American Airlines traveling excessively abroad without normal restrictions, then you have a very suspicious potential. Later, when Harrington joined NISCO, he began running his fingers in and out of the international shipping business also, so we think we have good reasons for our concern," Linda interrupted,

"Okay, it seems like a stretch to me, but I'm still listening." Knowles was hearing about Harrington's money problems and navy restrictions for the first time, what could Harrington have done to receive that kind of curtailment? Seemingly reading her mind, Davis continued,

"The US Navy won't release definitive information concerning Harrington's restrictions, they only say he was 'somehow involved in an unresolved ship incident' and they 'thought it best to remove him from active sea duty assignments'. Our questioning of confirmed the Navy's reasoning, but we can't rule out the some type of sabotage…"

"Sabotage, you made a big leap there Agent Davis. Don't you believe the sailors you've interviewed?" Linda said.

"Yes, mostly, but with all Harrington's qualifications and opportunities I'm sure you can understand the FBI's concern about his possible involvement with sabotage or espionage by collaborating with another country, to include terrorism implications when he started working for NISCO."

"This sounds like an overly-expanded brainstorming-session. Did you tap Harrington's phone?"

"No, we didn't have probable cause, only our growing concerns. And you're right the FBI's initial focus is wide spread, we don't want to be surprised later in the investigation with something we might have overlooked."

"I think you're really overdoing this, are you tapping Sally Harrington's phone now that her husband's dead?" Linda asked, sarcastically, but Davis answered seriously,

"No, not at this time, but we are presently in the process of getting a court order for communication surveillance of Sally Harrington and several of Wilber Harrington's former associates, including Stephen Irons. Anyone like Irons, with motive, training and experience should be a suspect. All HE needed was opportunity and he could be the 'prime' suspect." Davis said the last with the emphasis of a teacher summarizing before the final exam.

Knowles decided again to wait on providing Harrington's navy character's association in the 'Pacific' book. She needed to have a better look at the FBI's entire report before she offered more. Right now she wanted to focus on the basics of the investigation she must have missed, so she asked, "You said you were here to help, you mentioned Harrington's financials, 'a lot of debt', you said. What were Harrington's money problems?"

"I'm surprised you haven't turned them up." Davis said with a small smirk initially, then, he immediately corrected his expression and went on, "Sorry, he was paying $1,000 per month to his ex wife, Lydia, in Franklin, Virginia. There was a divorce decree agreement in 1985, after two years of marriage, requiring alimony and child-support. It remained in effect until July of this year, when their son Wilber Jr., turned 21…" Linda interrupted,

"Harrington has a kid?"

"Yes, its all in the report, Harrington has paid over a quarter million dollars in alimony and child-support but he stopped the allotment in August. Harrington was also involved with a character in Portsmouth, Virginia that operates an antique sale and repair shop, we believe this guy, Donald Adams,"

"Donald Adams, who's he?"

"Adams and Harrington operated a business together and have a life insurance policy on each other for $250,000 to be paid to the survivor upon the death of one partner. Adams, is about to collect on that policy, so there's motive for you, although, the business is co-signed by Sally Harrington, so she's the legal partner now. Maybe the insurance pay-out is for the business, we don't know yet. Additionally, Harrington had a policy with his son as the beneficiary for $100,000 and another for Sally for $500,000. Those policies alone cost Harrington about $400 per month. All the insurance payments and alimony debt were paid for through military allotments, a lot of big money reasons for several people to want Harrington dead."

Linda stopped writing notes and said, "You called Adams a 'Character in Portsmouth', what's he done?"

"Nothing, major, he was pleaded out for disorderly conduct in Norfolk and has some recurring business-permit violations, some late tax payments, that kind of thing. On the disorderly, Adams did Community Service at the Virginia Zoo. His business seems okay now we just don't know the whole story. He'll definitely profit from Harrington's death, so he's a suspect too."

"I'm not sure I agree with you about Adams, his position hasn't improved much, he just has a new partner, Sally. The business will probably be paid off benefiting both he and Sally Harrington, if we rule it wasn't a suicide since most life insurance policies have a 'suicide clause' in them. Is there anything else Agent Davis?" Linda was beginning to tire of Clayton's presentation, he had provided a lot of new information and raised obvious case implications that she had missed.

"No," Davis began, then, his cell phone *BUZZED* and he said, "Sorry, I'd better take this, excuse me please." Davis said as he moved out of the room into the hallway. Linda sat back down at the conference table and strained to hear, but Davis was too far away.

In the hallway, Davis answered, "Special Agent Davis," 30 seconds, listening, then, quietly he responded, "Irene, where are you?" 10 seconds more

"What, who let you in my room?" 20 seconds

"Okay, okay stay there, the weather's a mess, but I'm downtown too ." 10 seconds,

"Yes, I've missed you too Irene." Clayton closed his cell phone and pocketed it as he returned to the conference room.

Linda was reading the FBI's lengthy report as Davis returned and he offered, "Sorry Linda, that was a local colleague, I've got an important meeting. What you suggested sounds reasonable to me. I'll be in your office at 9AM on Monday and we can start again. You have my contact information on the FBI Report please call if I can help you before we get together on Monday."

"Okay," Knowles said as she stood and strained to look level with Davis. She rose up on her toes, but fell short of looking eye-to-eye by an inch or so. Linda put her hand out and Clayton shook it without much ceremony. "See you Monday," Linda Knowles offered as Special Agent Davis turned quickly and departed the room.

Linda began to gather up all her papers as Janet walked in, "Agent Davis head out?" Janet asked.

"Yes, he had another meeting with a local colleague,"

"Well, I know he's got a 'colleague' named Irene waiting for him in his hotel room, I just overheard his side of the phone conversation." Janet offered as she collected the coffee maker, cups and paper products, put them on her tray then said as she left. "Have a great weekend Linda, say hello to Ella."

"Yes, thanks Janet, you too," Linda replied as she pondered the information she would need to deal with the Harrington case and Special Agent 'HUNK' Davis.

CHAPTER THIRTY THREE

POLICE OPERATIONS CENTER, 4PM

Detective Knowles arrived at her office after twenty minutes of driving through the nor'easter that was lumbering into Norfolk. The storm was bringing heavy rains and winds, definitely causing a lot of downtown flooding. She entered the office, shook out her wet coat and umbrella, opened her large tote bag and took out her cell phone. She dialed Shirley Knowles' home phone and left a message, then she tried Shirley's cell phone, but it was turned OFF.

Getting no answer at either number Linda became concerned, there was no way those two were still at the Norfolk Botanical Garden for a horticulture tour during all this mess. While Linda attempted to dry her damp hair with some paper towels she remembered Millers and Bradshaw were scheduled to check two leads Sally Harrington and Stephen Irons had offered during their visit Wednesday. Tiring now from fruitless efforts Linda sat down at her desk and called Bradshaw's cell phone. "Morris, how's it going in the storm?" Linda then listened for 30 seconds,

"Okay, but don't stay out long in this mess, my meeting with the FBI turned up some information I've got to check-out myself. Sheriff Os was there and told me one of his deputies had a group of prisoners working Lakewood Park the morning Harrington died. One of the prisoners saw a UPS truck arrive around eleven and added that 'he saw a brother driving', maybe that was the dead guy, Chin. The kids said the driver had a dark face… Anyway, the witness is Carter Moore, AKA Bull, try to go by the lock-up and interview Deputy Belton and Bull, okay?" 30 seconds,

"Sure, see you Monday morning at 7:30. The FBI will be here at nine. Oh, Morris, Sheriff Os said Stephen Irons was considering a job with NISCO, is Millers checking NISCO out?" 30 seconds more,

"Okay, I'll give him a call. Stay dry, if the storm continues you can wait until Monday to check out the jail." Linda closed and now tried Millers' cell.

"Sam, how's it going with NISCO?" Linda listened for 30 seconds,

"Yeah, it's this weather. I'm sure their operation's been restricted. Check with James Carlson out there or maybe Charles Taylor downtown, they were both at Harrington's Memorial Service. Another 20 seconds,

"Sam, at my meeting Sheriff Os mentioned Stephen Irons was being considered for a job with NISCO, if you talk with Taylor find out what that's all about," 20 seconds

"Thanks Sam, call me if you get anything, I'll be home in a couple of hours, or I'll see you Monday at 7:30, the 'feds' will get here at nine. Oh Sam, the FBI mentioned a Portsmouth character who was an associate of Harrington's, a guy named Donald Adams… You're from Portsmouth I thought you might have heard of him." Linda listened to Millers give a negative reply then he disconnected. Linda shook off Sam's abruptness, must be the weather she thought. Defensively she began to wonder why she hadn't told either of her people about Harrington having an ex and kid in Franklin. Oh well, she'd tell them Monday.

After the calls and some more drying and combing out her damp hair she took a full minute's walk and approached the door to the Norfolk Police Department's Accounting Office. Linda entered and said, "Abby, how's it going?"

"Doing good Linda, hanging around until the wind and rain let up. Hope the info we provided you helped some," Abby Wertz said.

"That's why I'm here, Abby, it helped, but, I've just been told by an FBI Agent that Harrington had money going to his ex wife and son totaling $1,000 a month until he stopped it a couple months ago. He also had $400 in payments to insurance companies we didn't know about. How'd we miss all that?" Linda asked.

"The FBI's in the case?" Abby asked, but Linda remained quiet. "Okay, the confusion must come from Harrington's military allotments we can't get that information without a federal order. If you recall my initial report, I noted that his monthly deposit from the Navy was pretty low for a retired Commander with 20 years in. That's got to be the reason. Harrington had allotments taken out before the pay balance was sent to his bank."

Linda began to see the error and said, "I should have covered that base myself, but this is my first real investigation into a military guy's money picture, I guess I'm still learning, how about a little help?"

"Sure, Harrington probably had the $1,400 automatically taken out of his pay and disbursed before his bank deposit which would make the $1,600 he WAS getting from the Navy a more reasonable figure. Do you remember his NISCO salary from our sheet?"

Linda looked at the accounting information and found the data, "Here it is. He was making $45,000 a year from NISCO."

"Okay, after taxes probably a deposit around $3,000 per month, or a total for

NISCO and the Navy of $4,600 to checking, that matches our information." Abby began putting figures into her small calculator and transferring some of the info to a sheet of paper. "He's paying the first mortgage and a second automatically, that totals up to $2,900. His checking account shows a current balance of about $1,300 with no savings account listed. I guess he and his wife could have a joint safety-deposit-box, but we'll need her approval to look there,"

"I don't think that's a problem, what else?"

"Harrington's credit card payments ran about $600 per month, so after those expenses he's left with about $800 a month for automobile and other loose ends. Their utilities and household miscellaneous are probably another three to four hundred and I don't see any checks to them. Sally Harrington's probably paying those or he'd be under water each month. Yep, his financial picture's worse than we thought with those allotments. Sally probably buys the groceries and some personal stuff for them, maybe home and yard care, unless they do that work themselves… I'll bet she handles their travel expenses through American Airlines, but we didn't have authority to check her out. You want us to go there?"

"Maybe we better, Harrington's life insurance was almost a million dollars with beneficiaries being; his son, Wilber Jr. for $100,000, a business partner for $250,000 and his wife Sally for $500,000." Linda offered then added, "Most companies like NISCO carry a life insurance policy on their staff, usually about twice their salary, that would be another $90,000, so his Life coverage is pushing the million dollar mark."

"Interesting," Abby speculated, "The $500,000 plus the NISCO $90,000 would certainly cover the house and second, so his wife can pay that off and be okay. I doubt her airline salary would let her continue to carry the house, Harrington must have known that. The $100,000 for his son is probably for college, how olds the kid?"

"The FBI said he turned 21 in July, Harrington stopped the allotment going to his ex for family support in August…"

Abby interrupted, "Whoa that could make her mad if she'd forgotten it was going to happen when her kid turned 21. I'm sure she'd gotten use to an extra $1,000 per month, even if some of it helped raise the kid. Who's the business partner?"

"A Portsmouth guy named, Adams, runs an antique store and restoration business. They had each other insured to pay off the property, but the property is in Harrington's name."

"What's the name of the antique business? I can probably check that out."

Linda looked back at the FBI Report and replied, "Adams Antiques, it's on Effingham in Portsmouth."

"Give me a minute, I'll check the tax records, they're open access." Abby stated, then, she worked with her computer for about 5 minutes while Linda waited. "The business property is tax appraised at $300,000, Harrington and his wife Sally signed as co-owners, I guess Adams is acting as the antique business owner and business property manager. That insurance money must be to pay the property loan off, I wonder if Sally is listed anywhere in the documents, did the FBI say?"

"They only mentioned Harrington and the Adams guy in the business but they did say Sally signed as co-owner of the property." Linda replied.

"There're no payments from Harrington's checking into this commercial account so either Sally's involved for the mortgage payments, or Adams is paying with the business proceeds. Oops, something else here, looks like they're in hock to the city of Portsmouth for about $3,000 in back taxes. What's the partner's full name?"

Linda shuffled through the FBI report again, and replied, "Donald L. Adams the FBI said he had a short sheet from four years ago, some Norfolk disorderly conduct and city-permit problems, probably like the taxes you're talking about with Portsmouth. Adams was pleaded out for Community Service at the Virginia Zoo, then, he moved the business to Portsmouth when Harrington bought the property. Except for the tax thing you mentioned, he appears clean."

"We'd need another court order to go after more on Adams and the business, but if he's in arrears for $3000 and his business is set to inherit $250,000 from Harrington's death, Adams' has a big motive." Abby Wertz offered then added, "You better check with the life insurance company, a lot of life policies carry a 'suicide clause'."

"Thanks Abby, I'll get the Federal Order for you on Monday, I appreciate your efforts, have a great weekend, after you swim your way home." Linda offered as she exited the room and headed for her car.

Linda drove north on Granby Street toward Shirley Knowles' home to pick up Ella. The wind and rain were still blowing in from the northeast and traffic was sparse but her visibility was restricted. She had her wipers on FULL but the driving rain still made her travel poor and slow at best. She crossed the Granby Street Bridge, drove past the Willow Wood intersection then turned off Granby onto Arden Street, into the Belvedere section of Norfolk, where Shirley Knowles lived.

Arriving, Linda turned in the driveway and was pleased to see the garage door open and Shirley's Van parked inside with space left over for her car. Linda entered the garage grateful for the shelter, parked her car and walked into the house calling,

"Hello, Shirley, Ella, where are you two?" Shirley's cat, Henry, a big yellow haired Maine Coon came around the corner, "Hello, Henry, where're the girls?"

"Mom, mom," Ella yelled as she followed Henry's arrival, "we had a great time, mom, Grammy took me to the Botanical Garden to learn about all the flowers, but it was like too wet for the tour so we listened in a big auditorium. They talked about all their flowers... Yuck Mom! You're like all wet too!" Ella exclaimed after grabbing Linda around the waist.

Shirley Knowles made her way into the kitchen, picked Henry up and said, "Hello Linda, looks like it's still a mess out there. Why don't you two stay for dinner, Henry and I'll make some spaghetti and we can all share our day?"

"Please, please Mom, you know I love spaghetti." Ella begged.

"I think that's a great idea, Shirley," Linda stopped and adjusted her thoughts, "sorry, thanks, Mom we'd love to stay for dinner."

CHAPTER THIRTY FOUR

CIA HQ, FRIDAY, 9PM

Craig Cooper continued to pace in Dr. Kale's front office, he was becoming concerned with the urgency of this impromptu meeting. Kale's secretary had reached him as he was leaving his apartment for a dinner date and requested his appearance for a discussion at 9:15, no other information was provided. After canceling his dinner date, with promise of a quick rescheduling and much groveling to the disappointed red head, Cooper drove through the DC downpour to CIA Headquarters to wait for Dr. Kale. When Cooper parked in the secure underground area he noted the DCI Limo waiting near the Executive Elevator. The big boss is here too, Cooper thought, and from that moment on apprehension accompanied his travel to Dr. Kale's office. Cooper's elevator incident with Deputy Director Rollins was likely the reason for this late night meeting.

"Damn," Cooper said in Dr. Kale's empty office, "someone needs to help get me out of this town!"

After a short wait the large door to the office swung inward and Merriman, Dr. Kale's Personal Bodyguard and Driver, entered carrying two large leather satchels physically pad-locked with classified documents. Dr. Kale entered behind Merriman and Cooper watched as their mutual boss tossed his wet topcoat and hat onto the leather sofa then, he said,

"Leave the cases Merriman, Cooper will put them away." Dr. Kale directed.

"Yes sir." Merriman answered as he placed the two cases down next to Cooper, "Anything else sir?"

"No, take a couple hours, come back and pick me up in the Executive area, we'll be done by 11:30, midnight at the latest." Dr. Kale concluded. Shit, Cooper thought as Merriman departed the room, something's definitely up.

"Cooper, open my office door and take the cases in, I'll be right back. Fix a couple of drinks, I'll have a scotch and two splashes of soda, there's beer in the small 'frig' if you'd rather," Dr. Kale added as he walked down the small hallway leading to his private bathroom.

Cooper opened Dr. Kale's office and placed the cases behind the desk, turned the small desk lamp ON then moved to the refrigerator in the closet. He checked the frig, got a bottle of Dogfish 60 IPA for himself and a small bottle of soda water and several ice cubes for his boss. He dropped the cubes into a crystal tumbler, poured a generous amount of CARDHU Single Malt Scotch over the cubes and added two splashes of soda as Dr. Kale returned. Dr. Kale took the proffered drink, walked to his desk and sat down. Cooper popped the cap from his beer and closed the closet door as his boss loosened his tie, unbuttoned his shirt collar and raised his glass toward Cooper, "Good news, bad news Coop, bad first." Cooper put his beer down and got ready for the elevator incident to drop on his head,

"The FBI Director called our DCI complaining about your unfortunate altercation with Deputy Director Rollins," Cooper started to speak, but Kale held his hand up and stopped him, "Fortunately for you your good news took over and our DCI personally apologized to the FBI Chief, getting you, and me, both off the hook."

"Excuse me sir," I'm grateful, but why?"

"Actually the 'good news' is kudos from the DCI, Coop, you hit the nail on the head with your pondering choice, it was right on the 'Chinese Money' so to speak. The DCI was duly impressed." Kale stated then raised the tumbler to his lips and drank a healthy amount. "Your puzzler was the actual result, 'a great teaser', the DCI said. When the Chinese did what you optioned, we were ready to negotiate with strength and the Chinese finally shut the damn machine down. After that the FBI's call was easily absorbed by our boss. Your buddy Bordeaux and his people performed well and passed on the monitoring information that let us know the device was still operating at a low level. That knowledge began the negotiations that ended with our 'threat to destroy the device publicly'. The Chinese capitulated an hour ago." Dr. Kale took another healthy swig, inclining his tumbler toward Cooper with, "Good job, Cooper."

"Thank you sir, I'm glad everything worked out for our 'boss'…"

Cooper began to reply but Dr. Kale interrupted him, "You can certainly call me 'boss', but the Director is always THE DIRECTOR or the DCI for you, don't make that mistake again Cooper." Then, he added with a calmer voice, "The Vice President monitored the operation and was impressed when our DCI responded with pre-planned and quickly executed action. It's kudos for all of us, but in your case, the coin has two sides," Dr. Kale paused and Cooper, still smarting from referring openly to the DCI as 'boss' got ready for the worst,

"Right now, you 'walk on water' for me, the Director and the Vice President, but your submission got you another challenge. Sit down and relax while I take you through this operation, then I'll tell you about your add-on responsibility."

For the next 45 minutes Cooper listened as Dr. Kale recapped the CIA beliefs concerning the continuing rise of Chinese influence and the resultant challenges for U.S. Security Policy and quoted Foreign Policy Analyst, Thomas J.

Christensen:

1. "Since the early 1990's American scholars have debated whether the Peoples Republic of China (PRC) will pose a security threat to the United States and its regional interest in East Asia in the next few decades. Although many have focused on intentions as well as capabilities, the most prevalent component of the debate is the assessment of China's overall future military power compared with that of the United States and other East Asia regional powers..."

2. "For the pessimists, the Chinese military of the twenty-first century is replacing the Soviet military of the pre-Gorbachev years and the Japanese economy of the 1970s as the next big purported threat to American global leadership..."

3."In 1993 Chinese military officers made two observations about American military power: first, that it was unrivaled and likely to remain so for a long time; and second, that during the Gulf War, the United States moved many of its most important assets, especially logistic assets, out of East Asia. This would have made it difficult to fight simultaneously in a country such as Korea, China or Japan...So even if we were to focus on relative military power in East Asia, we should start with the understanding that overall military assets are often not a useful basis of comparison to judge whether Beijing will perceive itself as able to use force effectively against American interest in East Asia. Actually, with certain new equipment and certain strategies, China can pose major problems for American Security interests, without the slightest pretense of catching up with the United States by an overall measure of national military power or technology..."

After Dr. Kale's dissertation, and interspersed quotes from Mr. Christensen, he pressed on with the issue at hand, "China's development of fusion technology, coupled with their beliefs concerning US capabilities and vast commitments led them to attempt even greater influence over the world by launching operation 'Deep Dragon' five years ago..." Cooper finally ventured an interruption,

"Sir, if Deep Dragon was in operation for five years, why did we let it go-on so long before we reacted?"

"Deep Dragon was launched on September 11, 2001, most likely under the cover of our frenzied responses to the 9-11 attack. That distraction allowed the Chinese effort to go undetected. Three years later we received information from a Chinese source which was corroborated by one of our 'domestic part-timers' confirming the program's specifics. When we evaluated the Chinese program's operation, the influence of the device was judged negligible and the notable increase of problematic weather was believed to be cyclical. Having that information and knowing Deep Dragon was expensive for the Chinese to initiate and maintain we decided to just watch and wait. That policy got us to where we are now when the physical response from several Chinese agents, attempting to keep Deep Dragon a secret, led to the murder of our 'part-time source' in

Norfolk, Virginia. Making any sense?"

"Yes, sir, I believe so." Cooper answered, waiting for the next shoe to fall.

"Good, now, because of our Director's emphasis 'to open up new communication efforts with the FBI, NSA and Home Land Security', you briefed Deputy Director Rollins on the Chinese program," Cooper nodded embarrassed at the mention of Rollins' name again and Dr. Kale went on, "The FBI's reaction was to send a Special Agent to the Norfolk area to help with the murder investigation. Their agent's direction was to help solve the murder, but steer it away from Chinese embarrassment or responsibility. Our sources now assert that a Chinese Agent IS actually involved and that more killings will follow if the FBI continues to shield the Chinese,"

"Excuse me sir, why did the FBI attempt to protect China?" Cooper asked,

"We share that blame, Cooper, helped steer the FBI in the wrong direction. There's enough blame to go around. So, your new assignment is born." Dr. Kale handed Cooper a package, "In addition, complicating things further, there seems to be several Norfolk locals supporting the Chinese effort, and sharing responsibility for the happenings in addition to the Chinese agent that's recently been directed to halt the interference." Dr. Kale paused and finished his drink then resumed, "The Chinese agent has also been told to 'sever all possible ties to Deep Dragon, so, we need to help stop any further Chinese attempt to 'sever all ties' by exerting more violence," Dr. Kale paused again, waiting for a response from Cooper, but Cooper remained quiet so Kale went on,

"This is not a normal effort for us, too damn 'domestic' for my taste, but the Chesapeake Bay's a perfect area for smuggling, infiltration and spy recruitment and its right here in our own back yard. As some wise authority once said, 'there's no more vicious an enemy than the one turned that you believed was your friend.' Anyway Coop it's your assigned task because you were involved initially and are familiar with our recently deceased 'part-time' source, Commander Wilber Harrington, who eventually came to work for us by monitoring the Chinese through the Joint Service Staff College in Norfolk, then, after he retired, through an international shipping company in the same city." Dr. Kale watched as Cooper's eyes lit up with anticipation.

"We're not certain why Harrington was killed, but the Norfolk Police are beginning to focus their efforts on the Homicide with help from the FBI. We do have a 'control asset' locally and that information and access channel is covered in your folder. Betty Boles will be your local point of contact, I'm sure you remember Betty, don't you?"

"Yes sir." Cooper replied as he recalled Betty's big brown eyes.

CHAPTER THIRTY FIVE

LAKEWOOD, SUNDAY, OCTOBER 8

"STEPHEN IRONS"

I'm sitting in Sally's kitchen waiting for the time to pick Ella Knowles up for our visit to the Virginia Zoo. I've just read The Virginian-Pilot article concerning the Virginia Lottery's broken promise to Virginia taxpayers in the year 2000 when voters approved an amendment to the state constitution requiring state lottery profits be spent on Education. The article said,

"At the time Virginia voters felt this would add much needed money to the school budget, when in fact instead of acting as a supplemental infusion, most lottery profits just replaced the money the state was already spending on education through the General Fund,"

I began to see that the state of Virginia played the old shell game, taking tax money being used for Education, put it back in the General Fund and replaced it with the Lottery profits, certainly no added help for Education. I read on,

"This budgetary swap has left some Virginians–and Virginia lawmakers feeling deceived,"

"Deceived?" Thornton said, looking over my shoulder, "That's too damn soft of an accusation, Rusty, it's more like LIED TO! Politicians are just 'moving deck chairs around on the Titanic' certainly no help for Education's sinking ship." I had to agree with Thornton, I became angry, crumpled the paper and threw it to the floor and said,

"Damn, its state sponsored deception, just like Virginia's car tax fiasco!" I looked around and Thornton was laughing at my tirade. I picked up the paper and smoothed it out so Sally could read it when she came home from church. "You want to come to the zoo?" I asked Thornton but he was still laughing at my frustration. So I ignored him and went to pick up Ella Knowles on my own.

Driving to the Ghent area there was a lot of standing water Friday's nor'easter, but without Thornton's interference I was able to make my way down one of the most elevated streets in Norfolk, Church Street, then down Princess Anne Road to Ella's home. When I arrived Linda acted distant and looked at me funny, like she wanted to ask me something but couldn't take the time. I reasoned she was still confused by my quick departure the last time I was here. I asked her for a progress update on Wilber's case, since Sally and I had provided her additional information on Wednesday.

"Sorry, Stephen, there's no reportable progress," Then she excused her self with work to do. No damn wonder Charles Taylor's concerned about the investigation getting stalled and wants to hire me to look specifically at NISCO. I decided to let the case rest for the day and headed to the Virginia Zoo with Ella.

When we arrived it took ten minutes to clear the gate area. The day had turned nice and the lines were lengthy, probably responding to a general feeling of celebration after surviving Friday's storm. Finally after clearing the entry congestion Ella took my hand and pulled me toward the zoo's rotating 'globe' in the middle of the entrance plaza saying, "Come on Steven let's go here first." She commanded, now stretching out her eight year old legs and pulling on me. She looked back, flashed her blue eyes expectantly and added, "Hurry up Stephen, you're like too slow."

Approaching the rolling globe I saw what I thought interested Ella, there was a man in his 60's with two young kids, probably his grandchildren, playing near the zoo's world. The kids were yelling and running around the spinning globe, pointing to some elusive spot on the tumbling world. Ella seemed fascinated by their activity and as we moved closer, she exclaimed, "Hi, I'm Ella, what are you guys pointing at?"

The kids were probably 5 and 8 and the youngest child, the boy, replied, "We're looking for our Nana, she's in China," When he answered and the grandfather began to laugh, offered his hand to me in greeting and explained,

"Hi, I'm John. These two are my grandkids, Ethan and Rebecca. Right now they're trying to locate their grandmother while she's on a trip to China." John offered the explanation as Ethan and Rebecca followed the rolling point on the globe they had identified as China. I watched as China rolled and tumbled then travel up and down sometimes disappearing under the globe's supporting water flow. Ella and Thornton joined the kids pointing and cheering when they all saw the traveling grandmother's location re-appear from hiding.

After ten minutes of discussing individual naval service experiences with John, I saw Thornton walk away from the kids. He looked exhausted and was heading for an empty bench. John excused himself also and said to his grandkids, "Come on kids, were off to see the elephants." Ethan and Rebecca stopped 'China Chanting' and Ella came back to where John and I were standing. "The elephants are Ethan and Rebecca's favorites," John explained as he took the kids hands and began to walk north, toward the area known as the Okavango Delta, where the zoo's elephants reside.

"Have a great time." I offered and Ella waved to Ethan and Rebecca before we began our own adventure. When Ella pulled us away from the spinning world, we took a few slow steps as she caught her breath and said,

"Look Stephen, that's Joseph's Coat," I looked for some kid's discarded clothing, but Ella was pointing at flowers surrounding the Fountain Plaza area, "And over there, that's 'Flower Carpet Roses.'" To my astonishment, as we got closer to the two areas, she was correct. Placards confirming her knowledge and my surprise were located in the flower beds she had pointed out.

"I'm surprised, Ella, how do you know so much about zoo flowers?"

"My Grammy Shirley took me to the Botanical Garden during the big rain, we couldn't tour, so we stayed in a theater where they showed pictures of all their flowers and some here at the zoo. I like took notes Stephen."

"Did they let you pick the flowers?" I asked remembering Wilber's photograph.

"No way Stephen, you were a sheriff, you know that's like up against the law." Ella announced and pulled me toward other exhibits. As we began to walk I saw Thornton leave his bench and amble over behind us. He smiled and offered,

"You better watch out for this little one, bud, she's definitely figured you out." I turned away from Thornton's smart ass remark but continued to think of Wilber waving a bunch of wild flowers and remained just as confused as Sally had been.

After touring several exhibits, while working our way toward the lions, we had seen: prairie dogs digging and scurrying around their enclosure, walked by the large pond holding a group of transient ducks and geese, some turtles and the zoo's resident black swan. Thornton was still staring at the zoo's two flightless eagles that now resided in an open area across from the large pond. He seemed fascinated by the birds that were the representative symbol of our country, and his 'ultimate sacrifice' in Afghanistan. Ella joined Thornton to watch the eagles and I recalled visiting David Thornton's parents in Annapolis, Maryland after my return to the states in 2002. They had been told of his death two months earlier,

We all three cried about his loss as I hesitatingly recapped the ambush that separated us, recounting the events that took his life and isolated me until I was rescued. His parents asked a number of questions centering mostly on Thornton's dedication to his country and out lengthy friendship. I expected to be confronted about the events that caused our separation and his loss, but my nagging guilt drove me to say, "I should have tried harder, I'm so sorry that I couldn't bring him back with me…" I wanted to go on but Mr. Thornton interrupted my unburdening,

"We don't blame you Stephen, you were very close to our son David and we love you. You're part of our family now and we love you like you were our son. Up there in heaven, David loves you too." After visiting for a couple of hours we parted and I started the drive back to

Norfolk. I crossed over the Chesapeake Bay Toll Bridge, east of Annapolis and turned south on Route 60 through Cambridge and Salisbury, Maryland then connected with Route 13 South. Soon, I needed gas and a bathroom break and stopped on the Eastern Shore in Virginia near the town of Cape Charles. I filled up and used the station's rest room and when I returned to the car, shockingly, I found David Thornton sitting in the front-passenger seat waiting for me.

After getting over my shock at his presence, dressed as I remembered him before his loss, Thornton smiled and said to me, "Thanks for visiting my folks, Rusty, they're much better now and you're my best bud ever. I've miss being with you so I'm gonna' check on you from time to time, like 'good buds' should."

I fought back my tears of remembrance as Ella and I resumed walking. We traveled a good distance through more flowers that were being tended by one of the zoo's horticulture staff. And as we watched the lady work in the surrounding flower beds, Ella decided to brag about her own flower experiences and began lengthy comments on the various flowers and flower gardens throughout the Norfolk Botanical Garden and the Virginia Zoo. The flower lady, by her zoo name tag, Marie, appeared impressed by Ella's knowledge and listened patiently until Ella asked "Can you teach me something else?" Amused, Marie answered,

"Well Ella you know lots about flowers, how about trees?" Ella began to pay closer attention and replied,

"Not so much, but I'm a quick learner, teach me trees."

"Sure, I'll teach you 'bout one tree problem," Marie offered with a growing smile. Then, she pointed to a distant tree that I recognized as a Crepe Myrtle, and asked Ella, "What do you-all that tree's problem is?" Ella stared at the distant Crepe Myrtle that looked like it had just been pruned and she replied,

"I'm not sure, but it's real small,"

"Well, you're close Ella, it's been over-pruned by one of our staff, and I call that tree's problem, 'Crepe Murder'!" Marie laughed shook Ella's hand then pushed her flower cart off to another zoo area.

After recovering from Marie's joke, which Ella promised to remember and tell her mom, we moved past the 'Butterfly Garden' and up a concrete pathway, arriving at the meerkat exhibit. The three small meerkats were busy digging and running around their enclosure. There was a red headed Virginia Zoo Docent watching their activity. She was wearing a light blue sweat shirt that identified her as 'Amy' and she was leaning over the enclosure wall humming or chanting in a high pitched murmur. While docent Amy chanted the three meerkats climbed up onto three large rocks in the center of their exhibit and stared vigilantly up into the clear blue sky. I became curious and asked Ella,

"What's that docent doing Ella?" Ella watched for a minute, listened to Amy's high-pitched chanting then replied,

"She's warning the meerkats about a hawk, it's like her job, Stephen." I started to laugh, but docent Amy turned and offered me a sly smile saying,

"Ella's right, it's my job. Have a fun-day Ella." She said and left Ella and I alone with me still confounded by Ella and yet another zoo female.

We made our way up the concrete path leading to the overlook of the lion's large exhibit and paused to watch the two large 'cats' move about their enclosure. The lions at the zoo are named Mramba and Zola. Mramba has been here a while, he's a young male about 24 months old and Zola is a younger female, perhaps 18 months. Ella watched for a minute then asked, "Do you think the lions will have babies, Stephen?" I looked around quickly to see if anyone was within earshot of our conversation, but there was only Thornton, snickering and giving Ella a thumbs-up for her question. Comforted by the lack of a real audience, I started to reply, but a zoo announcement came on the PA system and saved me, "Good morning everyone, thank you for visiting your Virginia Zoo, we'd like to announce the special feeding of our elephants at 11:30. Please join us near the elephant yard to see our keepers interact with our three elephants. We know you'll enjoy the event." My luck was holding, Ella went another direction with her next question,

"What's that announcement about Stephen?"

"I'm not sure Ella, but if you look over there," I pointed directly across the lion enclosure to the northwest toward the elephant yard, "we're not far from the elephants and its twenty minutes past eleven, we could walk right over and watch the feeding, okay?"

"Sure, I like elephants. Maybe we'll see Ethan and Rebecca again."

We walked past the lion area around the back of the enclosure for the rhinoceros and zebras, then a concrete walkway that led around some termite mounds until we came to a large wooden walkway that led us up to the deck area that overlooked the elephant yard. Gathering, near the top of the deck we could see a group of about 40 visitors waiting for the elephant feeding and as Ella and I edged closer for a better view, I looked for John and his grandkids but couldn't see them in the crowd. The 'China family group' could easily be hidden so I checked for Thornton but he hadn't come with us.

Directly below our position; separated from the three elephants by a large fence made of 12' tall telephone pole-type pilings buried deep in the ground and connected with heavy steel cables; stood three of the Virginia Zoo's Elephant Keepers. The keepers were all dressed in low-top work boots, short khaki pants and khaki shirts with collars. On their shirts was some white stenciling of a zoo rhino and probably the keepers' names. One of the keepers, a very tall, muscular woman, with long dark hair pulled severely back into a pony tail, was waving a steel pointed rod up toward the crowd to get our attention. Watching her I remembered Wilber explaining the rod she held was called an 'ankus' or 'elephant-stick', and it was used to encourage the elephants to focus on their assigned task when they were non-responsive. Ella saw the same 'stick', and asked,

"What's she got in her hand, Stephen?"

"It's called an 'elephant-stick', if the elephants don't do what the keepers ask them to do, they use the stick to poke the elephants and get their attention,"

"My teacher at Montessori School has a ruler she pokes Teddy Dobbs with when he doesn't do what he's supposed to do. Hers must be a 'Teddy Stick'." Ella ended laughingly. I let the issue slide and we both refocused on the three keepers. As the tall gal motioned for quiet, I estimated she was over 6' tall, but it was deceiving looking down from fifteen feet above her position.

The crowd quieted as a light breeze picked up from the north and the tall keeper said, "Good morning everyone, I'm Ursula Volk the Virginia Zoo's Elephant Manager. With me are two of my elephant keepers, Dennis and Jill." Ursula paused and we applauded all the introductions. It was easy to hear Ursula with the breeze coming our way, but the breeze also carried the unmistakable smell of the elephant holding yard directly behind her position. Ella looked up and whispered to me,

"What's that smell Stephen? It's really bad."

"It's the elephant yard Ella, forget about the 'elephant poop' and pay attention to the elephants and the keepers." Ella seemed okay with my request, she smiled wiggled her nose a bit then refocused back down to the group below.

Concentrating myself I could see Dennis was a big guy but not quite as tall as Ursula. He was in his early 30's, goat-tee bearded and a bit over 200 pounds. You must need to be big to handle elephants, I thought. Then, as you might have guessed, I focused more on Jill. She was a small sharp looking gal with medium length dark brown hair, very petite and very pretty. She reminded me a lot of Debra Winger in 'Officer and a Gentleman'. So now I had to figure that if you weren't big, then you had to be both 'pretty' and 'pretty-well-educated', to handle the elephants. Responding, Jill and Dennis waved up to the growing crowd and Ursula went on,

"My Elephant Keepers have the responsibility of helping me care for and training our three elephants, Monica, Lisa and Cita," At the sound of their names, and hand signals from the three keepers, each of the elephants moved a step forward toward the fence and raised a long trunk, saluting up us with what can only be described as a very loud, vocal rendering,

BRRARRAAP, BRRARRAAP, BRRARRAAP, rumbled up from the yard, sounding like three gigantic Darth Vader's in one of the 'Star Wars' movies.

Ursula continued her talk about elephant training and behavior then the keepers fed the elephants some fruit, corn, and sweet potatoes. Finally as Ursula completed her talk the keepers gave each elephant one big orange colored pumpkin and Ella whispered to me, "They're too loud Stephen, and did you see everything they ate, no wonder their 'poop' smells so bad." Thornton arrived and was laughing at Ella's commentary, but I decided not to respond further. Thornton had figured out my tactic and said,

"You better answer her Stephen or she'll hit you with a 'Stephen-stick'." I ignored them both and once the elephants finished smashing the pumpkins all over the yard, they trumpeted a final *BRRARRAAP* to the crowd and Ella put her hands over her ears. When the three elephants moved off into their exercise yard to browse and forage for other hidden treats, I ventured,

"Do you want to stay and watch the elephants some more, Ella?"

"No way Stephen, they're too loud and smelly, but, they did make me hungry. Can we get a hotdog at the Africa Restaurant?"

"Sure, that works for me," I replied and Ella took my hand and we began to move away from the crowd and out through the top level of the elephant barn toward the Africa Restaurant and a much needed tour-break.

CHAPTER THIRTY SIX

VIRGINIA ZOO

"STEPHEN IRONS"

Thirty minutes later Ella and I are sitting outside the African Village Restaurant. We're at a small table and have just finished the last of our hotdogs while we 'people watch'. Conversationally I asked Ella, "What did you do yesterday after you did your homework?"

"I don't have homework Stephen. My Montessori School doesn't do homework. But Saturday I couldn't go out in the storm, so I listened to mom's Sky-radio, you know the radio that goes up in the sky then comes back down, like, to your house, or your car," Surprised by the fact that Ella's school didn't force homework on kids and their parents caused me to think more positively about her school's desire to concentrate and focus on their students' education when the kids were actually in school. That would certainly encourage more 'family bonding activity' at home. I smiled and replied,

"You mean Satellite Radio, the one that plays great music with no commercials."

"No not music Stephen, a kids' program on Saturday, you know, pretend stories on the radio, like, Cinderella or The Three Pigs but yesterday it was 'The Problem Princess',"

I started to ask Ella what she meant, but several children, Ella's age, ran by with their mother, or a Sunday School Teacher, chasing quickly behind them. Ella paused and watched the kids until they settled down and headed into the restaurant, then, she offered, "Hey, I know one of those kids. He's the Teddy I told you about." She said, then, she refocused on her story, "The Princess was eight years old, like me, but she was always getting in trouble. Her mom and dad did everything for her, she was like spoiled. Everyone told the Princess she should do things for herself, not be spoiled, but, the Princess kept causing trouble and getting people to do things for her." Ella paused here, thinking back, then,

"One day the Princess was kidnapped in the park. Two bad guys took her to the 'bad land' and kept her in a tall tower. They locked her door and told her to keep her room clean or she couldn't have any food. The Princess cried and yelled for two days not doing anything they wanted her to do. Then, she finally got real hungry and cleaned the room to get some food," Ella paused for breath and focus then went on,

"The bad guys told the Princess' mom and dad they could have the Princess back if they paid 300 gold pieces. Her mom and dad thought they could raise the money and tried for a week by asking everyone in the 'good land' for help. But, the economy was bad and most of the people had been tricked by the Princess, so her mom and dad could only raise 100 gold pieces... The Princess continued to work for her food, but, she like kept screaming and hollering at the bad guys. So the bad guys said 'okay' to the 100 gold pieces to get rid of the Princess," Ella paused again, I kept quiet as Thornton joined us and sat next to Ella before she continued the story,

"The bad guys told the Princess' dad to meet them on the big bridge between the 'good land' and the 'bad land' and put the money down in the middle of the bridge then go back to the good side. The bad guys said they'd pick up the money then let the Princess go.

"After the Princess' dad put the money down and went back to the good side, both bad guys showed up. The biggest bad guy held the Princess' hand real tight, so she couldn't get loose and the small bad guy yelled at the Princess' dad to stay where he was. The small guy started to walk up the bridge to get the money. The Princess, like, yelled as loud as she could and kicked the big bad guy's leg so hard that he let go of her hand and grabbed his hurt leg. The little bad guy turned back to see what happened and the Princess ran right by him, grabbed the money and hurried down the bridge to her dad." Ella finished then said,

"That's it Stephen, like, Happy Ever After."

"Wow, what a great story," I said as the three of us began to walk away from the Okavango Delta toward the entrance area to the zoo where the fountains and the zoo's rolling world were still in full operation. Thornton decided to join several young kids jumping in and out of the water fountains. I dismissed Thornton's actions, I'd seen enough water over the past two days and it really wasn't that hot.

As we walked out I began thinking about Ella's story, and said, "That's a super radio program, Ella, no wonder it's your favorite."

"Stephen, is the Princess story like a little girl shouldn't be spoiled?"

"Yes, plus maybe one more lesson," I answered. Thornton joined us again, he was drying off from the fountains but anxious to listen to my explanation, "Even if you are a Princess you should always be ready to act in your own defense. Do you do play any sports, Ella?"

"I go to ballet, oh, that's not sports," Thornton shook water from his golden curls and began to laugh at her initial reply. Ella paused a second or two then she exclaimed, "But I do karate! My mom says it's for self-defense, just like you said. Is that right, Stephen?"

"Yes, Ella that's right." I offered as she took my hand and we headed for my car. Ella had softened my mood. I was encouraged by her story and wanted to find out why my personal story with Linda had gone wrong, I definitely wanted a chance at Ella's, 'That's it, a Happy Ever After,' ending to my story too. Thornton was smiling as we walked away from the zoo. He was still shaking his head, now mostly at my efforts to stay ahead of an eight year old. I ignored his smirk and signaled for him to 'zip it up'.

CHAPTER THIRTY SEVEN

GHENT GARDEN CONDOS

"STEPHEN IRONS"

Linda greeted us at the door hugged Ella and offered me a big smile and her gratitude then she asked me to stay a minute to talk. Ella gave her mom one of her funny looks, then, she thanked me for a fun day. After that, Ella mimed a 'karate-chop' followed by a 'karate-kick' motion and laughed loudly announcing, "Protect yourself, Stephen, it's gonna' be a Crepe Murder!"

When Ella marched off to her room, Linda gave me her own funny look and followed her daughter down the hall. I was certain I'd hear more about Ella's joking display since Linda's detective skills had been challenged. When Linda returned she had a small smirk on her face, she said to me, "You and Ella are both a little nuts."

"Maybe so, but we're just kids," I replied pushing a smile across my own face, "Actually you have a wonderful daughter, she's LIKE, great!"

"I do have a wonderful daughter but don't start saying 'LIKE' in the middle of your sentences to copy her and aggravate me." Linda stated and I relaxed a little, the ice seemed to have melted. I began to focus my concentration on Linda, she was dressed casually, blue jeans and a light blue t-shirt that clung seductively to her well proportioned figure adding a definite 'pop' to the effect her blue-gray eyes were having on me. My mood too had softened and I began to hope for an opportunity to advance from desire to arousal with even more Norfolk Police involvement.

"You wanted to talk?" I asked as Linda sat down on the couch I occupied.

"Yes, the FBI and Sheriff Os have provided some information I want to share with you, but I've got a few questions before sharing, is that alright?" I was a bit confused by her offering, but I nodded and remained attentive, "Okay, first Os mentioned you were being considered for a position at NISCO, is that true? What kind of position?"

Her tone wasn't exactly friendly. It wasn't confrontational but it seemed orchestrated to put me on the spot, like I was in an interview room suspected of some crime. I felt the warmth of eagerly anticipated feelings for Linda dissolve and turn chilly as I felt my face reddened, "Why does it matter if I go back to work? What has the FBI told you about Wilber, or me, that would make you ask a question like that?" I tried to calm myself, but once again I felt like looking for the EXIT sign out of Linda's Condo.

"I'm sorry you took it that way, Stephen. I actually want to share information about Wilber but, not if a conflict of interest at NISCO could jeopardize my investigation."

"Linda, if you think I'd take some job to cause a problem for your investigation, you haven't been hearing me." I felt I was controlling my voice, but Ella and Thornton appeared in the hallway and Ella said,

"Is it okay? I didn't mean to stay too late mom, we like had a great time at the zoo." Thornton stood next to Ella, crossing his arms in front of his body waiting for Linda's reply,

"No, darling, I'm not upset with you or Stephen for staying late. I know you had a great time and I'm happy you did. We're just discussing some work things, that's all. Please go back to your room and read, we'll step outside to finish our talk." Ella smiled, waved at me then Thornton followed her back to her room. Linda pointed toward the back door that opened out to one of their community park areas and we headed that way.

"We need to get some things straight Stephen." Linda said as she led me outside. She closed her back door and walked a step ahead of me, leading us across the small park. The weather was beautiful, as it generally is in October, with the trees flashing red and gold colors against the disappearing sunlight. We moved into the park and sat under a live-oak tree. The large tree was allowing the setting sun's rays to filter in through its dark green leafing, highlighting Linda's golden hair. As she sat down on a park bench, Linda watched me, probably until she felt I was gaining some aspect of calmness then she went on,

"First of all you must know how important this case is to me, I've gone out on a limb pushing for it to be classified a Homicide and now when I finally get the 'green light' the FBI jumps into the case and with a lot of speculative information. But, they've also provided some basic facts I shouldn't have missed." She paused here waiting for some comment from me. She'd lost some of her 'interrogator aura' and I'd calmed a bit too, I was now willing to listen. Linda seemed to sense this and went on, "In addition to the FBI's information, Os mentioned your job opportunity at NISCO and immediately I'm floored by something I would have hoped you would have shared with me. Why have you kept that information from me Stephen?"

"Well, it just happened, there's been no decision, I'm still thinking about the offer."

"How long have you had the offer?" Linda asked, trying to pin me down.

"Since last Tuesday but I made no specific decision at that time. Sally and I saw you at Police Ops with our information on Wilber's book ideas. I was trying to focus on helping Sally, and your investigation, not sharing my employment opportunities." I offered the last with a little sarcasm so she'd know I was still irked.

"Okay, but you've got to see my side of this. We were beginning, as you've implied, to become 'friends' then, I find out about you getting a job offer from an organization that could possibly be involved in your brother in law's death. I know, I know, I'm stretching now, but you should be able to understand my problem with you withholding the information." Linda's statement was given as a question, raising her tone at the end of the sentence to show my withholding information offended her as a friend and as the detective in charge of the investigation. I replied carefully,

"I guess I can see your point, and you're right, Charles Taylor wants me to be his 'personal representative' at NISCO to find out who in his organization might have had a reason to want Wilber dead. He wants me to question NISCO associates, using his authority, to determine who at NISCO could be responsible for Wilber's murder. Or, if it's not a murder, then he wants to know why Wilber became so depressed that he took his own life. Taylor feels your investigation will look at NISCO, but not as concentrated as I could as his direct representative. I honestly don't see why this would be a problem for your investigation." I concluded looking for a little, can't you see I'm hurting here too, edge over her. So far she was way ahead in that department. Linda continued with her own agenda,

"Would your information be available to me?"

"Of, course, Taylor specifically addressed that requirement," I overstated my ability to pass on information without Taylor's approval, but if that became a problem, I'd quit.

"Do you need this job, Stephen?"

"Well, it's only temporary, but I can use the money and the benefits. I can't live forever with my sister. Her plans may change soon and as you must know my pension and medical benefits aren't that lavish."

"You said temporary, what did you mean by that?" She interrupted, continuing to ask without responding. Linda wasn't going to stop being the 'questioning cop' but I tried to remain calm and said,

"Once your investigation is complete to Taylor's satisfaction, my job's over. Unless," I quickly added, remembering Taylor's instructions, "Unless you end up ruling Wilber's death WAS a suicide then I'd refocus on why Wilber was in such a state of mind as to have killed himself. But, I know Wilber didn't kill himself." Linda responded,

"Good, thanks for sharing that. Now, I do think it's possible for us both to operate in separate capacities and still cooperate to solve Wilber's murder." She paused with one of Ella's, 'You're a funny guy Stephen' look, then she continued, "Here's three 'ground-rules' I believe need to be followed so YOUR job will NOT interfere with MY investigation and insure our possible 'friendship' is not jeopardized. Are you willing to listen, Stephen?" Linda asked and smiled again like we had ironed out some differences but she wanted me to know she was still in charge. She was certainly in charge of her investigation, but for the continuation of 'our friendship', I wasn't ready to give up my ability to have an input there. So, silly as it might seem, I smiled, and crossed my fingers behind my back, out of her eye sight. Then I replied,

"Sure, I'm good with all that. Go ahead with your 'ground-rules'."

"Okay, number one, any information you discover must be given to me or one of my people immediately." She watched my face, I didn't react I just smiled and squeezed my hidden fingers tightly together.

"Two, any information I gain during my investigation will be made available to you once I determine its disclosure wont negatively impact the progress of my case." Linda took extra time here to watch for a reaction. I smiled again and continued to squeeze on my crossed fingers. I was happy to be able to receive information but I knew ahead of time she wasn't going to jeopardize her case. So far she hadn't surprised me, but I had no idea where she was going with the third 'ground-rule' so I still kept my fingers captive,

"Third and most important," She paused again, insuring my belief that I was right to worry about this potential deal breaker, "you and Ella should continue to be friends, she likes you and I know you like her too or you wouldn't have spent all that time at the zoo just to get in my good graces. So, how's that for three, simple rules Stephen?"

I uncrossed my fingers, knowing I could handle the third one without childish protection. "I have no problem with one or two, and I totally LIKE number three." I proclaimed reaching to shake her hand in agreement. As she smiled and reached over to shake my hand, I pulled her closer and kissed her gently on the lips. She was surprised, but didn't reject my new act of friendship.

"Sealed with a kiss, huh?' she replied and continued to smile. I smiled too and thoughts of arousal began, but I could still see her facial tension and concern. She had more to explain. Linda continued to hold my hand, but it wasn't the feeling of intimacy I hoped for, it was similar to the first night in her office, a sure sign of offering comfort for what was about to be revealed, "Stephen, what I'm about to tell is in confidence, the information will come out later in the investigation, but I think you should know it now." My returning warmth didn't stand a chance and the approaching flood of warmth receded into cold-water normality. She released my hand and said, "Wilber had some debts that were hidden until the FBI provided the information. He had military allotments going to his ex wife for alimony and child support at $1,000 per month," I started to interrupt, but Linda held up her hand to stop me,

"Yes Wilber and his first wife, Lydia have a son, Wilber Junior. Junior turned 21, in July, so Wilber stopped the allotment in August of this year, but he was also paying life insurance premiums of about $400 a month for almost a million dollars in coverage. Those premiums were also allotted from his military pay."

I began to understand why Linda hadn't known about these allotments, the military's very 'close hold' about that kind of member information. Linda elaborated, "Wilber's life insurance policies are: $500,000 to Sally, $100,000 to Wilber Jr. and $250,000 for an antique business' property called 'Adams' Antiques'. There's also another $90,000 from NISCO. Sally must know about the ones payable to her,"

I couldn't wait any longer, "Linda, I'm sure Sally knows about policies with benefits to her, but why do you think she knows about the antique business or Wilber Jr.? I've never heard her mention either."

"Wilber and Sally actually own the business property jointly. They both signed for the bank loan so she must be aware of the business. The third partner, or property manager, is Dave Adams and our accountant believes his business proceeds must pay for that loan, since those payments don't appear anywhere on Wilber's bank records." Linda paused, "I guess Sally could be making the payments, we haven't looked at her records yet."

The 'yet' startled me. The FBI had looked at Wilber's military information but not at Sally's. Shit! How about me? I wondered, and asked, "How much is the payment on the business property?" I tried to calm myself, wanting to immediately jump to Sally's defense. Wilber was gone and they obviously had a lot of information on him that I wasn't aware of, but Sally's information, concerning her employment income, was another thing.

"The property payments are $1,600 a month." Linda answered.

"There's no way Sally's making those payments, she told me she pays the utilities and most of the groceries, plus all of their vacation cost when they go on trips. Her take-home pay is about $2,500 a month the rest goes to taxes, health insurance, union dues, uniform purchases, Americans' commuting charges and her 401K retirement fund. Sally couldn't be paying for any business property loan."

Linda thought a minute, considering my response, then, she said,

"Abby, our accountant figured the same, so you're both probably right, the business must be doing well enough to carry the loan." I was floored from all this information but my mind finally got back to the ex wife and the kid.

"Wilber never told Sally about having a kid, much less paying out $1,000 a month... He and Sally have been married for five years I can't believe he kept that from her. And, the business insurance stuff, that's a shocker too. I can understand Sally as Wilber's beneficiary, even Wilber's kid, but what's the life insurance involvement with the property manager?"

"Abby figures it's to pay off the business loan if one partner dies, I'm not sure if Sally's involved with the policy, but Wilber and this guy Adams are,"

I jumped in again, "There's a damn motive for you, are you looking at Adams?"

"Yes, and this is for your information only, we'll see him next week."

"Damn, you don't suspect Sally do you, the NISCO insurance money and the $500,000 policy on Wilber's life?"

"No, Stephen, I don't suspect Sally, but the FBI is looking at everything. They think, because of Wilber's career in the Navy, his job in San Diego, his assignment at the Staff College here and later his position at NISCO, that his heavy debt could have pushed him into something profitable, but illegal."

"Jesus Christ, they think Wilber could have been some kind of spy? That's nuts!" I was wound up now, standing and becoming more vocal. I looked toward Linda's back door but didn't see Ella. Thank god Linda was smart enough to bring us our here for this discussion.

"Stephen, I know this is upsetting but you've been involved in investigations, you know the FBI will look at everything if they think there's a possibility of Espionage, Sabotage or Terrorism in this case."

"Wait a minute! Where in the hell would they get Sabotage?"

"Wilber was taken off 'sea duty assignments' because he was held partially responsible for a submarine running aground,"

"Linda, that's bullshit, Captain Westerly told Sally that Wilber was taken off 'sea duty' because he was training the sub's Assistant Navigator that WAS on duty during the incident, Wilber was actually sick and in his quarters when the ship ran aground. Three officers, including the captain, were removed from the ship and restricted," Linda stopped me, placed her hand on my arm, eased me back down onto the bench and offered,

"Thank you for that information. I know this is upsetting to you, Stephen, and most of it's removed from the effort we should be exerting to find Wilber's killer, but the FBI has opened this can of worms and I have to deal with all the slimy critters they've let out."

That helped me some, but if I had found out about Wilber's lying to Sally when he was still alive, I would have gone after his ass myself. Friend or not, he was being dishonest with my sister and I know how Sally hates dishonesty. Then it hit me, I looked into Linda's blue-gray eyes, now only a foot away from mine, and said as calmly as I could,

"The FBI thinks I found out about Wilber's secrets and the possibility of his being involved in something illegal. They think I had the motive and means, and because of my background and training, they think all I needed to kill Wilber was the opportunity, is that right?"

Linda took both my hands in hers and nodded slowly in the affirmative. Shit, I began to think, what a damned mess this has turned into.

CHAPTER THIRTY EIGHT

NISCO, DOWNTOWN NORFOLK

Charles Taylor sat in his downtown office reading the morning paper. He was upset by the headline article in the Hampton Roads Section of The Virginian-Pilot concerning a multinational corporation's proposal to build a large garbage port directly across the Elizabeth River from his building. Charles gazed out his Portsmouth facing window and shook his head in disgust as he read to confirm his disappointment,

"The COVANTA Energy Corporation, based in New Jersey, part of the larger COVANTA Holding Corporation, wants to build a local Trash Port in Norfolk's neighboring city of Portsmouth, Virginia," Charles pushed the paper away and added, "Damn why didn't I know about this development?"

Charles had tried several times this morning to call Sonchi Zimchi in Shanghai. He was concerned why Sonchi had not informed him about these new efforts in Hampton Roads. Sonchi would have known about COVANTA, their corporate ties to China were well known. Charles pressed the intercom button on his phone bank, "Betty, have we heard from Zimchi Shipping?" He asked, hoping for a positive reply from his Administrative Assistant, Betty Boles.

"I'm sorry, Mr. Taylor, Sonchi's secretary, reminded me it's 9 PM there and she was alone in the office. Mr. Zimchi is traveling in Africa and is unavailable. She promised to call when they reestablish contact. She did ask if 'Gong Ju Zimchi, Sonchi's oldest son could help'. So I'm certain she's sincere in her desire to assist. I told her you were calling on a matter of mutual interest to Zimchi and NISCO, I hope that's okay."

As Betty's reply came through his intercom, Charles relaxed a little, he was sure Betty had been reading from her detailed notes, she had always been focused on protecting NISCO and himself. "Yes, Betty that's fine. Are the Kroger girls on schedule to meet with me before Sheriff Irons arrives at 11:30?"

"Yes sir, I spoke with Margarete, they'll leave James Carlson in charge and be here for last weeks review at 10:30. Margarete sounded excited, do you think Sheriff Irons will come to work for you, sir?" Betty asked.

"I hope so Betty, he could be a big help getting this Harrington mess cleared up. Let me know if we hear from China, I'll be on e-conference for an hour."

"Of course, I'm certain your conference will prove beneficial." Betty replied and closed the connection.

Switching OFF the intercom Charles began to wonder if Betty was psychic or just so well in-sync with his operation that she knew everything he knew as soon as he knew it. Well, he reasoned, he'd hired her away from a career with the CIA, so he expected her to be smart and resourceful. But, there were a few things Betty might find out that could cause him a real problem.

Betty Boles stood and moved away from her desk toward a small cabinet located along the back wall of her office. Betty's 5'– 5" frame, trim and attractive carrying about 110 pounds, moved across the room quickly. She paused to view her window reflection and thought her dark hair and short Prince Valiant cut definitely gave her the look of Catherine Zeta Jones in the movie "Chicago". Her large brown eyes flashed and she smiled even broader as she opened the lap-top remote providing Charles Taylor's e-conference communication through wireless technology. The information automatically triggered an 'f drive' disc copier and transferred it to Dr. Kale's office. Taylor's e-conference had been going for just under an hour now, and as Betty checked her remote screen for the print version, she was certain that Charles Taylor's use of his nine-month-old email ID, 'mermaidlover', was associated with a female employee of Norfolk's downtown Nauticus facility. Betty was certain Charles was having an affair with the marine science expert Charles had been seeing for the past few months. Dr. Peggy Turner had been hired a year ago to supervise the Oceanographic and Maritime related programs for visitors to Nauticus and the adjoining exhibit of the retired Battleship Wisconsin now berthed alongside the Nauticus facility. Betty was certain Charles' on-going relationship with Dr. Peggy Turner, and some of his other secret involvement with Zimchi Shipping, would surprise and anger Charles' ill tempered wife Millie… Betty believed the positive confirmation of Charles' secret involvement with Dr. Turner and Zimchi Shipping could create a financial account for her, like a hidden 401K for her. Betty closed her remote lap-top as the Kroger twins entered the office,

"Betty Boop," Margarete greeted, misstating Betty's last name intentionally to make a joking reference to who she believed was Betty's look-alike cartoon character, "how's it going with ole' Charlie-boy this morning? Has he seen the article on COVANTA?" Margarete asked as Elizabeth smiled and remained quietly at Margarete's side providing a beautiful reflected image.

Betty watched the two tall slender figures attired in thinly gray striped, charcoal black business suits, and smiled back as she suppressed her thoughts of wanting to jerk Margarete's hair out by its natural roots. "Good morning ladies, Mr. Taylor's been on e conference all morning, I'm not certain he's had the time to read this morning's paper. Margarete dear, you should clue ole' Charlie-boy' in on the COVANTA news, I know he'd love to hear it from you." Betty took her shot at getting Margarete in trouble but Margarete wisely turned on her heel and marched, into Charles Taylor's office announcing,

"We're here Charlie-boy." She offered as Elizabeth followed her twin sister in.

Alone Betty began to plan how to get back at the twins. She suspected Taylor and the twins were up to no good, but proving it might be above her pay-grade. Maybe with Dr. Kale's help, it could happen. Betty put that prospect on hold and dialed the downstairs reception,

"Robby, it's Betty at NISCO we've got Sheriff Irons visiting at 11:30, please Valet Park the sheriff and direct him up. Thank you."

CHAPTER THIRTY NINE

POLICE OPERATIONS, 10:30AM

Linda Knowles sat at her desk, her meeting had been delayed but she still dreaded the rescheduled conference. She was certain Millers would cause her problems with Special Agent Davis, and now, Stephen Irons might be taking a job with NISCO, trying to do her work for her. What a balancing act; she had a murder to solve but most of her energy was spent evaluating information and passing it on to other people so they could remain civil and do their own jobs. Chief Beck had ruled Harrington's death a Homicide just before Special Agent Davis called to delay their meeting until 11AM. Davis said he was expecting a conference call from FBI Headquarters to shed new light on several aspects of her case. Knowles called Millers and Bradshaw and informed them of the delay, asking them to get other assignments scheduled for this morning. She knew her challenge was to keep everyone pointed toward her ultimate goal of bringing Harrington's murderer to justice and her mind continued to tumble around this challenge as her phone rang,

"Knowles," she informed the operator then, "sure put him through," she pressed the SPEAKER ON and continued scanning her notes, "Hello Morris,"

"Morning Boss, I got a positive ID from Irons on the Chin guy and a possible from the Lakewood kids, sounds like we've gotten Chin tied into this mess, he could have been Harrington's killer."

"That's great, I'm not sure the kids could have given you a positive being so far from the UPS vehicle, but a possible helps. Anything else,"

"Dr. Ski she has some new info on Chin. I'll stop by before I come back to Ops,"

"Did she tell you what it was?"

"Eh, no, she just said it was interesting. See you later,"

"Morris, wait, check out the City Lock Up, you remember Bull, Deputy Belton's worker? Show him your photos, try to get another ID. That could make a solid case."

"Yeah, I almost forgot, sorry, Boss, Sheriff Os told me anytime this morning. I'll go by on the way to Dr. Ski's."

"Can you make the 11 o'clock?" But Morris was gone, she decided to try Millers and dialed 9 for an outside line and punched in Millers' cell number, heard two rings then,

"Millers, is that you Chief?"

"Yes Sam, anything from NISCO?"

"Nothing new, I called Carlson got some input from him, but the other three are tied up somewhere downtown."

"Okay, Bradshaw got a positive from Irons on Chin and a possible from the kids. He's on the way to the lock-up to question Bull then see Dr. Ski about some new development. Do you think you can make the 11 o'clock?"

"Not sure, but I'll try. The ID's good, I wouldn't have expected the kids' to be a positive but it's a connection. And, who knows what a 'city con' will say, Sheriff Os has a tight reign on that mob... What's new with Dr. Ski, or is it just Bradshaw's early morning hormones?" Linda laughed in response, a little louder than she intended,

"We've got to give Morris a break Sam he sees this Chin connection as a biggie,"

"Yeah, maybe, but he's got another 'biggie' in his pants if he's off to see Dr. Ski." Knowles had to laugh again as Sam disconnected, but he was probably right about Bradshaw and Dr. Ski. Linda mused about her own relationship with Stephen Irons and their Sunday, discussion. She didn't envy Stephen having to tell Sally about the FBI's concerns about Wilber Harrington. Linda began to think about the possibility that Stephen could be involved with Harrington's death, that he could have known about Harrington's secrets and confronted him about the lies, then, killed him. No, she concluded, there's no way, Stephen's not that good an actor. Linda was certain he had been genuinely upset yesterday. He was too emotional he couldn't have faked that surprise.

11AM, still no word from Special Agent Davis, he must still be tied up on the FBI conference call. Another thought crossed Linda's mind and she reached for a small black book that contained the names of several Norfolk Confidential Informants, street-wise locals she and her husband Dwight had dealt with over the past few years. She remembered someone at the Tazewell Hotel they had both used. She figured it was worth a chance, tapped the SPEAKER ON and called the hotel, Becky answered, "Tazewell Hotel, this is Becky, how can I help you?"

"Becky, Detective Linda Knowles, Dwight's wife, do you remember me?"

"Yeah, Hi, long time no talk, how are you?" Becky said,

"I'm well Becky…" Then Becky interrupted,

"How's Ella, she must be a big gal now, is she hard headed like Dwight? I do miss talking to him every week or so,"

"I miss him too, Becky. Ella's eight now, she IS a big girl, very smart and very pretty. She reminds me a lot of Dwight, smart, strong willed, inquisitive and bull-headed,"

"That was Dwight, except for the pretty part, how can I help you Linda?"

"You have a guest at your hotel named Clayton Davis," Becky interrupted,

"Yeah, I definitely know him, he's FBI and good looking, but don't get wrapped up with him Linda, he's a 'player', he's already hit on me once. Flattering, but as Dwight said about some law enforcement guys, *you don't want to spend any time in that guy's handcuffs*.'"

"Thanks for telling me, I'll keep Dwight's message in mind. Anyway Agent Davis was sent here to help with an investigation I'm doing on a local Homicide, please keep this all confidential but I'd like to know what he's doing when he's around the hotel, you know who calls, who visits, where he goes when he leaves. Stay friendly-like, not too pushy, he's trained and I don't want him to know we've had this conversation. Okay?"

Becky talked five minutes straight, Linda got a pen and note pad and began taking notes. Talk about hitting the jackpot Linda thought as Becky finally ended her lengthy report and agreed to provide all she could on Davis' activities as long as he stayed at the Tazewell. Linda had just hung up the phone when Clayton Davis walked into her office,

"Sorry I'm late Linda hope I didn't upset the schedule." Clayton said.

"No, Clayton I'm just a small-town cop trying to muddle along on my own, but, believe it or not I've learned a few things without you." Clayton looked confused but he remained silent, he was sure his lateness was the reason Linda was upset.

"I've just talked with HQ Linda, they informed me that the FBI knows specifically why Harrington was removed from the Navy's Sea Duty List, he," Linda held up her hand,

"Well, let me guess, he was training a young navigator who was on duty along with the Boat's skipper when their sub ran aground in a foreign port. Harrington was actually off-duty due to illness, but all three officers were removed from the sub and sea duty assignments, unless, all three were in a conspiracy, is that how the FBI sees it?"

"How in the hell did you learn that? It took putting some heavy pressure on the Navy to get the information!" Clayton exclaimed displaying a temper Linda hadn't seen before.

"Well Clayton, we got our information from Sally Harrington,"

"Okay, Okay, I'm sorry I'm late, I'm sorry I screwed your schedule up and I'm sorry I thought I had something you'd be pleased to get. How about we start over, how can I help with what's left of the morning?"

"Alright, here's Harrington's ex's phone number, give her a call and get her in here for an interview, tomorrow would be good. Dial 9 when you get the tone, she's in Franklin so you'll need to dial a 1 then the area code and number." Clayton did as he was told then he activated the SPEAKER ON function, he wanted Linda to be impressed with his ability to function in her investigation. The speaker broadcast two rings, then a connection,

"Hullo," a female southern voice replied,

"Is this Mrs. Harrington?" Clayton said.

"Yes, this is Lydia Harrington, who's this?"

"This is FBI Special Agent Clayton Davis calling for Detective Knowles of the Norfolk Police Department, we would like to talk to you concerning your ex husband's recent death, can you come in to the Police Operations in Norfolk tomorrow afternoon?" Clayton's question was followed with a string of laughter,

"We're all flooded here with a lotsa' backwater, Mista' FBI, I can't get out and you-all can't get inta' Franklin 'less you got a row boat. Try next week, I can make it then."

Clayton was getting upset, nothing had been accomplished. He looked at Linda Knowles, but she was hiding her face, offering nothing, Clayton responded,

"We have utility vehicles that can make the trip, Mrs. Harrington I'll call you when Detective Knowles and I will be at your home. Thank you for your cooperation." Lydia Harrington's laughter could be heard from the speaker, quickly followed by a definite hang-up.

Linda smiled and said, "Well that went well Clayton, what's your next act?"

"Don't worry Linda, Agent Lance can supply the transportation we need, I call him on my cell and get back to you."

CHAPTER FORTY

LAKEWOOD

"STEPHEN IRONS"

After I started the car, on the far right side of the Volvo's Indicator and Warning Light Display, one of the caution lights stayed ON. I leaned forward for my eye test and read 'Check Engine'. "Damn," I said to Thornton sitting in the passenger seat, "I don't have time for this." He grinned back but gave me no reply. I reached across Thornton into the glove compartment and retrieved the VOLVO C70 Manual. Leafing through the Contents listed on the second page, I located Chapter 2 titled Instruments, Switches and Controls, on page 15. I immediately turned to page 15, not there, flipped the page and saw the Indicator and Warning Lights listed, my light was #21, Malfunction indicator lamp, and read, 'See page 18 for more information. I grimaced, Thornton laughed and I changed pages, **'The warning lights described on page 18 and 19 should never stay ON while driving.'** This great news was in bold print and when I checked the panel again, sure enough the light was still ON. I found the further instructions:

'Take the car to your AUTHORIZED VOLVO DEALER as soon as possible.' "Shit," I voiced and made a mental note to eventually do as I'd been directed, but Barry's Performance Imports (BPI) would have to wait, I was in a big hurry right now.

Despite the warning light glitch, I was excited about identifying my airport attacker. Sergeant Bradshaw said when the guy's body was found in the Lafayette River and during the autopsy the Medical Examiner had discovered an elastic knee support on the guy's left knee. Bradshaw showed me the drowned guy's photo. Wow, this confirmed my recovering physical ability! The guy who had attacked me, someone I wanted another shot at had already been punished. He was found stone dead. How, if in any way, did this guy fit into the mystery of Wilber's death? That still confused me. Bradshaw said the guy's name was Eric Chin, but he wouldn't share other information. Maybe Linda would honor our new arrangement and tell me more.

Driving now I smiled and just took pride in the fact that my response to the guy's attack had caused him some pain before he died. Thornton read my mind laughed and said, "You're still a killing machine bud." I joined in Thornton's laughter as we drove down Huntington Place, turned right on Willow Wood and mingled into the sparse traffic flow headed across the Willow Wood Bridge. I cleared the intersection at Granby and traveled south on Granby past where Eric Chin had drowned, then past Lafayette Park and the Virginia Zoo. I veered right onto Monticello and saw another long line of coal cars moving slowly to the Lamberts Point docks. But this time I was safe headed to the Monticello underpass. After clearing the underpass I was forced to stop for a RED light on Monticello and 20th Street. And as I waited for the RED traffic light to change, I looked to the right at Doumar's Drive-in Restaurant. "This drive-in was a meeting place for me and all my high school buddies in the mid eighties." I said to Thornton, but he seemed disinterested. I could have told him that Norfolk has changed a lot since I was in high school when the city was still trying to come to grips with the heavy influence of the Navy at the end of the Viet Nam War. Bars, Tattoo Parlors, Street Girls and Sailors were everywhere and every sailor was looking to fall in love or get in trouble. How ironic was it that after all the negative thoughts we had about the navy I still volunteered-in, right after my own high school graduation. Thornton read my mind and offered, "Your reaction was probably to piss-off your father and get as far away from Norfolk as possible. I know I felt the same way about Annapolis and my dad."

I didn't know about Thornton's rebellions against his father, but I cut my nostalgia short, continued south driving past the SCOPE Arena on St. Paul's Street and as traffic flow started to increase I slowed my progress until I was able to turn right on Main Street now headed toward the NISCO downtown office building. I was running late but their building had Valet Parking and when I drove up the Attendant was waiting at the building entrance. He opened my door, allowing me out and as he handed me a ticket he said,

"The Valet Park's on the house, Sheriff Irons. Mr. Taylor and the 'super-model gals' are waiting up on the seventh floor, room 707. Great car, sir, but you've got a CHECK ENGINE light on, you better see your mechanic."

CHAPTER FORTY ONE

NISCO, DOWNTOWN NORFOLK

"STEPHEN IRONS"

"Sheriff Irons, I'm Betty Boles," the attractive receptionist said as I entered the NISCO office. Damn, I thought, Charles Taylor is no slouch when it comes to picking pretty personnel and I began to wonder if Wilber had ever been tempted... Of course I was thinking of Sally's earlier concern about an affair Wilber might have had with a flight attendant friend of hers and the surprises Linda had shared concerning some of my brother-in-law's personal and financial secrets.

"I'm Mr. Taylor's Administrative Assistant it's very nice to meet you, Sheriff Irons. I'm very sorry for your loss. Wilber was a wonderful person and a fine co-worker, a true loss to NISCO and to me personally." Previously I had only looked at Charles Taylor's professed regard for Wilber's work, but now here was a co-worker genuinely affected by Wilber's death. I mentally prepared my self for more of that type of response after I began my new job. I smiled and replied,

"Thank you for your kind thoughts and please call me Stephen. I'm sure I'll have plenty of time in the future to speak with you about Wilber and his work here." I offered in response to her kindness. I had only meant it as a casual reply, but Betty saw beyond my words and said,

"So, you're accepting Mr. Taylor's offer, I think that's great. Welcome Aboard, Stephen, Mr. Taylor will be so pleased." Betty shook my hand and smiled up at my slightly reddened face.

"Yes, thank you, but please let me tell Mr. Taylor," I stammered, thrown off guard by her quickness and my verbal slip.

"Certainly," Betty responded, then she marched to the large door, opened it and announced to the occupants, "Mr. Taylor, Margarete, Elizabeth, Sheriff Irons is here to see you." She turned and smiled again as I entered Charles Taylor's office.

Charles' seventh floor office overlooks Norfolk's Harbor and the USS Wisconsin, which could be seen through one of the two large windows that drew my attention. The office floor was hard wood and covered like his NIT office.

The furniture was minimal, a chrome and glass desk, where Charles now sat, plus three other chrome and canvas chairs, one empty and the remaining two presently occupied by two striking blondes, the Kroger twins. Charles, Margarete and Elizabeth all stood to greet me and my pulse began to race…

For the next 20 minutes it was hard to keep my eyes and mind focused on Charles Taylor and his response to my acceptance, because the excitement that my joining NISCO created for the Kroger twins. Margarete and Elizabeth both apologized for their earlier prank when they tricked me into believing I had only met Margarete during their orchestrated sequence of deception. I must admit, looking at and trying not to look at the ladies during the 20 minutes they were allowed to stay, was one of the most difficult tasks I've ever had. Sensing that the 'ladies' had intentionally chosen to NOT duplicate their hair styles; Margarete's was a free flowing 'pony tail' and Elizabeth had fashioned hers into a single French Braid. This differential styling made them easily distinguishable leading me to believe their apology was sincere. Now, trying hard to remember details from my earlier encounter with the twins, I had the feeling that they had also shown differing hair styles, probably as a hint to anyone not totally overwhelmed with their beauty. Of course, like meeting the NIT gate guard Fred, with his name tag boldly affixed to his shirt, I had missed all those clues.

After the ladies had congratulated me and promised to help with anything I might need in the future, they each shook my hand once again and departed the office with Thornton in trail. After their departure I was emotionally exhausted, but physically charged with the energy the twins had provided the conversation. Let me adjust my statement, the energy was provided by Margarete, Elizabeth had only smiled and looked at me intriguingly with her striking eyes. Margarete's eyes are also striking, but her energy level is so high I became more flabbergasted than intrigued by her presence. So I took some comfort by just looking and swimming in Elizabeth's eyes. These two gals were everything the US Navy had been training us to fight for. Getting us back on track, Charles said,

"You're a bit taken by Elizabeth, eh Stephen?" I had no answer, I just grinned. "Well she is the intriguing one," Charles continued using my own descriptive thoughts, "but they're both beautiful women. Don't let their beauty fool you, they're very bright and like most beautiful women they know how easily the male of our species can be distracted and manipulated. Trust me I've seen their manipulative talents quite often," Charles paused, watched for my reaction, then went on, "In retrospect Margarete did show some 'physical interest' in Wilber, you understand, flirting and excessive attention, but, I honestly felt it was not reciprocated. I believe Wilber's behavior showed he was a very loyal person, God rest his soul, and Margarete is not only striking…" Damn I was beginning to think Taylor was like Thornton, he could read my mind too. But, I finally surmised Charles was just another man that had also fantasized about the Kroger twins. He smiled at my obvious embarrassment and continued, "She's a bit overwhelming, like trying to take a small drink of water from a fully functioning fire hose," Charles laughed here at his analogy then went on,

"I'm certain, knowing Wilber as I did; he much preferred a quieter, more restrained woman, very much like my impression of Sally. And, please do give dear Sally my regards and my sympathies when you see her again…"

"Actually, Charles, if I may continue to call you Charles now that I'm your employee." Charles smiled and nodded, "I'm now living with my sister so I'll certainly give her your warm regards. I thought this arrangement would be the best for Sally since she's planning on returning to work in a month or so," I wanted to offer some of the information I'd learned from Detective Knowles. Thornton had finally returned and shook his head NO concerning my thought-out intention. He whispered,

"Rusty, that's family business. You should keep it to yourself until you and Sally have not discussed it. You've got to start thinking more about your little sister's feelings." I decided Thornton might be right and remained quiet as Charles responded to my news about living with Sally,

"I'm a little surprised Sally will continue to live in the house where Wilber died. Even though the circumstances of his death remain unresolved, I was sure she would be thinking about moving to a smaller place. Their home most likely has appreciated in value, along with all waterfront property in Norfolk, so a property sale could be easily accomplished," Charles seemed to be speculating, maybe sensing a financial opportunity for himself or some real-estate friend, then he rethought and refocused, "But, I've gotten us off track. How do you see your investigation shaping up?"

Charles' real estate comments, then his abrupt change of subject took me by surprise. Sally's moving was a possibility especially once she found out about Wilber's lack of honesty and his neglect to share information about his wife and son, Wilber Junior. That information was going to hit her hard. And, what about his involvement with a business I was certain Sally knew nothing about? Thornton sat down next to me now. He seemed interested in Charles Taylor, and he offered confidentially,

"No damn wonder the FBI suspects you Rusty, if Wilber wasn't already dead, you'd be strangling him yourself." I ignored Thornton and tried to be open but non specific in my answer to Charles Taylor,

"Sir, I have a general process in mind with detailed interviews to be scheduled with your self, the Kroger twins, James Carlson, Betty Boles and some of your dock-workers. After that I plan on following any direction those inquiries take me. I've tried to establish a cooperative effort with Detective Knowles…"

Charles immediately interrupted, "You've shared your employment status with this detective?"

"Yes, sir," I answered, thinking I was about to be fired, "There's no possibility our separate investigations won't cross paths, so, I thought it best to be up front with Detective Knowles. Does that concern you?"

"No, now that you've explained yourself, I'm sure your instincts are correct. I was responding as a typical businessman, worried about my company and trying to keep everything close to the vest, but please continue with your thoughts."

"We do have a 'sharing agreement' but I'm not so naive to think that Detective Knowles will openly share ALL. But some information that has already been provided through the FBI is very enlightening and may be crucial to the case," I watched Charles' expression change with my mention of the FBI and he said,

"The FBI's involved in the case? That points toward a Homicide, doesn't it?"

"Well, Detective Knowles told me Wilber's death HAS been declared a Homicide. The FBI is actually concerned with the possibility of some type of espionage or terrorism aspect to Wilber's death. Detective Knowles said the FBI entered the case in an advisory capacity only," Charles interrupted again,

"Espionage, there's no way Wilber would have been involved with that type of activity. But, I can see you were wise to have reached an agreement with Detective Knowles, do you know him very well?" At this point, Charles' intercom sounded, he held up a large open palm to stop my gender corrective response and picked up the phone,

"Yes," Charles answered, then listened for about 20 seconds and turned back to me, "Stephen, I've just received some important information I must respond to immediately. I may be in Richmond for a few days, please see Betty, she'll help you schedule meetings with our people. Give yourself a few days with that effort, and checking back with Detective Knowles, then, come back to me later in the week, possibly on Friday. Sorry to rush you off like this but I've got to make some calls." Charles rose looked straight into my eyes. With several inches of height advantage he took my hand between his two large palms as Betty reentered his office,

"Betty, please help Sheriff Irons set up some meetings over the next few days, then keep some time open for me, perhaps late Friday afternoon when I've returned from Richmond. Thank you."

Betty took my arm, nodded to Charles and led me and Thornton out of the room. I began to think about how Charles was focused on one thing then gets a call and runs off toward something new. He was actually speculating about the sale of Sally's house, then, concerned about Detective Knowles, then, a call and he's on the way to Richmond.

While Betty went through her schedule books Thornton whispered to me, "I'll bet Wilber looked at Taylor for one of his books, Rusty, he's like Os they're both pompous, unpredictable and manipulative as hell, must be their damn William and Mary background."

Thornton could be right, about Wilber and his books, Taylor's actions and schemes would be interesting to a reader, just what Wilber was looking for in a story, something startling to put on a jacket cover to make a person want to buy his book. Thornton smiled at my giving him some credit then he added,

"You forgot to tell Taylor 'Detective Knowles' is a good looking blonde gal, didn't you Stephen? She's just like the Kroger gals. Shame on you Rusty you still think you need some all-night police protection, don't you? You're still thinking about sleeping with a cop".

Thornton had made a great joke, but his timing was off. "Try that joke again when I'm not here." I offered without mirth.

Startled and confused by my comment to Thornton, Betty said, "Excuse me…"

CHAPTER FORTY TWO

NORFOLK CITY JAIL

Sergeant Bradshaw stopped by the Norfolk City Lock-up and talked with Deputy Belton about the Saturday morning Wilber Harrington was killed. Bradshaw felt like a little kid as Belton's six foot ten stature led his five six frame to see Bull, who was presently being held in the jail infirmary. Covered with extensive bandages and braces Bull was recovering from what Belton called 'an in-house disagreement'. When questioned, Bull explained in forced incoherent utterances that he and three other inmates had a difference of opinion that led to his present condition. He tried to smile as he offered,

"Yu shou' see tha ot'er gu's!" But his reply came out pained and garbled. Bull stuck to his story nodding affirms and negatives to Bradshaw's questions with forced and painful head gestures. Bull had seen a 'brother driving a UPS truck down the street called Huntington Place around 10 AM the Saturday morning Wilber Harrington was killed. He looked at Bradshaw's photo array through red, hemorrhaging eyes, but sadly moved his head from side to side indicating no recognition.

Bradshaw asked Bull about the possibility that Deputy Belton or Sheriff Os might know more about that morning? Bull got a startled look in his swollen eyes and shook his head NO. Bradshaw thanked Bull completed his notes and placed his small green notebook in his pocket. He took out one of his newly printed Norfolk Police Department, Homicide Division cards, gave it to Bull and asked him to call if he remembered anything else.

As he was leaving Bradshaw told Bull "You need to be more careful picking your friends", Bull offered as Bradshaw signaled the jailer for release,

"Wern... NO friens'...did this ta... me."

———————————

Sergeant Bradshaw traveled across town and entered the Medical Officer's building. He was excited, like a kid going to school on Valentine's Day, carrying a secret affection card hidden in his lunch box. He wanted to show Dr. Katherine Kowalski how he was beginning to feel about her but he was going to keep his card hidden until he was sure she could feel the same. The front desk was vacant, Dr. Kent Clark must be off today, Bradshaw thought as he ventured into Dr. Ski's examining area and she waved,

"Morris, come in, glad you could make it so soon. I've got some interesting info to share. And I was anxious to see you. How've you been?"

"I've been great, Kat, I missed you too, looking forward to Wednesday night at the Chrysler," Dr. Ski took his arm and turned him around,

"Let's go up stairs for coffee, Morris and I'll fill you in on my findings." Not the excited response Bradshaw was looking for, but he did enjoy Kat taking hold of his arm.

"Okay, I could use a little down time, Knowles has got me and Millers running all over Mermaid City."

Arriving at a small cantina, they pulled two chairs out at a small table and after Dr. Ski had gotten coffee and a large Danish pastry to share, Bradshaw continued proudly, "I got a positive ID from Stephen Irons on the guy that attacked him at the airport. He said, 'his attacker was your dead guy Chin'." Bradshaw waited, wanting some validation of his efforts and a return to Dr. Ski's earlier statement that she was anxious to see him again, but she went a different direction.

"Bad news first Morris, the city's sending me to Richmond on Wednesday and Thursday for a medical conference, how about we slip our date until the next Wednesday night, or maybe some other night would work?"

"Will you be back by Friday?" Bradshaw asked, seeing an opportunity slipping,

"Sure, the conference is over late Thursday, I'll return Friday morning."

"How about Friday night, we can go out to dinner somewhere, you know a nice restaurant in Norfolk?"

"Great, you pick the place and surprise me. You still have my address and home number, don't you?" Bradshaw smiled and nodded, yes. "Okay you can call and leave the time you'll be by for me on my recorder, will that work?"

"Sure, I'll find a super place, unless you want to offer a suggestion?"

"No, No I want you to surprise me," Dr. Ski replied, smiled and got down to business, "As for Chin, the interesting stuff I've found is from his work boots.

The boots have a heavy cleat type rubber sole that had some foreign matter stuck to the bottom of the sole, you know in and around the cleats,"

"It didn't wash off in the river?"

"No, he was a big guy, weighed 220# and had walked in this stuff for some time. The foreign matter got embedded, at least enough for me to make a cursory analysis."

"What kind of analysis?" Bradshaw asked and sat his coffee down and took out his small green notebook.

"It's animal fecal matter, and some urine, most likely from a hay-burner…"

"Whoa, Kat, I understand fecal matter and urine but I'm a city kid from Boston, what's a hay-burner?" Bradshaw asked.

"You know, Herbivore, a plant eater, any animal consuming vegetation: bushes, trees, grasses and hay, that kind of stuff. I first thought about a farm with horses, cows and pigs but there was some indication of different kinds of fruits, some digested bamboo and a lot of vegetables," Bradshaw started to laugh and interrupted,

"So, this guy Chin was working with animals that eat grass, hay, bamboo, vegetables and fruit? That's a weird animal maybe we should call the zoo." Morris continued to laugh at his own humorous response.

"You're right, Morris, we'll call the zoo they'll have a Veterinarian to help us."

"Eh, I was joking Kat, but okay, let's try them." Bradshaw stated, then he pulled out his cell phone and punched in 757-555-1212, then, he hit the SPEAKER ON button and placed the phone on the table as the call connected,

"Information, what city and state please?" The phone company recording asked,

"Norfolk, Virginia." Morris responded, then, after a few seconds,

"What listing please?" A live operator now requested,

"The Norfolk Zoo, the Veterinarian's office." A pause of 10 seconds, then the operator came back,

"The Virginia Zoological Park, 3500 Granby Street in Norfolk," the operator corrected Bradshaw, then, added, "Sorry, I don't show a separate listing for the Veterinarian's office, only the main number, 757-624-9937, I'll connect you now."

A pause again, then, two rings sounded as Morris jotted the number down, then,

"Virginia Zoo, this is Jean, how can I help you?" Bradshaw smiled, gave Kat a 'thumbs up' signal and spoke to the cell phone,

"Jean, this is Sergeant Bradshaw, Norfolk Police, please put me through to your Veterinarian,"

"Our vet's off today, Sergeant Bradshaw, he should be in tomorrow. Do you want to leave a message?"

"No, just let me speak to the zoo Director, please."

"Well sorry again, we're between directors right now, our old director just left and we're waiting for the new one to arrive permanently, probably another week or so,"

Jesus, Bradshaw thought they're giving me a run-around, "Okay, who's in charge of the animals while you're waiting?"

"That would be our Curator, just a minute, please." A ten second wait then, "Okay, I'll put you through to her now." The operator activated the connection and dialed an extension, there was a moment's pause then, a ring and the connection completed itself.

"This is Louise, how can I help you Sergeant Bradshaw?" Bradshaw explained their problem and the possibility that the zoo's veterinarian could help them figure out what animal their fecal and urine samples could be from. Louise told them the veterinarian was part-time but his Vet Tech was here today. She offered to call and have the Vet Tech meet them at the Animal Clinic Building and gave Morris directions. Bradshaw thanked Louis, hung up and asked Kat to go along for the visit to help with scientific questions. Dr. Ski agreed and they departed in Bradshaw's Crown Vic.

CHAPTER FORTY THREE

VIRGINIA ZOO

Sergeant Bradshaw was hopeful the zoo staff could help find the origin of the fecal matter Dr. Ski had discovered. He was also certain he was now pushing a boundary that his partner, Detective Sam Millers had talked about. Bradshaw turned right off Granby Street toward the zoo entrance and could see the Animal Clinic and Admin Building down another road to his left. He made the turn left toward the facility, went a hundred yards or so and parked the car opposite the two story building. As Bradshaw and Dr. Ski headed toward the building a young woman standing by the door wearing khaki shorts and a tan zoo shirt waved at them. The gal was almost Bradshaw's height, about 5'- 4" which seemed to relax all three of them,

"Hi, I'm Leah, the zoo's Vet Tech, how can I help you?" The young woman said.

Bradshaw shook hands and made the introductions as the three entered the building. Dr. Ski explained her findings and asked if Leah could help them narrow down what animal they might be dealing with. Dr. Ski showed Leah the four slides she had preserved and Leah set up her microscope to check it out.

"This could be our elephants or maybe the bongos, they're both in the same general area, but since there's fruit and bamboo that points to elephants. I can run a 'float' check for an elephant specific parasite called *Fasciola jacksoni*, to make sure. Do you have a larger sample?"

"No," Dr. Ski answered, "that's all I could recover. Is that a problem?"

"Maybe, it generally takes a large sample to expose the parasitic eggs, but I'll try with what you have here. It could take me a few minutes if you don't mind waiting."

"No, we can wait," Bradshaw replied then added, "But, since you mentioned elephants, you must have them here at the zoo, and, what's a bongo?"

"A Bongo is a large African antelope, and yes, we have three female elephants." Bradshaw removed the two photos from his brief case and told Leah how Chin was found drowned in the Lafayette River several days ago and that the fecal matter had been removed from his boots.

"Have you ever seen this guy, his name was Eric Chin?"

"No, I don't think he works at the zoo, but, we have a lot of volunteers that help as Education Docents, Keeper Aides and Horticulture Aides. But, if it is elephant fecal matter, he could have been a Keeper Aide for String Three. That's the group of animals that includes our elephants." Leah led Morris to the break room, picked up a large black notebook and continued, "We have a certification process before volunteers become Keeper Aides and we have a time-sheet for their volunteer hours in this book. We should have some documentation here." After looking and finding no paperwork on Eric Chin, Leah added, "Maybe the paperwork got misplaced, but one of our elephant keepers would know if this guy was a volunteer."

"Who's the keeper in charge of the elephants?" Bradshaw asked.

"That's Ursula Volk, she's called the 'Elephant Manager', but she's away for a few days. I'll call String Three and see who's still here today." Leah activated a hand held radio and said, "Leah calling String Three." Then all three heard,

"Leah, Dennis here, go ahead,"

After a few minutes of conversation Dennis agreed to meet in the Admin building in 15 minutes. Bradshaw stayed in the break room while Dr. Ski and Leah returned to the Vet Lab to begin the 'fecal float' process on the small sample Dr. Ski brought to the zoo.

The large break room was centered with several tables placed together to provide a conference type setting and Bradshaw began reading a paper on the table concerning the care of elephants. He started to read an article on 'Protective Confinement' for AZA elephants as Dr. Ski and a big guy in zoo clothing entered the room.

"Morris, Leah's still checking 'the float', but this is Dennis, he's one of the Elephant Keepers. Dennis this is Sergeant Bradshaw." Dr. Ski offered.

"Hi, how can I help you?" Dennis asked as they shook hands and Morris looked up at another tall guy as he pulled his photos from his briefcase,

"Do, you know this person?" Morris said, showing the two photos of Eric Chin to Dennis.

"Sure, that's Eric. He's a new Keeper Aide volunteer that Ursula's checking out. Actually, it's the second picture I recognize, I never saw him without the glasses. He's a big guy, taller than me and very strong. What happened, to him? He looks dead..."

"He is." Bradshaw replied then asked, "How long have you known Eric?"

"Well, a couple of weeks, I worked with him a few times here. How'd he die?"

"He drowned in the Lafayette River last Sunday. Just how many times have you seen him here at the zoo?"

"Three or four, once in this building when Ursula introduced him then a few more times when she was training him to work with us. The last time was Friday, I think... Ursula left, a few days ago, but she mentioned that Eric failed to show up to help her Sunday night. She said she would report his absence to the Volunteer Coordinator... Now I guess I know why he was a no-show."

"Where's Ursula Volk now?" Bradshaw asked,

"She's at an Elephant Sanctuary in Tennessee for some cross training. One of their staff members is a good friend of Ursula's. She's expected back Friday or Saturday... Do you want her to call you?"

"Yes, do you know anyone else that might have known Eric while he was volunteering here?"

"I can ask Jill and Jason, the other two keepers, but Ursula was supervising his check-out, I only know him because I happened to be here the day he started, then a few more times when he worked my scheduled time with Ursula."

"How long had Eric been working here?"

"Can't be over three or four weeks, I'm certain we have the records. Did you look in the Keeper Aide Book?" Dennis asked.

"We looked there, but there's nothing on Eric Chin."

"That's odd Ursula's a stickler for paper-work, but I'm sure she can answer these questions when she gets back." Dennis replied and Bradshaw gave Dennis his business card, a copy of Eric's photo and three extra cards for Ursula and the other two other elephant keepers.

On their way out Morris and Kat stopped by the Vet Lab and told Leah that Dennis had identified Eric Chin from the photos. Leah said,

"Well, you were lucky Sergeant, I'm still having problems with the 'float', there's not enough fecal matter make a positive on the parasite eggs."

"No matter Leah, Dennis knew the guy and it was your suggestion that got us started with the elephants, thanks, we're grateful." Morris offered as they departed the clinic.

CHAPTER FORTY FOUR

NORFOLK

"STEPHEN IRONS"

Sally and I had been to AW Shucks for dinner. I was anxious to discuss Wilber's secrets and share my new employment information. I figured one of her favorite sea food restaurants would be the perfect spot for full disclosure. We had two of their 'Specials'; Grouper with extra Succotash for Sally and Corn Chip Breaded Catfish with Beans and Rice for me. After we munched on fried calamari and toasted Wilber's memory with some Brown Estates' Zinfandel that the restaurant owner, John Boggs, served us, I told Sally about my new job. She seemed reluctant to understand my desire to work there until I explained how Charles Taylor believed Wilber's death was in some way related to NISCO. After John served the food we spent the next 40 minutes enjoying each others company and our meals.

After returning home, we're now in Sally's den sharing a small glass of Port. The warmth of the Port brought remembrances of sibling bonds, which led us to the unknown challenges ahead for both our futures.

"Sally, because Linda has been willing to share some of the information the FBI provided her investigation, I want to let you know a few things the FBI's concerned about, okay?"

"Sure, I want to know everything that's going on. Do they have a suspect?"

"Well, like any investigation, the early part looks at everything possible. Investigators use statistics from past crimes of a similar nature to determine the most likely type of suspects. They look at the financial background of the victim and they look for other motives and opportunities plus the physical ability or means of a suspect to commit the crime."

I watched closely as Sally listened, "Some of the information the FBI turned up examining Wilber's bank account and his Military records, led them to believe Wilber was financially strapped. He owed on several credit accounts and was involved in some business property investment I wasn't aware of,"

"What business property?" Sally interrupted.

"Wilber was in partnership with a guy in the antique business in Portsmouth.

Did you know about that? The FBI thinks you're part owner of the property."

"Oh, yeah, I remember now, the papers are in our safe-deposit box. Will wanted to help a friend from high school get a loan for his business but the friend had bad credit. We co-signed for the property loan. The guy's like a renter, you know he takes care of the property makes the mortgage, insurance and tax payments with his business income. Will brought the papers home for me to sign, Sorry, I'd forgotten about it. Has the business gone bad? Is that the financial problems you're talking about?" Sally asked.

"No, I don't think the business is in trouble, especially now, Wilber and this guy had life insurance on each other, I assume the business property will be paid off now. Were you on that life insurance policy too?" I ventured, working toward one of Wilber's secrets.

"No, I don't think so. Will just wanted the property covered so I wouldn't have a problem if something happened to him," Sally began tearing then she smiled through her tears and offered, "I guess Will was smart to make the guy buy the insurance."

"But, Sally, it's going to be your property now, unless you and Wilber had some other agreement with Donald Adams,"

"Donald Adams, oh my god, yes, that's the guy!" she exclaimed, "I knew I'd met the guy I saw at the memorial service. He said 'he read about Will's death in the paper and came to the service to pay his respects'."

"Did Adams say anything about the property?"

"No, we didn't speak any more at the service, but I remember Will wanted me to sign the property over to Adams if something ever happened. I'd forgotten about Adams' Antiques. Why is this so confusing to the Police?"

"Adams is a suspect now he had a motive to kill Wilber. Wilber's death paid his business property off," I said, but then it hit me, Wilber's death didn't pay off Adams' business property, it paid off Sally's property. "Sally, I'm wrong, Adams doesn't have a motive unless you've got a paper giving the property to him after Wilber's death. Or, maybe the Police think he's after both of you." Sally was visibly shaken, but she offered,

"I don't know of any paper about the property being turned over to Adams, it was just a hand-shake agreement by Will and Donald Adams. I wanted to tell Will not to do this, but, he said Adams was a close friend from Franklin that deserved to have his own business."

"I'm sure you're right Sally, but we've got to call this guy Adams, Linda told me the Police are going to see him next week, I'll call so we can try to go see him too,"

"When do you start at NISCO, Stephen?" Sally said.

"I actually started today, I've got some interviews scheduled and I'll meet with Taylor's admin assistant tomorrow, you might know her, Betty Boles?"

"I think I met her at a Nauticus party. She's short, real cute, looks and dresses like a 1930's flapper with short dark hair and big brown eyes?"

"Yes, that's her. I'll call her tomorrow for my schedule but we should stop by your bank and look at the Portsmouth property deed too."

"Good idea, I'm glad we had this talk, Stephen, we'll get it all straightened out tomorrow." Sally offered.

Thornton looked at me and said, "See that wasn't so hard was it Rusty? It's a good start, but, you haven't told her everything, have you?" Thornton was right, so I took Sally's small hands and said,

"Sorry, Sally, but there's a lot more you need to know..."

CHAPTER FORTY FIVE

RICHMOND TRAIN STATION

TUESDAY, 11PM

The gusty wind from the northeast brought a chilling downpour that had voided the station of warmth and travelers. The gusts were propelled by a northeast wind that spun the moisture into spherical coverings surrounding the globe shaped station lights and created an angelic halo atop each wrought iron column that stretched along the lengthy platform. The wind picked up and began to destroy the columns of halos and rattled trash containers throughout the small depot as a black limousine cut through the downpour and stopped directly under the one of the linear station lights. Several station workers rushed out from the depot pushing baggage trolleys and carrying rain-slickers for the three arriving guests as the limo driver and two additional workers hurried toward the car's opening trunk.

Brandy in hand, Morgan Folds watched from his private rail-car as Gerda Von Richter exited the limo directly under one of the flickering lights her long legs perfectly shaped and covered by what appeared to be a lengthy trench coat that surrounded her high-topped leather boots. Morgan's memories connected the beautiful vision to his own youthful past and momentarily he envied his youngest son's health and time-of-life. Morgan forced him self to recover and wanted to share the warmth of the returning memory, he called to Conrad Holmes,

"Conrad, come here, please," Morgan instructed as Conrad turned from preparations for their meeting, "you must see this vision. She will no doubt be beautiful entering the rail-car, but outside she is a goddess haloed by the street lights and clothed in the gossamer glitter of the swirling rain."

Conrad smiled at Morgan's poetic offerings, dismissed his meeting preparations and joined his boss at the depot facing window. As they both watched the approaching goddess Conrad's peripheral vision picked up Sonchi Zimchi and Gunter Wilhelms being assisted from the opposite side of the limo. As his attention refocused on Gerda he was immediately riveted by the beauty that refused proffered rain covers and walked briskly toward the rail car with trench coat flying open and oblivious to the swirling rain. "My God, Morgan, no wonder Gunter's besotted and speaks so glowingly of her, she's a bleeding masterpiece, look at that body, those smashing legs and all that hair, I'm definitely hearing 'Lara's Theme' in my fantasy."

"Yes, a very appropriate analogy Conrad, this should be interesting, don't you think? The three hour drive from DC with Gerda, must have set Sonchi's pacemaker on 'ALERT' several times." Morgan joked,

"Sonchi will definitely need a drink and a quick lie-down," Conrad responded laughingly as he moved toward the door to assist the arrival of their newest partner.

Thirty minutes later the warming affect of the private car's small fireplace had all but removed the chill of the storm as it cast an amber luminescence over the dark stained Philippine mahogany appointments evident throughout the private car. Soft leather furniture added to the welcomed comfort now enjoyed by the weary travelers and after Morgan's welcoming presentation and his excitement informing them of their prospective visit to one of the most famous sites in Virginia, The Monticello Home of Thomas Jefferson, near Charlottesville, Virginia, Conrad began the 'Power-Point' presentation as Morgan's narrative highlighted the many beautiful structures and prominent architecture that had been the center of American Culture over two hundred years ago.

After the Monticello presentation a new excitement took over the gathering, the excitement of Gerda Von Richter on center stage for the first Executive meeting of 'BUCK'. Gerda, minus outer adornments, began her presentation wearing a dark blue silk skirt and blouse, with double stranded Pearls. The blouse highlighted her deep blue eyes and the shortened skirt showcased her star quality legs. Intentionally she twisted her pearls, smiled and began,

"Thank you for the warm welcome. Gentlemen my presentation is quite short for I am pleased to announce I have completed the engraving and testing of the first set of twenty pound notes. I chose the Isle of Man currency for I believe it to be the most difficult note to duplicate. Intricacies of the Queen's crownless portrait, on the 'show side' of the note, and the obscured watermarks and features of Douglas Bay on the 'off side'," Gerda paused here and removed from a large storage tube the uncut sheet of 100 twenty pound notes, handing the sheet to Morgan who began to check them out with a jeweler's loop before passing the loop and the sheet to the remainder of the group. She then used her long supple fingers to remove what appeared to be a hand full of circulated 20 pound notes and passed them around saying,

"The large uncut sheet contains the authentic notes gained through Conrad's sources in England," Gerda paused and applauded Conrad who bowed with his recognition. "The individual twenty pound notes being circulated are my submissions and are printed on the paper supplied by our friend, benefactor and most gracious host, Mr. Morgan Folds and his resources in the great state of Virginia. As I hope you will agree the results are fantastic and will be improved with better ink."

After that the remainder of the corporation reported on their efforts and progress: Conrad spoke of the continuing development of the security arrangements for China the US and Africa and volunteered aid for South America, if needed. Morgan, still overwhelmed by the presented notes, talked of purchasing the mentioned inks in Tennessee and procurement of the printing site, a large warehouse in Fredericksburg, Virginia. Then he concluded with the arrangement for domestic and international transportation of all supplies needed to put the project into full operation.

Gunter spoke of 72 affirmed purchasers, at five million US dollars each, already secured, and his optimism for securing the remaining 28 for a total investment reward of 500 million US dollars. Gunter then diagramed the distribution routes from product receipt in Mombassa, Kenya, spreading out like the un-leafed branches of a wintering Acacia tree, reaching upward through all of Africa and into the lower continent of Europe and beyond.

Finally, Sonchi assured the group of the paper acquisition and the shipment of their final product from Fredericksburg, Virginia to Mombassa for Gunter's distribution tree. Sonchi mentioned the use of a local US shipping agent, Norfolk International Shipping Company, and that their CEO was unaware of 'BUCK' and would remain that way with no impact against the $500,000,000 the group was scheduled to divide. Sonchi asked for questions or comments and Gerda stood,

"My dear friends, after the exciting presentation and the detailed security proposals by Conrad, I fear my preparations for Brazil's security could prove inadequate, if at all possible I request Conrad to extend his security umbrella to cover my operation" Morgan stood and said,

"An interesting request, I feel Sonchi's security preparations in China are also further complicated by the approaching Olympic endeavors for 2008, but I'm confident that Conrad and I are well prepared to assist in that effort. Conrad is also confidant concerning Gunter prep work for Africa and our preparations for America, so the extension of security efforts to include Brazil is certainly possible." Morgan paused only long enough to envy Conrad's opportunities, then he added, "Gerda, please consider your request approved, Conrad will make the adjustments and arrangements to accommodate your needs." Conrad smiled fantasizing his accommodation of Gerda's needs and quickly nodded his agreement.

Morgan approached Sonchi alone while the others shared their congratulations, and offered, "Sonchi, I'm pleased, but I remain concerned about our transportation aspects and control over the manufacturing operation in Fredericksburg, I believe they are the most vulnerable portion of BUCK. I think this is where NISCO and Charles Taylor will assist our effort. As you have mentioned many times before; 'The teachings of Tai Chi offer that a significant move in your chosen direction is oft best begun by a subtle move in the opposite direction'; So, I believe this required diversionary move can be the assistance gained from Mr. Charles Taylor and NISCO, most likely involving our extensive research into laboratory produced diamonds… But that is yet to be determined.

"Are you certain we have control over Charles Taylor?" Sonchi asked

"Yes I believe so and you'll see also. After our other two guests depart, I want you and Conrad to remain one extra day. Charles Taylor will arrive soon because he seeks my information and support to achieve his greatest desire, unrivaled business success and unlimited riches. Charles will be here for a day or two then Conrad can travel back to Norfolk with him to prepare for our diversion. So, in two days you'll know for yourself just how much control we have over Mr. Charles Taylor."

CHAPTER FORTY SIX

VIRGINIA RT. 58W, TUESDAY, 11AM

Detective Linda Knowles rode in the 'shotgun seat' while Special Agent Davis drove the Ford Expedition he requisitioned from the FBI's local Motor Pool. After they passed by the City of Suffolk, along Route 58 West, larger patches of standing water began to appear along the highway. The backwater flooding of several nearby rivers was continuing to make its presence known throughout the area. Similar to the aftermath flooding from Hurricane Floyd, in 1999, excessive water was pooled everywhere. Linda remained skeptical about this visit and said, "I think we could be overreacting, I would have preferred to interview Lydia Harrington at the Ops Center,"

Clayton cut her off, "We need this interview now, Linda. We've let it slide too long."

"That's bull, Clayton, we're not going to learn much from Lydia Harrington she'll just confirm what we already know. She was continuing to take money from Harrington at $1,000 per month for alimony and child support until he shut it off a couple months ago,"

"You don't believe there's motive there? Harrington also had an insurance policy for her kid for $100,000." Clayton immediately responded,

"Well, it's possible, but that money's intended for a college education for junior, I'm not sure you can deduce motive from that."

"You've talked to the insurance company, you know there's no legal restriction on the money, it'll go to Wilber Jr., or his mother, not to a college. She could have known that."

"But, that would put the motive on junior, he's past 21, he'll receive the money, his mother can't intercede, he's not a minor in the eyes of a Virginia Court."

"That's why we have to talk to them both. Lydia Harrington said she would have Wilber Junior there today, so the trips definitely worth the effort."

They both kept silent for a few miles, then, Linda gave up on nagging, and asked, "Do you have FBI weapons in this vehicle, Clayton?"

"I don't think so, it's a Motor Pool issue, but I'm not certain."

"Great, some Special Agent, you are." Linda joked, "Do you even have a personal weapon, other than you're disarming looks and obsequious charm?"

Clayton smiled finally Linda was relaxing enough to joke with him. "I carry a GLOCK 17, Linda, like your back-up weapon."

Linda was impressed that he knew what type weapon she used in reserve, but she wasn't caving in, yet. "My back-up's a GLOCK 26 Clayton. What do you shoot with your nine-mil?"

"I score 900 at 15 yards, but I shoot 1000 at 1 yard." Clayton replied with a sly smile creeping onto the corner of his mouth.

"Damn, Clayton, I shoot 1000 at 15 yards, and NO PERP will ever get within 1 yard of MY weapon." Linda said, trying to suppress her laughter.

After exiting 58W and 15 minutes of travel through parts of 'Flooded Franklin' they arrived at Lydia Harrington's home. The house was a medium sized clapboard and brick Victorian Cottage with an expansive front porch featuring several large white columns leading up from the wood flooring to a wealth of gingerbread scrolling under its peaked roof system. Linda noted the 1985 Ford Mustang and a 2002 Dodge Caravan parked in the driveway, and she assumed both the ex wife and her son must be home. Linda offered,

"I guess you were right to encourage this interview, but let me lead the discussion, I'll call on you if I need to." Linda stated as she rang the door bell.

"No problem." Clayton answered as he straightened his tie and adjusted his blonde hair, by remembered feel.

"Good morning'," Lydia Harrington said as she opened the door. "I'm Lydia Harrington, you must be Detective Knowles."

"Yes, and this is Special Agent Davis of the FBI, thank you for seeing us on such short notice, may we come in?"

"Of course," Lydia stated as she shook Clayton's hand and looked him over. Obviously pleased she eased back from the doorway and allowed them to enter. Lydia Harrington was of medium height, about 5'- 6" and 120 pounds. She had the look of rural America, with long, dark brown hair, wide-set eyes and sun-dried, deeply tanned skin. She appeared to be in her mid to late forties. A bright sparkle entered Lydia's eyes as Clayton shook her hand.

"Can I get you-all some coffee? I got a new pot brewing." Lydia announced.

Linda indicated no, but Clayton replied, "Yes, that would be wonderful, thank you so much, Mrs. Harrington."

"Please, call me Lydia, I'll just get the coffee for you and me, then," Lydia said, "I could use another cup myself. Allen is here and I'll call him when you're ready." She departed through the dinning room toward the open kitchen in the back of the house.

"Who's Allen?" Clayton whispered to Linda.

"I am," A tall young man said as he entered the living room from the hallway. Allen appeared to be only nineteen or twenty slightly younger looking than his actual age of 21. He was 6-2, lanky, dressed in jeans and a Norfolk Tides sweatshirt. "I'm, Wilber Allen Harrington Jr., I prefer Allen." He stated as Lydia Harrington reentered the room,

"Oh, Allen you're here, did you meet everyone?"

"Yes mom, I met your guests."

"We're so sorry about your loss," Linda began as Lydia served coffee to Clayton and asked Allen if he wanted anything. When Allen shook his head, no, Lydia sat down across the coffee table from Clayton and Linda noted Lydia had taken the opportunity to redo her hair while she was in the kitchen. Her long brown hair was now tied back in a silk scarf that looked to be a Hermes'. She had put on lipstick applied facial moisturizer and added a pale eye shadow, now appearing ten years younger to Linda.

"Thank you for your kindness," Lydia began, "we remained fairly close to Wilber over the years, he was continuing to help with Allen's education and we often talked of old memories together." Lydia provided but Allen stayed quiet and distant.

"How long were you married to Commander Harrington?" Linda asked.

"A little over two years, we were married in June, 1983 at the Naval Academy Chapel. It was a beautiful ceremony, with an arch of swords," Lydia's eyes glazed with the memory, then, she regained reality and continued, "Allen was born in July, 1985 just after Wilber was qualified to go on extended submarine duty so we didn't see much of each other after that. The continuing separations were stressful so we decided to split up and I moved here to Franklin in 1986, and Wilber continued to help us until Allen turned 21 this year,"

"Allen, did you see much of your father when he returned to Norfolk?" Linda asked shifting the conversation focus,

"Not too much, he came by several times, real surprised at my growth. Of course he hadn't seen me for almost 20 years, but you know he was pretty short..." Allen offered, and Lydia quickly interrupted and added,

"Allen takes after my dad, god rest his soul. He was 6' 3" and a basketball star for Franklin High in the 60's, he got a basketball scholarship to Old Dominion, but couldn't go, he had to stay and work at the paper mill,"

"My granddad was great," Allen interjected, "he taught me how to play basketball. I tried out in High School, but I wasn't quite good enough, or tall enough really, I'm only 6' 1" and a half". Allen offered, looking up at Clayton's 6'3" height for some understanding. His comments about his grandfather were his first sign of genuine respect for someone, Linda Knowles thought, so she asked,

"When your father did return to Norfolk, Allen, did you do any sports or other activities with him?"

"He took me to a few baseball games at Harbor Park, bought me this sweatshirt, but not much else. He only saw me when his new wife was away on a trip... I did see her at the memorial service, but I've never really met her. Pretty poor of him, I thought, not wanting his own son to know his new step mother. I did call to talk to her once, but he answered, so I just hung up."

"Allen, I didn't know you did that, but I told you your father wasn't really family-orientated, it's the main reason we divorced. I'm the oldest, from a big family but Wilber was an only child, quite a difference in upbringing wouldn't you think?" Lydia offered. Linda remained quiet, but Clayton nodded, smiled and said,

"But as you said, Commander Harrington did provide for Allen's education and care, a thousand dollars a month for 21 years is a sizable sum, don't you think?" Lydia's face darkened and the immediate look on Allen's face was total surprise. Lydia Harrington responded quickly,

"He was buying us off to ease his own conscience. It's not cheap to raise a child... I've had problems working, and we needed the money,"

Responding before his mom finished talking, Allen got up, looked quickly toward his own room as he announced, "Excuse me, I've got to go." and he left the room headed back toward his own bed room. Clayton got up and followed. Lydia stood, started to protest then resigned her self with this new turn of events.

"Do you think Allen's upset learning the extent of his father's financial involvement?" Linda said.

"Allen knew Wilber was providing money, he just didn't know how much. He's only 21 he doesn't have a clue how expensive it is to raise a family."

"Does he want to go to college?"

"Not sure, he works at the YMCA. He's a lifeguard and basketball coach." Lydia offered and Allen remained out of sight. Linda could no longer see Clayton down the hallway so she assumed he had followed Allen into his room.

"You don't know about the insurance policy Wilber took out for Allen's college education, do you?" Linda asked.

"What, Wilber had a policy for us?"

"No, actually the policy's for Allen, he's the beneficiary. The wording suggests it's for a college education, but that's not legally binding, it will go to Allen and he can decide what to do with the money. Hopefully you can help influence that decision."

"How much money is the policy for?" Lydia asked skeptical of this new information.

"The policy's for $100,000." Linda answered and watched as Lydia began to go a little slack-jawed and Allen ran back into the living room,

"Mom, did you hear? My dad left me $100,000! God, I can't believe it, that's super, I can quit that damn job at the Y. This is great!"

"Yes Allen, Detective Knowles just told me, it's wonderful for your future. We'll have to put in the bank. Your father wanted it used for college…"

Lydia began, but Allen interrupted her, "Yeah, the FBI guy told me, but he said college wasn't legally required AND he said the money's tax free! I can get a new car! I guess my dad wasn't the total asshole I thought he was." Allen finalized and headed back to his room.

"Kids," Lydia said, "they've got no concept of money, only about the things money can buy them right this minute. It's one of the reasons I never told Allen what his father was providing our family, he wouldn't have understood." Linda got up from her chair,

"I'm sure the insurance company will contact you, but here's their name and phone number. There was some concern when it was first believed Wilber might have taken his own life, but his death has been ruled a Homicide. Do you know of anyone who might have wanted to profit from Wilber's death? Perhaps his business partner, Donald Adams, do you know him?" Linda asked as Clayton returned.

"Good God, my brother, Donnie? Why would he want Wilber dead? Wilber was helping him with his antique business." Lydia answered truly confused and upset by all the morning's disclosures.

"Did Wilber have a policy for Donnie too?"

"There was a business property policy on both Wilber and Donald's lives," Linda replied as both she and Clayton hid their surprise at finding out Donald Adams was Lydia Harrington's brother.

"How much is that policy?" Lydia asked showing more frustration at this news.

"I'm not authorized to answer that, but it's scaled to pay off the loan on the property. Our understanding is that Wilber was not paying for this policy, your brother was. Do you think Wilber and Donald got along okay?"

"Yes, Of course, Donnie was just happy Wilber was willing to help him get a bank loan, you don't believe my brother had anything to do with Wilber's death do you?"

"We're not sure what to believe but we're going to talk to your brother on our way back to Norfolk. The insurance proceeds are legally restricted to paying off the mortgage on the property, which is now owned by Wilber's wife Sally,"

Lydia interrupted, "Sally, that airhead, she's not involved with the business."

"Actually she is as far as the property is concerned. Sally signed the papers too, she and Wilber co-owned the property," Linda assumed Lydia had referred to Sally as an 'airhead' because she works for American Airlines as a Flight Attendant, but she withheld further comment as she and Clayton headed for the door and Lydia Harrington offered,

"You two messengers brought a worse plague than the damn flood!" She said as she closed the door behind Linda and Clayton's departure.

CHAPTER FORTY SEVEN

ADAMS' ANTIQUES, PORTSMOUTH, VA

Donald Adams worked over a large tank of wood-stripper solution, the fumes were noxious, but several large fans operating in his shop, carried the eye-burning vapor toward a large open doorway. Things were looking up for Donald, he was sorry about Wilber's death, but grateful Wilber had insisted on the life insurance policy. Donald had struggled with the $100 per month it cost but that was not a problem now. His only problem was he had no idea what Sally would decide to do now that the property would be paid off and she alone would own it outright. Wilber said Sally had agreed to turn the property over to him if something ever happened and Donald had wanted to talk to Sally about the agreement after Wilber's Memorial Service, but he hadn't had the heart at that time. Donald made up his mind to think positive now. Things would be alright, Sally would live-up to Wilber's verbal agreement and it would all work out.

Donald decided to take a break and go outside for a few minutes and breathe some fresh air. As he removed the heavy rubber gloves that protected him from the acidic stripper solvent, the phone rang. He checked the ID read out, it was his sister's number. He touched SPEAKER ON, then said, "Adams' Antiques, is that you Lydia?"

"No, Uncle Donnie, it's Allen." Came the speakers reply,

"Allen, hi, where's your mom?"

"She's gone to see her lawyer, she's really upset. Guess what Uncle Donnie? I'm rich!" Allen screamed through the phone line. Donald was fairly certain why Lydia would be upset and his nephew was elated.

"You're talking about the life insurance your dad took out for your education, right?"

"Yeah, but the FBI guy said I don't have to use it for school and he should know he's the FBI." Shit Donald thought, what's he talking about, FBI? He ended the thought as he watched a black Ford Expedition pull into his parking lot.

"I've got to go Allen, we'll talk later. The police and your FBI guy are here now. Say hello to your mom and have her call me, okay?"

"Sure, Uncle Donnie, see ya." Allen finalized.

Donald disconnected his phone and picked up a towel to wipe his hands as the two officers approached. "Hello, I'm Donald Adams, are you Detective Knowles?"

"Yes, and this is Special Agent Davis of the FBI." Linda offered as she shook hands with Adams.

"Hi, what can I do for you?" Donald then quickly added, "My nephew, Allen, just called, said you made his day. You told him about Wilber's life insurance, didn't you?"

"You also have a life insurance windfall, don't you?" Clayton said, interrupting Linda's response.

"Is that why you're here? Am I a suspect in Wilber's death?" Adams asked.

"You're certainly a 'person of interest'. Where were you Saturday, September 23rd? What kind of work do you do here?" Clayton asked rapidly jerking Donald's attention toward him as Linda turned to look inside the building.

Linda walked in the large open door and heard the large fans running. She immediately smelled the noxious odor coming from the stripper-tank and turned back to ask about the tank, but saw Clayton still pressing Donald Adams, forcing him back against one of the large doors to his shop. Linda turned away and took a handkerchief from her jacket pocket, covered her nose and mouth and began to wander through the large building.

The shop was separated into two sections with the first area where the stripper tank was located, seemingly devoted to repairing and refinishing antiques. As she ventured further into the building the odors were diminished and she could once again breathe normally. She made her way past the lathes, table saws, band saws, belt sanders and gluing stations. Broken and in-need-of-repair pieces were evident everywhere including a large maple armoire positioned in the middle of the aisle where she was traveling.

Moving into the second portion of the building, Linda saw antiques positioned together in an attempt to section off various chairs, dressers, beds, dinning room tables, side pieces, living room furniture, kitchen furniture, wicker of all sorts and one small section with a large pile of assorted old carpets. Linda shook her head at the large number of the pieces stored in the building as she passed a small office area with a large desk piled with invoices, catalogs and antique brochures.

To the right of the desk area she saw a small bathroom with several rifles stacked against one of the bathroom walls. Linda braved the dinginess of the bathroom to take a better look at the capability of the weapons but discarded her thoughts of concern as she noted the weapons were all in need of significant repairs to make them usable.

Turning back toward the doorway she noticed a copy of the life insurance policy covering both Donald Adams and Wilber Harrington lying on Adams' desk. She pushed the small office door open from the inside and walked toward Adams and Davis, still in a heated conversation. As she got closer she could see Davis poking his long index finger into Adams' chest and she heard,

"Look, I want to help you, Agent Davis, but Wilber wasn't just my friend, he was my brother-in-law, the father of my sister's only child. He did nothing but try to help me with my business. There's no way I would ever harm Wilber, even if I was anxious to have his business property paid off,"

"So you say, Adams, but you've dealt with the authorities before and you know how we operate. We cast a wide net at first and you're one of the squirmy fish caught up in that cast." Clayton explained as he prepared to poke Adams again. "Stop evading my question and tell me where you were on the morning of Saturday, the 23rd of September."

"I'm not evading your question, and stop pushing me around," Adams demanded, looking toward Linda for some help. "I'm just insulted by your accusations. I was disruptive a long time ago but since then I've kept my nose clean!" Adams turned toward Linda and added, "Detective Knowles, I was at an antique auction in Asheville, North Carolina, about 4 hours southwest of here, on Saturday, September 23rd."

"Who can verify that?" Linda asked calmly now entering the discussion.

"Several dealers from this area were at the show, most of us went the night before. We stayed overnight in a Motel 6, so we could be there early." Linda walked closer as Adams answered and she abruptly changed the subject,

"Did you get that large maple armoire at the auction?"

Adams became confused, thought a moment, then relaxed a bit and shifted his mind to business, "No, no I bought that locally from a military customer leaving the area. Why? Are you interested in it? It needs some repair work, but I can make you a great deal…"

"Give me your business card, when I call, have the names and numbers of two dealers we can check with about your trip to Asheville." Adams nodded and handed Linda a card. Linda saw Adams relax a little and quickly added, "Do you have a hand gun in your shop?"

"Yeah, an old Colt 45, it was my dad's gun..."

"Do you have a permit?" Clayton demanded.

"No, I don't need a permit for my dad's old gun," Clayton was close to Adams reaching out to physically take his arm, but Linda moved to stop Clayton and instructed,

"Never mind Clayton," She shook Adams' hand and said to him, "I'll call you about the armoire and the dealers, Mr. Adams, thanks for your help."

Driving away after trying to calm himself Clayton asked, "Why'd you close that interview? He doesn't have a permit for the 45, we could have hassled him some more, put him under some more pressure,"

"Wake up Clayton, this is the state of Virginia, you're in the 'WILD, WILD EAST' now, Virginia's an Open-Carry state, anyone 18 or older, who can legally own a gun, can carry their weapon in public holstered and visible. Adams doesn't need a permit to own it."

CHAPTER FORTY EIGHT

NORFOLK INDUSTRIAL PARK, 2:40PM

Detective Sam Millers sat in his car in the parking lot of the Norfolk UPS facility. He was early for this meeting and decided to take a short break. As he lowered the driver's window and reached for his briefcase cumulous clouds drifted in front of the sun and the cooling effect gave him pause to review his notes from yesterday's visit to Regent University and this morning's interview with Richard Milligan, a Virginia Zoo Education Docent that had known Wilber Harrington. Millers' written notes were cryptic, but they brought back the limited information he learned from Mr. Jeffery Cullen at Regent University. Millers had asked Cullen several questions concerning his boss, Pat Robertson's, involvement with FEMA, his publicized call for the assassination of President Hugo Chavez of Venezuela, his purported relationship with the Dictator of Liberia. When asked about the allegations of fraud voiced by two of Robertson's former 'Operation Blessing' pilots, Cullen had stated,

"Mr. Robertson and Mr. Robertson alone can comment on those subjects."

Millers had thanked Cullen and departed certain that Pat Robertson wasn't going to be helpful to the investigation. Millers shook his head with frustration and took out a second notebook, this one on Richard Milligan. Millers retrieved his tape recorder, touched REWIND to insure full interview coverage, then, he hit PLAY,

"Richard, thank you for meeting me, do you mind if I record this conversation?"

Millers heard himself ask, then,

"No it's okay detective, do you mind if I do the same?"

"Well it's not normal procedure for the interviewee to record the Police interview, but, I, have no real objections. Why do YOU want a record of this interview?"

"In 1998, two former pilots for 'Operation Blessing' were asked about their allegations that the tax-exempt cargo plane was being used illegally by Pat Robertson. Both stated that 'the plane was also being used for coordination and support of Robertson's diamond-mining operations during the plane's charitable efforts'. Later there was a lot of conjecture that went well beyond the real questions and answers during the interview, so I'd like to be protected when I talk about MY time working for 'Operation Blessing'."

"This interview's more about Wilber Harrington, Richard, but I understand."

"Thanks, detective, okay, how can I help you?"

"I'm investigating Wilber Harrington's murder and I think you knew about a book he wanted to write, called 'The Devil on Angel Flight', is that so?"

"Yes, two years ago I met Wilber and his wife Sally when they started training to be Education Docents at the Virginia Zoo. Wilber and I became friends. He talked about the Navy and I told him about being a commercial pilot. He asked a lot of questions about that."

"Okay, did Harrington share a lot about his Navy career?"

"Not so much, he was secretive about that aspect of his life, but he did say he'd just retired and had a new job with NISCO. He also told me 'he met his wife Sally in San Diego when he was stationed there', but he didn't share anymore."

"Did you know Sally was his second wife?"

"No, but I knew Wilber was a lot older than Sally, is that a factor in your case?"

"We don't know yet, but we're finding out, as you said, Harrington was secretive about a lot of things. How did your discussions get on the subject of his writing a book?"

"Well, answering Wilber's questions let him know a lot about my being a pilot for 'Operation Blessing' and he told me he wanted to write a book about criminals transporting human organs harvested and bought cheaply in foreign countries, then brought in illegally to the United States under the cover of some humanitarian effort. He said he was thinking about the criminals being associated with the UN, the Red Cross, or some other big charitable organization during their international travel..."

"Was that how he came up with 'The Devil on Angel Flight' as a title?"

"No, no, that was his proposed title for a non-fiction expose' about Pat Robertson and Regent University. Wilber told me 'a non-fiction expose about a local personality might sell more books than a fictional account of international organ smuggling'."

"Harrington was all about selling books, wasn't he?"

"He had problems with his first book. It only sold 400 copies so I guess he had to focus more on writing books that would sell. That made sense to me."

"Did he ever mention any other book he was working on?"

"Not really, Wilber was secretive about a lot of things. I asked him later-on if he was still pursuing 'The Devil on Angel Flight' but he seemed taken-back by my question. He said he'd placed that book idea on hold, and a new, hotter topic, had taken my interest... We didn't have a chance to talk more because Wilber and Sally were getting ready to take 'Apollo' out for show.

They had their hands full."

"Who's Apollo?"

"One of the zoo's llamas, he's an Education animal we like to show-off."

"Okay, thanks. Do you think anything in the Devil book, or the other book he was focused on, could have gotten him killed?"

"I have no idea what his other book was about, but I know a lot more about Pat Robertson than Wilber did and no one's threatened me..."

Millers shut the tape OFF, remembering that he had done the same just before he thanked Richard and departed their meeting for the interview here at UPS.

CHAPTER FORTY NINE

NORFOLK UPS FACILITY, 3:15PM

As Detective Sam Millers closed his notes, his cell phone rang; Knowles was calling on her way back to Operations. Their staff meeting was still scheduled for 4:30 and Sam told her he should finish up with UPS and make it back on time. Millers closed the phone call with Knowles, exited his car and entered the UPS building and spoke to the receptionist,

"Good afternoon, I'm Detective Millers please let Mr. Williams know I'm here to see him." Sam said as Williams entered the room,

"Hi, I'm Williams," the young man said as he wiped his right hand on the side of his khaki shorts and shook hands with Millers.

"Thanks for meeting with me. I'm Detective Sam Millers, Norfolk PD. I'm here to check your delivery truck traffic for Saturday, 23 September in the Lakewood area."

"Okay, Sam, I'm Billy, we've got to go to the records center area to check on that."

"I'm interested in a van that might have been in Lakewood that Saturday morning, around 11 AM. That area was the scene of a Homicide we're investigating."

Looking in the book Williams said, "We normally deliver late in the afternoon there, but I don't show any deliveries to the Lakewood around 11 on that Saturday. Do you have a tracking number?"

"No, there was a fire that probably destroyed the envelope, how about your drivers, would it be worth the effort to interview them about that day?"

"Well, that'll be a big effort, why don't you tell me what you really looking for?"

"Okay, three kids, practicing soccer in Lakewood Park saw a UPS truck come out of the area where a small fire was observed in one of the homes. When the fire department responded they found a man shot to death. Is it possible someone could take one of your trucks and use it for a period of time without you knowing it?"

"It's possible, but unlikely. Our drivers are with their trucks all day, if they stop somewhere to eat, they lock it up. Could someone have used a van with a UPS logo?"

"Yeah, we thought of that, but the kids said it was a 'real UPS truck'. Maybe the guy stole one of your trucks, even one of your uniforms. Do you have an old shirt I could take to check against some fibers we found under our victim's fingernails? The 'PERP' could have used one of your trucks and a uniform then just dumped them both somewhere. Do you have records on trucks that get stolen?"

"Yes, but it doesn't happen much. I can get you a shirt too, khaki like mine?" Sam nodded and Williams replaced the scheduling book, then he got a khaki UPS shirt and the incident sheet. He handed Sam the shirt and began to go through the sheet for the week of 18 to 25 September. "There was nothing taken during the week before your date, oh, wait a minute, one of our repair facilities noted the absence of a vehicle that day, but the entry adds that it was out on a test run after some repair work. Could that be it?"

"Possibly, could you give me the address and a contact name at the repair facility?"

"Sure, glad to do it. Let me know if the shirt and van info help." Williams pulled off a blank routing slip and wrote the repair facility information down and Millers departed. It was 4PM, if he hurried he could make the meeting, he'd call the repair facility during his drive back.

CHAPTER FIFTY

NORFOLK POLICE OPERATIONS

Detective Linda Knowles moved around the small conference room preparing for her 4:30 meeting. Millers and Bradshaw promised to be here on time and Davis was returning the Ford Expedition to the FBI Motor Pool. Linda looked at her notes and prepared to construct a matrix on a large chalk-board to guide their discussion. She'd fill the left hand side of the board with people of interest that tied Wilber Harrington and Eric Chin's deaths together. She suspected Chin killed Harrington but believed a broader conspiracy existed. A matrix, listing of known and unknown relationships, could give her a start...   Down the left hand side of her board Linda listed the people of interest:

Wilber Harrington

Sally Harrington

Stephen Irons

Donald Adams

Lydia Harrington

Allen Harrington

Charles Taylor

Pat Robertson

Eric Chin

On the right she listed Harrington's book projects and several local organizations:

Pacific Secret

Honorable Service

Devil/Angel Flight

Adams' Antiques

Virginia Zoo

MacArthur Museum

NISCO

Regent U

UPS

Next, in the middle of the board, she placed subjects to connect everything. Connections would help determine motives, opportunities and people that had means or ability to accomplish the killing.

Wilber Harrington's Life Insurance Policies:

$500,000 – Sally Harrington

$90,000 – Sally Harrington (NISCO)

$250,000 – Adams' Antiques

$100,000 – Allen Harrington

Eric Chin – San Diego Police concerns:

Possible foreign connection (China)

Assault, Burglary & Manslaughter suspicions

Wilber Harrington's Secrets

Child from 1st marriage with Lydia Harrington

Alimony/Child Support of $1000/month for 21 years

D. Adams & Lydia Harrington, siblings

Just as Linda finished writing Adams and Lydia Harrington's relationship the conference room phone's intercom buzzed. Linda looked around the vacant room, selected SPEAKER ON and touched TALK and said, "Linda Knowles,"

"Stephen Irons is calling Detective Knowles,"

"Put him through, please." Linda answered, then, "Stephen I'm alone in a conference room and you're on SPEAKER."

"Afternoon, Linda," Stephen's familiar voice responded, "I talked with Sally, she DID know about Adams and the antique shop. She showed me the documents…"

"What do the documents say Stephen?"

"Basically what you thought, Sally will own the property and the life insurance will pay it off... But, she said Wilber wanted the business property given to Adams if anything happened to him. It's not spelled out but she wants to do what Wilber asked, except,"

"Except she didn't know about Wilber's ex and son living in Franklin did she?"

"No, she's very upset and trying to deal with that now," Linda interrupted,

"Stephen, does Sally know Donald Adams was Wilber's brother-in-law?"

"Shit, ah sorry Linda, Wilber having a kid and Sally not knowing was enough to set her off. I can't believe Wilber kept Adams being his brother-in-law a secret too. Wilber told Sally that Adams was just an old friend. Damn, Donald Adams is just like me, a brother in law to Wilber. What else have you found out?"

"Not much yet, but I have a meeting in a few minutes to find out more. I CAN tell you a lot of the evidence points to Eric Chin, the guy that attacked you at the airport," Linda paused, then came right back, "Sorry, Stephen, I can hear my people showing up now, I've got to go,"

"One more thing Linda, there was a lot of cash in the safety deposit box with no explanation. Sally had no idea about the money, it totaled over $127,000. Sally said Wilber dealt with the box,"

"That is weird, thanks Stephen I'll try to call you later." Linda disconnected as Sam Millers entered the conference room.

"Hi, Chief, ready for the meeting? I see you getting a matrix set up I guess it's as good a way as any to deal with all this information. Where's everyone?"

"They'll be here soon, Sam. I'm counting on you, Morris and Clayton to help me get this all sorted out," Davis and Bradshaw entered and Bradshaw said,

"Hi, Boss, oh, you're setting up a matrix," Davis forced himself to concentrate on Linda's matrix and offered,

"It's actually been proven that the Matrix Comparison Method is one of the most efficient ways to deal with an excess of information..." Clayton stopped mid-sentence as he saw Linda's reference to the San Diego Police and the possibility of a connection between Eric Chin and China, "Linda can I use the phone in your office, I need to check on something before the meeting, I'll just be a minute." Davis exited the room,

"Couldn't you have left that jerk in Franklin?" Millers offered,

"No, Sam, Clayton was actually helpful. I'll just wait 'til Davis finishes…

Millers interrupted, "Come on Chief, you saw his reaction. Davis saw something on your matrix and had to call the Hoover Cross Dressing Society," Millers and Bradshaw began to laugh, Linda indicated quiet, but Millers jumped back in, "Okay, what's on your matrix to set him off like that?" Linda considered the comment and replied,

"You could be right Sam he did look at the matrix and immediately decided to call," Millers interrupted,

"There's an FBI elephant in the room we're not seeing, something Davis saw got his attention and he had to report it. The FBI has a 'big' hidden agenda Linda, and if we figure out what that connection is we'll know why they got involved." They all heard the door knob turn, paused, then, the conference door opened and Davis walked back in.

"Sorry for the delay Linda, I was concerned when I saw your reference about Eric Chin being associated with China, so I checked with my people. Chin was suspected of being a minor criminal in California but no association with a foreign country could ever be verified. You can scratch that reference off."

"I think I'll leave the reference," Linda replied, "at least until I have a chance to call San Diego myself. Or," Linda adjusted her thinking, "Sam you make that call while I finish the chart, it's after 1PM there so they'll be back from lunch. Morris, get some drinks for us, please, I'll just finish my notes and we'll start when you both get back. I've got to add Sally Harrington to the list concerning Adams' Antiques, she now owns the property."

When both were out of the room, Linda changed her matrix to show: Adams' Antiques, D. Adams (Mgr.), Sally Harrington (Property Owner), then she added $127,000 under Wilber Harrington's secrets. Linda put down the chalk, stepped back and said,

"What's the deal Clayton? You walk in here, see a reference to Chin and China and you bolt out of here to call home. What's going on? Are we treading into an FBI sanctuary? The comment from San Diego seems valid to me."

"Well sure, I just wanted to save you some effort, you're pressed for time and short staffed, but it all looks pretty cut and dry to me," Millers and Bradshaw reentered the room. Linda decided to delay the confrontation and said,

"Okay, lets get started, Sam you fill us in on your findings and I'll connect things.."

CHAPTER FIFTY ONE

POLICE OPERATIONS

After an hour and thirty minutes the four investigators had reported the following: First, Millers spoke about talking with Mr. Jeffery Cullen at Regent University and a Virginia Zoo Docent named Richard Milligan concerning Pat Robertson, Operation Blessing and the book idea Harrington called, 'The Devil on Angel Flight'. Neither witness was very helpful but Milligan said the book Harrington was first working was put on a 'back burner' to develop the story line for the 'devil book', then the 'devil book was preempted by another book idea', possibly 'Pacific Secret'. Millers said he was still checking on a UPS van that could have been taken from one of their repair facilities, used in the murder and returned later. Fibers under Harrington's nails could be from a UPS shirt that was now being checked by the Police Lab's Micron Spectrometer. In closing Millers added, that Wilber's Publishing Agent, Cecil Li, provided no additional information about Harrington or the navy connection to Stephen Irons, but the San Diego Police Department stood by their Eric Chin's China connection. Millers was scheduled to see Charles Taylor and work his way down the NISCO corporate structure, but had been delayed because Taylor was presently in Richmond.

Second, Bradshaw covered the information provided from samples of the foreign matter found on Chin's shoes and the knee brace on his left knee. He confirmed the ID of Chin as Iron's airport attacker and the possible ID from the Lakewood kids. He added that Chin had a connection with the Virginia Zoo where he had been a volunteer under the supervision of Ursula Volk, plus he discovered that the pair had worked together in San Diego previously. The San Diego Police found no indication of criminal activity by Volk, but added to Millers' previous information that Chin had gotten in some drug related trouble when he worked for the San Diego Wild Animal Park where Volk had been in charge of large animals. Volk was still out of town at a seminar in Tennessee and would be contacted when she returned. Bradshaw stated he also had concerns about Chin's California history of suspected assault and drug and alcohol abuse and he submitted a photo of Ursula Volk from the Virginia Zoo's employment files. Linda put the photo on the board next to the two photos of Eric Chin.

Last, Knowles and Agent Davis participated, giving their impressions of Donald Adams, Lydia Harrington and her son Allen. They followed with Adams'

Antiques, and the business property now owned by Sally Harrington. After Davis' remarks about Allen Harrington's elation and new respect for his dead father for having an insurance policy that provided him $100,000; Knowles reported that she had called the Mac Arthur Museum's Chief Historian but found no knowledge of Wilber Harrington's book idea "For Honorable Service". The historian had laughed and declined comment on Harrington's idea that General Mac Arthur's staff, and the newly formed CIA, had plotted to place an Atomic Bomb near the Japanese Emperor's Palace, ostensibly to force the Japanese to comply with the World War II Surrender Treaty. Knowles closed the presentation by suggesting that Millers hold off on Harrington's NISCO associates since Irons was interviewing them and would share the information.

Davis and Millers finally agreed on something, both objected to information being gathered outside their own investigation and warned 'they weren't sure they could trust Stephen Irons as far as Knowles could throw him'. She responded to their remark,

"You might be surprised to know that Stephen has turned up the fact that Sally did know about the business called Adams' Antiques, but unknown to Sally or Stephen, Wilber had accumulated the one hundred and twenty seven thousand dollars in cash they found hidden in a safety deposit box. Hardly the 'financial problem' the FBI said Harrington had."

After a lengthy discussion Linda's chart was now filled with connecting lines and notes implying Harrington and Chin's deaths were most likely the results of a larger conspiracy between known and unknown individuals. New questions had been raised but it was getting late, so Linda popped the last can of soda and said,

"We've pretty much confused this issue now so let's take a break, think about it separately then, tomorrow we'll get back into it fresh,"

"Sorry to interrupt," Clayton said, "but I have to go back to Washington for a couple of days, I should be back late Friday," Millers moaned and Linda cut Davis off,

"Okay, Clayton, you said this all looked cut and dry, that?" Clayton stood, and said;

"Even before we knew about the money and you drew your lines of connection on the matrix, it seemed obvious to me that the most likely solution is some involvement between Sally Harrington, Stephen Irons and Donald Adams. The money connection is obvious and now Bradshaw has turned up the zoo as a common point with Eric Chin. The Virginia Zoo connects Wilber and Sally Harrington, Stephen Irons, Eric Chin and surprisingly, the Community Service of Donald Adams. So, #1, Wilber Harrington hid a secret life and a lot of cash from his wife. #2, Our knowledge of the navy training and experience of Stephen Irons, when that's coupled with #3, The likely possibility of extreme anger being Irons' reaction to learning all this information about Wilber Harrington's secrets, we end up with a group-conspiracy right in front of us. If your ID of Chin, holds up, then the 'conspiracy group' learned about Harrington's money, got Chin to do the job on him, then, Irons backed out of paying Chin for the murder and Chin's answer was to attack Irons. After the airport attack failed, then, Irons took care of Chin himself. We need to look in Irons' direction a lot harder. Irons had motive, means and opportunity to get all this done in a partnership… To me that's 'cut and dry'." Clayton smiled, put on his jacket, and left.

Millers gave Davis' fashionable performance the 'middle finger salute'.

CHAPTER FIFTY TWO

NISCO, NORFOLK OFFICE, TUESDAY 7PM

Craig Cooper knew Betty Boles was still working in her office, he could hear her through the door tapping on her computer. He listened for a minute wondering if Betty would be pleased to see him, their parting three years ago hadn't been as friendly as he would have liked. They had been intimate for over a year, then, while Cooper was away on an assignment Betty had decided to affect a split-up. She had either been frustrated by their lengthy separations or attracted to someone else, Cooper wasn't sure which. Upon Cooper's return and Betty's surprise declaration of estrangement, Cooper quickly found someone else and moved-on, but he wasn't sure about Betty. Cooper had given up judging people 'on their face-value alone' now he patiently waited for their actions or reactions, especially with Betty. She had continued to work for Dr. Kale and Cooper had seen her from time to time, but they remained no more than just casual, work-related friends. Then, a few months later Cooper heard Betty found another job in her home town of Norfolk and left DC for that opportunity. Cooper didn't know exactly why but he now knew she still reported to Dr. Kale. After receiving Kale's briefing and the packet concerning his Norfolk assignment, Cooper was pleased that Betty knew he was coming. Cooper knocked on the door and opened it a crack, leaning in to announce himself,

"Betty, it's Craig Cooper, can I come in? Dr. Kale sends greetings…"

"Hey, Coop, it's good to see you. I've been expecting your call, but it's great you stopped by. Cooper hadn't changed much, Betty thought, he's obviously nervous about our meeting after three years of separation."

Cooper began to feel a little better with Betty's cordial reception to his arrival. But as Betty turned toward his entrance and smiled, she remained seated, exerting no effort to rise and greet him physically. "I've missed you Betty, it's been a long time, I'm glad we have this chance to reacquaint." Cooper offered smiling a bit too much.

"Me too Coop, but I'm tied up tonight, finishing some work for Taylor. How about tomorrow, 7 PM at EMPIRE? You'll see the Bistro next to the Tazewell Hotel when you meet with Davis, that's where you're going isn't it?"

"Oh sure, that's where I'm headed," Cooper replied now knowing Betty probably knew as much if not more than he did about this mission, "You're right, I've got to make contact with Davis. Have you met him?"

"No, I've steered clear of him,"

"Well, I'll check him out, anything you can add?" Cooper knew information was Betty's 'coin of the realm', she had always been that way. Betty offered,

"Davis is about to leave for DC, you should hurry if you want to catch him tonight. We'll meet tomorrow night and compare notes, okay?"

"Okay, anything more on Harrington's death?" Cooper tried one more time to extend the conversation.

"No, but he's a big loss to the company. He provided a lot of confirming information about NISCO and some of Taylor's local associates, including a Judge named Knutson. Taylor's in Richmond on business now, could be a connection, don't know yet." Dejectedly Cooper turned again to leave, but Betty stopped him once more with, "I'm really glad to see you, Coop."

———————————

Clayton Davis entered his hotel room and began to get his things together for his trip to DC. He wasn't certain he'd been able to continue diverting attention from the Chinese but he needed an update and more guidance before he continued to try to control Knowles' efforts. Clayton was beginning to have doubts about the security of his daily activity now, how could Knowles have known about the reason for Harrington's removal from sea duty unless his phone was being tapped or she had an inside FBI source. Lance could be the problem. Clayton heard a loud knock echoing from the door and he responded, "Who's there?"

"It's Lanss, open up." Cooper responded hissing his voice and covering his mouth with his hand. Clayton wondered about this late visit, and he wasn't sure about the voice, so he drew his GLOCK and moved to the door to make sure he was protected.

"Just a minute, Lance ," Clayton placed his weapon up against the door frame with his left hand, hiding the fact that he carried it and opened the door inward with his right... *SLAM* the door banged totally open and Clayton and his weapon were knocked backwards, both landing hard, but separately on the carpeted floor. Clayton groped toward the gun but a man entered and stood between him and his discarded GLOCK. Looking up carefully Clayton saw a man about ten years his senior, probably 6'2" and maybe 200 pounds, tanned complexion, sandy hair, dressed casually in jeans and a dark gray jacket. Under the bottom of the guys left pants leg Clayton could see strapping that most likely held the ankle rig for a small caliber weapon. The intruder extended his hand to help Clayton up, smiled and announced as Clayton sensed the man's arm and grip strength grab onto him,

"Sorry about the physical stuff Davis, I'm Cooper CIA." Cooper released Davis' left arm and handed him his CIA Credentials as he continued to help Davis up. "I know your boss, Rollins, you can check with him later, but we need to talk now. Here let me help clean you up." Cooper brushed Davis' coat off and secretly slid Davis' wallet from his jacket as he retrieved his own ID, and placed Davis' lifted wallet and his own ID back in his pocket. Cooper then picked Clayton's weapon up from the carpet, smiled and ejected the GLOCK clip onto the bed and ratcheted the slide back, popping the chambered round onto the bedspread next to the extracted clip. Cooper handed Davis his neutralized weapon, and said,

"Nice weapon Davis, no safety on a GLOCK, so you were serious answering the door. Makes sense to me but I personally prefer the 38, it's got the same hitting power and a safety feature too… But I'm old fashioned. Here, sit down a minute you need to be brought up to speed before you see Rollins in DC."

Clayton sat on his hotel bed forced to listen to Cooper's enlightenment concerning Deep Dragon and the recent shut down of the secret program brought about by the combined efforts of the National Security Council, the CIA, the FBI, and in no small part, the US Navy. Cooper explained that Davis' initial, misguided efforts to steer the Harrington investigation away from the Chinese, through no fault of his own of course, was just that, misguided. Cooper said that the CIA was now laying ALL their cards on the table and requesting a combined effort to help the Norfolk Police put a stop to the killings that were continuing, seemingly to protect the Chinese involvement in Deep Dragon from becoming public knowledge.

As he listened Clayton began to focus on the real possibility that Harrington had actually been an agent for some foreign power and after clearing over $127,000 his further attempts had gotten him killed. Clayton finally felt comfortable enough to venture a question into the discussion, "I'm not saying I believe everything you've said, but it does seem my people have left me a bit uninformed concerning Harrington's involvement with some foreign power. Can you tell me more on that aspect of the case?"

"I can tell you some, but you should ask Rollins, the FBI knows a hell of a lot more than they've told you. They have our file. It's not a certainty that Harrington actually worked with a foreign government, but he did post letters to foreign military contacts he made at the Naval Amphibious School in California highlighting his experience and knowledge of US Nuclear Submarine development. He then requested a meeting to discuss possible employment." Cooper paused, then added, "Harrington was quick to stipulate he would NOT remain in the US Navy as a spy for the country, but he would actually defect and help them better understand the future opportunities for their own Nuclear Submarines," Clayton interrupted,

"I can't believe this. What countries are you talking about?"

"I'm not at liberty to answer that question, Davis, but your people have copies of the letters, again, you should ask Rollins. Sorry about the manhandling, but I wanted to get your attention to tell you about the letters." Cooper slapped Davis' shoulder and slipped the lifted wallet back into Davis' jacket, minus Clayton's FBI-ID card. and left.

CHAPTER FIFTY THREE

ZOO CURATOR'S OFFICE, WEDNESDAY, 4 PM

Louise was working on revising her budget estimates for the next three years. Greg, her new Director, was still out of town arranging his permanent move, but his initial requirement was to update the previous budget forecasts adding specific emphasis on Virginia Zoo improvements and expansions, to include permanent-facility building-projects and the acquisition of several new animal exhibits. As Louise was beginning to learn, Greg's goals were: raising the local awareness of his zoo, physical improvement and expansion of the zoo, and the addition of new exotic animals to create excitement for zoo patrons. Louise shifted some paperwork as her phone rang and she picked up, and touched SPEAKER ON, then said, "Good afternoon, this is Louise, how can I help you?"

"Sorry to bother you Louise, its Ursula Volk calling from Tennessee, there's a problem with my parents in Germany. My dad had a stroke and I've got to go back to help my mom for a few months, I'm sorry,"

"No problem Ursula, but I'm so sorry about your dad, how can we help?" Louise put away her budget estimates and took out a small note book as Ursula replied,

"Thank you, I'll need a leave of absence for a couple of months, I don't expect salary of course but I'd like to talk with you and the new director about returning to the Virginia Zoo, or possibly you could help me find another AZA position when I return,"

"Are you comfortable with Dennis managing String Three and the elephants while you're gone?"

"Yes, of Course, he's been very good assisting, I've relied on him to do the scheduling and we've conferred on almost everything else. Dennis is experienced, knowledgeable, well respected and very capable."

"Thanks, okay, we can talk later about your return here, or help you find another position, but don't worry about that now, it's important for you to get back home to help your mom and dad. Will you leave for Germany soon?"

"Yes, my friend Alex will give me a ride to the airport to get me started, thanks for being so understanding, Louise, it's a big help."

"You're welcome," Louise replied then quickly remembered something important, "Oh, Ursula, the Norfolk Police were here asking about a volunteer of yours, an Eric Chin, they found his body in the Lafayette River. It looks like an accidental drowning but could you give them a call? I know they'd like to talk to you before you leave."

"Sure, give me their number, I'll call. Sorry to hear about Eric, but he wasn't working out for us, he missed several scheduled training days before I left... I didn't even get to do the paperwork on him. I apologize about the paper work, but I was probably more concerned about my dad."

Louise thought Ursula was a little callus concerning Eric's death, but that was Ursula , all business. But then, funny about the paperwork lapse, she was usually so meticulous. Louise gave the information to Ursula from Sergeant Morris Bradshaw, then, asked her to call if there was anything else the zoo could do for her then Louise hung up. She put all Ursula's information aside and picked up her on-site radio from its recharging unit, "Louise for Dennis," After 10 seconds the radio reply came back,

"Dennis here Louise. Just finishing in the barn, what's up?"

"Stop by my office before you leave Dennis, we need to talk about a few things."

"Okay, see you soon." Dennis finalized.

Louise placed the radio back into the charger unit and got back to her budget revisions. Ursula being gone a few months would save the zoo some money. Ursula was well qualified but highly paid by AZA standards. Louise was sure Dennis, Jill and Jason would be enough to handle String Three for a few months and if this change became permanent they could train or hire another keeper part-time and still save the zoo some money.

Louise heard a soft knock on her door, checked her watch, 5 PM she looked up as Dennis opened her door, "Dennis, come in, you're just in time for good news, for the next few months you're the new Elephant Manager and the overall Supervisor of String Three. It's not a permanent change yet, but it's a step in the right direction and certainly well deserved."

Dennis was pleased, but a bit taken back by this sudden change and asked, "How'd this happen, Louise?"

"Ursula's taking emergency leave of absence. Her father has some medical problems she has to help with. I just finished talking with our new boss Greg and he concurs with my decision to make the temporary change… But Greg thinks this could end up being permanent so we'll probably move someone from another string to help you out temporarily. We'll honor Ursula's request to wait a few months before we make a permanent decision, so congratulations."

"Thanks, sounds like a great opportunity for me. What did Ursula, say, you must have talked to her about this change,"

"She said you'd have no problem with the job. My guess is she knew this family issue was coming up but put the decision off until it was absolutely necessary. Anyway, it's done for now, you're the new boss until we hear more from Ursula. Would you prefer the announcement came from me?"

"I think it would be better from you, Louise. I've got tomorrow off. Jill and Jason open up at seven and they have Angie coming in to help."

"Who's Angie?" Louise asked.

"A volunteer Keeper Aide, a hard worker, efficient and thorough, she's actually Ursula's favorite. Anyway, Jason's scheduled to close, so you should be able to explain this to everybody tomorrow. Thanks again for the opportunity Louise."

CHAPTER FIFTY FOUR

EMPIRE LITTLE BAR BISTRO, 7:15PM

Craig Cooper sat at the corner of the bar waiting for Betty Boles. Robert, EMPIRE'S bartender for the night, fixed him a Beefeaters Martini, Straight-Up, with 'excessive olives' while Cooper watched and waited. Betty was fifteen minutes late so far. As Cooper savored the gin, and munched on gin-soaked fruit, he saw several taxis turn down Tazewell Street headed toward the Wells Theater. When the line of theater patrons and taxis piled-up all the way to Granby Street, one of the cabs stopped in front of EMPIRE. Cooper could see the silhouette of a dark haired woman in the back of the cab. Her hair seemed too long to be Betty, but Cooper wasn't sure, so he jumped up and hurried outside.

Arriving curbside, still unable to tell who was behind the opaque windowed cab, Cooper reached down and opened the rear door. The young lady arriving looked up at Cooper and said, "Well, thank you, handsome," then, she began to stand to her full height. Cooper could see this gal was way taller than Betty and he became fascinated by her height and beauty as he assisted with the unfolding of her lanky body and long legs when she exited the cab. The gal turned to Cooper, standing very close now and added,

"Hi, I'm Audrey, I've got a theater date, but if you want to try me after the show..." Audrey began, but she was interrupted,

"That want be necessary, Audrey," Betty interjected as she crossed Tazewell Street and took Cooper's arm, steering him back toward EMPIRE'S front door, "Cooper's definitely new in town, and he may be looking for a theatrical performance, but tonight he's 'all sold out'."

Betty smiled and finalized her remarks as Cooper reached the front door for entry, "You just can't be left alone, can you Cooper? I guess I should know that by now!" Finally Betty smiled up and offered, "Its okay Coop, sorry I'm late let's go in for a drink."

Entering and sitting at the bar, Robert refilled Cooper's martini' and poured some Beefeaters gin on a pile of ice cubes for Betty. Cooper allowed Betty a large sampling of her drink before he ventured a further explanation, "Sorry about the stupid mistake Betty, I just saw the dark haired gal pull up in a cab and thought it was you,"

"Don't worry Coop, I'm actually flattered, Audrey is gorgeous and you were attempting a little 'gallantry'. I'm just happy to see you again, Cheers." Cooper and Betty talked quietly as they finished the last of their drinks. Cooper placed two twenties on the bar and took Betty's arm and led her to the small table next to the front window that faced out onto Granby Street. As he eased Betty into her chair, Cooper offered,

"I'm glad to see you too, Betty, it's been a long time. What, three years?"

"Almost four, Coop, I left in December '02 for the job here. Your packet must have told you I'm here in a 'limited administrative capacity' for Dr. Kale and the company, which has recently suffered a set-back with Wilber Harrington's murder. I actually began as his cut-out then took over as handler," Betty paused as their waitress showed up and offered,

"Hi Betty, its good to see you again," Then to Cooper, "Hello, I'm Jocelyn. Here's a list of our New Fall offerings. Do you want to continue with martinis or would you like to see the wine list?" Jocelyn asked as she delivered two glasses of water, two small plates with heavy silverware and chop-sticks all rolled up in a black linen napkin.

"I think I'd like some wine, how about you Betty?" Cooper said.

"They stock some great Cabs, Coop, how about a red? Betty answered.

"We've just gotten some Napa Rosenblum, it's by the glass too, if you'd like to try it." Jocelyn replied and Cooper said,

"I know the vineyard, we'll try a bottle. Do you have their '02?"

"I'll check. Would you like to order some food while I check on the wine?"

Betty looked up to see who the chef was but the crowd blocked her view, so she asked, "Who's your chef tonight?"

"Natalie's working tonight." Jocelyn replied.

"Great, have her fix Pot Stickers for me and her Tenderloin, rare with blue cheese and garlic mashers, for Cooper... Oh, we better have a bread order too I don't want to lose any of Natalie's sauces. Is that okay, Coop?" Cooper nodded his approval and Jocelyn smiled and moved away letting Betty ask Cooper, "How'd your meeting with Davis go?"

"I got his attention. He's leery of all his bosses now. Does the FBI know about Harrington's connection with us?" Cooper asked.

"I doubt if anyone does, including Harrington's wife, Wilber kept a lot from her. I'm sure another secret was a drop in the bucket for him. Did Dr. Kale tell you we wanted to approach Sally about running a Safe House in Frankfurt? Her job gave her a perfect cover." Betty said,

"No, he didn't talk specifically about either one of the Harrington's, what happened with her recruitment?"

"We had to run it through American Airlines, but they stalled too much, so we went another direction. If it had worked we would have told Sally about Wilber during the 'vetting' process," Betty paused as she saw Jocelyn return with the wine and two small glasses.

Cooper noted the Cab was a Napa '02 and nodded for Jocelyn to open it. Receiving a slight pour Cooper swirled the wine around in the small bowl of the glass, sniffed a little and tried a bit on his tongue, then he took in a little more, moved it around over his palette, swallowed, and said, "It's very nice but do you have better glasses, maybe with a larger bowl? It needs to breathe a bit."

"I'll ask Robert, he's an owner and picky about his reds too." Jocelyn responded.

"Thanks," Cooper replied, "you don't mind the wait do you, Betty?"

"No, Coop, I was just remembering how you know the right way to treat 'reds', wine and women both." Betty said as Jocelyn provided the new glasses and poured the wine.

"Hope you enjoy the wine," Jocelyn said and departed. Cooper swirled his wine glass and said,

"Cheers Betty, Reds ARE great, but I want to try harder with dark haired, CZ Jones look-likes too!" They touched glasses and Cooper went on, "Here's to Norfolk, and enjoying the adventure." Cooper tried a small offering, "Very nice, I think you'll like it Betty."

"Your toast wasn't bad either Coop, did my red-head remark scare you a little?"

"No, Betty, I'm sure our past separation was mutually agreed-upon, not alternatively driven, I just don't have any hair color knowledge in your case."

"You're right, Coop, actually he was bald. Doesn't matter now, it's great to see you again, lets just, 'forget and forget', no 'forgive' is necessary."

"Good!" Cooper responded as Jocelyn brought their bread and tapas orders.

"Natalie says hello, Betty, enjoy. Please call if you need anything else. Hey, we've got 'Jan's Chronic Cake' if you want dessert."

"Thanks for the heads up, what's 'chronic' about her cake'?" Cooper asked.

"You know, 'chronic', the cake keeps coming back on demand because its moisture aged coconut cake, very healthful and really scrumptious."

"We'll think about it, thanks." Cooper laughed and answered as Jocelyn departed. "Betty, can you tell me a little more about Harrington?"

"We'd be better off some place else, maybe my place later this week, but I can tell you I was asked to follow up on Harrington in December of '02, after he returned to Norfolk. He wasn't interested at first, but I put a little pressure on him when we vetted his history and turned up some things he was trying to hide from his new wife. So, I used them to convince him to come to work for us. I did push patriotism you know, the 'do all you can for your country bit, and still be able to keep secrets,"

"I tried patriotism in California, but it didn't seem to get his attention. Did you personally drop Wilber in the 'honey pot'?" Cooper said.

"No, nothing involving MY feminine charms, although I'm certain that would have worked too. He was actually hiding an ex wife and child living close by in Franklin, plus the fact that Wilber was paying big bucks for alimony and child support while he continued to communicate with his Franklin family when Sally was away on her trips. Anyway, we learned a lot by the time I talked with him again and our new knowledge flipped him. That plus the money was good. Wilber already had access to some of the information we wanted verified, information we were already getting out of China plus some new hints of things the Chinese were involved with. That's how he picked up on Deep Dragon, Wilber was the one who put a 'confirmed annotation' on that," Betty stopped as Jocelyn returned and said,

"Just thought I'd check on you two, how about some of Jan's coconut cake?"

CHAPTER FIFTY FIVE

POLICE OPERATIONS THURSDAY, 10AM

Linda paced back and forth in front of the matrix, she had tried to cross reference her data and narrow the possibilities down, but her chart was a mess with erasures, cross-outs and a lot of add-ons. She hated to admit it but Clayton's assessment was starting to make sense. All the indications led to a broad-based conspiracy, and yes, Stephen Irons could have put it all together. Clayton could be right about all those people associated through the Virginia Zoo. The conference door opened and Special Agent Clayton Davis walked in, "Clayton, you're back early I didn't expect you until Friday, something new?"

"I should have called but I decided to come back and talk to you in person Linda. First, let me apologize for passing on some flawed analysis in the initial part of your investigation that led the FBI to rule out the possibility of Chinese involvement. We've received additional information from the CIA that confirms Harrington was attempting to either join or infiltrate a local Chinese group,"

"The CIA, what are you talking about?

"Yes Linda the Central Intelligence Agency is involved,"

Linda interrupted again, "Okay, you said join or infiltrate, you don't know which? And what did you say about a local Chinese group? Is it a business or a spy ring? Sounds like you're being intentionally misleading again Clayton."

"That's just it Linda, the FBI's not sure at this point, but, the CIA's gained some information from China that they're willing to share. Harrington was attempting a liaison with some local Chinese connection, but we don't have definitive information about his motive for seeking the involvement, or if he actually succeeded. This was passed on by the CIA to keep your investigation open to the possibility of Chinese involvement,"

"Was Harrington some kind of an agent for the CIA?" Linda asked.

"The CIA will neither, confirm or deny, but, it's possible. Harrington could have attempted a connection with China on his own, or for the CIA. But, for the FBI and myself personally, I apologize."

"You learned all this when you returned to DC?"

"Yes and here in Norfolk from a direct briefing with a CIA representative." Clayton admitted, remembering Cooper's control of that conversation. Clayton took out one of the folders passed on to him by Rollins and offered it to Linda,

"Clayton, that a Classified Government Folder! I'm not cleared for that kind of information."

"I know, but we've determined it would be beneficial to the resolution of your case for you to be made aware of some of our information. The pertinent information concerning China's interest in Harrington and his attempt to connect with China is clearly annotated for you to use openly. The other information provided to support the validity of the folder remains CLASSIFIED. Only you and I, and other authorized personnel locally are free to discuss the total contents of the folder,"

"What, the CIA has an agent in Norfolk?" Linda interrupted as she took the folder.

"That's all spelled out in the document, Linda. Please sign the cover sheet showing I've briefed you on the classification. Do you have a personal safe in your office, one that you alone have access to?"

"No, Clayton I'm a cop, not a political jerk with a lot of secrets, why do you ask?"

"Okay, you can read the document in my presence, you can do it now or we can go to a local FBI office downtown and openly discuss the document. How do you want to do it?"

"How about both I'll read it here, then we head to your downtown office to meet with the CIA rep and I get to ask a few questions, how's that?"

"It'll take some time to set up, but if I do this for you, you've got to do something for me, okay?"

"Alright, let's hear it Clayton." Linda said sarcastically,

"I take you to dinner Friday night, my treat." Clayton offered.

"Damn right it's your treat, but my restaurant choice." Linda replied.

"Okay, it's a done deal!" Clayton answered as he handed the folder to Linda and turned to his cell phone to call Agent Lance and set up the downtown meeting.

CHAPTER FIFTY SIX

FEDERAL BUILDING, NORFOLK, 2PM

Special Agent Rachel Finn, Agent Lance's Norfolk Assistant, found an empty conference room on the third floor of the Federal Building and opened it up for Special Agent Davis and his guests. Davis arrived early carrying his classified folder in a small briefcase. Davis fidgeted around the room checking all the obvious areas for cameras or recording devices, he was certain Lance was leaking some of his activities. Agent Finn entered escorting Detective Knowles,

"Your first guest is here Agent Davis. I'll watch for Mr. Cooper then Agent Lance will bring him up. Do you want water, coffee, soft drinks?" Clayton looked at Linda, got no indication one way or the other and responded,

"Just some water, if it's not too much trouble Agent Finn."

"Sure, Agent Lance will bring the water when Mr. Cooper arrives." Rachel departed and closed the large conference room door.

"Clayton is the FBI always so formal?" Linda asked.

"Not really, but Lance and I don't get along well, so I'm formal with him and his staff... I've actually gotten the feeling that Lance has a different agenda, but that won't affect your investigation, just my comfort level."

After a ten minute wait, Agent Lance appeared carrying several water bottles and leading a tall sandy haired man in his mid-forties. The guy in tow was wearing a casual suit and a big smile across his well tanned face. Lance offered, "Detective Knowles, this is Mr. Craig Cooper, Cooper, Detective Linda Knowles, I think you've already met Special Agent Davis. Agent Davis, please buzz Agent Finn if you need something else." Lance instructed and turned to leave the room.

"Thank you Agent Lance," Clayton offered as the large door closed behind Lance's departure. Linda and Cooper shook hands and after Cooper showed Linda his CIA credentials, Linda sat down and opened the classified folder, Cooper remained standing.

"If I may call you Linda," Cooper began, "Clayton told me he let you look at Harrington's folder, and I see you have it there, so I'll try and answer any questions I'm permitted,"

"Alright, how long have the CIA and the FBI been concerned about Wilber Harrington, his wife Sally and her brother Stephen Irons?"

"That's a lot of questions, Linda but let's start with our primary interest, Wilber Harrington. We first looked at Harrington in March of 2001 when he posted a couple of letters to representatives of foreign governments offering his services basically as a military consultant. He stated that 'he was being underutilized by the US Navy and wanted a more challenging role in another country's nuclear submarine development'. I'm at liberty to tell you that one of his letters went to China, the other country remains classified beyond your investigation. But both letters went out after a visit to the Naval Amphibious School by China's President and several other Chinese dignitaries,"

"Did you interview Harrington about the letters?"

"We did know of his recent restriction to shore duty and his directed assignment to the Naval Amphibious Base and that Harrington's letter stated that 'he wanted to defect, not become a spy for the country he solicited.' Having said that, our experience has shown that such reactions to negative career events, such as Harrington's restriction to shore duty, are not uncommon,"

Linda interrupted, "Wait a minute, you mean if a military person gets upset with what's going on with their career, then he or she fires a letter off to become a paid consultant for another country?"

"Certainly not every time, actually, such solicitations from military women are rare, almost non existent. To your gender's credit, Linda, women seem more inclined to fulfill their obligations and work within normal channels to address their issues." Cooper added,

"Well, I'm pleased, but did the CIA approach Harrington about the letters?"

"We approached him in August of 2001, specifically about China. We proposed that if he were contacted by representatives of China, we wanted to 'hire him' to learn what the Chinese wanted to know and what they might be doing with his information,"

Linda interrupted again, "Did Harrington agree to 'spy' for the CIA?"

"It got a little more complicated than that. I met Harrington in San Diego, introduced myself and basically tried to appeal to his patriotism and desire for a more challenging job by offering him one with the CIA. Wilber was amused by the offer, he wasn't surprised about us knowing about his letters, but he showed me a copy of a recent letter he sent to China withdrawing his initial offer. The copy indicated his recant went out a week in late July,"

"He changed his mind?" Linda asked.

"Linda, excuse me, I want to be responsive but please let me finish my answers before you put your 'detective hat' back on and interrupt me with another comfort distracting question. Okay?"

"Sorry Cooper, it's a hard habit to put on the shelf, no disrespect meant."

"Okay, none taken, but concerning Harrington's removal of his original offer and your question, this was August, 2001, Wilber had met Sally Irons earlier in the year and told me that 'she was young and very beautiful and he had fallen in love with her and asked her to marry him'. He explained that he only had a few more years to get his 'twenty' in for retirement and he was no longer upset with the Navy for sending him to San Diego. He actually credited the assignment as helping him find someone he wanted to spend the rest of his life with," Cooper paused and Linda felt safe enough to ask,

"Did that end it?"

"Not really, I told him that if the Chinese saw a use for his position and expertise they would probably contact him anyway, so we still wanted him to come to work for the CIA, part time, or possibly on a retainer. Again, this was in August, 2001 and next month, of course, September 11th happened and everything hit the fan. Wilber married Sally in October and early in 2002 they moved to Norfolk for his last Navy assignment. Wilber arrived here in March and I came to see him later in June at the Staff College. I asked him if either country had contacted him concerning his letters but Wilber said 'no' and informed me that he was retiring next year and had been offered a job with a local international shipping company, NISCO. I wished Wilber good luck and asked him to keep our offer in mind. He asked if we would keep him under surveillance and I told him we would turn some information over to the FBI but basically we would put his file on hold unless we heard from him. That was three and a half years ago. I personally didn't see Harrington's name again until his death."

"So, you believe it's possible that the Chinese could be involved with Harrington's murder?" Linda asked.

"I believe some of the information Harrington was going to use as fiction for the country of Japan came very close to a secret Chinese Program,"

Linda couldn't stand it she interrupted Cooper, "What secret Chinese Program?"

Cooper smiled and gave Linda a quick, abridged explanation concerning the possibility that pressure exerted by the United States recently had forced the Chinese to shut down a secret program that Harrington had helped discover. He informed her that he couldn't answer any further questions, but he did add, "We now have knowledge of one Chinese agent operating in the Hampton Roads Area,"

"If you know this, why don't you arrest the agent and allow me to question him about Harrington's murder?"

"Actually it's a bigger problem than just this one agent and your investigation. There are several other locals helping the Chinese and we're trying to find them and at least monitor, or preferably put a stop to their involvement. In repayment for our disclosures, concerning Harrington, we're asking for your cooperation in this effort." Cooper said, then sat down and tried some water himself.

"Was Eric Chin a Chinese agent?" Linda now asked.

"Eric Chin, who's he?" Cooper replied and Linda looked at Clayton for the FBI's input. Clayton was embarrassed but after a short pause he stood and offered,

"Eric Chin was a Chinese transient found drowned in the Lafayette River. He's also been identified as attempting an assault on Stephen Irons and is one of the suspects in Wilber Harrington's murder. Chin's father was a Chinese sailor that met Chin's Danish mother when visiting the port of Copenhagen in the late 60s. They married and the family moved to China when Eric was about eight years old. Chin's father died in '03 but his mother still lives in China."

"Linda, did your investigation turn Eric Chin up?" Cooper asked.

"Yes, one of my people saw a drowning incident sheet from the Norfolk PD and talked with the construction boss where the body was found. We followed up with a photo array of the victim with Stephen Irons, who confirmed Chin was his airport attacker. We believe Chin was also Harrington's killer from that ID and some fiber evidence we found under Harrington's fingernails. We're following up to determine if Chin's drowning was a drug related accident or another Homicide. The information Clayton just provided about Chin's background is news to me, the FBI's been withholding that information from my investigation."

Cooper stood, looked directly at Clayton and asked, "How long have you known about Eric Chin?"

"Just recently for me, but the FBI thought Harrington and Chin were somehow connected, so when you talked about trying to hire Harrington, the FBI wasn't sure about the ramifications of that connection and I was told to keep quiet about Chin until we knew more. Sorry, Cooper."

"You mean the FBI told you to keep quiet until they found a way to use the connection without letting us know about Eric Chin's complete history." Cooper said, then, he turned to Linda and offered,

"Linda, I'm sure you know the CIA's a never-ending maze of compartmentalized puzzle boxes within other puzzle boxes. If there's even one person that knows the entirety of our operations with the Chinese, I'd be very surprised. Having said that much, the CIA puzzle box I operate in has a limited amount of information concerning Wilber Harrington and MY personal attempts to recruit him. I can honestly assure you that I've told you everything associated with MY personal relationship with Harrington, but as I implied, my information is limited to my puzzle box." Cooper waited for Linda's response,

"Cooper, I appreciate your frankness but it opens up the possibility that Harrington's death could have been caused by some country or countries, who wanted to put a stop to his involvement with China… Chin may have been Harrington's killer and he may have been an agent of China, but, at this point I don't think I can yet rule out any country's involvement with the death of Wilber Harrington, either, foreign or domestic."

CHAPTER FIFTY SEVEN

NORFOLK, THE BISTRO, FRIDAY, 5:30PM

Charles Taylor sat at the far end of the 'L' shaped mahogany bar in one of the most popular happy-hour spots for working suits and skirts in downtown Norfolk. THE BISTRO; located directly across from the Nauticus Maritime Center had been a show place since its grand opening three years ago and was judged to be the 'Premier Chef Owned and Operated Restaurant in Mermaid City'. A lilting background of TGIF chatter filled the dark mahogany enhanced room as Charles Taylor turned westward to observe the sunset. Paula, THE BISTRO'S bar manager, delivered Charles' extra large Grey Goose Martini and said,

"Here you are Mr. Taylor, are you expecting someone this evening?"

"Yes, Paula, Sheriff Osborne, I'd like to save this seat, if that's okay?"

"Sure, just put your briefcase on the seat then no one will bother you... I'll fix the curtain so you'll be able to see the sunset." Paula came around the bar and pushed her long black hair away from her classic features as she edged her slender figure by the patrons occupying one of the three window tables opposite the lengthy bar. Stretching across one patron, Paula smiled as she began to raise the filmy linen drapery that protected the bar's interior from the afternoon sun.

THE BISTRO'S chef and owner stood at the small reception podium near the entrance to the restaurant. He was checking the reservation list for this Friday the thirteenth when he noticed Charles sitting by himself. He came over, shook Charles' hand and immediately felt the intimidation of strength from the two-handed clasp. "Charles, great to see you, you've been away for a few days haven't you?"

"Yes Todd, but how did you know?"

"The Kroger girls were here a couple nights ago, they must have told me you'd taken a quick trip. How was it?"

Charles was about to answer when the thought struck him, how did the twins come in here together? They're in charge while I'm gone, one of them should always be on duty, unless it's a Tuesday or Friday night when I work the late shift. Maybe they put James Carlson in charge for a short time, Charles' thoughts speculated, but that was not what he wanted to happen. "The trip was exhausting, Todd, a lot of driving just for a couple of meetings in Richmond then up to Charlottesville for a tour, then back. But, it had to be done. Things are changing on our waterfront and I wanted to know what was coming." Charles saw Todd's face darken, and added, "Don't worry Todd, no matter what it's just more business for you."

"Glad to hear that, we've got a lot of great restaurants in Norfolk, but I don't want to lose my edge. Are you waiting for someone? Who's coming in your wife Millie?" Paula was nearby, heard Todd's question and offered,

"Mr. Taylor's waiting for Sheriff Os, boss, I can get another Gray Goose for Mr. Taylor and a Bombay Sapphire for Sheriff Os, if you'd like."

Todd nodded his okay, then, "Charles, you and Sheriff Os enjoy the sunset. Are you joining us for dinner?"

"No, we both have other commitments tonight we're here to discuss an employee I've recently taken on,"

"Not a problem, I hope, I wouldn't want one of my employees at cross purposes with Sheriff Os." Todd said.

"Nor, would I," Charles answered ignoring Todd's question, "thanks for the drinks, Todd, I'll give Os your best."

"Please do." Todd said as he worked his way around the bar greeting guests, then, he sought a conference with Paula's husband, Roger, THE BISTRO Sommelier.

Paula offered, "I see Sheriff Os coming Mr. Taylor, I'll get your drinks now."

"Thanks Paula," Charles replied as he turned back to the window that looked out toward the setting sun. With the drapes fully retracted, the fading glow washed over the fantail of the resting Battleship Wisconsin and Norfolk's Pier Side Apartments. Charles glanced up at the familiar apartment complex, raised his almost empty glass and whispered, "Cheers, Peggy, my Little Mermaid, sorry about last month, I promise to do better. See you Sunday night with flowers."

"Did you say something?" Paula asked then she turned toward Sheriff Os and added, "Good evening Sheriff Os, you look great in those civvies." Os smiled, wearing a light tan sport coat over a dark brown silk shirt and khaki Dockers' slacks and said,

"Well, thank you 'Pretty Paula', I don't often venture out so artfully attired, but your comment has encouraged my continued effort."

"You've got a 'Bombay' on the way Sheriff Os, Todd's compliments."

"Well, Charles," Os began, as he shook hands with Charles, "you've gotten us started off right. How's your world after the Richmond trip?"

"I met with my landlord and primary shipper, Sonchi Zimchi, and our major rail partner, Morgan Folds, they've just returned from a hunting trip in Africa…"

"I thought African big game hunting was quarantined." Os interrupted,

"Mostly, but 'money talks' and those two have enough money to filibuster the entire African Continent. So, I'm certain they found a way to go there and kill something."

Os smiled at the comment then asked, "Did you learn anything about what's happening here in Norfolk?"

"I know more about COVANTA, Sonchi Zimchi clued me in on some of their plans while we visited Monticello, but I didn't learn enough to put me at ease. I tried to talk with Morgan Folds before coming home, but he's got this new security guy, some Brit named Holmes, who rode with me coming back to Richmond. He didn't talk much business, typical Brit, lot of dry humor, kept his business opinions to himself. I'm sure it'll all work out for NISCO, but there's something else going on. I've seen Folds and Zimchi when they returned from Africa before, they always looked spent, you know sun burnt and grimy faced like they've been forced to ride in an open jeep for a week or so. But, this time they looked refreshed, like they'd been to a European Health Spa. Something's in the works for them now. They promised NISCO would eventually be involved, but it's still got me worried."

"You worry too much, Charles, it's probably like you said, these guys are rich enough to hunt in Africa even with the restrictions, so I'm sure they're rich enough to travel in-style without the inconvenience of heat and dirt."

Charles watched Os take a sip of his drink and decided he needed to clear up a few other things and he asked, "How's your business, Os? We don't ever talk much about you. You're always listening to Judge Knutson and me but how's your work going?"

"I'm a political animal Charles you should know that by now. I'm focused on the Sheriff and his constituents, you know, listening to them, looking for political leverage somewhere," Os laughed a little at his own reflexive honesty, "But, right now, with the Portsmouth Sheriff's Office still dealing with their old 'harassment reputation', I guess you could say the Norfolk Sheriff's Department is flying well under the public radar. So, my work's going well." Os smiled then offered, "You mentioned the Judge, are you still concerned about him?"

"Yes, he's slipping again Os, like when we decided on the 'drastic measure' last March, before Irons stepped in and nixed the effort," Os interrupted,

"Charles we both believed the Judge was remorseful after 'that incident' and we jointly agreed to suspend our effort. You're always quick to decide on an action, but your decisions usually place the ultimate closure on my shoulders." Os was becoming upset, but this wasn't the place to show that emotion, so he forced himself to calm and offered, "Give it some more time Charles. I'll check on the Judge personally, I've got as much to lose as you do, trust me here, let it ride a little, okay?"

"Sure Os, it's just that he called me at work and,"

Os interrupted, "Just let it go Charles I'll work it out." Os finalized then slid his attention to another topic, "Speaking of work, how's Stephen Irons, working out for you?" Charles was upset about Os continuing to interrupt him, but he wanted to talk about Stephen, so he answered,

"To be totally honest I wasn't sure he was the right person when you recommended I hire him, but he's jumped in with both feet so far. While I was gone he talked with the Kroger girls, James Carlson, several of the dock workers Wilber supervised and my Executive Assistant Betty Boles. I've been told he's found no obvious NISCO lead to Wilber's killer yet, but he's only had a couple weeks. I'm sure he'll eventually make the connection and brief me personally."

"Why are you sure Harrington's death has something to do with NISCO? What did Harrington really do for you?"

"Primarily he worked for James Carlson, my Logistic Controller. Wilber was his scheduler, you know, scheduling and supervising the arrival of container ships. But I actually hired him to handle some 'Special Projects' for me. Wilber had served long enough in the Navy and supervised a lot of on-shore and at-sea replenishments, so he knew how they were choreographed efficiently. I asked him to look at our rail loading and container ship off-loading and come up with suggestions to make it all more cost effective,"

"So, he got to know all your shipping ins and outs, your domestic and foreign carriers incoming and outgoing cargo manifests,"

Charles interrupted, "No, Os he actually didn't have to know much about the cargo itself. Of course, he could have gone to Carlson for that, but he didn't have to know what was in the containers to do his job. But for the 'Special Project' he was assigned, he compiled a lot of data and took hundreds of pictures of our operation. Then he studied our employees and their on and off-loading protocols and suggested how we could revamp both processes. His suggestions actually saved us about a million dollars the first year, it was very impressive."

Os listened, thought a minute about his erroneous assumption then tried again, "That's good for NISCO, but I thought your concern was that Harrington might have found out about something illegal being shipped, or he might be involved with something illegal himself? Something he found out about..."

"No, Wilber wouldn't have been involved in anything criminal. Maybe he was tempted by industrial espionage for another company," Charles thought about telling Os more about his personal belief in that possibility, then he pushed his own suspicions aside and continued, "But, to answer your original question, I'm, not sure why I believe someone at NISCO is involved in Harrington's murder, it's just a feeling I have, you know Os, like the feelings we got playing defense for William and Mary, you on the line and me at safety. Remember, how sometime we just knew the play was coming our way? We killed a lot of end runs with those feelings, remember?"

"Yes, those were a couple of great years for me before I became a Sheriff's Deputy. I certainly remember us playing for Stephen's dad, working our asses off to shut down UVA, Tech, Richmond and even Maryland. Those were great times."

"Well, like our old football instincts," Charles began, "I think Stephen's instinctive too. I'm looking at him as my defensive Captain and I think he'll find out who's really calling these offensive plays against me, then, he'll find where the next play's going and help me sack the play calling quarterback."

Os listened to Charles' analogy, thought it bullshit, but he was happy to have steered the subject away from the Judge. Os was intrigued that Charles might have suspected Wilber of industrial espionage, he could use that knowledge. Os shifted his thoughts, "I'm glad Stephen's doing well, I'm sure he'll dig up anything there is to find, I told you he was resourceful. Sorry I have to go now," Os shook hands with Charles again and dropped a $20 on the bar for Paula, then, he turned to go,

"Great to see you Os, by the way, have you seen the Kroger twins in here together lately?" Os paused and turned back to answer Charles' question.

"I don't come in here that much, Charles, a few times for the Virginia Sheriff's Association meetings and maybe an occasional Friday, like tonight, when you're working the night-shift. Other than that, if I see one of them, it's usually Margarete with some guy, you know, for drinks or dinner. Why do you ask?"

"Nothing, really, Todd said he saw them in here. Said that's how he knew I was on a trip. I just wondered because one of them should have been on duty while I was gone,"

"Charles, you know the twins, they're always messing with someone's head. One of them probably told Todd she was Margarete then changed her hair or added a scarf and became Elizabeth, just to confuse him. You know Todd's planning a trip to Thailand so right now his witness testimony, outside the kitchen, is probably compromised…" Os was upset having to 'parry' Charles' question about the Judge and the Kroger twins, so he said, "By the way, how's Peggy doing?" He asked knowing of Charles' involvement with Peggy Turner and Peggy's growing concern about how Charles was beginning to treat her.

"I haven't seen her for a few weeks Os. Our last meeting wasn't good, totally my fault, but I'm anxious to do better." Charles offered. There was a hint of sadness and even a little shame in Charles' voice and Os knew the reason, but he just said,

"Well, thanks again for the info on Stephen, give my best to Millie, and don't worry about the Judge I'll go see him in a couple of days and get back to you." Os waved and headed toward the kitchen to thank Todd for the drinks.

Leaving, Os noticed in the far corner of the restaurant Detective Linda Knowles and Special Agent Clayton Davis were being seated by a waitress named Caitlin. He'd talk with her later maybe she'd hear something of value for him.

Os met Charles at the front door and they exited the restaurant together. He held the car door for Charles and waved him off as he drove away, then Os turned to walk toward the Pier Side Apartments and his own meeting with Peggy Turner.

In the Kroger apartment, the living room phone rang twice then, "Hello, Kroger residence, you've got Elizabeth, Margarete's at work 'til seven." Elizabeth offered as she noted the ID readout, 'Private Caller'. She listened for 30 seconds, recognized the caller's voice, and said,

"No, No, Mr. Folds, that's not true, Margarete and I weren't out together this week. One of us is always working, unless Charles is on duty like tonight. But you know that Sir." A full minute of respectful listening and nodding her head silently to the phone, then, Elizabeth replied,

"Yes sir, that's possible, WE could have done that." She replied quietly, then, "No sir, I know that's dangerous, I promise it will never happen again. Please forgive us sir and please don't send Conrad to talk to us. Elizabeth listened for 30 more seconds then,

No sir, please don't tell Margarete, I promise I'll take care of this personally.

You have my word, it'll never happen again." Elizabeth hung up the phone, then, she shouted toward the condo's kitchen,

"Christina, we just got BUSTED! I told you we'd get caught sneaking out together!"

CHAPTER FIFTY EIGHT

LAKEWOOD, 7PM

"STEPHEN IRONS"

Sally has just joined me watching the sunset from her back yard where I've been relaxing for an hour. I've got my shirt off and the sun's warmth is helping to ease the stiffness from the abdominal scarring of my operation. The scar looks like crimson colored football lacing now taking on a purplish tint as the evening twilight washes over me and the northern edge of their property. 'Their property' funny my mind's still referring to Wilber in the present tense… I guess it'll continue that way until I become so disheartened by the secrets he kept from Sally that I just wipe them, or him, from my memory bank. There's got to be another reason why Wilber was so secretive, he can't have been the total asshole he appears to have been toward my sister.

Sally's been quiet for some time now, gazing northward, watching several rowing crews from Norfolk Collegiate Academy as they work their skulls eastward back toward the Lakewood Park boat ramp. I wanted to engage her in conversation to lessen her depression, but she surprisingly asked me, "Stephen, can you take me to the airport?"

"Yes, of course, do you have something to pick up?"

"No, I'm going to Dallas for re-qualification training." I couldn't believe what she'd just said, this was the first indication I'd been given that she was ready to go back to work. I was certain she was still upset with the recent disclosures concerning Wilber and his secrets. I wanted to be supportive, but I didn't understand why she had to leave now.

"Sally can you delay this? I'll quit NISCO if that's upsetting you."

"No Stephen, I decided to do this yesterday when I finished cleaning out a lot old navy stuff in the garage and checking for khaki shirts for Detective Knowles. I didn't find anything for her but his navy stuff went to the Navy Relief earlier today. I just need to get away from Norfolk right now. Your job doesn't bother me I just want some time to get my mind straight about why he thought it was necessary to keep personal secrets."

"I sorry too Sally and I feel the same, there's more to all his secrecy, maybe it's as we thought with the antique business, he just didn't want you to worry about it."

"Maybe about the business, maybe that's where the money came from. But he had an ex wife living nearby and a son he never spoke of, what reason would he have to keep that from me? I can only guess he thought their living so close and his meeting with them when I was gone on a trip was a threat to our life together. It would have been different Stephen; I would have supported him seeing his family." Sally paused and I began to notice how we were both hesitating, reluctant to actually say Wilber's name when speculating about his secrets. Sally continued, "I just need to get away, Stephen, get immersed in my work again. My job and the time away from Norfolk will help clear my mind and give you and the Police some time to solve his murder. Possibly it has to do with why he kept so much of his life a secret from me. Does that make any sense?"

"Sure, but Sally you were still working a few weeks ago, why do you need to get retrained, is it your annual certification time?"

"No, American recommended a few counseling sessions before I return to work, most likely a couple of days, then I expect to be back on the regular schedule. Can you watch Willy-nilly and the house for me?"

"Okay, but do you have to leave tonight?"

"I want to Stephen I've got a room set up at American's Flight Academy. I'll write all my contact information down for you. Excuse me now I've got to go finish packing. Thanks Stephen, it's really what I need right now."

Sally departed for the house, and I muttered to myself, "Damn you Wilber!" Thornton interrupted my mumbling,

"You've got to get hold of yourself Rusty, Sally's got to get her life back, all this business about Wilber is getting to her. There's got to be more to this than what we know right now. We've got to make the effort to get this damn mess straightened out before she returns. Two weeks, bud, it's got to get done by then."

When I took Sally to the airport, Security restrictions wouldn't allow me to go with her to the gate, so she asked me to drop her off in front of the Terminal. As I helped her out of my car she handed me a small packet of papers and said, "When the Navy Relief people picked up his clothes they found these papers inside the lining of one of his uniform hats. I've put my contact information on another piece of paper for you." Sally handed me several small sheets of paper, her contact numbers were on a new sheet but the other papers were old and had been folded many times obviously used. Sally added, "There's a set of books, some Navy

Correspondence Course of his in the garage, could you throw them out please, Navy Relief didn't want the books."

I told Sally okay, kissed her good-by and she turned and pulled her roller-suitcase into the Norfolk Terminal. I moved back to my car, sat down and folded her contact information up and pocketed it as I began to look at the other papers Sally had given me. The sheets were about 5X8 inches in size and had been folded lengthwise into four sections. Opening up the folds, the first and second columns were the alphabet, A-Z and the numbers 1 to 26 vertically corresponding to the number of letters in the alphabet. I exposed the third column on the second sheet which was the alphabet in reverse.

As I opened the paper more, some object tapped on my windshield startled me, *TAP, TAP, TAP,* "Hey, sir, are you, waiting for a flight?" A cute gal in a TSA uniform asked as she tapped on my windshield with her flashlight. I lowered the window and answered,

"Hello, Miss, sorry, I was trying to read a note from my sister. Am I blocking traffic?"

"Not yet, but you're giving me reason to ask you to move on, so, do it NOW! Go somewhere else to read your note!" She stood up straight and motioned with her flashlight for me to move on. As I raised the window, shoved the old paper into my shirt pocket and started the car the TSA gal stopped her retreat, smiled and moved back toward my car. She must have more to say, I thought looking for another female connection, maybe she'll apologize, I hoped as I lowered the window again and she leaned down and said,

"Sir, your Check Engine Light is ON, you better see your mechanic soon."

Some apology, I made another mental note to get an appointment with BPI and drove away.

Thornton and I went into Sally's garage. The garage space held their car on one side and the rest was a work space, neat and clean like you'd expect an Ex Submariner to keep all his stored gear. There was a long work bench extending the back length of the garage and on one side of the clean work bench was the navy correspondence course. I began to thumb through each page of the twelve volume set called, JOINT SERVICE CHALLENGES FOR THE US NAVY. I began to find loose $100 bills and by the time we had finished laughing and checking the entire twelve volumes thoroughly, I had found a short note from Wilber and over ten thousand dollars in one hundred dollar bills and Wilber's short note to my sister,

Sally Dear, I don't know where I am now, but if you're reading this note I'm probably gone and I'm sure you've found out about my ex and son Allen living nearby. I'm so sorry about not sharing my son with you. It was stupid of me but I thought I had to keep his existence a secret. My fear of losing you because of my age and the responsibilities I carried when we first met, kept me from being totally honest with you then. Sadly that fear never really left me. I'm sorry that concern about my age and the support money I was paying forced me to act so stupidly. Now I'm certain you would have understood, but my need to impress you was overwhelming. I'm hoping you and Stephen will be able to forgive me and you'll have also found the other money in our safety deposit box and know about my effort to do more for my country than my Naval record indicates. Maybe I'll get the nerve to tell you this in person, but I want you to know that I love you Sally and I'm grateful to God for sending you to me when I needed you the most. All my love always, Will

Thornton shook his head and offered, "Damn Rusty, Wilber was some kind of SPOOK. We better watch our step in this mess."

CHAPTER FIFTY NINE

STARFISH MOTEL, FRIDAY, 8PM

Ursula Volk had driven 14 hours straight, she was tired but she knew if she was going to act, now was the time. She didn't know the names of all the people involved but she was certain her immediate threat was Sergeant Morris Bradshaw. She had called Bradshaw earlier from a pay phone at the Memphis Airport in case he checked on the origin of the call. She answered his questions about Eric explaining that he showed up a month ago asking for her help getting him a job at the Virginia Zoo. Because she knew of the trouble Eric had caused in San Diego, she admitted that she had been skeptical, but had agreed to take Eric on as a volunteer while she tried to help find him regular employment. Bradshaw had asked how that worked out and she replied, 'okay initially, but a week ago he let me down. He was a no-show'. After Bradshaw confirmed that Eric Chin had been found drowned near his apartment last Tuesday, Ursula responded with genuine regret. Bradshaw told her Chin's death appeared accidental with some alcohol and a lot of drugs found in his system. Ursula had explained that drugs had been Eric's problem in San Diego and she gave Bradshaw a contact at the San Diego Wild Animal Park to confirm her information. Ursula had been impressed when Bradshaw boasted tracing Eric to the Virginia Zoo from the elephant fecal matter embedded in the soles of his boots before he thanked her and asked for a future contact number. Ursula informed him that her dad was transferring to an unknown nursing facility in Frankfurt but she promised to provide a follow-up address through the Virginia Zoo's Curator. Bradshaw seemed inexperienced to Ursula. He was overly preoccupied with his successes so far, like a little kid looking for praise, wanting to please everyone. He had seemed easily misdirected but she remained concerned since Bradshaw had her name.

After Bradshaw's phone call Ursula and Alex split up at the airport and Alex took Ursula's ticket and ID and flew to Dulles International Airport, in Washington DC, to show-up for Ursula's booked flight to Frankfurt. Alex would arrive at Dulles, check in with Ursula's ticket for her Lufthansa flight, then, return to Tennessee. Ursula's booked seat to Frankfurt would go empty, but she didn't believe it was necessary to distract the Police beyond the Dulles Airport check in. She couldn't ask Alex to delay her return to work any longer, that extra delay could cause a problem for both of them.

Arriving in the Hampton Roads Area, Ursula took Route 13 North through the Chesapeake Bay Bridge Tunnel and stopped at the Starfish Motel. Ursula rented a room for a week to plan her next moves. She was concerned about the connection Bradshaw might make between his investigation and her main mission remembering Iron Man Cheng had been adamant, *"There can be NO chance these two separate missions can be connected,"*

Ursula had her orders and she was determined to close out this chapter of her life. As she rested, pondering her next action, her cell phone rang. The phone's ID told her it was Alex,

"Hi, Sweetie, everything okay?" a full minute of listening, some notes on a pad of paper, then finally,

"That's good, I'm sure both our butts are covered, now. Don't worry about Bradshaw, I've been told he's a fill-in guy for Homicide and can be manipulated, you know he's like a 'dumb duck' kind of guy," Ursula and Alex both laughed, then, Ursula listened for another 20 seconds,

"Yes, Honey, I'll be back and we can do Atlanta. Thanks for everything I'll see you soon." Ursula closed her cell-phone and it immediately rang again, this time the ID registered 'VA cell'. "Damn", Ursula voiced and flipped the phone open a second time,

"Yes, who is it?" Ursula knew very few people had this number, it could be a mistake, a misdial, but she was cautious. It was no misdial she heard the demandingly pompous voice and knew she was in for an extended lecture. She listened patiently for 20 seconds of the long-winded diatribe then she replied,

"No, I'm not in your area I've gotten my orders too. The zoo thinks I'm on a leave of absence to help care for my family in Germany, so don't me call again."

Ursula's demands were quickly silenced as her caller interrupted and told her of the FBI's involvement in the case then spelled out her instructions, direction after direction and threat after threat. Ursula listened for another full minute before her caller finished, then, closed with demands for her to get the job done, and hung up.

Alex had told her that Bradshaw called and she had been there to cover his questions but Ursula wasn't sure Bradshaw believed Alex totally. Now, Ursula thought Bradshaw might not be a 'dumb duck', now he seemed more curious, like a cat that could possibly follow up at Dulles Airport and find she hadn't departed on her scheduled flight. If Bradshaw did that, then he was a definitely a 'curious cat' threatening to end up spilling all her cream. Well, curious like a cat, he may be, Ursula thought, but he doesn't have 9 lives, and now, I know exactly where he is, I can kill his curiosity soon enough.

CHAPTER SIXTY

THE BISTRO, FRIDAY, 8:30 PM

Kat was surprised by Morris choosing 'The Bistro' for their date. Maybe, she thought as they sat at the bar waiting for their table to open up, he could have asked Linda Knowles because Kat had seen Linda here several times. But, she finally decided to give Morris full credit and let her mind go along for the fun of the date. 'Little Todd', as he was called by the Bistro's staff and regulars, was Kat's favorite waiter and he came by the bar and introduced himself to Morris saying, "I'll be your server tonight, Sergeant Bradshaw, but I'm tied-up right now, so Caitlin will come by and escort you when your table opens-up."

Kat smiled noting Morris' dark blue suit, crisp white shirt and bright red tie. He was spicing up his image for her by wearing such a bold tie. Then, as Morris turned in his seat to order their drinks Kat noticed his bright red socks with white lightening bolts spiking down both sides of each ankle and pointing to his highly polished cordovan loafers. Spicy indeed, Kat mused. After Paula delivered two dry martinis at the bar, the waitress Little Todd mentioned arrived, "Hello you two, I'm Caitlin, your table's open now and Little Todd asked me to lead you over, WOW, those are GREAT SOCKS sir!"

Their show-booth was located near the front of the restaurant and that pleased Kat, who was still smiling to herself about the waitress' remark and Morris' embarrassment over his 'RAVE' socks. His face hadn't turned as red as his socks and tie, but it had definitely flushed a blood-rush-pink. After Caitlin seated them, Kat saw Little Todd with the chef-owner talking in the Bistro's expansive kitchen. 'Big Todd' was busy but Kat caught his eye and he waved a small copper pot toward their booth in a friendly greeting. Kat smiled, waved back and Morris saw her gesture and asked, "Who're you waving at, Kat, our waiter?"

"No, Big Todd, the chef." She replied.

"You know the chef and owner of the restaurant?" Morris said.

"Of course, I come here often it's one of my favorites. I actually followed both Todd's from their earlier restaurant, 'Bistro 210'. They always have the best places."

Kat looked great to Morris she was still tanned from the summer and wore a filmy black dress with thin string-like straps. Morris fantasized that he could pull the dress up and off her small taunt body if she'd just stand-still and hold her arms up straight. The fantasy evaporated as he became concerned about both these Todd characters and the fact that Kat had followed them here from some other restaurant. His detective instincts got the better of him and he asked,

"So Kat, you know Big Todd, because you come here often, and you come here often because you followed both he and Little Todd from some other restaurant, is that correct?"

Kat regarded Morris' string of question then said, "Be honest with me Morris, did you really pick this restaurant yourself?" Morris smiled at Kat's turning the table on him and replied,

"Well, I had some help from Detective Knowles," Just then Little Todd returned, and announced,

"Our Chef would like to buy you two a drink," Little Todd said directly to Bradshaw, "or maybe dessert, after dinner?" Kat smiled and answered for them,

"Please thank Todd for his kindness, but we're going to my house for our dessert, we'll just have two more of Paula's perfect martinis." Kat said as she laid her hand gently on Morris' thigh and squeezed provocatively. Then she added, "Is that okay with you Morris?" Morris' face flushed for a second time and his mind sent his concerns about the two Todd's into a dumpster for bad ideas.

"Sounds like a plan," Little Todd responded, "You two look at the Menu and I'll get your drinks and be right back with the evening specials,"

Morris was excited about Kat's 'dessert offering' and the feel of her fingers squeezing his thigh. She was definitely showing him her own Valentine Card. Morris wanted to impress Kat and brag about his follow-up chasing down Ursula Volk and her information... After talking to Ursula, Bradshaw found out more by phoning her friend Alex, but then, when he checked the friend's information, he lost Ursula's trail at the Dulles Airport. Ursula had arrived and checked in with Lufthansa, but didn't actually make the flight. The ticket agent remembered paging Ursula several times but, her seat had gone out empty. Bradshaw was certain there was more to be found out and he was anxious to tell Knowles and Millers when they would meet on Monday to update the investigation. Morris had written it all down in his notebook and knew Millers would be pleased that he had actually gone back and 'touched' those seemingly empty bases.

Little Todd returned for their order and Kat suggested that Morris have some of The Bistro's famous Oyster Stew. They all laughed at Kat's second 'sexual' suggestion and Morris agreed and accepted the recommendation from Little Todd about the special entrées featuring Thai spicy seasoned lamb chops for their meal.

During their dinner, Linda Knowles walked by their booth and said hello. Morris and Kat were both surprised. Linda told them, she was here with Agent Davis discussing some new information about the Harrington case. Bradshaw was immediately tempted to jump in with his own information about Ursula Volk, but decided to remain focused on Kat. So he restrained himself, once again agreeing to meet on Monday morning for the group's scheduled briefing.

After their meal, on the way to Kat's home, she sat very close to Morris dreaming about a Norah Jones' song, 'Yes' she thought, 'my heart's definitely drenched in wine and we're going to my house of fun'.

Arriving Kat thought she might have to make some coffee to 'pep' Morris up for their 'house of fun' adventure. She thought that until she opened her front door entered, and Morris closed the door and bodily picked her up and carried her to the hallway asking, "Which way to your bedroom?"

CHAPTER SIXTY ONE

LARCHMONT CRESCENT DRIVE, 11:00 PM

Ursula Volk had been hiding outside Dr. Kowalski's home when the unmarked Crown Vic pulled into the driveway. She watched as Bradshaw struggled exiting his side of the car, stumbling slightly, then catching his balance on the left front fender before fully recovering. After Bradshaw righted himself he came around to open the door for Dr. Kowalski. Jesus Christ, Ursula thought, why the hell was I worried about him, he's an uncoordinated Munchkin. As she watched Dr. Kowalski exit the car, she laughed to herself again now knowing this was going to be two very small jobs.

Ursula, wearing dark clothes a knit cap and dark surgical gloves, had been hiding between a hedge and cold concrete wall that separated Dr. Kowalski's property from her next door neighbor. Ursula was certain this job had to be done. The connection Harrington's death might make with her primary mission had to be eliminated. She moved toward the house and peered in through a side window watching Bradshaw hurry down the hallway carrying the small doctor. She could imagine the pleasure they were anticipating and immediately thought of her 'friend' Alex and how their passion re-flamed with each reunion. Thoughts of Alex and how easy this 'new task' was looking began to monopolize her tired mind as she worked her way toward the front door.

Ursula carried a small bag in her right hand containing a short, wide pry-bar and the 22 caliber Colt she had taken from the teenage punks. The Colt was loaded and now fitted with a modified silencer. In her left hand she had a lock-pick tool designed to open a number of standard front door locks. She reached from behind a decorative hedge and tried the front door, the knob turned within her grasp so she pocketed the lock pick and soundlessly eased the door open, sliding around the edge of the small porch and entering the home quietly. She closed the door as began to concentrate on the sounds of the house.

Standing in the small entrance area, she could make out the large living room to her far left and directly ahead she saw the dimly lit hallway the couple had hurried down. She continued to listen, now hearing amorous sounds that again reminded her of Alex. Ursula 's mind now focused on Alex's small taunt body, her exciting aroma and her anxiousness to please and she made the decision to wait. These two were just little people, like Alex, so for Alex, she'd allow them a final pleasure then once they had exhausted themselves, she knew they'd be an even smaller challenge.

As her eyes became accustomed to the dim lighting of the house she moved left, seeking the comfort of a large wing back chair standing deep within the fully darkened living room, well away from the faded hall lighting. Ursula eased into the living room and removed the silenced revolver from her bag now holding it loosely in her hand as she seated herself and felt the warmth of relaxation begin to enter her body. Soon her tiredness and the icy coldness of the concrete wall left her muscles and bones and she began to relax and fantasize of telling Alex this story when they reunited. As Ursula sat quietly listening, the loving sounds softened and diminished to near quiet as Ursula's long 28 hour day took its toll and she drifted off to sleep.

———————

Morris and Kat slept, exhausted, sexually fulfilled and free from known care. They were unmoving for a few hours, then, Kat's slumber was assaulted. Certain she heard a noise she awoke, drowsy and forced herself to glance at the bedside clock. The clock's glow offered 4:15AM and Kat eased herself up and traveled across the co-mingled clothing that spread over the floor and the bed. She moved quietly to her adjoining bathroom, closed the door and slipped into the red silk robe that hung on the back of the door. She clicked one small night-light ON and peered into the dimly lit mirror preparing to cream her whisker burned face.

Morris had been mostly driven by his own needs, but he had shown gentleness carrying Kat to fulfillment. Kat had been anxious, hastily drawing Morris into own body and feeling the increased rhythm move up and down her spine believing she had finally found her destiny, her own motivating force to drive away her lack-luster past. Yes, she decided, this was her force; Morris, red socks tie and his lingering insecurities; were going to be her saving force.

After cream application she washed her gritty eyes and quietly brushed her teeth. Refreshed, she turned OFF the water and light, opened the bathroom door and reentered the bed room. Remembering the noise she had thoughts of checking the front door, she was uncertain she had actually locked the door earlier. Quietly she proceeded down the dimly lit hallway past the edge of her darkened living room straight to the front door. Everything remained very dark as she checked the lock, barely turning the knob. She sighed quietly to herself and noiselessly turned the latching mechanism to the locked position. She couldn't honestly remember not locking the door but the excitement of Morris, martinis and red wine had fuzzed her memory.

Kat's small, bare feet padded quietly back down the hall and reentered the bedroom pushing the door almost closed so that only a small opening separated the door's edge from the dimly lit hallway. She moved toward her dresser, picking up her little black dress and Morris' discarded trousers from the floor placing them on a chair. The dim light brought Morris' relaxing features into focus and as Kat neared the bed she kicked a pathway through their remaining clothing, propelling his' red tie and 'rave socks' softly toward the wall. Her eyes followed the clothing flight and saw, on the edge of the bed, the reflection of leather and composite metal in the subdued lighting. Kat retrieved Morris' holstered weapon and laid the GLOCK 17 and holster on the carpeted floor near her side of the bed. As she eased back in under the sheet, her red silk robe fell gently to the floor, covering Morris' holstered weapon.

CHAPTER SIXTY TWO

LARCHMONT CRESCENT DRIVE, 5 AM

Ursula began to move in the chair as she awoke. She listened, but heard no sound from down the dimly lit hall. She tapped her digital watch and the responding glow told her 5AM. She was shocked she had slept for five hours and got up and moved quietly toward the front door. She tried to turn the doorknob and found it now locked, someone had been there. Her teeth clenched and her heart began to drum rapidly against her rib cage as she made the conscious effort to slow her breathing, momentarily closing her eyes and fighting to regain control. The deepening pulses of her heart resounded less and less as she began to calm, preparing to complete her small task. As she moved slowly down the hallway she eased her way past the open kitchen area toward the bedroom door now partially closed allowing only a faint, amber light from the hallway into the room. The hallway's muted glow was joined by the pre-dawn purpling tint as the first rays of the emerging sun began to wash its soft vermillion haze through a small easterly facing window. Framed pictures and documents attesting to Dr. Kowalski's Medical Service and Police employment were barely visible in the dawning hallway and Ursula focused on the nearly closed bedroom door and prepared herself for possible discovery as she raised the weapon and silently cocked the hammer.

Ursula eased the door open barely illuminating the shadowed room as she extended the weapon's silenced barrel into the bedroom moving the gun barrel slowly from side to side seeking a final point aim. The readied Colt was rock solid in her right hand as she moved up closer and much more personal. Approaching Bradshaw's side of the bed the dawn's soft glow highlighted both sheet covered bodies and Ursula was surprised how much Dr. Kowalski continued to remind her of Alex lying quiet and deep in sleep. She discarded the intruding thought and began to watch Bradshaw's chest rise and fall in the dim lighting. Momentarily his eyes trembled and she tensed to fire until the dim lighting revealed only a REM sleep response, Bradshaw was also deeply dreaming. Easing closer Ursula placed the silenced gun gently against the left side of Bradshaw's head and fired the weapon. The quiet *POP* was muffled by the silencer and head contact and hardly made a sound. But as Bradshaw's muscles jumped their last effort, Kat sensed the movement and jolted upright in bed, looking directly at Ursula. Ursula's minds-eye flashed again to Alex and she hesitated for the split second that allowed Kat to respond. Seeing and intruder with a weapon, Kat twisted rapidly, reaching down where she remembered Bradshaw's gun on the carpeted floor. Ursula shook off her distraction, shifted the muzzle toward the back of Kat's head and pulled the trigger once again. Ursula's delay gave Kat just enough time to stretch down toward the gun on the floor and her fingers actually touched the red silk robe that covered Bradshaw's weapon as Ursula's second muffled shot *POPPED*, sounding like a small Chihuahua's bark and sending a 22 slug into the base of Kat's skull, spilling her naked body over the edge of the bed and onto the floor, covering the silk robe and Morris' holstered gun.

Confident of her second kill, Ursula pocketed her weapon and began pulling open several drawers and throwing articles and clothing around the room. In the emerging dawn's light she grabbed loose jewelry attempting to leave the room in a ransacked and burglarized condition. Ursula paused momentarily and pushed Kat's body sideways with her foot, looking for a response but the body rolled slightly then fell back into its original lifeless position.

As the dawn's light increased its intensity, now beginning to expose the entire room, Ursula focused on getting this done and leaving. She moved to the hallway knocking picture frames from the walls onto the hard-wood floor as she traveled back down the hallway toward the small living room where she had slept. Arriving back in the living room she began looking for small, worthwhile targets of theft. She gathered in Kat's purse and a small DVD player, ripping the wires from the wall. Next she found an iPOD and a Blackberry device lying on the coffee table near two small sterling silver statues. She grabbed the electronic devices and the statues, placing them in her small bag as she removed the short pry bar and carried the bag toward the back door.

The early purple of dawn began to issue a yellowed warning to expose her departure as she worked exiting and closing the back door. Ursula used the pry bar to damage the door appearing she had entered here then she gathered her tools and bag and departed the rear porch area headed back toward the hedge and wall where she had originally hidden herself. A dog began to yap as she moved between the concrete wall and the hedge, but did not approach her position. Ursula continued to move away from the home toward her hidden car now confident that she had 'acted' to put an end to Bradshaw's curiosity and his threat to discover her closely guarded secret.

CHAPTER SIXTY THREE

PIERSIDE APARTMENTS, SUNDAY, 7 PM

Peggy Turner cooled down from her aerobic routine, toweled off and added powdered chalk to her taped hands as she approached the large floor mounted punching bag system. She took several deep breaths to focus her control and bent down near the end of the bag apparatus to release the clamp on the locking mechanism. The opposite end of the bag *CLANKED* loudly as it sprang upright and snapped the large punching-bag into a locked vertical position. The bag now towered over her 5' 8" statue, presenting a seven foot tall leather covered opponent, certainly larger than any Norfolk mugger she was concerned about. Os had promised this exercise would help her become less intimidated by an attacker's physical size and Peggy slid forward into a fighting stance as she moved toward the leather target and let fly a flurry of hands and feet rocking the bag to its hinges and Os' exaggerated instructions came back to Peggy's mind, echoing from Friday night's training session here in the Apartment Complex's Workout Area. His remembered voice was low and grinding, like stones banging around in a galvanized tub, *"Peggy, my gal, you've got to be quicker if you're going to protect yourself!"* His voice remained in her mind, guiding her now as it had motivated her efforts during the past six weeks of her training. Peggy sometimes wished she and Os could get back together, but they had gone their separate way and Os had introduced her to Charles soon after they split. Os had said, *"Peggy you'll be good for Charles and he could be a comfort to you,"*

The new relationship had grown to be wonderful for Peggy and Charles, at least until Charles began to worry: about his wife Millie, about threats to his business, and most recently, about the death of one of his employees. In Peggy's mind, Charles now worried about everything but her. His admirable qualities of caring, concern and consideration had deteriorated into personal disregard and even disrespect. Peggy had wanted to turn to Charles when she became worried about the recent increased crime in downtown Norfolk, but he was too busy, too preoccupied, so she turned to an old friend. Os had agreed to train her in self defense, to help her restore her feeling of security and her natural self confidence but only if she was 100% committed. Peggy was strong, she was quick and she was motivated, she knew her experience as a field hockey athlete in high school and college would serve her well and she announced to the empty room, "I'm going to get my confidence back," she offered the punching bag, then, continued building her skills, striking the bag forcefully between each statement, "I know it's not ALL your fault, Charles,' but, I can't keep dealing with your personal problems and business enemies, real or imagined. I've got to make my own without your baggage."

Peggy's clenched hands forced powdery spheres to form around them before her right fist shot forward and slammed the leather target with a twisting force that penetrated the leather bag barely one inch, before she retracted her strike. The elasticity of the leather had no time to recover from her initial strike as the ball of her left foot slammed into the exact same spot on the bag. The softness and pliability created by her initial thrust, prepared the leather for a penetration, this time, of over three inches, a crippling strike.

After several punches the turbulent sequence was over and Peggy released the clasp and pushed the upright bag back to its stowed position. She towel off her face and arms and headed back to her apartment determined to end her weakening relationship with Charles and get on with her life. Soon, she would break the hold that was pulling her down in a spiraling loss of confidence and self respect. Soon she and Charles would be a thing of the past. Perhaps she and Os could get back together, yes perhaps that could happen.

Charles Taylor checked his watch, exactly 10PM. He stood at the front door to Peggy's apartment, determined to control his jealousy and temper. After his knock the door opened and there framed by the interior lighting was the old friend he hadn't seen for over a month. His mouth dropped open as he fumbled to offer the roses, hoping for Peggy's forgiveness. Her short, dark hair, still damp from a shower was stroked back away from her oval face highlighting the angelic appearance he had fallen in love with several months ago. Charles barely heard Peggy's "Thanks for the roses," as she invited him into her apartment. "They're so pretty, Charles, I do love them, but we need to talk." Peggy continued to offer as she pushed Charles down into a chair and departed the room for the kitchen.

Charles watched as Peggy reentered the den carrying a pitcher of martinis and two large iced martini glasses. She placed the iced glasses on the table and leaned over to hand Charles his drink. Peggy's shirt front fell open and Charles spilled his drink groping toward the open shirt.

"No, Charles, none of that, we've got to talk, you've got to be a gentleman," Peggy's chiding was interrupted as her door bell sounded an interrupting *RING,*

"Excuse me Charles, I'll check this out and be right back." Peggy moved across her small living room, opened the door and stared at Charles' wife Millie standing in the doorway with a nickel plated 32 caliber automatic held in both hands.

Peggy started to slam the door closed, but heard, "I'll get you, Whore," were the last words Peggy heard as the nickel plated 32 fired twice, CRACK, CRACK and Peggy took the bullets directly in the face and neck. Two muted echoes bounced through the apartment and Peggy's cervical spine snapped shutting down her brain from the spinal cord impact. Her head flopped limply as Peggy fell dead to the apartment floor and Millie exclaimed,

"Not so pretty now Bitch. I told you she's a WHORE Charlie, its damned good to be rid o' her. You get to a phone Charlie we need some Wizard stuff right now!"

CHAPTER SIXTY FOUR

NORFOLK, SUNDAY 10:15PM

Judge Anthony Knutson was relaxing in his back yard, sharing a drink with his long-time friend, Master Deputy Sheriff Jimmy Osborne. The Judge nursed a tumbler of McCallum Single Malt as Os sipped Cognac and watched his old friend. Os thought of Charles' concern that the judge's mind was beginning to wander to old thoughts, the same thoughts that had caused he and Charles to 'act' earlier in March. But, Os was going to make his own assessment.

While they sat in the Judge's fenced-in back yard enjoying the evening and reminiscent conversation, a background noise from wind-flapped flags and evening-traffic could be heard from the nearby Brambleton Avenue Bridge. The reflecting sounds joined with the Elizabeth River's breeze generated waters-flow lapping of small waves against the concrete bulkhead directly across the street from the Judge's home. Os hadn't wanted to spend this much time with the Judge, but it was important to understand the Judge's present state of mind. Os' attention was gained as the Judge offered, "Os, we've seen Norfolk grow and prosper over our years, but don't you regret some of the missed opportunities that passed us by? You know opportunities to do better for Norfolk, to do more for our city," The Judge said as he contemplatively rolled the small tumbler of Scotch around in his liver spotted hands. His eyes were a cloudy blue reflecting the onset of cataract disease in the halogen lighting from his neighbor's security system. The opaque light gave the Judge an appearance of gauntness, a face of frailty, a look of the approaching 'end of life'. Os waited for the Judge to continue.

"My regrets, mostly concern the loss of my darling Estelle last year, but I do think of Norfolk at times. You know Os, you and Charles and I have surely done a lot for this town, but we've taken a lot too, it's been good for us. I don't regret our taking, we had that coming, but I do regret some of the 'means' we used from time to time. You understand Os?"

Os understood, he had been up close and personal with the application of most of those 'means', whereas Charles and the Judge were mainly involved in identifying the 'ends'. Like after the Judge's wife death, when the judge worried both about Estelle's loss and the 'means' they had used to gain several of their chosen 'ends'. Those types of things were regressing again. Charles is right, Os mused, there seems to be less drinking and more recrimination. Os was becoming concerned again like he and Charles had been in February, when the Judge wanted to publicly unburden his tortured soul for his wife's memory. They had counseled the judge to Reflect, Resist and Retire but Judge Knutson's attitude had continued its deterioration into a threatening melancholia and they had decided drastic action was needed to stop the deepening spiral. After their decision and attempt to 'act', the Judge's increasing urge to cleanse himself had miraculously vanished. Possibly, when Stephen Irons interceded to prevent the Judge from being shot dead in his own courtroom, provided the catalyst that had changed the judge's mind. Os' reflections ended as he took the last sip of brandy and his cell phone *BUZZED* and the Judge offered,

"Don't mind me Os, take the call, I need a little more ice in my scotch." Judge Knutson said as he rose and moved agedly toward his back door, up three short steps and into his home's breakfast room area.

Os flipped open his cell, answered and listened intently while in between Charles' sobs and Millie's background hysterics, the story of Peggy's death played out. Soon, Os had heard enough, and responded,

"Charles, get a grip now! Clean-up everything, get your clothes, get your personal things and get your ass out of there now! Can you do that Charles? Can you get that done and go home now?" Os listened as his old friend relayed that, he wasn't sure he could do what Os wanted without some help. Os asked to speak to Millie as he watched the Judge add ice to his drink in his kitchen. Millie answered and Os instructed,

"Millie, don't speak, just listen. It's life threatening to stay there. Get all of Charles' things, leave the weapon and close the apartment door, go home, now! Wait at home until you hear from me, don't call anyone and don't go anywhere. Keep Charles at home and wait for my call." There was no answer, only a pause before the line disconnected.

Os closed his cell as the Judge came back with a newly diluted scotch and said, "Os, can I get you another brandy? The evening so nice, I've not felt this comfortable in a long time."

"No thanks, Judge, it's late for me, I've enjoyed our evening too but I've got to go. Maybe I'll take a sip of your scotch." Os interjected, in need of a quick jolt to get him moving, "Then I've got to go. Are you okay Judge?" Os asked after sipping and returning the watered-down scotch to the Judge.

"Yes, thanks for listening to an old man's ramblings, I'm always grateful to you and Charles for your concern."

"You're welcome, Judge, I'll just let myself out now, you relax and enjoy the evening, Charles and I will come by tomorrow."

———————

In the Pier Side Apartments at 12:15AM, it had taken Os over an hour to get everything done. He had gone home, changed into athletic gear, picked up a large trash bag, gloves and a small crowbar from his garage. He drove his personal car to the apartment complex and entered the basement parking area. He was careful to park his car away from known video cameras, then, he let himself into the complex using the now familiar entry code before he proceeded up the stairs to the fourth floor where Peggy lived. He had been there many times lately, working with Peggy and he reasoned that if he were seen at this late hour again, he expected there would be no problem.

Wearing thin surgical gloves Os had entered the apartment, gathered everything he believed could point to someone else having been there, other than the burglar that had obviously shot Peggy after breaking into her apartment. Os stepped carefully around Peggy's body as he placed several articles of value, some electronics, some jewelry, Peggy's purse and exposed cash, along with the discarded weapon into the trash bag.

The apartment effort itself took forty five minutes. Now, standing outside the apartment, Os closed the front door and used the crowbar to pry it open. Dropping the crowbar, he removed and pocketed his gloves, grabbed the large trash bag and went to Peggy's phone to dial 911. The operator answered and Os said,

"This is Norfolk Master Deputy Sheriff Jimmy Osborne. I'm at the Pier Side Apartment Complex in downtown Norfolk and I've just discovered the body of Dr. Peggy Turner, murdered in her apartment, number 402. Send the Police NOW. I'll meet them in the parking garage of the complex." Os immediately hung up the phone and headed down the stairs to wait for the Norfolk Police.

CHAPTER SIXTY FIVE

POLICE OPERATIONS

"STEPHEN IRONS"

It's Monday morning and I'm sitting in Linda's office waiting for her arrival. The Duty Officer (DO) escorted me to her desk and informed me that 'Detective Knowles was observing the questioning of a witness.' The DO, Jack something, looked at me funny, like he wanted to tell me more, but he retreated to a safer option, smiled and left me alone to wait for Linda. I took out the notes from my side of the investigation and prepared to brief Linda on my findings since interviewing several NISCO employees that worked closely with Wilber. After that, hopefully, I'd learn the news she was willing to pass-on from her investigation.

Folded-in among my notes was the small group of papers Sally had given me Friday night, the papers she had found in one of Wilber's navy hats. I debated telling Linda about the papers, about Wilber's final note to Sally and about the additional money Thornton and I had found in their garage… But, I decided to hold those cards close for a little longer. The money was an increasing mystery but the papers could be some of Wilber's old coded submarine notes. Or, possibly some type of 'craft' he used to set up meetings, like Wilber's final note to Sally had implied.

Sally actually called from Dallas last night, she was very up-beat. She had spent the past two days visiting with friends that lived in the Dallas area and was certain she had made the right decision. She was scheduled to see her counselor today for the first of her sessions but already she sounded much better. Sally's friends, as I noted earlier, were strong and very supportive, and now they were helping her work her way through dealing with Wilber's loss and his secrecy. I was now more determined to get the mystery that surrounded Wilber's life, and his death, solved before Sally returned.

It took ten more minutes before Linda arrived, she shook my hand and asked for my patience while she accessed something on her computer. I sat down and began to connect Jack's earlier 'funny look' with Linda's need to get on her computer. I watched and waited while her computer took a long time coming on line. Her antiquated machine was sputtering and finally as all the clicks and whirs settled into a factual display and the requested data began to scroll across the screen. I watched it all happen as I tried to bring the small print into focus, but all I could make out was the familiar overall presentation of a Norfolk Police Report Sheet, possibly cataloging recent crimes.

After a full minute of asking, refining and asking again, Linda paused and said, "Damn Steven, your friend, and mine, Master Deputy Sheriff Osborne, found and reported the murder of a friend of his that he was visiting late last night, a lady named Dr. Peggy Turner," I was stunned but able to offer,

"I've heard Os speak of her, she's a doctor in some Maritime field of study. She works at Nauticus I think. What happened?"

"Os stated he'd been working with Dr. Turner, teaching her self-defense for the past month because she was worried about increased assaults in downtown Norfolk," I interrupted,

"Is that what you were checking for on the computer?"

"Yes, and Dr. Turner was right there have been increases. Of, course Os would know that too, so he would want to respond to a friend's request for help. Os' training has been going on for about five weeks, generally late at night so it fit into their busy schedules. When Os showed up around 12:15 this morning, he found the apartment broken into, ransacked and Dr. Turner shot twice, dead on the floor. He called 911 to report the crime and our logs indicate 12:23AM. Our preliminary examination of Dr. Turner's body places her time of death at 10:30 last night, plus or minus an hour. Os told the operator he'd meet the police in the garage. He told us he 'went to the basement to get his Sheriff's ID and wait for the police'."

"He left the scene unguarded?"

"Yes, he claimed an emotional error, finding a murdered friend and being anxious to greet the responding officers, but he admitted he wanted to take a quick look for suspects while he obtained his ID and his weapon. Os was, and still is in his work-out clothes."

"He's here now?"

"Yes, he's been here since 1AM. The Sheriff showed up an hour ago to check on him but we were still questioning Os so the Sheriff left."

I thought a minute about the situation, what concerned me was this weird feeling of curiosity I couldn't shake. "Funny, Os is generally not too emotional about anything... Dr. Turner must have meant more to him than he's ever said."

"It comes across that way, doesn't it? He's very upset and said his help was 'too little and too late'. You know him better than I do, Stephen, does that make sense to you?"

There wasn't a quick Yes or No answer to Linda's question, but after a short time I offered, "Maybe, if he really cared for her and feels partially responsible, I'm sure it was traumatic for Os to find someone he knew, probably cared for more than he's ever admitted, to find her murdered, you know like shoving his face into his own perceived failure. I felt the same when I lost Thornton." I wanted to elaborate, but I saw Thornton enter the room waiting for my explanation, so I changed my mind and went back to Linda's investigation.

"Are the police comfortable with Os' story?" Both Linda and Thornton gave me a funny look, like they wanted to hear more. Thornton continued to look perplexed but Linda replied,

"I think we believe him, I can certainly see it his way. The complex's security cameras have been on the fritz for the last week and the manager stated the fact has been kept a secret during their repair process. But the old security tapes show Os coming and going at the times he mentioned over the past few weeks. Since the cameras weren't functioning at the time of the murder and there were no eye witnesses we're stumped. There're only two large apartments on the fourth floor and the other tenant's away on vacation, so our only course is to canvass our area informants and local pawn shops to look for what we can ID as being stolen. The apartment break in looks like a crowbar we found was used to gain entry. Dr. Turner probably heard the noise and came into the room where she was shot before the intruder burglarized her apartment. She was dead on the floor when Os found her. She was dressed nice, you know casually like she could have been expecting someone other than a work-out partner. Os obviously noticed that too, but stated he doesn't know who she might have been expecting."

"Are you, or any of your people, assigned to this case?"

"No, they're leaving my small group alone," Linda began, then she paused and immediately shifted her thoughts, "Damn Bradshaw should be here now, he said he had some new information to pass on. I told him you and I would be here at nine,"

"Maybe he's tied up with some other aspect of your case and its dragging out longer than he expected."

"You're probably right, I saw him with Dr. Kowalski at THE BISTRO, Friday night, that's when I reminded him of this meeting." Linda offered, then, she added, "Well, I guess he could have forgotten he was really focused on his dinner partner..."

"Are they an item?" I interrupted and Thornton commented,

"Who the hell was Knowles' dinner partner, Rusty?" That nagged at me but she opted not to answer my 'item' question, and went to her cell phone,

"Damn, no answer for Bradshaw, and lot of rings before going to message." Linda reached her desk phone, and asked the operator to connect her to Dr. Kowalski, at the Coroner's office. She put the phone on SPEAKER and I heard,

"Medical Examiner's office, Dr. Clark, how can I help you?"

"This is Detective Knowles can I speak to Dr. Kowalski?"

"She's not here, detective, I've been expecting her, but no answer at her home or cell, I'm about to drive to her house in Larchmont, I'll have her call you when I find her. Okay?"

"Yes, thank you." Linda closed the call then she said, mostly to herself, "I'm going to call Sam, maybe he knows something,"

"Who's Sam?" I interrupted as she dialed out on her own cell phone this time,

"Detective Sam Millers, you met him a week or so ago when you and Sally were here helping us." Linda stopped in mid sentence, he must have answered, "Sam, have you heard from Morris?" She waited about 10 seconds, then,

"No, Dr. Ski's missing too, get her address, she lives in Larchmont somewhere, try her place and then check Bradshaw's apartment in West Ghent." I thought about Bradshaw living in West Ghent, the same area I use to live in, then, Linda instructed, "I'm in the office, call me back when you find them."

For the next twenty minutes Linda and I went over everything we had separately learned over the past week. Linda told me about her matrix and how that effort seemed to further confuse the issue. I took some notes and told her of my interviews with several NISCO employees, intentionally omitting physical descriptions of Betty Boles and the Kroger twins, she could have her 'secret restaurant rendezvous' but I could keep my 'other women' fantasies hidden too. She nodded to guy coming in the room and moved to answer the phone as she introduced us, "Clayton, this is Stephen Irons, he's helping us with the Harrington case, Stephen this is Special Agent Clayton Davis, with the FBI." We shook hands as Linda took her phone call, "This is Knowles," Linda listened to her operator for about thirty seconds, and she kept repeating, "Oh God No, oh God No," through the conversation. Then she closed with, "Yes, Yes, we'll get right over there!"

"What's going on?" Davis asked.

"Morris Bradshaw's been murdered at Dr. Ski's home, she's at Sentara's Norfolk General with a gun shot to the back of her head. She's unconscious, no prognosis yet… Come on Davis we're going to Dr. Ski's home." Linda finalized, and they were gone.

CHAPTER SIXTY SIX

POLICE OPERATIONS

"STEPHEN IRONS"

Left alone in Linda's office I became upset that she and Davis had departed for Bradshaw's murder scene without me. Linda had already shared some of her investigation's results with me but she hadn't shared it all. Thornton was still in the room and said, "Rusty you've got to look around her office, there's got to be a lot more about why all this is happening. I think they're still looking at you as a suspect. Do you think they know about Wilber and the 'cookie-factory' connection?" I turned my back on my old buddy, but he had a point so I began to lift various papers from her desk looking for something she didn't want me to know about just yet. I was being careful, trying to keep things as she had left them, when I heard,

"Hey, Irons, Knowles called and said you'd be a snoop. Leave her stuff alone! Shove-off before you get in real trouble!" Jack said to me as he stood in the entrance to Linda's small office, looking like the cat that had just caught a cheese-stealing rat.

"Jack, eh, sorry, our meeting was cut short. I'd given Detective Knowles all my information but she hadn't shared hers, I was just looking," I replied and Jack jerked his thumb motioning me away from Linda desk. So I added, "I'd like to wait for Sheriff Os, he'll need a ride back to his car." It was a guess on my part, but I knew Os' boss had been here and already departed, so it was a high percentage guess.

"Okay, you know where Interview Three is?" Jack asked, relaxing a bit.

"No I haven't had the pleasure," I quipped, "just point me in the right direction and I'll find my way."

"Not likely, Irons, I'll show you, you're bound to get me in trouble if I turn you loose in here. Grab YOUR stuff only, then, follow me." Jack said as I picked up my few papers folded them, put them in my shirt pocket. Then Thornton and I got in Jack's trail.

Standing in the hallway now, outside Interview Three, Thornton and I've been waiting for about ten minutes watching through the one-way-mirror-glass as two detectives continue to question Os. I wanted to hear what was going on, but Jack key-locked the speaker to the 'MUTE' position before he departed. Since neither Thornton nor I could read lips and no one in Interview Three was 'signing' for us, we were watching a silent movie of Os, in work-out sweats, responding to a new and different side of the interview process.

Os looked very tired as he continued to reply to the questions he was being asked. It was 9:30 AM and there were four Styrofoam coffee cups on the table near him, more than likely providing enough caffeine to set him on edge. Linda said 'she thought they had no problem with Os' story and his actions', but 'frick and frack', Norfolk's follow-up, good cop, bad cop pair, were still checking on his information. They weren't taking chances.

As we continued to watch, Os stood and stretched his body and the cop pair seemed to relax a bit. The one I'm calling 'frick' headed out of the room and the 'frack' guy, shook hands with Os and reached up and slapped Os' gigantic arm at the shoulder level. The access door opened and 'frick' leaned out, and looked around, "Who are you?" he asked, ignoring Thornton and focusing on me.

"A friend of Sheriff Os', I thought he might need a ride."

"What's your name? I'll tell him you're here."

"Stephen Irons." I answered and 'frick' turned back into the room. As we watched 'frick' verbalize my presence, I saw Os turn toward the mirror-glass, he smiled a little and his shoulders seemed to relax. He shook 'frick's' offered hand as Thornton entered the interview room and began to look around while Os marched out the door,

"Scrap, good of you to come, did the Sheriff call you?"

"No, I just happened to be in the area, thought you might need a ride. You Okay?"

"Yeah, let's head out, we can talk in your car." Os instructed then he headed toward the front desk where I assumed he'd pick up his belongings. I followed closely as we worked our way around corners and through the hallways until we rounded the last corner and arrived at the Operation Center's Reception Desk and Os spoke,

"Jack, Irons agreed to give me a ride back, if that's alright?"

"Sure Sheriff Os, anything else you need?" Jack asked. I could finally see his name- tag. Sgt. Jack Webber was advertised on his chest.

"Call your people and tell them we're on the way to pick up my car, if you've still got your guys watching it." I listened but I wasn't sure if Os' question was sarcastic concerning the Norfolk Police Department's lack of concern for his private automobile, or if he was implying that the Police might think his car could be 'evidence' in the crime.

"We don't have anyone watching your car Sheriff Os, here's your keys, badge and weapon, nice seeing you again, sorry about your friend." Jack concluded then offered as we departed, "Hey, Irons, Detective Knowles wants you to call her this evening she should be home by eight."

"Thanks, Jack." I finalized as we exited the Police Operations Center. Os was in a big hurry leading us out then he stopped, looked at me funny and allowed me to lead the way to where I had parked my car.

Outside the Ops Center, the day was turning nice, it was a bit cool, but for mid October not bad at all. I thought about putting the top down, Os might like a little fresh air after his last few hours cooped up in a small room, but Os cut off my thought as he opened the passenger door and said, "Why don't you get a grown-up car, Scrap, this little thing's like a torture box." as he folded himself up in order to squeeze his large frame into my passenger seat.

"Sorry Os, you want the top down?"

"No Scrap, we're not going to a 'parade', just get me to the Pier Side Apartments, next to The Wisconsin, so I can get in a real car." Os had made his point. He was in a hurry, so I offered,

"Os I'm sorry about your friend, I remember you speaking of her. Was she more than just a friend?"

"Long time ago she was more, then we went our separate ways, nothing dramatic, a mutual decision, but we stayed good friends." Os replied softly, "She was getting paranoid about crime in Norfolk recently and I was trying to help her get a better grip." Os added, with a show of emotion rarely expressed by him in my years of knowing him, "I guess she wasn't paranoid after all."

I didn't have a much better topic to shift to but I felt I should up date Os on Bradshaw and Dr. Ski. "Os, while you were 'interviewing', a report came in to Knowles, Sergeant Bradshaw's been murdered and Dr. Kowalski was shot in the head, no prognosis so far on her. She's at Sentara Norfolk, Knowles and Davis headed out to the scene,"

"What the hell's going on in this town?" Os almost shouted, "Has everyone gone crazy? When did this happen?"

"Knowles got the word about 9:30 this morning, but I think they'd been looking for the two of them for a while. I'm not sure about when, but it happened at Dr. Ski's home in Larchmont."

"Do you think this has anything to do with your brother-in-law's death, Scrap? They were both associated with that case." Os asked quietly, cutting his eyes toward me with a sad but curious expression.

"I don't know Os I hadn't gone in that direction." I answered a bit perplexed as we pulled into the parking garage and Os pointed me toward his parked car. Thornton was standing near Os' trunk. Curious, I thought but it brought me back to why I was transporting Os and I asked as he exited my car,

"Did the Police think you had something to do with Dr. Turner's death?"

"Probably, but they asked and I told them I had been with Judge Knutson's from 9 to almost midnight, they checked on it and finished up with me."

"How did you stumble onto Dr. Turner's death?" I asked now trying to figure out how Os got drawn into this mess.

"I was going to train her some, it was set up for midnight, I was running a little late, but that's why I showed up there...The rest you probably know,"

I watched Os get in his car and drive away. His question about the possible relationship between Bradshaw's death and Wilber's murder began to cause my head to throb. Then I remembered Knowles said she had seen Bradshaw and Dr. Ski at the Bistro just like Os mentioned. So they were all there at the same time, maybe Os would know who Linda was with, it was worth a shot. Thornton got in my car and climbed into the back seat, I guess he wanted to be chauffeured. "That was weird Rusty, Os asking you about all these killings being connected. What about Os initially leaving the crime scene?" I had no answer or comment, I just drove away.

CHAPTER SIXTY SEVEN

NORFOLK

"STEPHEN IRONS"

Thornton and I traveled west on Brambleton, turned right onto Colley and drove past Sentara's Norfolk General Hospital where Dr. Ski had been taken. It was 11:30 AM and traffic was picking up with people working their way into downtown Ghent's limited lunchtime parking spots. Travel was slow and after passing the NARO Theater, now advertising the upcoming Halloween replay of one of my favorites, "The Rocky Horror Picture Show" I had to stop at the light on Colley and 21st Street. Looking to the left Thornton pointed toward CRACKERS Little Bar Bistro and said, "How about that Ava Gardner look-alike Rusty? You know the one that waited on you and Os the day Wilber was killed. You should go back to CRACKERS and check on her. Knowles is too tall and too expensive for you, even if you had a fat wallet to stand on." Thornton laughed at his financially height challenged joke then he finalized, "Knowles ain't turning out so good for you bud," The light turned green and Thornton added, "Keep going this way, Rusty, I remember the radio chatter in Ops, Dr. Ski's home's on Larchmont Crescent, head north on Colley that'll take us to the scene."

I knew Larchmont Crescent ran parallel to Jamestown Crescent for about five blocks in length before crossing Hampton Boulevard, Thornton didn't know Dr. Ski's street number, but I was certain we'd see the Police activity.

Soon enough Colley changed to Jamestown Crescent after we crossed the Colley Avenue Bridge and we saw Police cars moving in and out of the area. I continued northwest and after watching two police cars exit Monroe Street, I turned south on Monroe and Thornton pointed out the crime scene on our left a block back toward the Colley Avenue Bridge. I turned left onto Larchmont Crescent and stopped less than a half block away from the police activity. I parked the Volvo in someone's vacant driveway and got out of my car and moved toward the police presence about a hundred yards away.

Yellow and black 'crime scene tape' enclosed what I assumed was Dr. Ski's front yard. It started on a fence that ran along the west side of her home, came out to the street, made a ninety degree turn, looping around a large tree trunk, then it ran along Larchmont Crescent, enclosing the front yard. A Norfolk Police un-marked Crown Vic was parked in Dr. Ski's driveway and as I joined the small, milling group.

"What's going on?" A young man standing near the crime tape wearing a sweat stained Navy flight suit asked me. I couldn't see his entire name tag but I did catch the Navy Call Sign displayed on his flight suit, it was 'TOOLS'. I replied,

"I'm not sure, but it can't be good, they're too many cops here for it to be trivial," I answered then added, "You're a Navy pilot, right? Do you live around here?"

"Yeah, I'm at NAS Norfolk, Lt. Rich Craftsman, Call sign 'TOOLS', funny huh, CRAFTSMAN TOOLS? Anyway I just got home from an earlier flight to check on my dog, Cod, now I'm headed back for a second flight."

"Rich, good to meet you I'm Stephen Irons, I was in the navy a few years myself, hope you're enjoying it, I sure did." I replied as I shook hands with the Rich. "Were you up early this morning for your first flight?"

"Yeah, Oh dark thirty, I had to be there at six, got up around five, gave Cod a short walk, some food and left for work."

"Did you hear, or see anything when you were walking you dog?"

"Not really, he barked at something moving over by that hedge, the one over there…" Rich pointed further east, back toward the other side of Dr. Ski's home, then he went on, "But, I didn't see anything, probably somebody's cat." Rich paused again, looked at his watch, "Oops, getting late I've got to go back, good talking with you Stephen, take care.

"Thanks Rich, have a safe flight." I offered as he headed toward his home, but he fooled me and climbed into a big Range Rover parked on the street and departed.

I turned to look back as Thornton arrived and looked over the crime scene. The yellow and black tape continued along Larchmont Crescent for the eighty foot width of Dr. Ski's yard, then, turned ninety degrees back toward the house around a smaller tree and ended up tied to a long hedge row next to a concrete wall on the east side of the home, probably the hedge row Rich's dog barked at this morning. Thornton began to walk toward a large Norfolk Police Forensics van parked in front of the home and I noticed several other police cars, nearby, including the one I recognized as Linda's. Two uniformed policeman were stationed close-by, one in Dr. Ski's front yard and one outside the crime-tape, patrolling the street. I approached the 'street side cop' and said,

"Hi, I'm Stephen Irons I'm working with Detective Knowles on another case. I'd like to speak with her, if it's possible."

The cop looked at me, then turned toward his partner, the cop inside the tape, and yelled, "Hey, Litton, this guy says he's working with Knowles, he wants to see her." Litton turned away from the house and walked until he was standing next to Bradshaw's car. Thornton joined me and from his perspective on the street he could see directly under Bradshaw's car,

"Rusty, look just inside the left front tire, there's small note-book. Looks like one a cop might carry to keep track of interview information," He's right I thought as I stared under Bradshaw's car and Litton approached, ignored Thornton, and asked me,

"Who are you?"

"Stephen Irons, I'm Wilber Harrington's brother-in-law and I'm working with Detective Knowles on some of the information we've gathered on the Harrington case."

Thornton chuckled and said, "Good tap dance routine Rusty." And Litton answered,

"Let me see some ID Irons." I held my driver's ID diagonally over the Sheriff's plastic, trying to cover the RETIRED, annotation, but Litton was too savvy for my smoke and mirror trick. "You're the retired sheriff, took a bullet for Knowles and the Judge, right?"

"Yes, that's me." I confessed now hoping for the best.

"What do you want Irons?" Litton asked missing my informational dance segment.

"I want to speak to Knowles for a minute to set up a later meeting. If you'll let me in, I can wait until she comes out. Maybe, I could stand over by the car?" I indicated implying the car was too far away from the actual crime scene to be of any consequence, "You know, so she wouldn't have to come all the way out to the street."

"You want me to tell her you're here? They're busy in there, could take a-bit."

"No problem, I'll just wait by the car, I can review a few of my own notes," I tapped my shirt pocket indicating the folded up notes I had, "I don't mind waiting." I began to lift the tape and slid under the barrier, so far so good.

Thornton stayed with Litton and they watched me, then, Litton turned back toward his partner to discuss something else as Thornton pointed directly under the left front fender of Bradshaw's car. I moved to the car and took out my own notes and turned facing the house as I checked out Litton and friend with my peripheral vision. Casually I dropped my notes to the ground and bent down shielding the front wheel of the car from Litton's view. I retrieved my own notes and the small green notebook so far eluding discovery. Rising back up I turned and smiled but Litton was still talking with his partner. Thornton gave me a 'thumbs up' as he headed toward the crime scene house.

As I congratulated myself for my own cleverness, I heard from the porch of Dr. Ski's home, "Hey Irons, Knowles asked me to check for you, her cars' over there," Detective Millers pointed toward Linda's car as Thornton walked past him into the home, "She wants you to wait in the car, said she'd be there in ten minutes."

"Thanks Detective," I answered as I waved my notes and the small green note book I'd just retrieved. Millers, wearing surgical gloves, crime scene booties and a shower-cap looking head-cover turned to go back in the house.

As I watched Millers follow Thornton into Dr. Ski's home I did remember meeting him last week when Sally and I had tried to help them sort out some of Wilber's book outlines. Millers acted like a smart-ass type and used some of our conversation time to 'rag' on FBI Agent Davis, I had definitely liked that about Millers.

I sat in Knowles' car for about fifteen minutes reading Bradshaw's notes. I knew most of the information from Linda's briefing just before the phone call about Bradshaw and Dr. Ski. Then, I came across Bradshaw's checking on some employee of the Virginia Zoo's named Ursula Volk... Yes, I remembered her being one of the Elephant Keepers Ella and I saw during our zoo visit. I scanned indications he had talked on the phone to her concerning Eric Chin, the guy the cops believed might have killed Wilber and had certainly tried to kill me. There were a lot of question marks around the information about Volk traveling to Germany, some more names, Alex, some friend of Volk's, in Tennessee, and then Volk's parent's in Germany, a Mr. and Mrs. Herman Volk. Finally, Lufthansa at Dulles Airport was underlined and a 703 area code number was written down. I'd just finished copying all Bradshaw's zoo info to my own notes as WAVY TV10 drove up and the outside cop stopped them before they got too close.

When I saw Knowles and Davis come out of the house Knowles motioned toward Litton and the TV crew and gave Litton some guidance before she headed my way. Thornton was with Linda and waved at me pointing to her and smiling like maybe he'd changed his mind about her being a waste of my time. Maybe he was starting to believe she could be the answer to all my emotional problems. I waited for Thornton to yell at me but he was comfortable just walking away from the house with Knowles and Davis so I bundled up the entire note package I had assembled and put it all back in my shirt pocket and got out of the car to wait for their arrival.

CHAPTER SIXTY EIGHT

LARCHMONT

"STEPHEN IRONS"

As I watched, Linda and Agent Davis left Dr. Ski's small porch and walked toward me. Both were wearing surgical booties and thin-skin investigator's gloves. Linda's medium length blonde hair remained covered by a protective cap as she removed her gloves and crossed under the crime scene tape. Davis paused, removed his gloves and cap, then he bent over and looked into the side mirror of Bradshaw's Crown Vic and began to straighten his expensively cut blond hair. What an asshole, I thought as Linda and Thornton got closer and Linda spoke,

"Stephen, sorry to leave you back at Ops, but I'm sure you understand. Dr. Ski's at Sentara, she's critical with a gun shot to the base of her skull, Morris Bradshaw died immediately with a shot to his temple. We're still examining the area,"

I remembered Os' question and interrupted, "Linda, I know it's early to speculate, but is there a possible connection to Wilber's murder here?"

She paused, thought a second, then, "Actually, the gun shot wounds are almost identical, extremely close range, star pattern from a small caliber weapon. But it's too early to speculate on anything except a back door break-in, murder and burglary,"

Linda was interrupted by Davis' arrival, "What are you doing here Irons? You're still a damn suspect in my book." Linda responded,

"Davis, get in the car, Stephen's here to talk to me, not argue with you... Sorry Stephen, we're all on edge. Call later this evening and we can talk,"

Davis wasn't through, "You're out of your league, Irons, you're a second rate deputy sheriff from a hamburger town and I know you're involved in all this," Thornton was standing in front of Davis, he was agitated and I knew if I didn't intervene he'd cause me big trouble. I pushed by Thornton and Linda and approached Davis.

"Why the hell do you think I'm involved, you big jerk?" I yelled up in Davis' face.

"Just like now, Irons, it's your rage! When you found out Harrington lied to your sister you freaked out. It's your military training,"

"You dumb ass!" I shouted as I cocked my fist, rotated my shoulder and thrust my arm forward, hitting Davis as hard as I could right in the chest, aiming the blow to impact his sternum, *THUMP* my fist slammed forward hitting him just above his pulmonary trunk, right at my shoulder level.

Davis looked shocked from the impact and that I had hit him first enough and strong enough to shut him down temporarily. Fortunately my punch did just what it was meant to do. It knocked the wind out of Davis and put his ass down on Larchmont Crescent's with a resounding *KER PLOP*.

As Davis frantically tried to catch his breath, not a pretty picture with all that red and blue facial coloration under all those expensively quaffed blonde strands, Thornton smiled and clapped his hands together. Linda was upset and shouted, "Stephen, knock it off! Litton, get over here!" Linda yelled for assistance and Litton pushed me away from the scene and tried to help Davis up. But, my punch had been too good. Davis' butt would stay on the asphalt for another minute or two. I smiled to myself as I felt a strong hand grip onto my shoulder and I heard Detective Millers say,

"Not bad Irons but come away before WAVY TV puts us all on the Six O' clock news. Let Knowles deal with what's left of 'pretty boy'." Millers smiled as he pulled me toward my distant car, "You've got to calm down Irons this is not just about your brother-in-law's death and your sister's tragedy, we've lost a fine Police Officer and another Police Official has been critically wounded. It may be tied to Harrington, like you want to speculate, but it's gotten beyond your interest in Knowles, or Davis being an interfering asshole." Millers kept his arm around my shoulders as we walked toward my car but I could turn my head back toward Linda, she and Litton had begun to help Davis up from the street and I answered,

"Detective Millers, I appreciate your stepping in, I waited for Linda because I wanted to give her some evidence I found under Bradshaw's car, but Davis jumped in and it all turned to shit," I offered this information as I handed Bradshaw's notebook to Millers. "I haven't had a chance to really look through it, so here, you take it. Please apologize to Detective Knowles." Millers reverted to cop,

"Where did you find this notebook?"

"At first I was told to wait for over by Bradshaw's car, then, while I was waiting, just after you told me to go to Knowles' car, I noticed the book under the Crown Vic near the front tire so I reached down and picked the notebook up. I looked for you, but you had gone back into the house, so I carried the book to Knowles' car and waited to give it to her." Thornton smiled, it all sounded plausible to him,

"You looked at the notebook?"

"Just enough to know it was Bradshaw's then I put it in my pocket to wait for Knowles. Davis came out and you saw what happened,"

"How did you know it was Bradshaw's? There's no name on the book."

"I saw the entry about him showing me his photo array,"

Millers interrupted, "After Bradshaw's notes on the photo array, what else did you see?" He wasn't going to give up until I offered more. I wanted to share but I wasn't ready to be totally honest so I said,

"Just some stuff about the Virginia Zoo, some names and numbers, nothing that made any sense to me. Okay?"

"Yeah, for the time being, but don't go shitting me, Irons, getting me in trouble along with yourself. I don't like Davis, but I do like my job, and I want to find the asshole that killed Bradshaw, so don't hang me out to dry. If you think of anything else, you call me. You hear me Irons, YOU CALL ME IMMEDIATELY!"

"Okay, one other thing, Detective Millers, one of Dr. Ski's neighbors was up early this morning walking his dog and the dog barked at something over by Dr. Ski's hedge. He's a Navy pilot, Lieutenant Rich Craftsman. Rich lives a couple of houses down from Dr. Ski. He's gone back to NAS Norfolk for another flight, but you should check with him."

"Thanks," Millers wrote the info down in his notebook, "I'll check into it, but you, stay out of trouble, Irons."

Thornton got in the front seat this time and I reversed the Volvo out of the driveway and departed as Thornton offered, "Good job Rusty, it's about time you showed Knowles you've got a pair of brass balls!"

CHAPTER SIXTY NINE

THE BISTRO

"STEPHEN IRONS"

As I sipped one of the best martinis ever I looked at the beautiful bartender who conjured-up the masterpiece and said, "Paula this is great, it's the best ever!" Paula laughed and tossed her lengthy black profusion of hair around her shoulders provocatively. She was a comforting distraction from just how bad my day had gone so far and allowed me to focus my thoughts on the welcomed affect she was having on me. Strikingly attired in black tuxedo pants and cummerbund, topped by a white pleated tuxedo shirt and black bow tie, her seductive image invigorated my system and brightened my evening. I had just met Paula, and was obviously 'smitten' by her beauty and grace. She and her 'best ever' martini were a bewitching combination for me.

While Thornton and I waited for Charles Taylor, he seemed interested in Paula too but seemed a bit restless looking back and forth from THE BISTRO'S entrance to Paula at the other end of the bar. Paula finally returned and asked me, "Which Kroger-twin are you waiting for Stephen? I'm guessing Margarete, you look like a redheaded hell-raiser to me."

Trying to gain Paula's interest earlier I had shared my present job with NISCO but her assumption about Margarete Kroger was her own. "Neither twin actually, I'm waiting for Charles Taylor himself, but he seems to be running late." I offered noting it was 6:15 PM, "Probably held up at the office, he just got back from three days in Richmond, must be a lot of catching up here," Paula interrupted,

"Okay, one 'Tanq Up' for Mr. Taylor, he just walked in," She said pointing toward the front entrance gaining my attention, "see, he's over there talking with my husband, Roger, he's THE BISTRO Sommelier." Paula offered the information, then, she smiled mischievously raising an eyebrow and narrowing her beautiful, dark eyes as she moved away to mix Charles' drink. Thornton decided to comment,

"What a vixen! She not only has a husband, he works right here at the same damn restaurant." He paused, with a nasty cackle then went on, "You're finally getting screwed, bud, too bad it's just a figure of speech." I smiled at Thornton's comments as I stood and shook hands with Charles.

"Good evening Charles, welcome back, Paula's bringing you a martini."

"I can definitely use it, this was a shitty week." Charles replied. Having known Charles only a few weeks and been impressed by his pompous attitude about everything, including his use of the English language, I was surprised at his descent to my comfort level. So, I searched for more about Charles' definition of the word 'shitty'.

"Your Richmond meeting was disappointing?" I asked,

"Not really, Stephen," Charles began then he took a long swallow and nearly drained his entire glass. "The meeting was informative but my sadness is due to losing a very good friend yesterday, she was murdered during a home invasion and burglary right here in downtown Norfolk, actually just across the street." Charles turned and pointed to the apartment complex next to the Battleship Wisconsin then he turned back toward the bar, finished his drink and positioned his empty glass toward Paula, who said,

"Yes sir, another for you Stephen?"

"No Paula, I'm fine, I'll let Charles catch up." Then I turned back to Charles, "Are you talking about Dr. Turner's death?"

"Yes, did you know her?" Charles asked, now giving me his full attention. I could see the formation of tears that cast a clear covering over his dark brown eyes, this was not the Charles Taylor I had come to know, so I answered carefully,

"I didn't know her but I heard about her death from Sheriff Os, evidently, they use to be involved and still remained good friends. I do know that Os had been training her in self- defense," Charles looked intently toward me now and started to respond, then, he paused, seemed to think better of it, retrieved his new martini and drank half as I went on, "You know Os found Dr. Turner and reported her death to the police?"

"Yes, he called us. Peggy was a dear friend to me and Millie. What did you say about self-defense training?"

"Os said he'd been training her for a few weeks, she was worried about crime in downtown Norfolk, so he agreed to work with her. He showed up to train with her and found her home broken into before discovering her body." Charles looked a bit perplexed, too much information about a dear friend I reasoned. He finished his drink, stood and wobbled a bit before offering,

"I've got to go Stephen we'll talk tomorrow or Wednesday, call Betty for a convenient time, sorry for the change of plans." Charles turned and was out the door.   "Charles had to go?" Paula asked as she returned and picked up his empty glass. I was still curious about Charles' reaction and didn't answer, Paula added, "Don't you want another drink now Stephen?"

"No, I've got to get something to eat, how much do I owe you Paula?"

"Twenty five fifty, how about something to eat here, at the bar?"

"No, I'm headed home," I replied and placed a twenty a ten and a five on the bar, "nice to meet you, Paula." I offered with very little enthusiasm. Charles' reaction to Os' training Dr. Turner and Paula's revelation of a husband, co-worker named Roger, had taken the wind out of my romantically billowing sails. I exited the Bistro, got my car back from the Valet and headed out. This day still wasn't going all that well for me.

As Thornton and I drove away, he pointed up at the Pier Side Apartments, where Dr. Turner had been murdered, and said, "Her death seems to have impacted two people you know a lot more than you thought it would. Obviously you don't know either Charles, or Os, that well bud." Thornton was right.

Headed home through the Ghent area, I turned right on Colley and passed the hospital, where Dr. Kowalski was most likely undergoing intensive care, probably under full police protection, and I began to wonder about Dr. Ski's condition. I wanted to talk with her to explore the possible connection between Wilber's death and her tragedy but, after my confrontation with Davis earlier today, I was sure Linda would shut me out of Wilber's investigation. Dr. Ski and Sergeant Bradshaw had been involved in Wilber's case too, so, Wilber's death, Bradshaw's death and Dr. Ski's shooting could be related, just like Os had implied. I shook off the thought of talking with her now, no way Dr. Ski's well enough, maybe later after things calmed down a bit.

Thornton saw my obvious concern and decided to speak again, "Rusty why is it every opportunity you've had to discuss the case with Taylor gets sabotaged by circumstances. His anxiousness to solve Wilber's murder's been preempted by a bunch of other events he claims are beyond his control. First the business run to Richmond and now the death of a close friend, it all seems really weird to me." Then he thought a bit and added, "You need a distraction, bud, let's try CRACKERS, maybe Cora's working tonight." Thornton finally had a great idea, so I decided to listen to him.

CHAPTER SEVENTY

CRACKERS LITTLE BAR BISTRO

"STEPHEN IRONS"

For a Monday night, CRACKERS was active. Late night smokers, allowed to continue risking their own lives and others after 9PM, hadn't arrived yet, but the place was lively with a large group of patrons and a lot of 'rock and roll music'. As Elton John sang 'Rocket Man', I waved hello to Steve, CRACKERS' bartender extraordinaire, and I looked for an empty seat at the bar. Steve pointed toward the far end of the bar and I seated my self with my back toward their side parking lot and looking forward into their small kitchen area. I watched Jeremy, CRACKERS' chef and one of his souse-chefs, perform a dodge ball routine as they prepared food orders and avoided hitting each other in their telephone-booth sized workspace. Steve approached me wearing another one of his outlandish shirts, this one with big black cats stretched-out over bright yellow cotton fabric. On cue Elton switched to 'Honky Cat' and Steve smiled pointing toward his shirt as he offered a greeting,

"Stephen, how are you? Haven't seen you in awhile, how's Sally doing?"

"She's fine Steve," I answered, "But, she's gone back to Dallas to work for American, I guess she needed to get away from Norfolk."

"I can dig that, most gals I know get really tired of this town." Steve offered his bartender's philosophy about Mermaid City and women. "What'll you have, maybe some of my 'High Shelf Booze'? Hey, how about Bombay Gin, up or on the rocks…"

I looked around the small restaurant and noticed a good looking gal with a pretty face, great body, and a lot of energy doing CRACKERS' waitress duty. This gal was taller than Cora and way-more energetic. She wasn't the Ava Gardner look-a-like I anticipated so I smiled and answered, "On the rocks, Steve, where's Cora, she not working tonight?"

"Not tonight, or a lot of nights, this one's Laura, she's new, works EMPIRE and CRACKERS both. Cora's gone Stephen she's one of those gal departures we talked about. Didn't know you knew Cora, never heard her mention you."

Thornton was standing behind me and laughed as he whispered, "Shit, that's all it took Rusty, I think tonight's recce-mission's a bust." Thornton was right again, I'd been turned down, misled, deceived and now abandoned. I grimaced at Thornton's comment but responded to Steve,

"I don't really know Cora, but she was kind to me the afternoon I was here with Sheriff Os. You know, you were working the bar when Os told me about Wilber's death. You must remember that, I got really upset."

"Yeah, I remember, that was tough for you, but Cora's out of here now." Steve replied as he moved off to fix my drink and pick up another order from the bar. Still moving away Steve stopped and looked back toward me adding, "Oh yeah, what do you want to eat Stephen, we've got those pot-stickers you like, you want some of them?"

One of CRACKERS' best is their fried pot-stickers with a spicy Asian sauce, but a red pepper pick-me-up wasn't going to solve my depression, so I joked back, "I'll just have the 'Bomb', Steve, then, I'm going home for some canned 9 Lives. I'm hoping for a better number nine, my first eight cans haven't gone so well today."

As Steve turned away Thornton laughed at my joke and pointed to one of the black cats on Steve's shirt, then, he pointed at the speaker still drumming-on with 'Honky Cat'. Thornton was certain he understood my 9-lives joke, but he'd skinned the wrong cat.

CHAPTER SEVENTY ONE

ST. MARY'S CEMETARY

"STEPHEN IRONS"

Sergeant Morris Bradshaw was being eulogized four days after his tragic murder. His body had been interned here at St. Mary's, now listed as one of The National Registry's Historic Places. They were established in 1854 and are also listed on The Virginia Registry, that particular recognition is highlighted by the challenges they faced responding to the 1855 'prevailing plague epidemic' that swept the Norfolk area.

The cemetery is centrally located on Church Street, right next to The Virginia Zoo. Linda's speaking now, standing in the center of a small platform in front of a seated group of mourners. She's tearing as she mourns the loss of a dedicated partner that was striving to help solve a complicated mystery. Linda gained control of her emotions and spoke of how Morris Bradshaw had been instrumental in achieving near resolution of their case before he was brutally murdered. It's obviously a very sad occasion for her personally, for the Police Department and for the entire city of Norfolk.

Due to Linda's publicity clamp-down on information concerning the murder of Morris Bradshaw, and the hospitalization of Dr. Kowalski, Bradshaw's service was restricted to the press and only attended by a couple dozen City dignitaries and several Norfolk Police Department personnel all formally dressed and exhibiting saddened faces and black arm-bands. A small, but honest tribute to a young man whose notebook had informed me how excited he was about a new job in the Homicide Division, a new love in his life and a complicated mystery he was totally involved in trying to resolve. His information allowed me a much closer look inside his life as he chased down a new and possibly case-breaking lead concerning Ursula Volk's misleading travel information. She wasn't on her way to see her parents in Germany, at least not on the Lufthansa flight she had booked. I began to wonder, as Bradshaw must have, what could have caused her to change her plans at the last minute? Now, as Wilber's murder and Eric Chin's death seem to intertwine, possibly this recent act of violence against Sergeant Bradshaw and Dr. Kowalski was also related.

Near the end of the service, as I sat in the back row of the small section of pre-positioned chairs, I watched the stage area where Linda continued speaking my mind drifted back to the phone call from Sally last night,

"Sally, I was beginning to worry, how's it going?"

"Its great Stephen, it was the right thing for me to do. The counseling went OK and all my friends are very supportive. I couldn't have done it without them. They've actually helped me come to grips with Will's death and his secrets. They've convinced me the issues can definitely resolve themselves in time." I interrupted here, I was happy to hear Sally's optimism and her ability to refer to Wilber by name once again, but I wasn't sure what she meant about issues being resolved in time.

"Sally, what do you mean by; 'resolve them selves in time'?"

"My friends and my counselor encouraged me to revisit and trust-in everything I believed about Will before the tragedy, you know what caused me to fall in love with him when we first met, what caused me to continue to love him before the recent shock of his death and all these secrets. They encourage me to trust the earlier feelings that helped me decide to spend the rest of my life with Will. All those feelings couldn't be wrong, there must be something more to these secrets,"

"I'm pleased with your decision, Sally. I also think there's more to this so your friends are probably right. But it'll take time to know why, I actually believe it'll take the solution to Wilber's murder before we can understand his secrets, not just who actually killed him, but why he was killed." I replied.

"Yes, somehow it's all tied to the reason for his murder. How's that investigation going, Stephen?"

"Not well right now. You remember Sergeant Bradshaw, the police officer working for Detective Knowles that came to your house with a photo array for me to look at?"

"Yes, has he found some clue?" Sally asked excitedly.

"I think he did, but sadly, he's also been murdered, he was found with another police official, both shot in the head, just like Wilber. The other victim is one of the Norfolk Medical Examiners and she's critical at Norfolk Sentara ..."

"Oh my god, Stephen I'm so sorry, do you think it has anything to do with Will's murder?"

"I think it's possible but I haven't been able to talk with Detective Knowles yet," Sally interrupted me again,

"Stephen, you've just said Detective Knowles, not Linda, twice in the last minute, has something changed your relationship with her?" She asked pointedly and I began to think about how insightful women are; Betty Boles picking up on my casual statement in her office and knowing I was going to accept Charles Taylor's job offer, Linda controlling our conversation a

week ago knowing how I would react to the FBI's belief I was involved with Wilber's murder, and now my own sister sensing something had changed between Linda and me. I decided to divert her concern,

'No, Sally, nothings changed, we're both just busy, and now with Sergeant Bradshaw's murder, Linda's really stressed. But something Bradshaw discovered could be important to Wilber's case and you might be able to help me check on it,' Sally jumped right back in. I knew that would get her attention.

'I'd love to help, Stephen, what can I do for you?'

My focus came back to Sergeant Bradshaw's Memorial Service as a now growingly familiar grip clasped onto my shoulder to gain my attention. I looked up to see Detective Millers standing beside me. "Irons, we need to talk, can you come sit in my car for a few minutes? It would be helpful."

Dutifully I rose and followed Millers to his vehicle, a carbon copy of Bradshaw's unmarked Crown Vic. We sat in the car, well away from the conclusion of the ceremony and Millers continued, "I've got a good deal bad deal situation Irons I'll start with the bad, if that's okay with you?"

"Sure go ahead."

"Knowles asked me to talk with you she's still pissed about you attacking Davis on Monday." He paused a moment to let that set in, but it wasn't startling news to me, so I just waited, "She said to tell you, quote, 'the deals off, she doesn't want anything more from you and you get nothing from her' unquote. Then, she added something I didn't understand," Millers paused here, looking in his own notebook, a small, green flip over, similar to Bradshaw's, "Here it is, another direct quote, she said, quote 'I'm not going to be part of Stephen's BLONDETOURAGE!' unquote."

Thornton and I started to laugh, both impressed with Linda's wit, obviously she was aware of the Kroger twins and expanded on the word 'entourage' to make it hair color specific. Millers laughed and went on, "Come on Stephen, what's a BLONDETOURAGE?" I felt a bit encouraged since he had now addressed me by my first name so I paused to form my answer.

"She's talking about a trio of blondes and the fact that she not going to be any part of that threesome. They're two other blondes I work with at NISCO, Margarete and Elizabeth Kroger they're definitely blonde and beautiful." I answered, then, added, "So what's your good deal part, Sam?"

"Well, Knowles said 'she didn't want anything from you and you couldn't have any thing from her', ha, ha." Millers cut his eyes and snickered suggestively like an old 'Monty Python, nudge, nudge, wink, wink, joke' then, he went on, "but there's no specific restriction concerning a certain Detective Sam Millers, so, how about a new partner, not so pretty but certainly more friendly-like?" I perked up at this offer, I was inclined to agree right away, but I hesitated, thinking, why is he going this direction?

"Sam, why would you want to partner with me?" I asked.

"Well, first, I'm sure your attacker, Chin, was also the 'PERP' for your brother-in-law, but he's long dead so he's not Bradshaw's killer, but I do think there's a connection between the two murders. The wounds are too much alike not to point at something shared, not the actual weapon but one similar, creating an almost identical star shaped wound. Secondly, and this might be a stretch, the wound and weapon similarity could signal some type of commonality in experience or training. I believe we'll find Bradshaw's killer at NISCO or the Virginia Zoo... I can follow up on Bradshaw's efforts at the zoo, but I think you can better ferret-out something from NISCO... And the two blondes sound exciting to me. You can't handle both of them can you?"

Millers was pulling out all the stops now, we were on a first name basis and he was using the group inclusive 'we'll' then going for the male bonding angle with the 'shared blondes' trying to draw me into his 'Murder Club'. He went on, "Another blonde bonus for me is I loved watching you 'cold-cock' pretty boy Davis. I'm definitely not a fan of his, or the FBI, I just want to solve these killings in spite of their involvement. So, how about it Stephen, how about we form a conspiracy, you know a secret pact to clean up this mess?"

"Sounds good, but is this some hidden offer coming through Knowles?"

"Are you shitting me, she'd have my ass, not to mention my balls if she knew about this. And don't flatter yourself, she's really pissed at you, this offer is definitely something I personally pulled out of my own butt."

Millers and I talked for another 20 minutes. During that time Bradshaw's Service concluded and all the participants cleared out. While I listened to Sam I watched Linda stop to talk to a uniformed Police Officer arriving on his motorcycle toward the end of the service. They spoke for a few minutes then Linda seemed agitated with the officer, shaking her finger at him before she rushed to her car and drove off. After the cop departed, Sam's car and mine were the only two vehicles remaining.

Sam and I discussed both sides of the investigation; I shared all the information I had already given Knowles plus the follow up I was attempting to involve Sally with in Germany. Next I told him about the money I found in Wilber and Sally's safety deposit box, and in Wilber's Correspondence Course books continuing to highlight Wilber's secrecy. Knowles had already told Sam about the safety deposit money, but he was grateful that I was being honest with him about the additional money.

Sam lived-up to his side of the bargain and told me that Dr. Ski was getting better and Linda had assigned three cops to rotate around the clock coverage during Dr. Ski's hospital recovery. Her doctors predicted she would pull through and be able to speak to the police soon. Jokingly, Millers promised to smuggle me into that interview if I could arrange a double date with the Kroger twins. Finally, Millers told me about Knowles' meeting with Davis and someone from the CIA. She found out the CIA had approached Wilber about coming to work for them, first when Wilber was stationed in California and then again here in Norfolk. After that we shook hands and promised to get together soon, he gave me his cell number and I gave him James Carlson's NISCO office number before he departed.

Jesus Christ, the CIA had talked to Wilber about a job, Thornton and I had come to the right conclusion after reading his final note to Sally. Wilber had actually worked for the 'cookie factory' and that was the catalyst for all the secrecy crap we were trying to deal with. We had both dealt with the CIA in Afghanistan and knew they were capable of almost anything. Then, I remembered the slips of paper Sally gave me when she left for Dallas. They were probably the code keys to some kind of 'trade craft'. My outlook brightened, the CIA's possible involvement began to give me hope that Wilber's secrets had not been solely directed at deceiving Sally. Maybe Wilber's motives were going to resolve themselves, as Sally and her friends believed.

CHAPTER SEVENTY TWO

SENTARA NORFOLK GENERAL HOSPITAL

Detective Knowles navigated up the back steps two at a time her increased anxiety came from her discussion with Officer Stokes after Bradshaw's Memorial Service. She had seen the roster for Dr. Kowalski's security effort and knew Stokes was scheduled to be on duty during the Bradshaw's restricted service. She tried to call the Intensive Care Unit to check on Dr. Ski, but they had put her on hold and played rap-music. That pissed her off so she hung up and decided to check the hospital herself. As she climbed the stairs Knowles began to think her concern could be misplaced since Stokes had explained that Sergeant Webber had sent another police officer, Corporal Carol Carlton, to relieve him so he could attend the services for Bradshaw who had been a close, hometown friend of Stokes'. But, something wasn't right Knowles was certain Webber would not have changed the duty roster for anyone other than a relative of Bradshaw's without telling her. But, maybe Stokes and Bradshaw were that close. They had both been cops in Boston before coming to Norfolk and Webber knew that, Knowles just wasn't sure.

As Knowles rounded the third floor landing, headed toward the fourth floor and Dr. Ski's ICU, she saw a tall female police officer posted on the intermediate landing about six steps down from the stairwell door onto the fourth floor, "Are you Carlton?" Knowles asked as she neared the officer.

"Yes Ma'am, Corporal Carol Carlton, I relieved Stokes 30 minutes ago," Knowles stopped next to Carlton her features looked familiar and Knowles reasoned she'd probably seen her around Police Operations. Carlton was tall, an inch or two taller and much heavier than Knowles. She looked very fit and capable for her size. Knowles began to relax as Carlton continued, "Stokes was a close friend of Sergeant Bradshaw's Ma'am and he asked Sergeant Webber if someone could substitute for him for a few hours, so I volunteered. I expect Stokes back around seven. Is there a problem Ma'am?"

"No Corporal Carlton, I'm just concerned about Dr. Kowalski's security, I'm sure I overreacted when Stokes mentioned this change to me." Knowles stated turning to go up six more steps and enter the fourth floor to check on Dr. Ski, then, she turned back to Carlton and asked, "Has anyone been on these stairs recently?"

"No Ma'am, Sergeant Webber checked in with me a few minutes ago, but no one has come out here."

"Thanks, let me know when Stokes returns, I need to apologize to him I'm sure I gave him some uncalled-for grief." Knowles offered as she opened the door to the fourth floor and entered the corridor leading to Dr. Ski's ICU unit.

"Yes Ma'am, I'll let you know," Linda heard as the stairwell door clicked shut and she headed toward the ICU.

Sergeant Cathy Curtis saw Detective Knowles walk onto the floor from the stairwell door and came over, "Everything is going fine Detective Knowles. Dr. Han was just here and told me Dr. Kowalski's doing much better today," Knowles interrupted,

"What time did Sergeant Webber send Corporal Carlton over to release Stokes?"

"I'm not sure I understand, Ma'am, Stokes was in the stairwell an hour ago, I was just about to check on him again when Dr. Han came out and spoke to me. I don't know any Corporal Carlton,"

"She's taller than me, dark hair, about 185#. She's in the stairwell now. Didn't you meet her when she relieved Stokes?"

"No way Detective Knowles, if someone other than Stokes is in the stairwell, I don't know about it,"

"Oh, damn it, that's why she looks familiar, that's Ursula Volk! Who's in with Dr. Kowalski?"

"Officer Murphy, he went in when Dr. Han came out,"

"Go in with Murphy. Don't let anyone in the room, do it now Curtis!" Knowles got on her communicator and called for Webber at Ops, "Webber this is Knowles, CODE RED, get more Uniforms to Norfolk Sentara NOW, we've got a security breach. There's an intruder in the back stairwell between three and four."

Before Webber or any other officer could answer Knowles pulled her 38 S&W from her waist holster and headed back toward the stairwell door. She eased the door open and two shots rang out, CRACK, CRACK, the echoing shots reverberated up the stair well as the bullets impacted the edge of the door shattering metal fragments into Knowles' face.

"Drop your gun Volk, you're trapped," Knowles yelled down the descending stairwell toward the quickening foot step sounds from the retreating imposter. Knowles saw a burst of light come up the stairwell and assumed it was Stokes returning from the Memorial Service. Knowles yelled again down the stairwell,

"Stokes, get your weapon out, your relief's a phony, she's wanted for Bradshaw's murder, get your gun out and stop her!" Knowles then heard,

"Detective Knowles, is that you?" followed by a loud impact as Stokes and Volk crashed into each other half way up the first set of stairs. "Jesus Christ," Stokes yelled as he began to defend himself.

Ursula Volk, posing as Corporal Carlton, attempted to use her upper body strength and turn her weapon down toward Stokes vulnerable chest. Stokes forgot about drawing his own 38 and fought to raise his arms against Volk's attempt. Ursula Volk spread her feet between two stair levels and locked her staggered stance in place as she continued to twist her weapon's barrel down toward Stokes' chest. She had the height advantage and was standing a step above Stokes, making it difficult for him deflect her effort as he shouted,

"Damn it Carlton, knock it off, what the hell's the matter with you?" Stokes screamed as Volk fired the weapon again, *CRACK*, another shot echoed in the stairwell and the bullet impacted Stokes' upper thigh causing him to twist away from Volk and spin her down toward the lower steps and against the wall.

Volk recovered and pushed off against the wall as she twisted out of the tussle. She heard Knowles scurrying above and heading her way and Ursula chose to run, she regained her balance and raced to the Exit door and was gone.

Knowles heard the third gun shot, smelled the cordite discharge coming up the stairwell and saw another rapid intrusion of light from the ground floor followed by the noise of the Exit door slamming shut. She rushed down the remaining flight and found Stokes on the bottom landing, holding his thigh where the bullet had slammed into his leg. Stokes' weapon was still in its holster, he hadn't had a chance to pull it.

"She's gone down the stairs and out the door detective, what the hell happened to her?" Linda grabbed her communicator,

"Police Officer down, back hospital entrance doorway ground floor, Building 701, get medics and back-up uniforms here NOW! Ursula Volk's here dressed like a cop, she's tall dark haired and she's armed and dangerous, Webber did you copy?"

"Back-ups on the way, Detective Knowles, I'm calling Emergency to respond to your medical. Who's been shot?"

"It's Stokes, he seems okay. She hit him in the thigh with one shot. She's fired a total of three from a Police 38 and she's running with three more in the chamber. .. "Hurry up Webber I'll stay until the medics arrive but we need to close this whole area off. !"

CHAPTER SEVENTY THREE

SUFFOLK, VIRGINIA, 7 PM

Cooper leaned on the kitchen counter watching Betty prepare to make martinis. She got the martini shaker and the Beefeaters Gin from the lower shelf of her freezer, filled the glass shaker with a few ice cubes then added enough gin to challenge their combined brain cell count. Betty then went into one of her cabinet shelves and withdrew a small bottle of dry Sherry and added one half teaspoon to the shaker. Betty smiled at Cooper, capped the shaker and handed it to him, "Here Coop, you do the easy part," then she turned back to the freezer and got two very small martini glasses heavy with freezer-frost.

Cooper shook the container rapidly until he was certain he had bruised the gin enough to commingle with the ice and Sherry. Cooper stopped and Betty pried the shaker from his chilled fingers and she poured the two small, icy glasses full of the syrupy cold liquid, and toasted, "Welcome to my home Coop, I'm sure we'll both enjoy your stay."

They clicked the toast and drank their small glasses down in one effort. Cooper, now amorously encouraged, took Betty in his arms and kissed her, leaving none of her teeth un-assaulted by his gin soaked tongue. It was as wonderful for Cooper as he remembered and Betty responded passionately when some old, smoldering embers reignited. Betty quickly said, "That was nice, Coop but let's have another 'little tuni' and talk a bit before we head down my hallway. You definitely need some time to warm those fingers before performing on my bedroom stage. Okay?"

"Sure, the martini's great, I'd love another. Your 'invite' is highly anticipated too, but we do need to talk. Full disclosure Betty, why am I here?"

"Harrington was recruited to report on NISCO and their foreign involvement, mainly Chinese financial initiatives. Somehow while reporting, he stumbled on Deep Dragon and passed the info on eighteen months ago. I sent the data to Dr. Kale and you know where that went. Betty shook the second martini herself, paused and poured another round, then, she said, "It all continued straight forward until Harrington got the bright idea to write a book about the Japanese using a similar technology to control weather. Wilber changed the players, but, we think the Chinese got wind of the book and decided to write a quick 'THE END' to his Wilber's novel."

Cooper drank most of his refill, Betty drained hers, nodded and placed her empty glass on the counter before she went on, "The FBI's checking into his book agent in San Diego, there may be some connection there, but when I heard about Wilber's book in June, I confronted him and he just laughed about it. Finally after a bit of soul searching he said 'he, was only playing around with the book idea and that he'd hold back until all our concerns about the Chinese were resolved,' I took him at his word, but Wilber kept writing and reached out for a publisher. It's a shame we lost him, he was able to verify and supply a lot of good info and he was very pleased with what he was doing." Cooper offered to shake another batch, Betty declined and continued,

"Now, even after Wilber's death there's still some unidentified local involvement with the Chinese... Wilber and I first thought it was Charles Taylor and a Judge named Knutson but when we informed Dr. Kale, he said that 'Wilber's murder may be a secondary action', he believes the primary Chinese effort in Norfolk is recruiting Navy personnel and gathering classified information, you know, like the Russian effort with the Walker family here in Norfolk. So, I need your help to positively identify and stop the local support group plus put some added pressure on the Chinese to close out their Norfolk operation." Cooper responded,

"One of the Chinese assets has been closed out already... Eric Chin was found dead in the Lafayette River and the cops believe he was Harrington's killer. Chin was also positively identified as Stephen Irons' attacker at the Norfolk Airport and was probably the one seen by some kids in Lakewood Park right after Harrington was murdered. The cops are sure Chin's the guy for Harrington," Cooper paused and took a final drink, then continued, "Chin worked at the Virginia Zoo for someone who has a history of ties to the Chinese, so Chin was probably directed to take care of Harrington's book idea then the Chinese connected zoo gal, Ursula Volk, probably took care of Chin. Volk was suspected by the FBI as a possible Chinese agent in San Diego three years ago, but they lost track of her. They should have guessed the Virginia Zoo possibility, not assumed she'd been recalled to China."

"This is new to me, why haven't I gotten any info on this before?" Betty said.

"Betty, you know the DCI initiative concerning increased communications with the FBI, the one supported by Dr. Kale and all the other big cookies," Betty nodded, "Well the FBI has been less than forth-coming with their information and that probably caused the delay on both Chin and Volk. I got most of this from Detective Knowles because Special Agent Davis held the Chin information from everybody. Or possibly his people kept him in the dark. Davis could be the FBI's 'tethered scapegoat' in case Norfolk turns bad for the Feds but the FBI doesn't really know about our involvement with Harrington."

"Okay" Betty responded, "but the Chinese efforts locally have cost us a damn good source, Wilber's inputs are gone, including our attempt to positively identify ALL the locals helping the Chinese, most likely some other city employees or more people at NISCO. On that subject, I got a final 'heads up' from Wilber, just before he was killed. His last drop confirmed the Chinese were willing to close down Deep Dragon but Wilber also provided a new suspicion of something creeping up on everybody's horizon, he referred to it as 'BUCK'."

"What do you think BUCK is?" Cooper asked.

"No idea, Coop, but it could be related to some of the local support group Dr. Kale wants us to shut down. Or, it might be something totally new and unrelated. I didn't know anything about BUCK until Wilber passed it on, posthumously."

"Is there any other place Harrington could have left more information?"

"No, The Norfolk Botanical Garden was his drop. Straight forward craft, nothing complicated. Maybe he had some other info hidden around his house, but I haven't had an opportunity or legitimate reason to check on that,

Cooper interrupted, "Did Sally know anything about his involvement with us?"

"I don't think so. Wilber loved keeping secrets, it seemed to empower him. Secrets were his real weakness. His Nuclear Sub background fostered that I guess. He did tell me that if Sally got the 'safe house' job we talked about, then, he was going to come-clean with her. Wilber was keeping a lot of other stuff from Sally, he said to protect their relationship, but honestly I think he just loved the secrets. So, it is possible there's some more information about BUCK around his house, I'm just not sure we'll ever get the chance to look for it."

"Yeah, you may be right about Wilber loving all the secrets, at least until he was ready to put them into a money making book." Cooper offered as he hoisted Betty up and headed down her nearby hallway.

"Oh my," Betty said coyly, "It must be 'SHOWTIME. I'll bet someone I know has a dangling-curtain, that's about to go-up-up-up…"

CHAPTER SEVENTY FOUR

LAKEWOOD

"STEPHEN IRONS"

I'm getting ready to read the morning paper, Willy-nilly got me up early to let him out. I'm in the kitchen enjoying a cup of Sally's German coffee and waiting for her cat to finish his outside business. On the second page of the paper I found a very small article covering the funeral services for Sergeant Morris Bradshaw. Bradshaw's limited coverage was probably as Millers said 'a public-restriction by Linda'. I'm reading the paper when Willy-nilly comes back and I let him in for his morning snack. As I close the door the kitchen phone rings. Damn early call, I think, then, I notice Sally's cell phone number on the ID read out. I hit the SPEAKER ON, and said, "Good morning Sally, you're up bright and early."

"Stephen, I've got great news." She began in a very excited voice, "I've just talked with a SKY MARSHAL going on our flight, Will and I met him three months ago and he remembered us," Sally paused here and I waited for the 'good news' to come. "He said he can try to check on the names you gave me when we get to Germany, he's got some connections with TSA and the local authorities in Frankfurt. He's going back before I leave on Saturday, but he'll check-in with me if he finds anything out. Isn't that great!?"

"That's wonderful Sally, are you still going to check the hospitals?"

"Yes, Vera's one of our German Speakers for my flight and she's going to help me call. I feel good about this Stephen, anything new where you are?" I debated telling Sally about my overzealous reaction to Agent Davis' provocation, but I decided to go positive,

"We're moving forward here, Sally, Detective Millers is helping me run down some of my leads and keeping me up to speed on the Norfolk Police progress with Wilber's case…" Thornton looked at me funny and said,

"I think Sally's going to pick up on you mentioning Sam and not Linda as your police contact, bud." Thankfully Thornton was wrong this time. Sally didn't go there she was in too big of a hurry.

"I've got to go Stephen we're getting ready for air-port pick-up, good luck and love to Willy-nilly," Before I could say, 'have a safe flight and your cat's right here with me', but Sally had closed the connection. I had a third cup of coffee and headed to the shower to clean up and dress for a visit to NISCO downtown and the completion of my earlier interview with Charles Taylor.

After my shower I called NISCO on the kitchen phone, activated the SPEAKER ON function again and Betty Boles picked up, "Norfolk International Shipping, this is Betty Boles, how can I help you Stephen?" Her voice was chipper and very upbeat,

"Good morning Betty, you sound way-up, how'd you know it was me?"

"Simple, Wilber's phone number is on the read-out, you're staying with Sally and she's away on a trip to Germany, so it had to be you. What can I do for you?"

"I'd like to come in and complete the interview with Charles is he available this morning?"

"He's at NIT, a conference with the Kroger girls, then later with James Carlson. He'll be out there all day. Do you want me to set up a time for you tomorrow afternoon here at the office?" Then she quickly added, "Oops I see his calendar has him at a Kiwanis Club meeting, that's probably going to slide into a dinner," she paused then, "I'm sorry Stephen but Friday he's tied up too, he's busy in the office all day and it's his night to work the late shift, the twins are off on Friday nights." Betty paused again and I could hear a schedule page or two flip over in the background noise, "How about Saturday afternoon, he always comes in the office after lunch, I'll tell him 2PM, okay?"

"I can make that work," I answered, "do you want me to call back to confirm?"

"No I'll just call Sally's house and leave a message, anything else?"

Thornton was fidgety anxious to make an input, "You should ask her if she knows about Wilber and the cookie factory, Rusty." I thought it was a good idea but I wanted to be a bit more subtle. I had several other leads at NISCO to run down, so that discussion would have to wait, maybe James Carlson or the Kroger twins could help, I'd love to see the twins again. So I just asked,

"Do you know if it's possible that Wilber could have been involved with some federal agency while he worked for NISCO?" The minute I finished asking the question I knew I had made a big mistake. I heard Betty's quick intake of breath, then,

"What do you mean, Stephen?" All her 'chipper' was gone and I envisioned rime ice and frost forming on the phone cradle. "You think Wilber was spying on us?" Her voice was full of surprise and hurried reaction. I tried to turn away from that direction.

"No, Betty, it's just a question that came up in a conference with the Norfolk Police, I guess because of his navy service they thought it was a possibility," Betty interrupted,

"That's preposterous! Wilber confided openly with me, I would have known if he was working with some other organization. Please don't go that direction with Charles or the Kroger girls, they're all business Stephen, they'll think 'industrial espionage' for sure and Sally could lose Wilber's benefits!"

"Jesus," Thornton said, "what a reaction! Then, a quick shift of subject to concern for Sally, we haven't thought about industrial espionage, only about confirming Millers' CIA possibility, you better drop-it bud."

"Thanks Betty, I'll say nothing to Charles but maybe you should warn him the police are looking at all possibilities." I said and her answer was the phone clicking loudly in my ear, ending the conversation. How weird, I thought, how defensive Betty had gotten when industrial espionage was mentioned, but wait a minute, that wasn't it at all, she got defensive because I asked about Wilber 'working for some federal agency' she was the one that shifted to industrial espionage. Damn there is something else going on,

Thornton said, "You should check with Millers again, Rusty, and how about your car? You don't want to be stuck without wheels." Thornton was right, so, I called Barry's Performance Imports for a Saturday morning appointment to get the car's Warning Light System checked out.

————————

I drove to the NISCO, NIT facility, said hello to Fred as I entered the main gate and headed for NISCO to talk with James Carlson in his underground office. For an hour and forty five minutes Carlson and I reviewed photographs and video clips of Wilber working around the docks for the past three months. The last portion showed Wilber standing on the dock giving hand signals to a crane-use operation, directing the off-loading of arriving containers. I watched as Wilber's closed fist was raised and circled in the air, then, he pumped his fist up and down rapidly before the operator rested the container gently on the dock. That was followed by Wilber's hand spreading five fingers before walking toward the control shed.

Carlson was helpful and tried to explain all Wilber's duties, ending with

Wilber giving the crane-operator a five minute break, but he admitted that Wilber was mostly a 'special-projects guy' for Taylor, so he wasn't sure about everything Taylor had him doing. Carlson shut the video system down and left me underground to make a few phone calls while he went to handle a new shipment arrival. I hit my forehead with the heel of my hand and immediately thought about Millers and his CIA information, if Wilber was connected with them then there's something Wilber would have 'known well' and could have written about. I hadn't been thinking of a CIA possibility, that certainly needed to be pursued some more. I used James Carlson's desk phone to call Millers' cell number. I tapped the SPEAKER ON. It rang twice then I heard,

"Millers, is that you Irons?" Jesus how does everyone know when it's me?

"Yes, Sam it's me, I won't even ask how you guessed. Can we meet tomorrow night, I've got some info we need to talk about you know, a new possibility. Maybe we can share a drink and some dinner?" As I finished my two questions, one of the Kroger girls came in. I could feel my face redden as she saw I was on the phone and started to leave. I quickly stood and motioned her to continue into the room. I felt certain my eyes were begging, my body temperature told me my heart was. Sam replied through Carlson's speaker,

"Sure, we're busy beefing up Dr. Ski's hospital security now but where do you want to meet? Downtown would be best." Millers said.

"You pick the place, Sam, drinks and something to eat tomorrow night, how about eight?" I watched Elizabeth take in our conversation, I was now certain it was Elizabeth, she was calm and demure, no hint at the bottled up energy Margarete carried around with her.

"Okay, let's do downtown then, how about EMPIRE on Granby, you know it?"

"Yeah, a downtown CRACKERS type place in the Tazewell Hotel, I'll see you tomorrow night," Before I could say another word, the connection clicked off and Millers moved on, so I did the same,

"Hi Elizabeth, it's great to see you. How've you been?" I offered as I moved toward her with my hand out in greeting.

"I'm good Stephen, how did you know it was me?" She replied as she took my hand and smiled brightly.

"Maybe it was a lucky guess, but more likely a hopeful wish." Elizabeth smiled again and I remembered her reaction in Charles Taylor's office when we first met formally, her smile had been so warm and inviting. Now, looking into her blue, blue eyes caused me to venture further, "If you and Margarete are free tomorrow night, why don't you join Sam Millers and me at EMPIRE, do you know where EMPIRE is?"

"Sure, and we're off tomorrow night, we might make it Stephen. I'll check with Margarete. Has James gone over to the docks? Charles needs him."

"Yes, he left just before you arrived,"

"Okay, thanks, we'll try to make it tomorrow Stephen." Elizabeth said, turned and she was gone.

What a morning, a big plus with Sally, an interesting reaction from Betty Boles, a possible clue from Millers and James Carlson about 'what Wilber knew well and could write about' and now the exciting prospect of dinner with two blonde goddesses.

Thornton smiled at me and said, "Won't Millers be surprised!"

CHAPTER SEVENTY FIVE

EMPIRE, FRIDAY NIGHT

"STEPHEN IRONS"

Good meeting choice, EMPIRE is beginning to fill-up with the sights and sounds of fashionable downtown workers taking the opportunity to relax after a long work-week. After speaking to Millers again to confirm the meeting time and learning more about Ursula Volk's attempt to get to Dr. Ski in the hospital, I was even more optimistic about tying this whole mystery together in one small neat package. I wanted to call Sally to explain the latest but she was probably sleeping on her Frankfurt layover, it was 1AM over there so I'd just wait until she called again.

I arrived at EMPIRE early to secure a four top table before the after eight crowd swarmed into the eclectic watering hole. I talked with Kristin, our server, another classy looking gal, tall, slim, bright eyed with prominent cheek-bones and medium length black hair that she'd pulled back into two short, fetching pig-tales. She had exotic fashion-model looks and moved toward me with a roll and sway that immediately grabbed my attention. After Kristin helped me select one of the four-top tables against the wall, I informed her that Millers would be coming and hopefully a later addition of the Kroger twins. She knew exactly who the Kroger girls were and said she might also know Millers. I offered Sam as his first name and her answer was quick,

"Oh, yeah, Sam the cop, hey, he just walked in." She turned, waved toward Millers' arrival and asked, "You want Robert to fix you a Beefeaters on the rocks Sam?"

"That would be great, Kristin, hi Stephen, what's your drink?" Sam asked as he shook my offered hand and sat down facing the small kitchen area of the restaurant.

"I'll have Bombay-rocks Kristin." I replied and she hurried off to pass the order to Robert this Friday night's mix-master for EMPIRE. Sam pulled his chair up and began to elaborate on the police encounter with Ursula Volk and the increased security they were establishing to further protect Dr. Kowalski. I listened for a minute then I asked,

"Are you sure that was Volk?"

"Who else, Knowles and Stokes ID'd her from her zoo photo and I'm sure Bradshaw was close to identifying her before he was killed. Now that Dr. Ski's getting better, she'll be able to do the same. Volk's in a corner, she's got to keep covering her ass locally or she's got to run." Kristin arrived with the drinks and Sam and I toasted Dr. Ski's recovery and our own good health. We continued our conversation and I watched the front of the restaurant, for the Kroger girls.

"Sam, I know you're concerned about Sally checking on the Volk family in Germany, but she called and she's getting an AIR MARSHALL assigned to her flight to help. He has TSA connections and law enforcement friends in Frankfurt to help search for Volk. She's also going to ask a German speaking flight attendant to call the local hospitals to look for Mr. Herman Volk,"

Sam interrupted, "Sally's not going to find Ursula Volk in Germany, but more information on her family could be helpful. We're sure Volk skipped her flight at Dulles and came back here to eliminate her problems and cover her own ass."

"I'm glad Dr. Ski's going to be okay, she is isn't she?" I asked,

"The doctors think she'll get all her physical abilities back, Dr. Han said her hearing will be a little fuzzy for awhile, but her vision's okay. He estimates four to six weeks of physical therapy to get the rest of it done. She was fortunate to be moving away when the bullet hit the back of her head," Sam stopped talking as he saw my attention shift to the front of the restaurant and I stood and watched the Kroger twins enter the restaurant. Sam's head swiveled as he tried to continue talking, but all he could say was, "Holy Shit, Stephen I owe you that interview with Dr. Ski, they're breathtaking."

Margarete and Elizabeth Kroger entered the restaurant wearing spaghetti strap 'little black dresses', except the dresses were cobalt blue, really popping' their god-given eye color. They both had employed blue satin hair ribbons; Elizabeth's tying a French plait and Margarete's securing a long pony tail, drawing more attention to their golden hair as everyone in the restaurant paused to gape.

Thirty minutes after introductions; seating Elizabeth on my right and Margarete on Sam's left, both on bathroom convenient aisle seating away from the wall; our table top was covered with EMPIRE'S special martinis, pot stickers, tenderloin rare, seared salmon with mango salsa and a grouper braised in a white wine sauce. Sam and I were definitely full of ourselves, and the Kroger girls knew they were responsible for our euphoric state. Margarete handled Sam's wise cracks and provided some of her own while my romantic thoughts drifted to Elizabeth's enticing charm. I was smiling at Elizabeth when Thornton caught my eye and pointed toward the Tazewell Hotel's adjoining door. My face went flush and my jaw line knotted as Clayton Davis and a good looking red-head walked into EMPIRE. Their clothes were rumpled-up and they were laughing and grabbing each other while Davis searched for a spot at the now fully occupied bar. Finding no space there, Davis began to scan the room for a table. When he spotted me, his face turned as red as his date's hair and he abandoned her and moved our way,

"Sam, Davis is here." I whispered to Sam as Davis arrived and said,

"Irons, what the hell are you doing here?" Davis was flustered and the wonderful flush that appeared on his face when his butt hit the asphalt on Larchmont Crescent, began to return. When Davis got about two steps from us Sam tried to get up to stop him, but Margarete had Sam pinned in against the wall so Sam directed,

"Davis, knock it off, go back to your girlfriend," Sam said, then, noting the gorgeous red head Davis had left standing a couple of paces back Sam added, "Better yet, leave her with us and you just go away, we'll take care of your friend."

"Stay out of this Millers, you Norfolk jerk, or I'll add you to my list!" Davis announced this very loudly, gaining the restaurant's full attention as he towered over our table. The red head tried to reach Davis' arm to pull him back, but feeling the unknown grab, Davis lashed out and pushed her away, shoving her into Kristin and a lot of food orders being tray-carried to another table. Immediately with the, *CLATTER* of the dropped plates and the *CRASH* of several glasses, Davis looked sideways and saw Kristin and his girlfriend falling away toward the floor, "Oh shit, Gay, I'm sorry." Davis offered,

As Davis turned and reached, Margarete stood up. I could see she was shoeless as she assumed a tightly coiled stance then rotated quickly, kicking out behind herself, directly into Davis' sternum, she'd probably read the same karate book I had. Davis *COUGHED* out an expelled burst of wind and his butt immediately hit EMPIRE'S cluttered floor. Sam could now get up and he showed his police badge as he moved around Margarete, then, turned to me and said, "Stephen take the girls home and call me later, I'll get all this done."

Standing over the choking Davis, after helping Kristin and the red head up from the floor, Sam turned to Elizabeth, shook her hand and said, "It's been a genuine pleasure Elizabeth." Then, once he knew Kristin and Gay were up and okay, he gave Margarete a big hug and said in a very throaty voice, "It's been the experience of my life, Margarete, thank you." Then, Sam knelt back down to keep Davis calm as the twins and I, amid a standing ovation from the excited crowd, departed EMPIRE'S front entrance.

Back home in Lakewood, I reflected on the evening; Sam had been right, 'the experience of a life time'. I took the girls home to their apartment and was invited in. As Elizabeth and I talked, the phone rang and I imagined it was Millers tracing down their apartment. Margarete answered and after about two minutes of responses, mostly, 'yes sir' she hung up excused herself and called Elizabeth into the kitchen. I listened hard, but could only discern a mumble of voices, I actually thought I heard three separate voices discussing the call and coming to some decision. After several minutes Elizabeth returned and apologized explaining sad news from one of their relatives in Richmond that required their immediate departure. Elizabeth kissed me passionately and promised a call soon to resume our relationship. I departed knowing the arousal problem I had been so worried about was definitely a thing of the past. I called Millers' cell and reminisced the evening. I told him about the twins' call to duty and gave him there address for his reference. He thanked me for including the Kroger girls in our evening, then, he started to laugh. When I asked him what was so funny, Sam replied,

"I've got a date tomorrow with Davis' red head. When I helped her up and got rid of Davis, we talked. It seems she likes southern gentlemen, plus the fact that we were with such beautiful blondes, was a challenging turn-on to her red headed sexuality,"

I closed off the phone call and memories of Millers and his fantasies come true, then I fed Willy-nilly and set the clock for 8AM, to go and get the Volvo fixed tomorrow.

CHAPTER SEVENTY SIX

LAKEWOOD, SATURDAY

"STEPHEN IRONS"

God, my head's killing me! I drank way too much last night, but remembering the evening did bring a smile to my face in spite of my aching head. When I recalled talking to Millers and found that he was hooking up with Gay, I imagined him taking great pleasure in besting Davis. But who was I trying to kid, Sam wouldn't give a thought to Davis he'd been swept away by Hurricane Gay.

After several cups of coffee I tried a piece of toast, brushed my teeth, fed Willy-nilly, then Thornton and I headed out with my ailing Volvo. We arrived at BPI after a five minute drive and parked near the front entrance. Barry laughed when I explained the Volvo's problem and told him my corrective action was to delay until the light bulb burned out. "Why are you laughing Barry?"

"Bless your heart Stephen with customers like you I'll be able to keep sending all my kids through college." I immediately took offense and demanded,

"What do you mean, what did I do wrong? And whisper your answer, you're pounding my sinuses."

"Sinuses ha, you're hung over, aren't you? Well, your emission system's fouled, could be a loose connection or a failed seal. You need an inspection and an oil change too. You were due in September for both! I'll let you know about the emission system."

Still fighting my headache, I went where all Volvo owners go when talking to their mechanics, "How much is this going to cost?"

"It might be $50 for the inspection and oil change, another $15 to reconnect, if that's the warning system's problem, but if one of the seals has failed, then, it'll go about $155 total. Not a full semester's tuition but certainly a good effort toward paying for a class or two. Go upstairs and read a magazine, better yet, take a nap. I'll call you when we're done." Thornton and I trudged up the back stairs to the 'customer waiting room' on the second floor. He was sympathetic to my condition and allowed me to fall asleep on a big sofa. After about fifteen minutes the sound of foot steps coming up the stairs woke me. I checked my watch, 9:45, not bad I needed the cat nap and 30 'mechanic' minutes couldn't cost so much, probably a reconnection. I stood and waited for Barry to come up the stairs, but I ended up watching Paula, the bar manager from THE BISTRO, complete the journey with Thornton right behind her, making curvy gestures with his hands as he followed her ascending figure. I gave Thornton a hard look as Paula greeted me,

"Hi, Stephen, Barry says, 'thanks for the tuition installment, it's definitely a dead seal', makes me want to call PETA and turn you both in." Paula offered with some laughter, "Barry said you'd know what he meant. It'll be another hour for you."

"Hi, Paula, what are you doing here?"

"I've got a '96 Saab, needs an annual inspection I'll be here an hour also."

"They don't look that busy Paula, why so long?"

"Barry wants to buy my car, so he always takes longer with it to make me think the car's having some nonexistent problem. It's got 36,000 miles and nothing's ever wrong with it. It's just a game we go through when I'm in here for an oil change or inspection."

"Well, it's great to have your company, a little more expensive than a couple of martinis at THE BISTRO, but enjoyable none the less." I offered trying to dismiss the bad thoughts of her roommate Roger that she hit me with the last time I saw her. As if reading my mind she sat down in a large chair opposite my position and said,

"I want to apologize about 'stringing you along' the other night, then hitting you with my 'Roger Stick', it wasn't meant to be nasty, but I think you took it that way. Did you Stephen?"

"Maybe a little, my relationships have been in a 'black-hole spiral' lately, our conversation was in hopes of you throwing me a life-line. But, your Roger response turned out to be just another heavy anchor. However, your gracious apology is accepted. I'm a big boy I should be able to handle it."

"I'm sure you will, but I was serious about the Kroger girls, you should be able to work with one of them to rescue you from the spiral, I'd really recommend Elizabeth, she seems a lot more intriguing to me, you know still-waters running deep, that kind of opportunity."

Damn, there was that word again 'intriguing'. Elizabeth must have 'intriguing' written on her forehead for everyone to see. I guess I missed looking at her forehead. I responded, "Actually, a friend of mine and I were out with the Kroger twins last night and I agree Elizabeth's the more interesting one. But, the twins got a phone call after I took them back to their apartment. They had to leave for Richmond, some kind of family problem," Paula interrupted,

"I don't think they're really twins, I think they're probably triplets not twins."

"Why would you think there're three of them?"

"Subtle things another woman who sees them a lot when they're relaxed would pick up on. You know personality traits, some small make up variances, physical mannerism changes and a few other little things that mount-up. Lately I've had the pair come in to meet guys, or just hang-out. A few times the one that says she's Margarete, is a lot quieter than normal. I'm sure Charles Taylor's starting to wonder too, I heard him ask Big Todd..." Barry interrupted her thoughts, shouting up from the ground floor,

"Paula your Saab's all set." And Paula added,

"Well, that was quick I guess Barry's given up on trying to scam me out of my Saab. Good seeing you Stephen, drop by THE BISTRO, I'll introduce Roger and buy you a drink. No hard feelings?"

"Thanks Paula, I'll do that. All is forgiven and thanks for the info, I'll let you know just how good your intuition is." Paula departed and Thornton said,

"WOW Rusty you sure can pick 'em, but they're all treating you like Rodney Dangerfield now, you're definitely getting NO RESPECT."

I'm beginning to hate it when Thornton overstates the obvious.

———————————

Two PM, I'm sitting at Betty's desk in NISCO downtown. I'm waiting for Charles to get off the phone and call me into his office. Earlier, at Sally's house; after paying $155 and driving home with an oil change, a new State Inspection and repaired emission system; Sally called to say she was back in Dallas and had some exciting news. She was coming home and asked me to pick her up at the Norfolk airport around 11:30 tonight. While I waited for Charles to call me in, I began to look around Betty's office area noting the vast amount of computerized equipment that she had at her disposal and knowing all the separate businesses and foreign countries NISCO dealt with. I was about to go over to a remote computer station of some kind, with an entirely separate WIFI system that remained ON and waiting for incoming communications, when Charles' door opened and called,

"Stephen, come in, sorry I kept you waiting, I was on the phone with Margarete, there's been some crisis in their family and the twins have been called back to California. They've submitted their immediate resignation so I've got a big problem to deal with right now. Betty's on her way in to help me find replacements, she has a large number of contacts in the Washington DC area… I interrupted,

"I was at the Kroger apartment last night when the girls got a call from Richmond but it didn't sound like a crisis. Would you like me to wait until Betty gets here?"

"No, Stephen, Betty's very capable, I hired her away from the CIA four years ago, she's always been able to help me in the past, I'm sure she'll come up with something," Charles and I both heard the outer door open and Betty called,

"I'm here Mr. Taylor I've gotten a couple of applicants ready for interviews," Betty paused as she entered Charles' office and saw me there, she'd probably forgotten about my meeting just like she had forgotten to tell me about her former association with the CIA.

"I'm just leaving Betty, but do give me a call at home before you head out, we definitely need to talk."

Thornton trailed behind me with his shit-eating grin spreading over his face. He began to laugh and said. "Rusty, we were right Wilber was tied in with the cookie factory!" I gave Thornton a return smile and nodded my concurrence as we continued down the hall.

CHAPTER SEVENTY SEVEN

LAKEWOOD

"STEPHEN IRONS"

I'm in Sally's den, Thornton and I are watching a lead up game to the World Series but I'm paying zero attention to the game. I've got a beer open, but I haven't had a sip. This new turn of events is too exciting for me to wash down with a beer, it really calls for champagne. I wanted to phone someone to share the information I'd gotten today but I just wasn't sure who. Thornton read my mind and said,

"You should call Linda, it's her case. This information is crucial concerning Wilber's affiliation with the CIA." I reminded Thornton that Linda and I were on the outs, so that call wasn't going to happen.

"Maybe Os, I replied, he's not really involved with the investigation but he's a close friend and concerned about my progress working for Charles Taylor…"

Thornton interrupted, "That's counterproductive, bud, too much explaining to bring Os up to speed, he's not going to know any of this."

Thornton might be right again, so I tried Millers' cell and got the following recorded message,

"Hello, you've reached Sam, I'm occupied right now and want be available for a couple of days. Leave a message if you want to, but I'll probably dump it when I return from Nags Head. Try me Monday, after nine, Cheers."

So, Sam's off to Nags Head for the weekend, damn, Sam was definitely under the influence of 'Hurricane Gay', that red headed storm has swept him up in her path of destruction. I couldn't blame him I could only envy his adventure. I was in the middle of feeling sorry for myself when Sally's phone rang,

"Stephen Irons," I answered after I looked at the 'VA cell' ID on the phone's display and touched the Speaker ON button so Thornton could listen.

"Stephen, its Betty Boles, I'm on the way to Sally's house, I'll be there in ten minutes, I'm bringing a friend. We need to talk!"

"You're damn right we do," I said into the phone's speaker, but Betty had disconnected. She's still a damn 'cookie' I thought to myself, all of the 'secret shit' with Wilber is about to come out. The 'friend' business had me confused, so Thornton said, "Double stuff, Rusty, we're dealing with 'two cookies' maybe the one Sam said Linda talked with."

As I waited for Betty and friend to arrive, a real sadness came over me. The CIA business could explain a lot about Wilber and his secrets, but it couldn't rationalize him keeping the existence of his son and ex wife from my sister. Even after finding Wilber's letter to Sally, it didn't make a lot of sense to me. But Sally was on the way home excited and optimistic, so I wasn't going to stay depressed. I cleared my mind as a four door black Toyota Sedan pulled into Sally's circular driveway and I watched Betty and friend move toward Sally's kitchen door.

"Betty, welcome to Sally's house, but you've probably been here before, haven't you?" Betty ignored my question as her friend a tall sandy haired guy reached his hand toward me and offered,

"Hello, Steve, I'm Craig Cooper an associate of Betty's, please call me Cooper, I don't much like Craig."

"Hello, Cooper, glad to meet you, you can call me Stephen I don't much like Steve, that's what my dad called me."

"Sorry, I should have remembered, your file indicates you and your dad didn't see eye to eye on too many things,"

Now I was getting pissed, no more joking banter, these two jerks had a file on me. Thornton laughed and said, "These two are definitely 'cookies' or some other 'federal food-chain-chum' you're going to have to deal with Rusty." I smiled at Thornton and said to Cooper,

"Okay, Cooper you've got my attention, it's obvious you have me at a disadvantage, but you and Betty better be prepared to come clean with me or this conversation's over. You've got a lot of info to share, but I've got some you don't know about, so show me yours right now."

"Fair enough," Cooper began, "We have your Navy history, we know about you losing your partner Thornton in Afghanistan, we know about the counseling you've gone through to deal with his loss before you resigned to come home and help your mom when your dad died. We know about your mom's death six months later and about the difficulty you went through qualifying for Sheriff's Deputy and the incident in Judge Knutson's courtroom this year. We sympathize with the mess you're going through trying to protect your sister and come to grips with Harrington's secrecy, so how about a drink? Sally has some 'adult beverages' doesn't she?"

Thornton was shaking his head, I'm sure he was surprised to hear his name mentioned in Cooper's dissertation. Personally I was turning redder with each fact Cooper threw at me. I should be really pissed by now, but I wasn't. I was just embarrassed because Thornton and Betty were listening to my life-history short-comings spelled-out chronologically. Oddly, my most obvious feeling was excitement toward what I was about to learn, so I answered, "Sure, Sally's got beer, wine and hard stuff, after your speech, I'm going for Bombay gin in the freezer, what can I get you two 'cookies'?" I replied. Betty looked startled but Cooper only smiled and said,

"Well, your brain cells have been working overtime" then he reached in his jacket and produced his CIA credentials, "I'll have gin with you, Stephen, maybe a wine for Betty?" Cooper began, but Betty cut him off,

"I'll do with cold gin too. I need a big, gulp right now!" I smiled and got out three tumblers, put in a few cubes and poured a generous sampling of Bombay gin into each glass. I handed the first to Betty, smiled and passed a second to Cooper, then, I offered, as I removed Wilber's picture in The Norfolk Botanical Garden, from my pocket and handed it to Betty,

"Cheers, I know you don't appear in this scene, Betty, but I'm certain you had a role in the overall production."

Sally's grandfather clock chimed seven as I cleaned up after my little 'cookie conference', I was a bit tipsy from the excitement and the gin but I was elated with the meeting's outcome. Finally, other than Wilber's personal reasons for keeping his wife and son a secret, I had it all pulled together. Betty had been encouraged to share her relationship with Wilber and his part-time employment by the CIA to report on NISCO, Charles Taylor, the Kroger 'twins' and their involvement with their Chinese associate, Sonchi Zimchi and a Richmond tycoon named Morgan Folds. Betty confirmed the Norfolk Botanical Garden as Wilber's 'drop' and laughed at Wilber's picture with the flowers and his message about me 'being proud of him some day when I figured it all out'. Well that day had come and I was proud of his involvement with the CIA, one that had helped shut down a Chinese secret operation, but the sad part was that his involvement and his quest for fame as a writer had gotten him killed. I shared Paula's theory about the 'twins' being 'triplets' and after much discussion Betty and Cooper came to the conclusion that Taylor and the Kroger girls were working two different sides of the street. The Kroger girls were working for Folds and Zimchi as industrial spies using their intimate knowledge of the NISCO operation to further both their commercial advantages and growing profit margins. Cooper confirmed the CIA believed that Chin had been brought to Norfolk for Wilber's murder and eliminated by someone locally, probably Chin's control agent, to cover up China's part in Wilber's death. Those events and Linda's investigation brought about

Bradshaw's death and Dr. Kowalski's near fatal injury.

After the 'cookies' departure, I understood why Wilber had gotten involved with reporting on NISCO operations and I WAS truly proud, as Wilber had predicted. Finding out about Deep Dragon and helping gain an edge over that Chinese operation was commendable, but Wilber's attempt to use a thinly disguised plot line to publish a book about that specific operation had cost him his life and most certainly sullied mine and Sally's belief in his good-character and honesty. Betty promised to share Wilber's CIA involvement to try and help Sally come to grips with his secrecy. That was the 'good' side of the close of our discussion, the 'bad' side was that I was now shoved into the middle, just where Wilber had been, I was recruited to be the newest 'temporary cookie' in the box and tasked with reporting on what I could learn through my investigation for Charles Taylor. I would report to Betty and Cooper about Charles Taylor and NISCO, searching mainly to find out what the hell BUCK referred to as Wilber's last message had suggested they focus on. Betty and Cooper still withheld a lot of information concerning Wilber's death but I felt they believed that Wilber's attempt to publish a book about a Chinese secret had cost him his life. Wilber's book was not a continuing threat to the security of the United States, but the CIA was still concerned with the information gathering the Chinese were attempting in Norfolk and they had no idea what 'BUCK' was. They never mentioned Ursula Volk by name when they spoke of the 'control agent' and the death of Eric Chin, so I kept quiet about Knowles' and Officer Stokes' ID of Ursula Volk at the hospital and Sally's present investigation through her sources in Frankfurt. They wanted to hold on to some of their secrets but I could keep a couple too,

"Hey Rusty," Thornton said interrupting my thoughts, "We're just starting to understand Wilber's manipulation of everything, you know, protecting himself and his CIA involvement, but, you better get your excitement under-control you don't want to end up like Wilber did."

I smiled at Thornton's input and checked the clock. Sally was coming home soon I was going to the airport to pick her up in an hour.

After I picked Sally up at the airport she was dead tired from her Frankfurt departure at 8AM German time, 3AM our clock. On top of the long, work day for her, she told me her trip to Norfolk had been on a 'jump seat' because the flight 'had an ass in every seat and a face in every window'. Riding on the fold down hard back, hard butt seat was the only way she could make the trip home. She was grateful to learn of Wilber's involvement with the CIA and the additional $10,000

I had found in his Correspondence Course books and when she read Wilber's note and cried a bit. She seemed pleased, but not totally comforted by his 'letter from the grave'. She did tell me that her friend Vera couldn't find any record of Ursula 's father in any Frankfurt Hospital or nursing home but her AIR MARSHALL friend, found out that Ursula Volk's parents had been dead for ten years and Ursula was restricted from returning to Germany for suspicion of anti-government activity. After that, Sally bundled up Willy-nilly and headed upstairs to her bed for a well deserved sleep.

I cleaned up the small mess that goat cheese and a couple glasses of red wine had made as I reflected on Sally's parting comment that, 'We needed to talk about Linda, but it could wait until tomorrow'. I was worn out myself and headed upstairs for bed. Thornton began to talk to me as we climbed the stairs,

"We've got to get this thing solved Rusty, Sally's hurting and I'm getting tired of all this, NO ACTION, JACKSON." Thornton was right again, I had to do something to get this investigation moving forward.

CHAPTER SEVENTY EIGHT

LAKEWOOD

"STEPHEN IRONS"

Willy-nilly got me up, walking on my chest and licking my nose until I fought my way out of the dream about Betty Boles making a batch of cookies that Wilber threw at some NISCO cargo off-loaders. I was glad to have been pulled out of that dream Betty and Wilber were wasting a lot of cookies on a bunch of grubby dock workers. I forced myself up and walked by Sally's closed door. I was sure Sally had ejected her small pest then shut her door and gone back to sleep. She needed a lot of sleep-time to catch up so I went downstairs and I let the little guy out. Outside, I saw Thornton standing down by the river's edge watching some early morning girl's rowing crew. I turned back inside and started the coffee while I spread out the Sunday paper for my own slow recovery from a late evening.

Minutes later, Willy-nilly was at the door, ready to come in the house, Thornton was gone, probably off on some other mission. The coffeemaker 'beeped' task complete and I left the newspaper on the counter opened the door for Sally's cat and got some fresh-brewed caffeine in my system. After my second cup of coffee the cat meowed and ran toward the stairs voicing his expectations when we both heard Sally's soft, velvet like foot steps start down the stairs. When she arrived in the kitchen, her long red hair was tumbling down around a soft oval face still filled with creases and push marks from a ten hour encounter with her pillow. I smiled at the long night-shirt she wore with the printed declaration of: **Flight Attendants are here to save your ass, not kiss it,** stenciled on the front. The sleeper shirt's rear sported a big red imprint of painted-lips that looked like an advertisement for 'The Rocky Horror Picture Show'. I and got up to greet my little sister.

"Morning Sleepy Head," I offered as I gave Sally a hug of welcome, "I'll get you a cup of coffee, if you're ready," Sally hugged me back, then, when I tried to release her and get coffee, she held on like it was far too soon to be alone. I responded and continued to hold her close feeling the bedroom warmth of her small body seek refuge, shelter and protection. I promised myself there was no way I was going to lose this dear sister to my own carelessness or disregard for my own personal responsibilities.

"Coffee would be good, Stephen." Sally finally said as she turned away and seated herself at the kitchen island holding Willy-nilly in her small lap. Sally nuzzled the kitten's tiny face and pulled his small body close against her breast. After a moment she seemed to regain her control and released the kitten to the floor, "Anything good in the paper?"

"Not much, but I did see an article advertising the 'BOO at the ZOO' next Saturday, will you be home for that function?" I asked knowing she would probably be asked to help out showing one of their Education Animals.

"No, I'm still scheduled for Germany Thursday, Friday and Saturday this month, it'll change for November but I haven't gotten the bid results yet, why do you ask?"

"Well, we spoke last night about Linda and I hoped you could call and ask her over, then, maybe we could take Linda and Ella to the 'BOO' event. I'm embarrassed to call her myself." I offered as Sally took her first sip of coffee.

"That's a great idea, but you'll have to wait a couple hours before I can make that call; I'm 'addle brained' from my trip, you know, I'm still functioning slow and not allowed to make any major decisions, or sign any legal papers for another couple more hours." Sally laughed at her own joke and I smiled, pleased my little sister was home.

Linda Knowles sat in a large tub filled with warm water and body soothing skin softeners. She'd been in the tub for 30 minutes relaxing, recuperating and recharging her intent to get on with the day. She was upset with everyone, Stokes and Webber for being tricked into allowing Ursula Volk access to the hospital and then learning about Davis' asinine behavior in a Norfolk restaurant, Becky from the Tazewell Hotel had called her yesterday about the downtown event, *"Sam Millers and Stephen Irons were at EMPIRE with two blondes I didn't know, they were very impressive twins."* Linda was certain that had to be the Kroger girls she had heard so much about, *"Davis came in with a local red head and tried to start a fight with Irons, but one of the blondes stood up and knocked Davis on his ass."*

After that disclosure Becky and Linda had a lengthy laugh and Becky had closed her call with the fact that, Millers stayed to pick Davis up and more than likely, Davis' red headed friend. Linda began to laugh again as she remembered Saturday afternoon when Sam called and asked for the weekend off to go to Nags Head to recharge his batteries. When she had asked Sam if his recharging unit had red hair? Sam had almost died laughing himself. She was still upset with Millers for

312

trying to pull something over on her, but she remained confused how the Kroger twins departed the scene and the red head entered Sam's picture. Men, what pains. Of course she was upset with Stephen Irons for being involved in another attack on Davis, through it seemed to be no real fault of his own, but she remained angered at Sam and Stephen for having dinner with two thirds of what she had jokingly called, Stephen's 'BLONDETOURAGE'.

"This is childish," she voiced to herself, "I should have talked with Stephen myself, now he's headed in a new direction, with a different blonde." Linda moved the lever that released the tub water to the drain and began to clean her self of residual soap with the tub's hand shower. She needed to get moving, she'd promised Ella Sunday Brunch AW Shucks and she was looking forward to fulfilling her promise.

As the large tub finished draining Linda replaced the hand shower and reached for a terry cloth robe. Leaving the robe untied she sat down on the tub's edge with a large container of moisturizing lotion. Reluctantly remembering the unwanted task of shaving her legs she placed the moisturizer aside and gathered in her electric razor for the task at hand.

Ten minutes later with smooth skin, she regained the moisturizing cream and began to indulge herself in a task she wished she had a man to help perform. She missed the manly touch her husband Dwight had brought into her life and she yearned for the right man to come along to help her regain sexual confidence. Linda could see in the full length mirror that she still possessed long muscular legs, firm thighs, ample bosom and an almost flat belly, certainly appealing to any man. She pushed her wet, short blonde hair back from her face letting her long fingers slide through to separate the newly cleaned strands. She saw her blue-gray eyes highlighted against her lightly tanned face and subtle cheek bones. She didn't have the provocative lips she envied in some other women, her mouth was smallish, adorned only with determination, not an inviting allure that she coveted. She had considered enhancing injections but had discarded the idea as she would discard any man that couldn't see, and be pleased with, her god-given attributes.

Finishing with self analysis and moisturizing Linda began to brush and blow-dry her hair. She toweled off briskly to get that 'natural' look then wondered why she was making this effort just to take Ella to a Sunday Brunch? No matter she assured herself she'd be back at work and dealing with her co-workers and the general public tomorrow and they deserved her best physical appearance. Linda exited the bathroom, tied her robe tightly around her body and called to Ella, "You can get dressed now Ella, we'll leave for brunch in about 20 minutes, Okay?" Ella responded,

"Okay mom." then the phone rang and Ella announced, "I've got the phone mom." Then Linda head Ella's voice in the next room, "Knowles' house, this is

Ella, - Stephen, Stephen hello Stephen. I've like missed you Stephen,"

Oh damn, Linda thought what the hell can he want? But an immediate warmness came over her body and she went back in the bathroom to brush her hair one last time as she waited to hear the next response from Ella.

"Yes, you can talk to her." Linda could hear Ella's small feet pound rapidly across the wooden floor, then, "Guess what its Stephen, tell him we miss him, mom, you like tell him mom!"

CHAPTER SEVENTY NINE

LAKEWOOD

"STEPHEN IRONS"

What an afternoon, 'Princess Ella' was charming of course, holding my hand and hugging me, it was a great reunion. She loved Willy-nilly and thought it was 'like super' that Sally had picked the name so she could still pretend to talk with Wilber, even after she lost him. She had turned to Linda and said excitedly, "Mom, we could get a kitty at the SPCA and name him 'Daddy' and I could always talk to him!"

Both Linda and Sally showed a glisten in their eyes and Thornton became emotionally reactive, looked at me wistfully and whispered, "Ella needs a real daddy in her life Rusty." I smiled at him but ignored his reevaluation of Linda's positive potential for my future. He was stating the obvious but his opinions were like my own thoughts, changing with each new event in my life. Linda accepted my apology for my Larchmont Crescent behavior. I wasn't proud of my confrontation with Davis but his efforts were disturbing. Neither of us mentioned Friday night at EMPIRE but I was sure she knew about that incident.

While Ella played outside with Willy-nilly, Linda shared revelations with Sally and me concerning her meeting with Cooper. Linda omitted the use of his name but I knew who she was speaking of. I showed Sally's photo of Wilber at the Norfolk Botanical Garden and reasoned how Wilber's quote finally made some sense. I WAS proud of Wilber's continued service to his country but when Sally asked what Wilber had actually accomplished for his country, Linda said, "Wilber helped uncover a secret Chinese effort against several countries, including the United States and actually helped bring an end to that Chinese effort."

Sally's sense of relief was genuine and Linda took notes when Sally explained her efforts through a flight attendant friend, Vera and the SKY MARSHAL assigned to her last flight. Linda added that Dr. Ski was recovering well enough now and had positively identified Ursula Volk as Bradshaw's killer and her assailant. Volk's friend Alex had been arrested in Tennessee and was being interrogated in an attempt to locate Volk before she could commit more crimes.

When Sally went outside to check on Ella, I told Linda about my second encounter with Clayton Davis at EMPIRE Little Bar Bistro. When I offered that the Kroger girls had been called away to California by their real employer, Linda asked "Do you think they could have anything to do with Wilber's murder?"

"No, I don't think so, I believe theirs was a business related plot of some kind, I'm sure Charles Taylor and Betty Boles are pursuing that." I offered Betty's name to watch Linda's reaction, but the name evoked no recognition so I added, "Taylor is very upset, he knows nothing of Wilber's involvement with the CIA and I don't plan on sharing."

"Good," Linda said as Sally and Ella followed Willy-nilly back into Sally's kitchen where Linda offered to Sally, "Thanks for the information Sally, I'll contact your SKY MARSHAL to learn his sources in Frankfurt if we need more on the history of the Volk family. Ella get ready darling, we've going to see your grandmother."

"Linda," Sally began, "would you and Ella like to go to the 'BOO at the ZOO' event on Saturday? I won't be here but I can get you passes and Stephen would love to escort you around the zoo's big Halloween Celebration…"

"Mom, that would be great," Ella chimed in, "Grandma could go too, if that's okay, Sally?" Ella asked assuming a positive reply from her mom.

"Of course, Ella, I'll get a zoo pass for your grandmother too."

CHAPTER EIGHTY

RICHMOND, VIRGINIA

Morgan Folds hung up the phone and said, "Sonchi, that call was from Gerda, she's gotten four of the six plates done and tested, she's very excited about the results." Sonchi nodded his head in response and Morgan added, "She's still concerned about her operational security and wants Conrad to come down and 'help her get her security organized as soon as possible'. Those were the exact words she used…" Sonchi interrupted,

"We can send him, but, don't you think it's going to take at least a week to arrange everything we need in Norfolk?" Sonchi asked as Morgan turned away from his friend and called to Conrad,

"Conrad, how much time for Norfolk?"

"Probably four to five days, to get Norfolk all fobbed off. A couple to gain Taylor's confidence and get him to introduce me to Judge Knutson, after that, a few days to set the scenery up and run the play. I've been warned the CIA and the FBI are snooping around Norfolk, not sure why, but they're cagy to a fault. If they've sussed-out our show, it'll get more complicated,"

Morgan interrupted, "Why haven't you mentioned the CIA before? We knew about the FBI, but are you sure about the CIA's presence?"

"I got the call-up an hour ago, Carlson wasn't aware of the CIA coming on stage, but a Washington source gave him the prompt. If both troops are in Norfolk, I think they have some other production, not BUCK, on their schedule."

"Is Carlson still functioning safely for us?" Morgan asked.

"Yes, he's keeping a close tab on Taylor and an eye on Irons' nosing around NISCO. He called about the Kroger girls' departure, so they've responded to your direction, Morgan…"

"What about Irons?" Sonchi interrupted, "Is he still reporting to Taylor?"

"Yes, and so far no one really knows if there's a connection between NISCO and Harrington's murder, including us. Carlson knew about Harrington's book but he's got no real idea about the plot, just some speculation it had to do with

317

Taylor's shipping business. The Kroger girls were trying to get it all sussed-out by getting close to Irons, but that door's closed with their departure."

"How about their apartment, have we cleared that out?" Morgan said.

"Carlson's stage-crew sanitized everything so that stage looks like 'only working twins' were there." Conrad said.

"Do you expect the authorities to look at their apartment?" Sonchi asked,

"Yes, Margarete had a physical confrontation with the FBI Agent assigned to the Harrington murder, so it opens up the probability of the FBI taking a more pointed interest in their former residence,"

Morgan interrupted, "What kind of confrontation?"

"Well, Margarete and Elizabeth were out with Irons and a Norfolk Detective name Millers when the FBI Agent, Davis, confronted Irons about some personal problem. At that time 'dear Margarete' took the lead and kicked Davis' butt. My guess is Davis might be too embarrassed to push extensive follow up on, but he'll probably check the twins out. Actually, when our distraction plays, most of the audience will focus on Taylor and Judge Knutson, as our Tai Chi diversion intends. That'll give BUCK a boost to get off the ground."

"Yes," Sonchi replied, finally satisfied with their progress, "the teachings of Tai Chi are sustaining on ALL levels and throughout ALL time."

Morgan now asked, "Conrad, are you concerned with the FBI and the CIA's involvement? I don't want an over-reaction to trigger a more concentrated look in our direction."

"Not to worry, sir, unless I'm cornered, I'll only deal with them quietly. Both troops ARE of interest to me but I've learned they're basically bureaucratic with too many secrets and too little cooperation between the bosses. Their people are well trained and can become formidable advisories when they act independently, that's more likely with the CIA, but I'll be cautious with either production. If I can't keep them back-stage, I'll just incorporate them into the play so our final act remains on-script… I might actually enjoy a little 'jousting' with the CIA if given the cue." Conrad offered then returned to his 'product distribution' lay out.

CHAPTER EIGHTY ONE

NORFOLK, DAYS INN

Ursula Volk was restless as she packed a small bag with several assorted tools preparing to leave the Days Inn. She had included her lock picks, she knew the police were keeping her hospital attempt a secret, but if they had informed the zoo of their suspicions the zoo might have changed some of their locks and her retained keys would not work. She had also packed the silenced 22 revolver she used to kill Bradshaw and send Dr. Kowalski to the hospital, but sadly now those thoughts brought back a lot of regrets.

What had she been trying to do last Wednesday? Her contact had expressed concern about Dr. Kowalski's ability to identify her once she had recovered enough to be questioned. Ursula had gotten names, locations and time tables to help her access Kowalski's hospital room. Her contact thought the hospital was the most vulnerable during the Memorial Service for Sergeant Morris Bradshaw and that had initially gone well. Officer Stokes had fallen for her reasoning to replace him as a guard at the hospital and had been pleased to get the time off to attend Bradshaw's Memorial. He hadn't even checked on her story with Police Headquarters. Ursula now blamed her contact's insistence 'that during the memorial service was the time to go'. She didn't like operating under someone else's direction and certainly not in broad daylight. She was certain that timing had been the main reason for her failure. She had wanted to go in at night, disguised as a doctor or a nurse and was now positive that would have been the best way to go. She remembered leaving the hospital and disposing of the Norfolk Police clothes, all but the 38 S&W, before getting this motel room to be near the zoo and the hidden computer discs. This should be her last day in Norfolk, after retrieving the three computer discs she'd head back to the small motel near Capeville, Virginia to plan her departure from the area. Iron Man Cheng had demanded that she should, *"Close everything out and return home via Canada or Mexico as soon as possible."* Ursula still believed that closing everything out still meant getting rid of Dr. Kowalski, but that option was becoming too difficult. Cheng's direction that she should come back to China was ominous. She was certain that trip would not be in her best interest. Her organization did not believe in second chances, Eric was the perfect example of that fact. She now thought if she couldn't get rid of Kowalski then the only way to protect her self was to secure some 'insurance protection' with her employers, which was definitely the three computer discs she had hidden in the elephant barn.

Ursula had dressed in her zoo keeper's clothing knowing her plan to get the Harrington discs back in her possession would protect and eventually reward her. She had hidden the discs in the small locked tool box located on top of one of the elevated hydraulic mechanisms that operated the large sliding gates in the elephant barn. She should have brought the discs out earlier, but her trip to Tennessee and her efforts with Bradshaw and Kowalski made that earlier effort impossible. Now she planned on going late tonight when there was protective darkness and limited security when the zoo was closed. She was certain a time after all normal animal-care activity had been completed would be the best time to attempt to retrieve the discs.

Craig Cooper watched from the Day's Inn parking lot as Ursula Volk left the motel room and headed for her car. He had been able to track her down with help from a local source and was anxious to close this business out as Dr. Kale had directed. Cooper knew he had to find the disc information that tied all these killings into the Chinese program the CIA had mistakenly allowed to continue for too many years. The discs were an important connection and Cooper was sure Ursula had them hidden somewhere local. Cooper thought about slamming his vehicle into Ursula's car to pin her down and take her in dead or alive, but Cooper noticed she was wearing zoo clothing. She's headed to the zoo, he thought, the discs must be hidden there. Cooper decided to follow Ursula and take her into custody when she had the discs in her possession, certainly a better way to go.

Cooper watched Ursula put the small bag she was carrying into her car and glance around the parking lot. There was a lot of traffic coming in and out of the motel, so there was no way she could have seen him. Ursula folded her large frame into the BMW, then, she headed out of the parking lot toward Northampton Boulevard. She drove across the Boulevard and turned left to head north on Route 13, in the direction of the Bay Bridge-Tunnel. He gave her a thirty yard start then pulled out in his black Toyota, trailing north in the early evening traffic. After a few minutes of driving north Ursula turned west on Diamond Springs Road, toward the eastern end of the Norfolk Airport, then she reversed on Diamond Springs and headed back toward Northampton Boulevard and the earlier intersection they had traveled through. "She's checking for a tail", Cooper voiced as he once again got in a long trail to follow. He rejoined the other traffic on Diamond Springs and watched as Ursula veered right back onto Northampton, this time headed east back toward her motel. Cooper mixed in with an RV and two small compact cars going along in traffic. Ursula weaved her way on North Hampton until she passed her motel and continued on eventually crossing Military

Highway where Northampton changed its name to Princess Anne headed eastward to Norfolk.

Minutes later Cooper became more cautious, they were approaching within five miles of the zoo and he stayed a football field back as they proceeded toward Church Street where she turned right passing in front of St. Mary's Cemetery, then drove on past the zoo's main entrance. When Ursula turned right at LaVallette Street by the Lafayette Park baseball diamond, Cooper still believed she was headed for the back entrance to the zoo and made his decision to pull into the 7-11 on Granby. Cooper got out of his car in time to see Ursula's car turn into Lafayette Park next to the tall perimeter fencing that enclosed the Virginia Zoo. Cooper locked his car and walked toward where he was certain he would find and apprehend Ursula Volk.

CHAPTER EIGHTY TWO

VIRGINIA ZOO

Ursula Volk parked her car in the northeastern area of Lafayette Park and walked the short distance to the back service gate into the Virginia Zoo. She paused near the gate and looked toward the Animal Care Building's parking lot about a hundred yards in the distance. The bright Halogen lighting showed there was only one car parked there at this late hour. Ursula was sure the car belonged to Dennis, her former assistant. He was probably working late trying to get a handle on all his new responsibilities. He was either in the Animal Care Building doing zoo paper work or at the elephant barn working on something for the next day. Ursula decided to chance discovery, she could handle Dennis if she had to and she needed those discs before she could leave.

Volk walked to the back service gate and tried her key, it still worked. She pushed open the gate and walked onto the zoo grounds, closed the gate and wrapped the chain back around the gate, leaving the lock open intentionally, she didn't need the extra time or effort required to re-open the lock if she got in a big hurry leave. Satisfied the lock and chain looked secure she began to walk along the back road leading to the elephant barn looking for any sign of human activity.

As she approached the elephant barn she could see the large entrance door was closed and locked, with no light coming from within the barn. Dennis must be at the Animal Care office as she first thought, so she continued. The barn door lock had not been changed either and Ursula used a second key to open the large door before stepping slowly into the dark barn carrying her small satchel. She placed a large cobblestone next to the door to keep it partially open to be able to listen for outside disturbances if she needed a quick reaction.

Volk could see Billy, Imara and Keana, the zoo's three giraffes, in their cages on the right side of the barn. She knew giraffes slept in weird patterns usually intervals of 30 to 40 minutes for a total about 4 hours a day, but at this moment all three seemed to be awake but quiet and would be no threat to her effort.

On the opposite side, at the far end of the darkened barn, Ursula could just make out the outline of one elephant in the last stall, a good 100 feet from her position. She was certain it was Monica and was careful not to make a sound as she moved along the wall of the first stall toward the area where she had hidden the discs. She inched her way close to the wall as moved toward the passageway corner where the back walk-way had a small metal ladder that led high up beyond the elephant's reach to the hydraulic mechanism controls and the small locked tool box near the high ceiling of the barn. As she approached the ladder she noted a faint light coming from under the back hallway's internal door to a work area in the barn. Damn, she now thought, Dennis must be in here, working on some project for the zoo. This complicated things, but she decided she could still get the job done without alerting Dennis.

Ursula took out the small penlight from her case and placed the case gently on the concrete floor. She held the small light and pointed its beam up the metal ladder toward the tool box located thirty feet higher. Placing the penlight in her mouth she began to climb the metal ladder. She got about eight feet up the thirty foot ladder when a big spot-light hit her, from below, fully illuminating her presence on the ladder and everything around her. Immediately she heard,

"That's far enough Volk, FBI! Stop climbing, I've got a 38 Automatic trained on your back. You're under arrest for suspicion of the murder of Sergeant Morris Bradshaw, climb back down the ladder NOW!" Cooper had made his way into the zoo and the elephant barn following Ursula 's trail, but he didn't want her to climb any farther, he had no idea where she was going but he couldn't take the chance of letting her escape through some upper level of the elephant barn he didn't know about.

Ursula glanced down at Cooper, opened her mouth, dropping her pen light to the concrete floor as Monica reacted to a strange voice and the bright light that flooded the other end of the barn. A loud, lengthy, *BRRAAPPTT*, trumpeted out through the barn.

In the adjacent room Dennis heard the commotion, opened the internal work area door and entered the barn carrying an 'elephant stick' yelling, "Who's in here?"

When Cooper became distracted by Dennis' entrance Ursula saw her chance and pushed away from the ladder as she vaulted down on top of Cooper knocking the Automatic from his hand and crashing him hard onto the concrete floor. Cooper recovered as well as he could and hit Ursula on her left shoulder with the large flash light he carried. Ursula flinched from Cooper's strike and yelled, "Dennis, help, this PETA guy wants to release the elephants!"

Monika recognized Ursula's voice and spread her ears wide flapping as she trumpeted the other elephants to try to join her, and *BRRAAPPTT, BRRAAPPTT, BRRAAPPTT* sounded-out through the elephant barn.

Cooper had lost his weapon and stood unsteadily after hitting Ursula a glancing blow. Ursula reacted and karate kicked out at Cooper catching him in the chest knocking him down again, but luckily toward his discarded weapon. Ursula decided it was time to leave, "Hit him with the stick, Dennis hit him now!" She yelled as she departed,

Dennis turned toward Cooper, prepared to respond in some manner but after Cooper stumbled with his balance he reached his weapon as Dennis said, "Stay on the ground," and threatened to swing the 'elephant stick'.

Cooper fought against collapse, rose up and hit Dennis a glancing blow with the flat surface of his gun. *THUD* the up-swing of the gun knocked Dennis out cold as Ursula ran out of the barn.

Cooper took a few seconds to completely regain his balance before running after Ursula, but she was gone. He rushed toward the service gate, now pissed at him self that he hadn't secured the gate or disabled Ursula's car before he entered the zoo. But it was too late now.

Arriving Cooper found the gate had been relocked and he could only watch as Ursula's dark BMW sped away through the park. Cooper returned to the barn picked up Ursula's small bag and helped Dennis up from the floor. He showed Dennis the FBI credentials he had taken from Davis and then focused on trying to find the discs he was now certain Ursula had hidden somewhere in the barn.

"Dennis, I'm FBI Special Agent Davis, sorry about the pistol slap, but I was trying to arrest Ursula Volk, she's suspected of killing at least one police officer and seriously wounding another. When I stopped her she was climbing up that ladder," Cooper pointed his flash light beam toward the ladder leading up to a large hydraulic mechanism, "I thought she was trying to get away, but, is there someplace up there where she could have hidden something?"

"There's a locked tool box at the top of the ladder, adjustments tools for the hydraulic mechanisms. She could still have the key. Something could be hidden there."

Zoo Security had responded to all the noise and one of the zoo's night security guards entered the barn, "Dennis, its Lawson, what's going on here?"

"Tom, this is Agent Davis, FBI," Cooper interrupted the explanations,

"Dennis, this is important, do you have a key, or a pry-bar to open the box?"

"I've got another key, Agent Davis, you can climb up and check the box I'm still too woozy." Dennis handed Cooper the key and Cooper holstered his weapon and climbed up with his flash light. Cooper yelled down as he climbed,

"Have Security call the Norfolk Police, I've got to head out for Ursula after I check the box." Cooper arrived at the top of the ladder, opened the box saw the three computer discs hidden there. He pocketed the discs inside his coat then he rummaged around making some noise before he relocked the box and climbed down.

"There's nothing but tools in the box, tell the police what happened here and have them get in touch with Detective Knowles, I'm working with her. Lawson, please come with me to open the back gate and let me out." Cooper said as he returned Dennis' key and prepared to leave the barn. Lawson went with Cooper opened the back gate and as approaching police cars pulled into Lafayette Park Cooper drove away with the three computer discs and Ursula 's discarded bag.

CHAPTER EIGHTY THREE

POLICE OPERATIONS

In the same conference room where Detective Knowles and her staff began to unravel the mystery of Wilber Harrington's murder over a month ago, Linda paused to reflect on what was now known and what was yet to be found out. Unlike Morris Bradshaw's sad fate Linda was beginning to understand how lucky she, Stokes and Dr. Ski had been when they confronted Ursula. And now Special Agent Davis had also confronted Ursula Volk at the zoo. The case was trying to solve itself, but it had better be solved quickly, Linda thought, any more delays would certainly cause more danger for the rest of her investigation. If Ursula was allowed to remain free, someone else was going to get hurt.

Linda looked at her matrix's listing of people of interest, but most of her original listings had been obscured by lines on the chart relating new factors and adding to her earlier assumptions. As Linda stared through the crisscrossing of connecting lines, underlines, quotation marks, circles and boxes now hiding much of the chart's linkage to her original listings her confusion mounted and she paused thinking, Where the hell is Davis? Why hasn't he checked in after his confrontation with Ursula? Now, a full day after that incident, why can't she locate him? The more Linda examined everything it all seemed to be spiraling to the 'Black Hole' of the Virginia Zoo. "Damn," Linda declared as she recalled seeing something in the paper this morning about the zoo, what the hell was it? She tried to remember as Millers entered the small conference room,

"Morning Chief, you okay? I know that hospital attack was a downer last week, I'm just glad you and Stokes are alright, not to mention Dr. Ski and now that jerk Davis. Hey, did you see the zoo's finally got their new director? Some guy named Greg. It's in the HR section of the Virginian-Pilot today." Millers said.

Linda flipped to the Hampton Roads Section and came across the new Virginia Zoo Director's 'Welcome to Norfolk' article. She read the caption, 'New Virginia Zoo Director wants more fun and more noise,' his statement was printed next to a picture of the director overlooking the giraffe yard at the zoo. Linda asked Millers,

"Did you find out what Davis thought Ursula Volk was after?"

"Davis' can't be found Chief. He's got to be back in DC. I've called his cell phone, but no answer. I tried his boss Rollins' office several times but the secretary won't confirm or deny Davis is in their area. I asked her if he'd briefed them concerning his confrontation with Volk but her answer was 'that's impossible', then she went back to Davis being 'presently on confidential assignment' and hung up. When I followed up checking out the zoo people, Dennis, the elephant keeper and a security guy named Larson, they both said 'they had no idea what Davis was looking for'. So with Dennis' help I looked through every closed cabinet or locked container in the barn, including the hydraulic tool box Davis had checked out. But nothing interesting was hidden anywhere. The FBI's still frustrating our efforts, Chief,"

Linda interrupted, "I don't want to believe it, but you could be right. Tell me again, what did Dennis and the Security guy say about the incident?" Millers took out his notebook, "They said,

'Davis showed them his FBI credentials' but then Dennis added that, 'Agent Davis got knocked to the floor by Ursula Volk, before she ran off yelling at me to stop the PETA guy trying to release the elephants, Then, when I did try to confront Davis he hit me under the chin with his 38 Automatic',"

Linda interrupted again, "Wait a minute was Dennis sure about Davis' weapon?"

"Yeah, he's a gun nut, like most guys, said he recognized the 38 even before Davis picked it up and hit him with it. Why?"

"Davis' carry's a GLOCK 17, I'm 100% sure. Did you ask the zoo people what Davis looked like?"

"Well, no, they both said he showed ID, then told them to call you, I was sure he was just getting rid of the responsibility, you know 'passing the buck'," Millers' statement was interrupted by Davis as he entered the conference room,

"What do you know about BUCK Millers? You'd better tell me right now, you're already on my 'shit list' for last Friday night,"

Millers stood up, confused about the 'buck business', but ready to physically respond to Davis' tirade about last Friday night, he was sure it was his turn to knock Davis on his ass. Linda immediately jumped in totally frustrated by their confrontation. She shouted,

"What's the matter with you two? You've both got to calm down, Davis go to the bathroom and get rid of the testosterone before you say another word! Millers you sit back down and hold your tongue until I ask you a question."

Millers sat down, he wanted to ask Davis if he was getting use to being knocked on his ass by civilians, but he let the retort slide. Knowles continued,

"You'll both calm down right now, or Millers, you'll be suspended and Davis will be on a bus back to DC with a formal reprimand in his briefcase. Do you understand?" They both nodded, so Linda asked,

"OK Clayton, tell us about the zoo confrontation, were you able to find out what Ursula Volk looking for?" Davis looked exasperated, shook his head and collapsed into a chair offering,

"I know what you're asking, Linda, but it wasn't me at the zoo. Cooper lifted my credentials and used them when he confronted Volk. It's not something I'm proud of, my boss threatened to suspend me unless I came back here and helped you clear up this mess." Linda wanted to laugh, but she was so upset, she fought the response. Millers, however, couldn't restrain him self,

"Cooper picked your pocket? Damn, Davis, you were probably standing there in one of your GQ poses when he 'lifted' your ass."

"Betty you've got to come take a look at this, I think Harrington was smitten with you." Cooper said as Betty entered her kitchen after her shower and getting dressed for work. Betty smiled at the comment, fluffed her short dark hair and glanced at Cooper, now checking his lap top's presentation of Harrington's book, "Pacific Secret".

"I've got to go, Coop, I don't want to be late today, too much going on with the desertion of the 'Kroger Girls' but talk me through the part of the book that makes me the 'fem fatale'. I don't want to miss any of Wilber's 'rave reviews'."

"If Harrington's book ever gets published everyone will be able to read about you flaunting your feminine wiles several times in the first 165 pages. Actually, that's all he's completed on this disc, 165 pages of the book, plus a full chapter outline of the entire book... Anyway, you're definitely in there as a CIA seductress. He had you pegged, right down to the CZ Jones resemblance,"

"I'm certainly flattered," Betty replied as she continued to brush her short black hair back away from her oval face, "but how about the Deep Dragon info, how'd Wilber get enough of that in 165 pages, to worry the Chinese into killing him?"

"Well, he didn't name 'that' project, other than calling it 'Japan's Pacific Secret'. He used the Japanese as his villains and his Prologue takes the reader through the installation of the device on the Pacific Ocean floor with the Japanese using a nuclear submarine right after 9-11," ˉ

"Damn, Wilber was brazen using the 9-11 timing and switching the Japanese with the Chinese... How did you see his involvement those 165 pages?"

"That was mostly through his chapter outline. Harrington followed it specifically for the completed pages and if you continue with the outline, he locates the support effort for 'Pacific Secret' in a 'NISCO like' organization in Norfolk," Cooper focused on Microsoft's 'edit function' and paged forward to the screen presentation to the chapter outline, then,

"See, here's where he gets a little too literal, this chapter's where the 'spy gal', Natalya Bolski..."

Betty interrupted, "Bolski, you mean like Boles?"

"Well close enough, Harrington probably screwed up the spelling to sound Russian and keep you from suing his ass. Anyway, his premise is 'the Japanese wanted to cause weather related havoc in Hawaii, Alaska and other west coast states by generating a continuous El Nino with their fission/fusion device'. It's damn close to China's 'real world effort' but it doesn't read like Harrington knew about Ursula Volk and the Chinese recruitment she's trying to set up here. That was another 'puzzle box' he wasn't privy to. No matter, the Chinese would have been worried about what he did know."

"Hold that thought, Coop, I've got to go." Betty said as she gave Cooper a kiss on the cheek as she continued with her departing thoughts, "Where are YOU going next?"

"I'm still trying to locate Ursula Volk, but until something turns up there I'm stymied. My guy at the Days Inn, the one that tipped me off originally, said 'Ursula didn't return, but she left some discarded junk in her motel room. Nothing revealing', he said, but I'm going to check it out myself." Cooper refocused his computer back to the written pages and offered, "I'm still trying to find a connection to Judge Knutson and Charles Taylor so I'll drop Davis' ID and Ursula's small bag off with Agent Lance's office then I'm going to see Taylor and Knutson to put some pressure on them, try to find out what they're really doing, see if there's anyone else mixed up in this with them. I'll be gone and my cell's OFF while I'm visiting. Hey, how about meeting at EMPIRE when I finish?"

"Sounds great," Betty said.

Cooper turned to the computer and made notes concerning the effort Wilber had made to turn 'real world events' into 'profitable fiction'. As he read Cooper mumbled to him self, "Wilber you devil, you were on the right track. Too bad you didn't see the 'Chinese bullet-train' coming up on your blind side."

CHAPTER EIGHTY FOUR

NORFOLK, 'THE HAGUE'

Cooper parked his Toyota off Colonial Avenue walked the block and a half to Judge Knutson's home on Mowbray Arch. He wasn't sure what he'd find here, but his earlier visit to the Taylor's home had been a shocker. Betty must be right, he thought, about Taylor's connection to this mystery. After taking a few digital photos to document the suicide and murder disclaimer, then, both bodies, Cooper got the hell out of Taylor's place. After that Cooper traveled to the Days Inn on Northampton where he found his contact was right, nothing but an unmarked newspaper and several empty beer cans remained in Ursula Volk's old motel room. He took one of the cans for a print check but there was nothing there worth his camera effort. Cooper took one last look around the parking lot, where Ursula's BMW had been parked, and found a discarded Chesapeake Bay Bridge Tunnel Ticket from two days ago. Cooper kept the ticket for another print check and placed it in a small plastic bag similar to the one with the empty beer can. He paid his contact $200 and promised more if further motel searches turned Volk up again. Cooper called Agent Lance's assistant, Agent Rachel Finn, and dropped off Davis' ID, Ursula's bag, the Colt 22, the tunnel ticket and the beer can. Rachel Finn was amused with Davis' pick-pocket misfortune and took possession of all the evidence promised to have Agent Lance call Knowles with the fingerprint and ballistics results as soon as they got it all.

Now as Cooper walked along the grassy area between Mowbray Arch and the Elizabeth River the moon was approaching a three quarter crescent that should 'full-up' in the next few days. Just in time for Halloween, Cooper thought as he spotted another guy headed his way walking a small Terrier type dog. The strolling guy didn't change pace, but did change the dog's lead to his left hand as he placed his right hand deep into his Pee-coat pocket. The stroller raised his head slightly to get a better look at Cooper, then, as Cooper watched the guy and the Terrier veered left, closer to the water's edge and away from street-light illumination. Cooper eased his own right hand into his fatigue pants pocket feeling past his small camera for the 38 Auto. He slid his left hand into the other side pocket past his 'lock pick' to the Kevlar Combat Knife, grateful both were accessible. With his right hand Cooper released the safety and rotated the 38 to point toward the stroller and his little dog. But, as the stroller continued closer, Cooper relaxed when the guy raised his empty right hand, touched his pull over cap and said,

"Proper night for a stroll, eh Chap,"

Cooper released the 38 grip and reciprocated the gesture, "Yeah, Mate."

The two similar figures smiled, as they half-saluted, like passing 'Knights' from the middle ages. Then the Brit and the Terrier made a right turn up Colonial Avenue toward where Cooper had parked. Cooper reversed his walk direction, until he could look north up Colonial Avenue where the stroller had gone but he only saw his own car parked half a block away under a street light on Warren Crescent, just where he left it.

Half past midnight now, the Judge was probably asleep Cooper thought remembering the Judges' age and his darkened home, this could be the perfect time to rummage through the Judge's papers. As Cooper walked toward the judge's house he shook his head in amusement recalling his earlier visit to the Taylor's home.

Cooper didn't stay long at the Taylor home once he found the two dead bodies and a long elaborate note from Charles Taylor. The note claimed responsibility for the murder of his wife Millie, then his own suicide. Taylor's note pointed the finger at Millie for killing some doctor named Turner then kept pointing toward Judge Knutson as the big reason for the trouble they were all mired-up in. There was a lot more about involvement in a scheme producing 'synthetically manufactured diamonds' to flood the US market, but Cooper settled on taking digital photos of the bodies and the letter, the damn letter was just too long and too tedious.

Cooper smiled and shook his head again to clear the memory as he eased his way up the two separate flights of brick steps and tried the large brass knob on the gigantic double door, no resistance. Cooper stopped and removed a small cell phone sized device from his shirt pocket, flipped open the cover, pressed ON and a soft glow emanated from the device's flat screen. He touched the 'Alarm' icon designation on the screen and the presentation went into a swirling purple spiral, then, changed to a steady green light. Not locked and No alarm. Cooper closed the small device as he turned the brass knob, and eased the large door open, "Shit a double door system," Cooper whispered before he tried the second door, no resistance again as he pushed down on the large latch lever system.

Once again he opened the small device and repeated his precautionary ritual. Again he was assured no functioning alarm locked door. Cooper replaced the alarm device and eased the large latch down. The second door opened and Cooper stepped softly into the entrance hallway. As his eyes became accustomed to the absence of artificial lighting, Cooper could make out a large, winding stairway in front of him spiraling up to the left. On the main floor, at the stairs very beginning, there was an ornately carved wooden, circular banister post system enclosing a tall, cylindrically shaped, steam radiator at the stairway's base. Directly to Cooper's right positioned on the hard-wood-flooring was a large Grandfather Clock echoing individual pendulum swings and presently indicating 12:45. Cooper immediately thought of Betty waiting at EMPIRE, he was running late and should call. But, he was fascinated by intricacies of the clock, the banister carvings and the uniqueness of the circular radiator.

Moving further into the home he could see a vast number of Victorian paintings decorating the open hallway, so, Cooper decided it was Betty's turn to wait. Glancing to his left Cooper focused on an expansive oak paneled dinning room, the highly polished table was unset but the held a large vase of fresh flowers above its veneered surface's high gleam luster. The moonlight filtering into the room through three large crystal-like lead-framed-paneled windows, cast feathery shadow patterns of the flowers onto the table and throughout the dinning room's interior appointments.

Cooper turned away from the 'museum-like-showcase' to look across the entrance hallway, past the clock and a large pocket door that opened into a library area with tall bookcases against one side and the far back wall. He crossed the entrance hall and stepped past the large clock into this new room, noting one large worn-leather recliner and two positioned wing-back chairs. With the moon's influence coming through more crystal windows Cooper could just make out a large desk facing him in front of the back wall's book-alcove. To his right Cooper saw a very large fireplace installed against what seemed to be the room's longest wall. The fireplace, dim with a gas-lit glow, was positioned to be the focal point of a surround with polished decorative tiles of muted pastels. The exposed tiles gloss surface reflected not only the muted gas light but the moonlight's affect on the tiles that covered the hundred year old hearth's front facing façade,

"Oh Shit!" Cooper voiced interrupting his own internal comments, there was someone sprawled across the top of the desk. He reached for his penlight, pointed it and moved toward the desk as he flicked it on, "Damn, another dead guy". Cooper whispered to himself as the crisp sound of another voice intruded his discovery,

"Don't flinch Mate, I've got a KORTH 9 on the back of your head, you know the weapon?"

"Yeah, big gun, 6 inch barrel, you've probably got the silencer and slide mounted laser, I can feel the hot spot," Cooper responded.

"Well, Bob's your uncle, you're right, I'm Holmes, friend, who are you?"

"I'm Cooper." Cooper offered but he was confused by the British 'Bob's your uncle' statement.

"You look a bit fuddled Cooper. Don't think about reaching for the Judge's weapon, just douse your torch and drop it to the floor." Cooper did as he was told and heard the small pen-light clatter against the library's hard wood flooring.

"Hands behind the head Cooper… Lace the fingers and squeeze tight. Good boy. What's your game Cooper?"

"Black bag job Holmes, looking for incriminating stuff on the judge,"

"Interesting, you armed Cooper?" Cooper nodded his head yes. "Find your voice Cooper. Don't let the stage go quiet here. Spell out the props you came with, item by item. Don't be 'clucky' and leave anything unaccounted."

"38 Automatic, right pants pocket, Kevlar combat sticker left pocket. I'm carrying a lock pick, a digital camera and a small digital alarm finder,"

"That all Cooper? Or, are you a liar down to your boots? I can shoot that boot to find the ankle strap,"

"Small caliber Beretta there Holmes, inside, left ankle,"

"My, my," Cooper heard Holmes say, then, he heard what sounded like Holmes taking a step forward. As Cooper tensed for an inevitable weapon spit, the Grandfather Clock *GONGED* out a deafening strike for 1AM. The clock gong was quickly over-ridden by a loud *SLAM* then a louder *CRASH* that echoed through the small room before Cooper heard,

"Bloody Hell," Holmes yelled, then, he heard a muffled *THUMP* as one of the large wing-back chairs toppled over behind Cooper. "Jesus, Cooper, you got a little chap in here that jumped the queue?" Holmes now voiced as he reacted to something crashing into him from behind.

Cooper felt the 'hot laser spot' disappear, pulled his hands down and began to crouch and turn reaching low for his ankle Berretta. As Cooper's fingers touched the small weapon he saw the dark-shadow of Holmes raise Betty Boles up off the floor, "Help me!" Betty yelled as Holmes sent her small body flying through the air, banging directly into Cooper's chest knocking both he and Betty into a rumpled two person pile hard against the front of the large library desk,

Cooper recovered and wanted to ask if Betty was alright, but she was out cold, probably hit her head on the desk when they both crashed to the floor. Cooper watched as Holmes righted him self then Cooper saw the big KORTH come up in Holmes' hand and the red laser line 'POP' back ON. Quickly the 'target line' steadied on Cooper's chest, Holmes had recovered and was back in charge.

"Cooper you a Cookie?" Cooper stared directly into Holmes' darkened face and nodded yes, "You've gone noises-off Cooper. Speak up. Is your little chap a Cookie also?" Holmes asked and Cooper nodded but quickly added in Betty's defense,

"She's an Admin Cookie, Holmes, not a trained asset."

"Lucky for me … Alright, grateful for your honesty Cooper, but its lecture time for Cookies; you and your 'chap' would be best served to leave my stage presentation intact. You check out the Charles Taylor Theater?" Cooper nodded,

"You get some pics there, scenery, cast and so on?" Cooper nodded yes once again, "Did you see any glaring miss-cues? Speak up Cooper." Holmes now demanded.

"No, Holmes, it was well staged, I'm sure THIS production's the same."

"Well, thank you Cooper. I'm not an expert guesser by a long chalk, but you're probably a 'theater stager' yourself, or maybe a 'theater critic' of some kind. Am I correct?" Cooper nodded his head in the affirmative. "Well then after your 'small admin chap' finishes her 'lie-down', you can get a few more pics, then, exit stage left behind me. You can surely stick to your 'black bag plot', if so inclined but I don't think you'll discover anything but the judge's 'scripted bits and pieces', you know, things I've had the pleasure of adding to the 'plot'. You get my 'off-stage prompt' Cooper?"

"Yes, Holmes, I hear you loud and clear. I assume it's time for 'curtain call'."

"Yes, very good Cooper, the performance is about to go 'dark stage', Judge Knutson was the final act. Straighten the theater up a bit before your pics Cooper I'd like the reviews to show my original staging, fair enough?"

"Just get on with it Holmes, the performance is a bit tiring."

"No doubt, by the by, old Chum, your chap's small but she felt quite nice, she must be a dear chap to come on stage like that. You know, untrained, unprepared, unrehearsed… I hope she brought transport for the cast, Cooper, your Toyota Taxi's been disabled, it'll barley do the 'speed-of-nought'." Holmes' British laughter invaded the small room but Cooper didn't answer, he was tired of listening to this English asshole and Betty was beginning to come around.

"No more remarks? Well Cooper that's fair, I'm talked-out too. Any question before I exit?" Holmes asked.

"Just one Holmes, is your little dog named, BUCK?"

Holmes began a small nasty laugh immediately, then, his voice turned to sharp threatening gravel as he turned to go out the large doorway, "No Cooper, he's Winston. But, don't get your knickers in a knot over 'BUCK', that one's worse than 'Pandora's Box' for you and yours. You understand, don't you Cooper? You do remember what happened when the 'players' opened that box?" Cooper offered no response, so Holmes said, "Cheers Cooper," and departed.

"Cheers Asshole!" Cooper finally answered as he helped Betty up from the floor. "You alright Betty, you took quite a tumble there?"

"Who's that British jerk, Coop?" Betty asked as she rubbed her head.

"Not sure, but he's the 'real deal' and he's definitely tied into BUCK, whatever that is. Holmes is quite 'Cheeky' as the Brits like to say, but he's earned an award for 'Staging' in two separate theaters. Did you come in your car, Betty?"

"Sure, I went to EMPIRE, got worried not hearing from you, so I drove here in time to see Holmes slash one of your tires before his little dog peed on it and they both walked away. He put the dog in a van and headed back this way so I followed and tried to jump-in when the clock-gong distracted him. I thought you could use some help."

"You did good Betty, but there's something else going on here, some specific message Holmes needed to send that he didn't want confused with our involvement or he'd have left us dead on stage with the rest of the cast. Let's straighten up a bit then I'll get some photos. We can get out of here and try to figure it all out over one of EMPIRE'S martinis, I definitely need a drink."

After a few minutes effort, the large Grandfather Clock emitted another sharp, solitary *GONG,* announcing 1:30AM as Cooper and Betty departed.

CHAPTER EIGHTY FIVE

VIRGINIA ZOO, SATURDAY, OCTOBER 28

"STEPHEN IRONS"

If my memory serves correctly, Halloween, or 'All Hallows Day' had its beginning in the British Isles during the middle-ages. At that time the last day of October was believed to be the eve of the beginning of winter when the Celtic pagans thought the veiled separation between life and death was reduced to the very thinnest of a curtain by the oncoming cold. And, during that winter's cold was when the pagans believed they were most threatened by the horrors of the dead that could now roam around the living world separated only by the thin curtain. Further analysis, probably influenced by flagons of ale, led the pagans to believe their most promising survival technique was to hide from the invading horrors by disguising themselves to look like the 'dead invaders' they feared. This tactic originated the Halloween costume tradition and pagan thoughts of 'begging for their lives' probably turned into 'trick or treat' demands from our now up-to-date, celebration of the Halloween's arrival of 'visiting horrors'.

Our own Halloween celebration began at 4PM as we entered the Virginia Zoo. Ella, Linda, Shirley Knowles and I encountered a celebration filled with zoo inspired 'Horrors' of the past: kids dressed as Ghouls and Zombies, Witches and Werewolves, Monsters and Vampires... On the 'Pagan Hero' side there were even more kids dressed as Batman, Superman, Wonder Woman and Spiderman. Holding my hand through all the good and bad was Ella dressed as the 'Little Princess' she was becoming to me.

"Ella, are you the 'Problem Princess' in your story?" I jokingly asked,

"No way Stephen, I'm like a regular Princess." I looked at Linda and Shirley for comment, but only received a grandmotherly giggle and a motherly smirk.

The Virginia Zoo had gone all out for this Halloween celebration, probably because they love to do this kind of thing for kids and their families but they were also anxious to impress Greg, their new zoo boss, with an ability to create 'more fun and more noise' as the new director's Virginian-Pilot article had stated was his desire. A dozen Scarecrows lined the pathway leading to the barn-animal enclosures where the 'petting zoo' portion of the Halloween displays began with goats, lambs, cows and the large black and white llama I had seen in Sally's photos.

All these furry exhibits were pushing up against the stockade fence, begging for their own Halloween treats. After a short time of petting and parading with other Halloween kids Ella decided it was time to pull us away from the barn area and back across the entry area, toward the zoo's Okavango Delta.

As we worked our way along the pathways leading to Africa, there were cut-outs of black cats, witches and ghosts dangling from the low branches of nearby trees and Ella's horticultural expertise surfaced as she and her grandmother discussed the various fall flowers growing along our route. After we passed by the large canvas tent-top used to house children-craft activities, we approached the African Village Restaurant and I saw a bony cardboard skeleton hanging down and pointing toward the small Education Center Annex. Ella saw the same display and pulled us to where she saw an old friend, Zoo Docent Amy, 'the meerkat whisperer' from our earlier zoo visit. Docent Amy was working the front door of the Education Center with a large white bird on her arm. She reintroduced herself, then introduced Casey the Umbrella Cockatoo who 'barked' like a dog before announcing that he was 'a pretty bird'.

When we moved inside to check out the Education Annex's interior we found several other zoo docents with Halloween appropriate animals... We saw several scary snakes, a few aquarium confined scorpions and spiders and in the back of the room there was a docent named Sandi with a large African Bull Frog she called 'Prince Charming'. Next to her there was another docent named Carla with a raccoon that sported his own black Halloween mask. Ella asked Sandi about the frog's Halloween appropriateness and Sandi explained,

"He was the handsome Prince that made a wicked witch mad and suffered the Halloween consequences."

I asked Ella what she thought about Sandi's explanation, but she just rolled her eyes at me and said, "Its all make believe, Stephen, just have fun." Then, she released my hand and ran out of the building. When I exited behind her I was sure Ella had seen WAVY TV 10's News crew filming the new Zoo Director talking to Docent Amy and Casey, but I was wrong. Ella was focused on chasing a small kid in a tiger costume that was running around growling at everyone. I watched Ella as she moved about attempting to subdue the little tiger's aggressive behavior with the magic wand she carried. That's when I noticed the kid was wearing those tennis shoes with lights embedded in the heels of his rubber soles. Every time the kid's foot hit the ground red and green lights flashed on and off. The kid was a running traffic signal, easy for Ella to pursue.

As I moved out of the annex, past the WAVY crew, I spotted Linda sitting at a small table with Grandmother Shirley and that asshole, Davis. Where the hell did he come from? I was beginning to tire of his presence in my life and silently wished for Margarete Kroger's reappearance to 'smack' his butt down again. While

I watched the seated group I saw Shirley get up to go after Princess Ella, who had now moved out of our sight line back behind the Africa Restaurant, still in pursuit of the tiger kid with the traffic light shoes.

I started to go after Shirley but I saw Sheriff Os, fully uniformed and having a confrontation with an adult cowboy and his little cowboy son. I joined the WAVY crew as we all shifted our attention and moved through a gathering crowd of bystanders as Os said,

"Walter you know better man. You can't come to the zoo with a real gun, where's your common sense?" The adult cowboy, about half Os' size, stood between Os and the smaller cowboy. The three of them actually looked like stair-steps, big, middle sized and little, leading down from Os' 6' 5" height to the kid's 3' 6". Walter himself, in the middle somewhere around 5'8", looked up at Os and replied indignantly,

"Sheriff Os you know Virginia's an 'Open Carry State' and I'm 'open carrying'. Our fore-fathers fought for this RIGHT and I served in 'Desert Storm' for it. Don't push me around just because you're a big guy Os, I'm standing my ground."

WAVY 's Dave Craft and I worked our way closer and I could see Walter actually had a post Civil War, single action Colt 44 in a belted holster, giving his cowboy costume some real authenticity. WAVY TV's camera focused on the gun as Os physically grabbed Walter, removed the weapon from its holster and cuffed Cowboy Walter on the spot. Then, Os demanded, "Don't say another word Walter, you're right about the 'open carry', but you're wrong to bring a weapon to the zoo, even as a joke." Os immediately put his wide black hand over Walter's mouth in case Walter didn't think he was serious. Then Os pocketed the Colt and turned to Little Wally, standing by his dad and watching up from his six year old perspective, Os asked, "Do you know who I am Little Wally?"

"Yes," Little Wally replied, brightly, "you're the Big Black Sheriff Os."

"Yes I am Wally and your dad's pretending to be a bad man, so as the Sheriff, I'm arresting him. Okay with you?"

"Sure, Dad's a bad man dad's a bad man," Little Wally's excitement was interrupted by the zoo's PA system announcement,

"CODE ADAM ALERT, all Virginia Zoo gates will be closed immediately, CODE ADAM ALERT, All zoo personnel respond immediately," I looked around for Ella and Shirley, came up empty and started to run toward where I last saw them. I left the TV crew questioning Os about the gun incident before the Code Adam changed all our focuses. Moving quickly around the far corner of the restaurant I saw Thornton standing with a Zoo Security person and Shirley

Knowles sitting on the ground being attended to by a zoo staffer named Wynn who was using his radio to call for more help. Thornton was trying to help Shirley up, but he was unable to get any kind of grip on her arm, his hands just melted through her body as he yelled to me, "Rusty get over here, I can't pick her up."

Shirley's face was scratched and there was some swelling around her mouth. She was obviously in pain and woozy. I disregarded Thornton's request to help pick her up and left her sitting on the concrete walkway waiting for some medical assistance. "Shirley, are you alright?" I asked, kneeling down next to her.

"He took her Stephen. The monster knocked me down and took my Ella."

CHAPTER EIGHTY SIX

POLICE OPERATIONS

"STEPHEN IRONS"

I'm sitting in Linda's office; Millers and Davis are investigating a call reporting a dark BMW with a tall person in some kind of scary costume driving away from the Virginia Zoo. The BMW came out of Lafayette Park headed toward downtown Norfolk and the call got Millers and a half dozen Norfolk Police cars responding. Linda was given a mild sedative and is still under its calming effect.

While I'm waiting for Linda to recover I recall Shirley Knowles' answers about Ella's abduction before she was eventually transported to De Paul Medical Center where she is now being treated for shock, a split lip and a sprained arm. Shirley's arm was wrapped and suspended in a make-shift sling while WAVY TV 10's Cameraman and the zoo crowd were being held back by Wynn and several other zoo staffers.

I was trying to help Shirley remain calm while Sergeant Curtis interviewed her and we all waited for De Paul's medical transport,

"Mrs. Knowles, are you calm enough to try to answer some questions now?"

"Yes, I'm okay, I know it's important for you to find out as much as you can right now. I want to help,"

"Try to remember everything you can, you said 'A big man in a Halloween costume took Ella', is it possible it could have been a big, tall woman, dressed like a man?"

"I don't know, but he or she was dressed like Frankenstein in a big ugly outfit, with those metal things sticking out on the neck. Ella was chasing a little kid with lights on his tennis shoes and I was chasing Ella. We were right here, just past the Mandrills when," Shirley paused she was out of breath or losing focus.

Sergeant Curtis gave her a minute and asked, "Are you alright Mrs. Knowles, do you want to stop?"

"No, no I'm okay, but I remember Frankenstein coming out of those bushes," she tried to point but her arm was incapacitated, so she motioned with her head, *"just over there. I thought it was a zoo Halloween trick, but the thing knocked me away and grabbed Ella. When I kicked*

at the monster and tried to take Ella back 'it' hit me hard and grabbed me, twisting my arm and knocking me down. Ella yelled and tried to get away but Frankenstein held her with one arm and ran away over there,"

"I know you think it was a man," Sergeant Curtis interrupted, "But is that because of the height and size of the person wearing the costume?"

"Yes and how hard I was hit," Shirley added, "It hit me so hard I was certain it was a big man."

"Alright, we'll leave that for a minute can you remember anything else, anything that seemed odd, you know different about the incident?" The medical people arrived and were helping Shirley up now, she did seem better but she was obviously still hurting, as she haltingly replied,

"The little kid, the one with the shoe lights, he just laughed when he saw Frankenstein, like he knew the monster was going to be there, he wasn't surprised or frightened at all,"

"Stephen," Linda said bringing me back to the present, "I drifted off, have we heard anything more? I'm so worried for Ella she must be so scared,"

"No Linda we haven't heard from Millers yet, but I can go and check,"

"No Stephen, stay with me now, I need your help Stephen, Ella and I both need you."

Millers' car lights were flashing and his siren was going full blast as he sped south on Hampton Boulevard just past 27th Street. The lights and the warbling tone warned the traffic to stop and clear the right-of-way for his vehicle. The flashing lights warned anyone nearby to clear out of the way. The car lights pulsated rapidly and the intermittent, *WAIL, WAIL, WAIL,* followed by a very loud throbbing of *WHOOP, WHOOP, WHOOP,* coming from the vehicle's siren system. Millers prayed it was enough to clear a path and kept his foot hard against the rubberized covering over the gas pedal. The Crown Vic was doing fifty, headed south on Hampton, but the BMW was pulling away and Millers shouted to Davis bouncing around in the front passenger seat, "If that's Ursula Volk and Ella's in there too, I'd be surprised either of them can sit still, even with seatbelts,"

"If Volk has Ella then Ella's probably drugged, that's Volk's way of doing things." Davis offered, "Volk's heavy into the use of drugs and violence, she's been that way from the time we've known about her,"

"How long has the FBI known about Ursula Volk and her use of drugs on people?"

"About two years now, ever since she left the San Diego Wild Animal Park," Millers interrupted as their car passed Red Gate Avenue, following the speeding BMW toward downtown Norfolk.

"You FBI assholes have known about Ursula Volk's association with an animal park near a navy base in California and you didn't think about the possibility of her just moving east to another coast, another animal park and another navy base?" Millers screamed at Davis over the roar of the Crown Vic's engine, the whooping of the siren and the increasing noise of the two lane traffic as they veered right and plunged into the Mid-Town Tunnel headed west.

Fifty feet ahead Millers watched the BMW speed alternately from the correct lane headed west toward Portsmouth and the adjacent lane bringing traffic from Portsmouth back east toward Norfolk, then back again, continuing to swap lanes when a gap opened up,

"Jesus Christ if Volk doesn't get herself killed she'll kill us," Millers stopped talking as a pick-up truck headed east, veered violently to keep from hitting the BMW and ended up head on to them in their west bound lane. He had no choice but to hit the brakes and pull the wheel hard left to avoid a head-on with the pick-up truck. Immediately Millers' Crown Vic slammed into opposite side of the tunnel in a tight left hand spin before it straightened out and hit the wall again. The Crown-Vic took a *SLAM* from another car from behind and began to flip-over, rolling twice then coming to rest pointed back toward Norfolk. The car ended up resting upside down with lights still flashing intermittently as the car's *WHOOPINGS* continued to bombard the hearing of everyone trapped in the tunnel, everyone but Millers and Davis who were both unconscious.

––––––––––––––

Ursula Volk slowed the BMW to a normal exit speed and turned south on Cedar Road leaving 164 West headed to Route 17 South. She had planned on doubling back and taking Route 264 to Norfolk's Downtown Tunnel, then, 64West and Route 13North to the seclusion of her motel room on the Eastern Shore. But, now as a Police car from the city of Portsmouth passed going in the opposite direction, Volk knew she'd be wise to alter her plans. She increased speed to just below the limit and moved onto Route 17 South and the comfort of mixing in with the slow weekend traffic making its way to and from Norfolk. In the mirror she spotted a Virginia State Trooper headed South in her direction. The trooper had his lights blazing, but no siren. He sped past her two lanes over and well above the posted speed limit so Volk turned left onto route 58, headed back east toward the small area known as Port Norfolk. Kidnapping Ella at the zoo probably wasn't her wisest response but Volk felt she was running out of options and needed some leverage while she figured out how to go back to the zoo for the computer discs. Hiding them there had turned out to be a big mistake but getting them back was her only guarantee of survival.

Trying to work her way into the elephant barn to get them back during the zoo's Halloween celebration had been the wrong way to go. But then the opportunity to grab Detective Knowles' daughter presented itself and that option seemed the perfect alternative.

Volk spotted a small almost deserted Days Inn on Route 58 and pulled in the parking lot far away from the office. She exited her car and stretched as any weary traveler would, opened the back door and got out a large-size tan raincoat to cover the remainder of her Frankenstein costume. Cleaning her face with paper towels she donned a ball cap and the large overcoat and headed for the office. She smiled at how slick it had been sending that kid with flashing shoes to lure Ella toward a side Exit while another distraction occupied the big sheriff and the rest of the crowd. Detective Knowles had thwarted her once at the hospital but now Ursula held the advantage, she held Knowles' daughter.

Volk checked on the quiet eight year old wrapped up in a sleeping bag still lightly sedated. All was going as planned except getting the computer discs could take a while now that she had stirred up everything at the zoo. But Ursula Volk counted on bargaining while she had Ella to give herself a safe departure after she had the computer discs to protect her future.

CHAPTER EIGHTY SEVEN

POLICE OPERATIONS, SUNDAY

"STEPHEN IRONS"

Norfolk Police Sergeant Jack Webber was working the duty desk as Sheriff Os and I entered the building. Jack saw us coming down the hall and rose to greet us, probably to greet Os, I wasn't one of Jack's favorite people.

"Sheriff Os it's good to see you under such bad circumstances." Jack offered and I presumed he was talking about Ella's abduction, but he continued in another direction, "I know Charles Taylor and Judge Knutson were friends of yours…"

Os interrupted Jack's information, "What are you talking about, Jack, what else has happened?"

"Our people went to see Charles Taylor to check on leads from Dr. Turner's murder and found Taylor and his wife both dead. A note from Taylor admitted his wife killed Dr. Turner before he cleaned the scene and left the apartment. His note said he killed his wife and took his own life because of Dr. Turner's murder and his involvement in some scam Judge Knutson concocted to swindle people with manufactured diamonds. The note was long, Taylor was really wordy,"

Os interrupted again, "Jack, stop the crap, tell me who's handling the Taylor shootings, and what did you say about the Judge?"

"It's not crap Sheriff Os, the Judge was found with a note too. He took his own life also, we found out late this morning. Taylor's note pointed at the Judge, so we went there and found the Judge dead, sprawled across his desk. In the desk we found all the information Taylor spelled out about the diamond business and how they were going to get people to invest in the scheme, sounded pretty clever too. Isn't your visit about these cases?"

"No, Jack, we're looking for Detective Knowles I saw her car outside, is she here now?" I asked.

"She's with her mother-in-law they just let Mrs. Knowles out of the hospital and Detective Knowles went to pick her up in Mrs. Knowles' van,"

"When will Detective Knowles be back?" Os now asked.

"She'll check on Millers and Davis first, Millers had a car crash in the Mid-Town Tunnel right after the kidnapping. He's okay, a sprained knee and broken arm but Davis is a mess, he'll be there a lot longer, didn't use his seat belt. I can try Knowles on her cell. She's probably still at the hospital."

"Christ, you got any more horrible news Jack?" Os asked.

"No, Sheriff Os, I think that's it."

"Jack, give me a ride to the Sheriff's office. I need my own car and Stephen wants to wait for Knowles." Os said, I started to object but Os pushed a big flat palm against my chest, encouraging my compliance.

Jack agreed to give Os a ride and I walked to the front door and watched Os fold his big frame into the Norfolk Police car. Then, the car pulled out onto Norfolk Square Street turned left on Virginia Beach Boulevard and headed downtown to the Sheriff's Office as I waved and silently wished Os better luck, so far, this hadn't been his week.

When I went back inside I turned down the hall toward Knowles' small office to wait. As I entered her office area I remembered the first night I was here, just after Wilber was killed and we were trying to find Sally, I began to think how even with Wilber's death and the problems facing Sally at that time, oddly what Linda had said then was one of my most comforting memories, *"I want to thank you for your court room response six months ago, I'm certain Judge Knutson and I owe you our lives."* But, Linda was still confronted with Ella's kidnapping and Shirley's injuries. If all that wasn't bad enough, the Taylor's and Judge Knutson were dead too and Dr. Ski was still hospitalized and vulnerable. Linda had lost Bradshaw to Ursula Volk and now, three other members of her investigation, Dr. Kowalski, Detective Millers and FBI Agent Davis were all injured while trying to deal with Ursula. Thornton stood quietly by my side probably reading my mind. He offered in exasperation,

"Rusty, Volk's probably got Ella now but there's a lot more going on: What about Wilber's death and Bradshaw's murder? What about Dr. Ski and now Millers and Davis? This mess is turning to shit! We've got to get Knowles focused on the big picture and bring Volk to justice. Ursula Volk thinks she's a Hammer and the rest of us look like a box of new nails."

CHAPTER EIGHTY EIGHT

SUFFOLK, VIRGINIA

"Cooper, what the hell are we going to do, Dr. Kale's NOT going to be pleased." Betty offered hoping for some solution from Cooper, lately he'd been her answer to everything.

"Betty, remember our directive from Dr. Kale?"

"Sure, find the Norfolk support effort for the Chinese and shut it down. If there're 'loose-ends' concerning inappropriate action, or lack of action, on the part of the CIA's protection of the Chinese and Deep Dragon, we should bundle-up those loose ends up and take them back to DC."

"Good summary, so I believe it's time for us to return to DC with the 'Pacific Secret' disc, it's definitely one of the bigger loose ends. We'll submit our report on successfully identifying at least two of the individuals involved in the local support group and confirming the termination of their involvement. We haven't found Ursula Volk, but we've got a lead about the Eastern Shore. I'll pass that on to Irons after I make a final check with my 'motel czar' to check on the information."

"How will this all play out with Dr. Kale?"

"Who knows Betty, but you need a vacation. Your Norfolk job is about to come under some serious reengineering and there's nothing around here for you to fall back on,"

"Okay, but how about Holmes and BUCK? They're a couple of rotten apples still in our barrel. What about them?"

"I've skirted that issue so far. BUCK, we were aware of, but Holmes is a new aggravation that I wasn't ready for. You know, like Ursula Volk when she vaulted down on me. Anyway, I'm avoiding those problems until I'm better prepared. Irons can help us with BUCK and I'll wait to 'stage my own 'production' with Holmes. Chances are BUCK and Holmes are tied together somehow, so when we find one, we'll deal with both of them."

Ursula Volk checked Knowles' daughter's blood pressure and pulse. She gently raised Ella's eye lids and saw the indication she was looking for, the girl was sleeping again under the influence of another small dose of Ketamine, an animal tranquilizer kept at the zoo. The first dosage allowed Volk to bundle the girl up and get her away from the zoo's festivities, but the girl had been a lot of trouble, yelling and screaming. Fortunately, Volk had an abundant supply of tranquilizing drugs and the girl was quiet again, back under for a few more hours.

Now, early in the morning Monday, October 30th seemed the right time for Volk to restart her travels toward the Starfish Motel, on the Eastern Shore. Work day traffic would be resuming from Virginia Beach and Chesapeake into Norfolk and from all over Hampton Roads into the Norfolk Naval Station. This was the perfect time to 'hide in plain sight' as she worked her way toward the Chesapeake Bay Bridge Tunnel.

Volk began to re-bundle the girl, now loosely tied with soft roping and wrapped up in a canvas sleeping bag. As Volk reached for her jacket to move the girl outside and into her car, her cell phone sounded, "This is Volk, go ahead,"

The guttural voice began in her ear, first with questions about the deaths of the Taylor's and Judge Knutson, then, admonishment for her rogue kidnapping action. Lastly Volk heard loud demands for the release of Ella Knowles and her own departure from the area immediately. Volk interrupted her caller,

"I don't know anything about those other people but I understand your concern about the girl. Here's what's going to happen, I'm staying hidden until I've gotten a few things sorted out, then I'll meet with you and release the kid. Now, leave me alone and don't call until later tonight. If you chose to do something different, I'll dump the girl, you understand me? I'LL DUMP THE GIRL" After Volk re-emphasized her threat, the caller hung-up and Ursula Volk was certain the caller understood her demands.

CHAPTER EIGHTY NINE

LAKEWOOD, MONDAY

"STEPHEN IRONS"

Willy-nilly is in Sally's front yard making his rounds, protecting her property from angry birds and pesky squirrels. I'm outside too, looking for The Virginian-Pilot paper. They missed Sally's house yesterday and today and as I reentered the house and glanced at the growing pile of mail for Sally and Wilber I thought there might be a payment request and delivery stoppage notice somewhere in the stack.

I've just finished a second cup of coffee when Sally's phone rang. I hoped it was Sally from Dallas before going on her next trip, letting me know about her schedule for November. But when I checked the ID, the read-out said it was Betty's number. I picked up hoping for more news about Charles Taylor and NISCO and touched the speaker function to ON and said, "Betty, are you alright?"

"It's Cooper, Irons, just checking in before Betty and I head to DC,"

"Damn, you're leaving? I thought you'd stay to help get Ella back, what's happening?"

"We've been recalled, probably updates on this 'BUCK' business, but the message didn't say. I want to let you know a few things, have you got a minute, this won't take long,"

"Sure go ahead," I answered as I saw Willy-nilly and Thornton at the side door and got up to let them in.

"Ursula Volk's still in the area, she'll probably stay awhile, she's after some of Wilber's information before she head's out," Came through the speaker and I interrupted,

"What information, Cooper? The stuff she was looking for in the elephant barn? The stuff you already have?" I didn't try to hide the anger and frustration in my voice.

"Settle down Stephen, it has nothing to do with Ella's kidnapping, Ella's a bargaining chip now to get Volk out of the area, she'll release the child soon enough. Do you know about Taylor and Knutson?"

"Yes, did you have anything to do with that?"

"No, of course not, it was probably as it appears, suicides, or if it was criminal, then Volk has another 'loose cannon' running around Norfolk. Someone who was threatened by Taylor and Knutson and decided to shut them up, have you got any ideas about that?" Cooper asked.

"I'm focused on getting Ella back. Knowles and her mother-in-law have gone through enough don't you think, they're the ones who need our help. How did you find Ursula Volk? It was YOU pretending to be Davis wasn't it?"

"Yes, and I feel bad about letting Volk get away, but she took me by surprise, she was more than I was able to handle at that time," There was a pause here like Cooper was searching for another point of clarification, or evasion before he continued,

"I actually found Volk through a local contact. That's why I called you. I also found some old Chesapeake Bay Bridge Tunnel tickets near where her car had been parked. No print or ballistic check back from Volk's weapon and the beer can I found in the motel room, but I'm certain they're hers. Keep all that in mind Stephen. She may have a base area on the Eastern Shore. I just wanted you to know. If I learn anything in DC I'll give you a call."

"Thanks Cooper, sorry about my anger, I'm just worried about Ella."

"I understand," Cooper paused a moment then, "Betty asks if you've deposited your $20,000 from NISCO?"

"Yes, is it going to bounce?"

"No, she said you probably got it in soon enough. The Feds haven't taken over NISCO yet, but you probably won't get another check. Betty left a package for Sally at the NISCO downtown office, go by and pick it up before the Feds start confiscating everything else, do it this morning Stephen. Betty left it at the security desk."

"What kind of package?" I tried to ask but Cooper was gone, so I got my car keys and Thornton and I headed out for the NISCO downtown office as I had been instructed.

"Have you heard from Holmes?" Sonchi Zimchi asked Morgan Folds, "It's not like him to leave us without word. I expected the Norfolk business to be completed,"

"Conrad called last night he should be here later this morning." Folds answered.

"I've been thinking about your suggestion Morgan and I believe it would be prudent to wait before launching BUCK. Gerda's almost finished, but she needs maybe two months more for all her testing and modifications. The paper's on the way to Hong Kong and the inks are in Fredericksburg waiting for the technicians to assemble the printing technology, so I think a delay until we're able to make sure we've gone undetected," Sonchi stopped as he heard the elevator sound then 10 seconds later, Conrad Holmes appeared,

"Good Morning Gentlemen, hope your weekend went well. You'll be happy to know our Norfolk loose ends have been clipped, actually 'fobbed off' permanently."

"Glad to hear it, so Taylor and Knutson are set up to take the fall for the manufactured diamond scheme we created?" Morgan asked.

"Actually they've been set-up, caught, tried, convicted and executed." Holmes answered with a self righteous tone.

"Spell it out Conrad, no more British humor, please." Morgan instructed.

"The Taylor's, both husband and wife, in addition to Judge Anthony Knutson, have all been found dead. I planted enough evidence of past and future-planned criminal activity to force the Norfolk Police and the FBI to focus on several unresolved investigations previously hidden by the Judge and his partners. Taylor killed his wife then he and Knutson both committed suicide because I planted all the evidence involving their fraudulent bond issues, both city and state, used to set-up the funding for the manufactured diamonds."

Conrad watched his partners, now looking for some form of disapproval. He saw none so he continued, "Taylor's lengthy confession and suicide disclaimer will help the police of course but it will create many hours of investigative diversionary time looking into all the allegations of their past and future planned activity. A perfect Tai Chi action in the opposite direction to allow BUCK to move forward,"

"We've been talking about BUCK and a possible postponement Conrad you know a 'pause' while you determine if our pending operation remains safely hidden. We want our security umbrella to be fully extended to Brazil and functioning properly throughout the remainder of our operation. What do you think?" Morgan now asked.

"I've always believed in striking while the iron is hot, sticking to the task until completed, but presently I am in agreement concerning a delay. What would you Gentlemen have me do?" Conrad asked seeing the possibility of investigation into the CIA involvement and of WORKING UNDER, Gerda Von Richter.

CHAPTER NINETY

LAKEWOOD

"STEPHEN IRONS"

Thornton and I went to the downtown NISCO office and picked up the small package with Sally's name on it. There was an envelope attached and I wanted to open the envelope at least, but I resisted. I placed the package on the kitchen counter as the phone rang and I noted 'City of Norfolk' on the ID read out. I touched the Speaker ON and responded, looking for a call from Millers, "Is that you Sam?"

"Stephen, it's Linda, Sam's off with my car, he totaled his," Linda sounded okay, not still groggy as she had been on Sunday. Hopefully she had some good news,

"Any news about Ella or Ursula Volk?"

"No, not about Ella, but I've got some other info for you and I need your help. Can you pick me up at Operations and give me a ride to get Shirley's van back from the shop? I'll be able to talk with you when you pick me up."

"Sure, I'll be there in ten minutes." I hung up the phone and grabbed my keys. Thornton moved with me toward the car, but he declined joining me and offered,

"You need to get a gun Rusty, you're not really prepared if you're running around naked." I slammed the Volvo's door and pulled out of Sally's driveway. In the rear view mirror I watched Thornton fade in the distance.

I saw Linda standing in front to the main entrance to the Operations Building as I turned right off of Virginia Beach Boulevard onto the small street that led into the Police Operations complex. I stopped and Linda got in the Volvo, "Any news since you called?"

"Not any more about Ella, but Shirley's van's Green-Gifford on Military highway it started running rough when I took Shirley home from the hospital so I took it in. It's ready now, can you drop me off?"

"Sure, I know where that is, what did you want to tell me? You mentioned something else on the phone."

"All this mess with the Taylor's and Judge Knutson doesn't seem right to me,"

Linda began but I interrupted as we crossed under the overpass and turned left onto Military Highway headed north, "Are you involved with those cases too?"

"Not really, but thinking about them is a distraction for me. The FBI's confirmed the weapon found in Ursula Volk's bag was used to kill Bradshaw and put Dr. Ski in the hospital, so we've got Volk dead-to-rights we just need to find her. Maybe she knows where Ella is."

"Do they have any idea where the weapon came from?"

"Millers interviewed a couple of 'gang bangers' who had a run-in with Volk, they were able to ID her picture. She took the weapon from them near Chin's apartment, probably right after she killed Chin and dumped him in the Lafayette River."

"Sounds like you've got Ursula Volk wrapped up, but what about the Taylor's and Judge Knutson?"

"I'm not sure, Chief Beck's running those, he promised to keep me up to speed on them."

"Could the suicides have been staged, you know, like Wilber?"

"I don't think so they seem legitimate," Linda began but her cell phone interrupted our conversation as we approached the Princess Anne/Northampton intersection that crossed Military Highway. "Knowles" she answered, paused 10 seconds and I heard, "Yes, that's great, where?" 5 seconds later,

"Yes, we're right there - Stephen, take a right on Northampton, head toward Shore Drive and speed it up," Knowles directed and got back to her caller, "How many other cars?" 10 seconds,

"You're joking! Okay, we'll do it ourselves, I'm with Irons in his car we'll check it out for you. Call me back if you get more." Linda closed her cell phone and said to me, "Some off duty cop thinks he saw Ursula Volk's BMW headed north, here on Northampton, no more than a couple of miles from us."

CHAPTER NINETY ONE

SHORE DRIVE

"STEPHEN IRONS"

I concentrated on my driving as we sped east on Shore Drive. Linda was getting antsy and said, "Stephen, I know I saw a BMW come off Northampton onto Shore, have you seen it since we turned off behind it?"

I searched the road for some sign of the dark BMW we were trying to follow before responding, "No, I saw it turn onto Shore too, but I haven't seen it since. We've gone a mile or so now, do you think they knew we were following?"

"No, I don't think so, but maybe, damn it, I'm just not sure. Looks like they may have given us the slip, let's double back and see if there was an earlier turn-off they could have taken." Linda instructed.

I came off the gas and pulled up on the emergency brake as I rotated the steering wheel hard left attempting to turn the small car rapidly around as we neared the Taste Unlimited outlet at the intersection of Shore and First Court Street. As I fought the little car's side-sliding bounce-attempt to give way to inertia and roll over, I came back hard right on the steering wheel, released the emergency brake and gained some traction-purchase immediately. I pulled the wheel hard left to compensate for the Volvo's bouncing inability to make the tight left turn without skipping its way across Shore Drive. After several more steering reversals and accelerations I was able to work my way back to the center of the road and straighten out my intended direction of travel. Now, reversed and under control, I pushed the gas pedal to the floor and sped back west on Shore Drive, back toward Northampton Boulevard. As we approached the exit we had taken earlier, Linda pointed at the first stop-lighted intersection, Shore Drive and Greenwell Road, the one we had sped through after turning off Northampton. Linda said,

"The BMW could have turned off Shore either way here, north toward the Bay or south down Greenwell. I remember the light was GREEN when we sped through, damn, Stephen do you think we're following Volk and she has Ella? It could have been her at the zoo, she's big, taller and heavier than me, she could have impressed Shirley with her size and strength. Stokes said she was strong and she could have gotten in and out of the zoo, she has all the keys. But she can't be doing all this on her own someone's got to be helping her. Lets give the Bay Bridge Tunnel a shot she's no more than 10 minutes ahead of us, head toward the tunnel entrance she could have someone she working with on the Eastern Shore."

"Good idea," Oh Damn, I thought about what Cooper had told me about the Bay Bridge tickets. I didn't want to involve Cooper, so I said, "Linda I forgot, to tell you, the FBI found some old Bay Bridge Tickets in the parking lot when they first picked up Ursula Volk's trail. She could be going that way to get out of the area, giving up on the computer discs." I watched Linda contemplate this information before she went another direction,

"Bridge traffic's seems slow, stop at the toll booth, there's a possibility for some information on the BMW." We drove up on to the Bridge access road to the toll plaza and I pulled off to the right of the toll booth and stopped, "I'll be right back," Linda said as she exited the car, holding her badge out for identification. Her short jacket flared as she removed her ID and I could see the 38 S&W she carried on her left side, butt end slanted forward, toward her right hand draw. She's definitely prepared, I thought, because I knew she had left her GLOCK 26 in her purse.

There were only a few cars processing through the toll plaza, traffic was very light in this direction and only two of the booths were manned. I remained in the car and watched as Linda ran toward the nearest booth with her badge out, "I'm Detective Knowles, Norfolk Police," I heard her announce as she approached the middle-aged toll operator and thrust the ID into the payment area of the booth. After the booth operator had assured herself that the ID was genuine, I heard,

"I'm Carroll, how can I help you Detective?"

"We're following a dark, late model BMW, tall gal with long dark hair driving it. Did a BMW come through your gate recently?"

"About 10 minutes ago, the tall gal driving seemed in a hurry, looking back toward the beach like someone was following her. You want me to call ahead, see if she's cleared the other end?"

"Can you stop cars exiting the Bridge?" I heard Knowles ask as a big FORD truck began to pull into the booth area where Linda was standing.

"Not without help, but my sister Mary's working the other side alone, not much traffic tonight, if the BMW was still in a big hurry, Mary might notice it coming off the bridge,"

"OK, check with your sister, I'm headed back to my partner's car, it's a private auto, okay for us to come through?"

"Sure, I'll tell the 'Head Troll' it was 'Police Business' but I've got a question detective," Linda stopped and turned to look back probably wondering about the 'Head Troll' comment. Then we both heard the toll lady yell,

"Look out sir!" she yelled to the driver of the large FORD 150 Truck as it lumbered into her toll booth area, "you've got to wait a minute, this is Police business," The FORD 150 stopped short of hitting Linda. Linda now looked pissed but seemed more anxious to see what the toll booth lady wanted.

"Is this gal moving drugs?" The Toll lady's question held Linda's attention, still blocking the waiting truck and she replied as she moved back toward the toll booth,

"I don't think so, why do you ask?" The truck driver began lean on his horn and honk, *BLARE, BLARE, BLARE,* Linda stopped her travel and approached the driver, showing her badge as he looked down on her from his high cab and I heard Linda yell,

"Sir if you don't knock that off I'll arrest you on the spot! Do you understand me, you asshole?" I'd never seen Linda react so strongly, she was definitely strung out about the interruption. The toll lady went on,

"The driver had a long package in the back seat all wrapped up in a dark brown sleeping bag could have been a lot of drugs," Linda turned and ran toward my car allowing the truck driver to process through the booth,

"Keep going north, Stephen, Ursula Volk's been through here and she's probably got Ella!" Linda exclaimed to me as she slammed the door and I floored the Volvo,

"The toll lady saw Ella?" I asked, not sure I overheard that part of their conversation correctly, because of all the truck noise.

"No, but she said the tall gal was in a big hurry and had a long package wrapped in a sleeping bag in the back seat. We're onto Volk, Stephen, we'll get Ella back."

I felt like crying for joy but I said, "Shouldn't you call someone on the Eastern Shore for help, State Trooper back-up, or surveillance?"

"I don't have any contacts there and my cell phone's getting weak, I don't want to waste a lot of calls trying to come up with a contact, but," Linda paused and decided to try Millers, he was off somewhere in her car. As she touched Speaker function I heard,

"Millers, is that you Chief?"

"Sam, I'm with Stephen and we're after a late model, BMW, we think its Volk and she may have Ella. We're headed north on Route 13, about to enter the second tunnel complex, damn," Linda's cell phone went dead as we became surrounded by the tunnel, "The cell just died, or it's the tunnel."

"Don't you think you should try to call from a real phone? Maybe when we get on the Eastern Shore?"

"Yes, maybe, but we've got to hurry now," she answered, and I could tell she wanted to do it all herself. "We've got to keep going until we find Ella. I'll call the State Troopers when we get on the Eastern Shore, you're right they could be our best bet."

I looked ahead as we cleared the second tunnel. Straining my eyes against the darkness and I could see the two large curving bridge structures that were lit up like strings of landing lights heading north, leading us onto the DELMARVA Peninsula to save Princess Ella.

CHAPTER NINETY TWO

STARFISH MOTEL, 7 PM

Ursula Volk placed Ella on one of the beds in the motel room, she was a very light bundle tied loosely and wrapped in a canvas sleeping bag. Volk watched Ella's breathing to make sure she was okay. Her breath came in calm drafts, deep and quiet, all the signs of restful sleep. Ella would be out for another 4 to 6 hours Volk thought as she laid Ella gently on the bed. She checked the time, it was just after seven. There could be some news on a local channel. Volk turned the TV on and cycled through local channels but there was nothing new, she paused on WAVY 10 to watch a report on the Saturday Halloween celebration at the zoo. Initially they were showing kids in costumes everywhere, then the focus of the coverage changed and the news program replayed an earlier segment concerning Norfolk Police Detective Linda Knowles' daughter, Ella, believed to have been kidnapped during the celebration. The local Police, and the FBI, were still searching in Hampton Roads for Ursula Volk, wanted for the murder of a Norfolk Police Officer and believed to have been involved with the kidnapping. The news segment closed showing a Virginia Zoo employment photo of Volk and a picture of Ella with her mother. The caption below Ella's photograph asked viewers to, CALL 1-888-LOCK U UP if you have any information.

"Lock me up? I don't think so," Volk laughingly announced to the TV as she clicked it OFF and her cell phone rang. She flipped the top of the cell open, hoping it was Alex she hadn't been able to reach her for the last two days. Volk was concerned about not hearing from Alex but sadly the phone's caller ID showed, 'VA Cell'. Volk sighed knowing it was her expected caller at least they'd waited as she had demanded,

"Volk, go ahead," she answered and then listened for 20 seconds.

"No, everything's good, no problem with the girl, she's sleeping." 30 seconds,

"Are you sure you want to do that tonight? I've got her and she's the leverage I need to get out of here, I think meeting right now might be a mistake." Volk listened for another 20 seconds to see how her caller would respond,

"Yes, yes, I understand. I can meet you if you'll help me out of here when I turn her over," She listened again, evaluating the opportunity to close this mess

"No, but we can meet near the zoo, at the back in the park would be good it's secluded, can you meet me there?" Volk listened again for 20 seconds thinking this was her last chance to get rid of the girl and pick up the discs,

"OK, I'll bring her near the picnic tables by the back service gate you can get her then." 10 seconds,

"Yes, that could work. Its 7:15 now and it'll take me a couple of hours to get back in your area. I'll meet you near the back gate at eleven." That should confuse everything, Volk thought, then, she listened 20 seconds more,

"Yes, they were following me earlier, but I lost them. Don't worry the girl's okay she's got at least four more hours of drugs in her, see you near the gate at eleven." Volk closed the phone satisfied with her conversation. She reached for her jacket and placed the cell phone and her room key in a pocket with the Police snub nosed 38 S&W she had reloaded then Volk exited her room and walked to the small restaurant to get a beer and something to eat.

CHAPTER NINETY THREE

ROUTE 13 NORTH

"STEPHEN IRONS"

We continued north until we passed a small motel on Route 13 and Linda told me to drive quickly through the parking lot looking for the BMW. With no luck there, we got back on Route 13 and headed north again. Now, in the distance, I could see a second motel, a much larger one, the neon sign proclaimed: Starfish Motel, VACANCIES NOW. Trying again to get help, I said,

"Linda, we've got to stop and call someone. This is dumb, how much longer are we driving north looking for Volk without calling for some help?"

"Okay Stephen, let's check the Starfish out." she answered, "I haven't been able to get anyone on my cell, I'm sure the battery's dead. I'll use the motel's phone to call the State Police and check on what's happening in Norfolk."

"I'm sure you're right, here's the Starfish," I said pointing up ahead on the left, "we can go in, you make your call and I'll ask people about the BMW."

"Sounds like a plan," Linda paused and touched my right arm lightly, then, she added, "Better yet, I'll go in and call while you check out the parking lot and let me know what you find." She grabbed her purse, exited the car and added, "No heroics Stephen, come get me if you find something."

"Okay," I said. I really wanted to stay with her, but she was right we could do a lot more separately. Linda got out and moved away toward the motel office and I headed to the southern most wings' parking area to check for the BMW.

There were about twenty rooms, ten on each of the two floors, and as I moved around the lower part of the motel wing, I noticed four cars and three trucks. It was dark and took me five minutes to make sure two big cars parked weren't BMWs then I moved around back to check out the rooms in the rear. As I rounded the corner area, noticing that none of the back rooms in this wing seemed to be occupied; there were no lights on and no cars parked nearby. I was headed toward the northern wing when I heard two distinct gunshots, *BANG*, *BANG* they sounded like a 38, could be Linda shooting. I reversed my tracks and ran back toward the office.

Thornton caught up and cursed me for splitting up, "Damn Rusty, when're you going to learn? You've got to stay and protect your buddy, at least as long as your buddy's still alive." Thornton words were sad, a condemnation about his own death and a reminder of my past and present errors in judgment.

I rushed into the office and noticed all the commotion was in the small café next to the office. I saw Linda, sitting on the floor, holding her right arm, her 38 lay on the floor next to her. I rushed toward her,

"It's Volk Stephen," Linda began slowly, almost a whisper, "I yelled at her with my gun out, but she shot too fast." One of the waitresses was coming to Linda's aid with a large towel to stop the bleeding from her arm. The motel manager, yelled,

"Hey, I called 911... Frank and MK are bringing their Emergency Unit from Cape Charles. Take 'em 'bout 10 minutes." The manager said. I bent down near Linda assuming Frank and MK were Emergency Medical Techs and began to help a short waitress, name-tagged Missy, place the towel around Linda's right arm. As I picked up her 38 from the floor and slipped it into my pocket, I noticed the small hole in her jacket, chest centered, near her heart. Linda had been hit with both shots. Lifting her jacket carefully I could see the chest wound was beginning to seep a small amount of blood onto her white blouse. Damn, I've done it again, I thought, I left my partner and this happened. God, I prayed it didn't hit anything major.

"Linda, she hit you in the chest too, are you alright?" I was afraid to tell her about the close proximity to her heart, maybe it was a lung shot,

"I'm feeling weak Stephen, hard to breathe, maybe my lung. In the purse, take the GLOCK, go after her Stephen, save Ella, please," Linda said, as she fell back into my arms. I'll be okay, Stephen," she barely whispered to me, "Find Ella, please," Linda tilted her head up toward my face, there were tears streaming from in her closed eyes. I helped the waitress place another towel under her jacket, and instructed,

"Missy, please keep pressure on the towel until the EMERGENCY TEAM gets here. The chest wound's beginning to seep, but you should be able to manage." Maybe the bullet did get a lung Linda was definitely having trouble breathing. A car noise startled me and I looked up toward the large front window and saw a dark BMW speed out of the parking lot and turn left onto Route 13, headed north.

"That's got to be her, what room?" I asked the manager, still standing by the phone,

"She's been here about a week she's in 207, in the back of the north wing.

Here's a pass-key." I took the key and paused, I had Linda's 38 in my jacket already.

I opened up Linda's purse, took the GLOCK and headed to room 207, "Missy, try to keep her calm. Keep the towels tight on both wounds, I'll check out 207 for her daughter. Have your manager call the State Police and let them know what's happening, the driver's wanted for murder and kidnapping." I put the GLOCK behind my back, tucked in my belt, and ran out carrying Linda's 38 in my right hand.

It took me and Thornton a couple of minutes to find room 207, the door was wide open. I entered cautiously, Linda's 38 held extended tightly in both hands, close into my body for stability and protection. I found a small half empty suitcase, several empty beer cans thrown around the room and impressions on both beds, they had both been occupied. One of the impressions was small, like it would be for an eight year old wrapped in a blanket. Thornton said,

"We've got to hurry Rusty, this shit's gotta' end soon!" We ran from the room, back toward the office, got to my car, started it and drove north on Route 13, Thornton was right, he and I would have to do this on our own.

Thornton and I had driven four miles on Route 13 North, when I sighted the Emergency Response Vehicle heading south toward the Starfish Motel with the vehicle's lights blazing brightly against the night's darkness. I breathed a sigh of relief and continued on. A mile later I spotted a State Trooper car, speeding south following the emergency vehicle. The trooper spotted me, reversed rapidly across the highway and came after me. I pulled over, stopped and he caught up in 30 seconds. He exited his state trooper car and approached me, "You Irons?" he asked,

"Yes," I said through the open window, I saw his name was Trooper Matthews, "I'm Stephen Irons."

"We've got two other Troopers after the BMW, Knowles is still unconscious, they're working on her and taking her to the Emergency Room at De Paul, in Norfolk."

"Is Knowles okay?" I asked,

"Not sure, but Chief Beck wants you to meet Knowles at the hospital. Troopers will do the search for the BMW. I'll catch up with the ERV and you follow us to DePaul." After the trooper sped around me and turned back after the ambulance, I was hesitating, wanting to go north after Ursula Volk and Princess Ella. Thornton saw my reluctance and turned to me and said,

"You've got to do what he asked, Rusty, the Troopers will get Volk, you've got to go help your partner." Thornton brought tears to my eyes, but he was right, so I reversed direction and headed south back toward the Chesapeake Bay Bridge Tunnel.

CHAPTER NINETY FOUR

CAPE CHARLES ERV, NORFOLK

With the state trooper leading, the Cape Charles Emergency Vehicle sped along at 60 mph turning right onto 64W working its way toward the De Paul Medical Center Hospital. The ERV followed the trooper car off the Tidewater Drive Exit then crossed Tidewater Drive with lights blazing and siren blaring out against the quiet night. MK, the attending EMT in the back of the small van was trying to keep Detective Linda Knowles stabilized, "Frank, her BP's starting to go to hell in a hand basket, she must be bleeding internally, is there a closer place?"

"No MK we're committed to DePaul, but I'll call again, we'll need a full 'crash team'. We just crossed Tidewater Drive, the State Trooper will probably go down Thole Street then left on Granby, to De Paul. I'm guessing three minutes MK,"

"We've got to hurry Frank we're going to need some BIG help soon."

Detective Sam Millers limped around the entrance area in the Emergency Room. He had a soft cast on his left leg and a heavy sling supporting the plaster cast on his left arm. He chastised himself, "Keep busy Sam try to find the doctors, the nurses, find out what's going on with Knowles. Do something Millers!" He mumbled to himself, then voice loudly, "Dr. Kramer, where in the hell are you, man?"

"Please Detective, don't use that kind of language," the small Catholic Nurse said, "You've got to move aside now, the Cape Charles ambulance is only a few minutes away. Dr. Kramer be here with the 'crash team' soon, please let them do their job." Millers backed off and out of the way as the crash team moved around him, then, he looked out the glass sliding doors and saw the state trooper and the ERV turn off Granby and pull-up near the Emergency Room entrance. Dr. Kramer and his staff hurried out the door to help the Cape Charles EMTs transfer Knowles.

CHAPTER NINETY FIVE

BAY BRIDGE TUNNEL

"STEPHEN IRONS"

As I cleared the Chesapeake Bay Bridge exit area, I was certain Ursula Volk was still headed north with the Virginia State Troopers in hot pursuit. I slammed my fist into the steering wheel I had missed the opportunity to ask about the BMW when I tried to pay the toll coming back. Mary, the gal working the toll booth, knew my car tag and cleared me through. She wished me luck and I was so moved by her concern for Linda that I pressed on reasoning I would have seen Volk's car coming back on Route 13 if she had reversed back toward Norfolk herself.

Silently I prayed for Ella, for the State Troopers after Volk, and for Linda, hopefully by now receiving emergency treatment at DePaul and fifteen minutes later, I was headed north on Granby Street and could see the Virginia Zoo sign on the right marking the entrance to the area where this mystery seems to be focused. I keep going north through the Riverview shopping area and over the bridge where Eric Chin's body turned up. I crossed the bridge and ran the red light at the Willow Wood Drive intersection, now just a mile from DePaul Medical Center, looking for the Emergency Entrance.

As I pulled in toward the ER's adjoining parking lot I saw another one of Norfolk's Mermaid statues guarding the side entrance to DePaul. This mermaid had beautiful golden hair with embedded mirror pieces as scales. The mirror pieces were reflecting near-by Granby Street light sources and when I got closer I could see the mermaid had a nurse's cap on and a stethoscope draped around her neck. Her face was Mona Lisa warm with a smile of welcome and compassion.

Parking I could see the two medics and the ERV from Cape Charles and decided to talk to them before I tried to see how Linda was doing. I approached their vehicle as the medics were climbing in, ready to leave, "Hi, I'm Stephen Irons," I said as I showed them my retired Sheriff's ID, "I was with Detective Knowles, how's she doing now?"

"Not that good, her vitals were slacking off," the long haired gal in the passenger seat said, "She's definitely some internal bleeding. She went into 'arrest' on me but I got her re-started and re-stabilized… The driver interrupted,

"The hospital's working on her now. She'll go to surgery then the ICU. I'm not sure they'll let you see her but there's another Norfolk Detective with her."

I breathed a sigh and asked before I headed in, "I saw you coming south on 13 when I was running north, chasing the shooter, did you happen to see a dark blue BMW headed north before you got to the motel?"

"That could be the gal we saw," The EMT in the passenger seat started to answer, but I interrupted,

"What do you mean 'gal you saw'?"

"We saw this BMW headed north, it passed us reversed to the south and sped up until it caught us. Then, she ran with us with her lights OFF all the way to the motel. We could see she was a big gal with dark hair, MK tried to wave her away but she just stuck to our right side until we approached the motel, then, she hit her lights ON and sped off toward the Bay Bridge Tunnel." The driver said.

"Shit, she was hidden behind your vehicle when I passed you I couldn't see the bitch." I exclaimed as I left the ERV crew and turned to head into the Emergency Room. I pushed past the large doors and headed toward Millers, standing half way down the hallway. "Sam is she going to be okay?" I yelled as I approached Millers, now standing near the Emergency Room desk with his left arm in a sling and his left leg in some kind of cast, his eyes were filled with tears, "Oh no, Sam, what's happened?"

"Nothing yet, I'm praying Stephen, you should too. She critical, but they're working on her now with a full staff." At that very moment, I knew I couldn't stand to lose another partner. All this killing had to end. Millers continued,

"I'm sorry Stephen, Linda hasn't regained consciousness yet, I know they're trying everything they can."

Sam helped me sit down on a nearby chair. I hung my head into my hands and my mind began to race about Ella, Linda, Ursula Volk and the Virginia Zoo. After a minute, I said to Sam, "I've got to go outside and get some air I've got to go sit outside." I offered, deciding to act on my own.

"Okay, you sit down outside, I'll be right there after I check with Dr. Kramer and the State Troopers. You sit outside, I'll be right there." I could hear Millers' voice fading away as I passed out the Emergency Room door and began to run toward my car. Volk had come back to Norfolk, she had to be at the zoo looking for those damn computer discs and she must have Ella with her. It was about time I went back for one of my buddies, it was time I went for Princess Ella. My mind flashed back to Linda's last words to me, *"Take my gun Stephen go save Ella."*

CHAPTER NINETY SIX

NORFOLK

"STEPHEN IRONS"

Tears were starting to block my vision as I drove away praying for the doctor to save Linda. I wiped my face dry as I sped past the nurse mermaid and got back on Granby headed south toward the Virginia Zoo and a confrontation with Ursula Volk. I felt in my jacket pocket, noted Linda's 38 and was further comforted by the biting pressure against my spine from her GLOCK 26 slipped into my belt under the jacket.

I drove over the Granby Street Bridge again, past the 7-11 on LaVallette and turned left headed toward the back service entrance to the Virginia Zoo. Turning right into the park, just past the tennis courts, I stopped on the grass area near the zoo's tall chain-link fence. I could clearly see the large structure known as the elephant barn and I got out and walked to the fence to look closer. The fence was very high, possibly 12' and topped with a two foot span of tightly stretched barbed wire slanting inward, not an easy climb-over for me in any condition.

Looking through the vines and small bushes, I could see Volk's BMW parked near the elephant barn. I looked around the car and saw the large door into the barn was propped open and there was a faint light coming from the interior, but no sign of anyone near her car. I returned to my car and drove to the back service entrance to the zoo hoping Volk had left the gate open. There was no Zoo Security in sight and the fence was gated and padlocked shut. Thornton was already inside watching me and said,

"Volk's still got a key Rusty, park your car near the gate so you can climb up on the windshield to get over the gate."

As I worked my way onto the car, I could see the Volvo was going to be too low to help me get on very top of the barbed wire gate and I thought about climbing the wire fence from the car but the extra height and barbed wire strands would definitely cause me some problems. I didn't want to be injured when I confronted Volk so I looked around for help of some kind to get me over the top of the gate. Near the back service entrance, about three feet from the gate, I saw a large garbage dumpster that held all the accumulated trash from the picnic areas in Lafayette Park. Near the dumpster there was a stack of construction materials being used to repair a stockade type fence nearby. I collected three of the 12' stockade rails and leaned them against the side of the dumpster then I moved the car close to the dumpster to help me climb up. Once on top of the trash dumpster I pulled the long stockade poles up, one by one, until I could fabricate a three rail bridge, slanting up from the top of the dumpster onto the top of the gate, a distance of about 8'. I lay prone on the fence rails and pulled my way up the rails until I was able to roll myself over the top of the back gate and hand crawl my way down the chain-link fence to the ground.

On the ground I checked my jacket for Linda's 38, still secure in my pocket. I felt the pressure from the GLOCK on my backbone but I reached around to assure myself it was actually there. Feeling the small automatic I caught up with Thornton and ran down the perimeter road. I was as prepared as I was going to be, Thornton yelled to me,

"Come on Rusty, we've got to save Princess Ella."

CHAPTER NINETY SEVEN

VIRGINIA ZOO, ELEPHANT BARN, 10:30PM

Ursula Volk tapped her digital watch as she moved in the dim lighting of the elephant barn and saw, 10:30PM. She had arrived at 10 and after looking for the three computer discs she was pissed to have found nothing. Someone else had been in the barn and taken the damn discs from her hiding place. It had to have been Dennis he was the only one who would have known about this hiding place and she was sure he now had a key to get in the tool box. Volk remembered the FBI jerk that stopped her from climbing up earlier, she had been lucky to get out of here then. But Dennis must have figured where she was trying to go and gotten the discs for him self. She'd settle with Dennis later, she knew where he lived.

After her failed search Volk decided to stay and have her confrontation here in the barn. She was certain her partner would see her car and know she'd changed plans. Volk had locked the three elephants out of the barn but the smell and residue from their earlier confinement was heavy in the air and on the floor of the now vacant stalls. The sliding door that separated the stalls from the outside holding yard was not completely closed, an opening of about 18" allowed Monica to swing her trunk vertically in the stall, smelling for Ursula Volk.

Volk had decided the barn would be a better meeting place than near the service gate. Much more hidden and she knew she could use the elephant's accessibility and her ability to control them as an advantage to close this business out before she departed to go after Dennis and the computer discs. After she dealt with Dennis and retrieved the discs she'd be glad to put Mermaid City far away in her rear view mirror before heading to Canada or Mexico. Everything was closing in on their operation and Volk knew this meeting would not go well. She got a six-foot folding stepladder, opened it up and placed it under the empty hanging net near the first elephant stall. The net normally held a bale of hay for the elephants to rip into with their trunks then devour the chunks of hay they were able to pull out with their trunk's excessive strength and grip. She undid one end of the hay net and let it hang open, ready to receive and hold Ella captive. She came down the ladder and moved back toward the large table where she had placed Ella. The elephants could be dangerous but Volk could use her ability to influence them to her advantage, even against one of her biggest human foes. Approaching the table Volk opened the top of the sleeping bag and noted Ella's eyes were beginning to flutter, she was starting to come out of the sedative. As Volk reached for Ella to move her to the hanging net, a voice from the darkness spoke directly to her,

"What are you doing Ursula?" the voice was totally familiar to her.

"She's starting to come out of it Os, I'm checking to make sure she's okay." Volk replied as she began to feel under Ella's sleeping bag, looking for the jacket that held her gun. Os was early and had found his way to the barn, not a big surprise.

Os stepped out of the shadows and began to walk slowly toward Volk with his weapon extended and pointed down toward the red-restriction-line on the floor of the elephant barn. In the dim light Os looked even bigger than Volk knew he was. "Ursula , you've got to cut and run here," Os said as he walked along the line moving closer.

Volk finally felt her jacket just under the edge of Ella's sleeping bag and maneuvered her hidden hand, reaching for the gun. The weapon still had four live rounds, the four that remained after she shot Ella's mother twice. The gun was in the jacket pocket, an S&W 38 Police Special, certainly enough to stop even a big ox like Os.

"Step away from Ella, you need to leave while you can. Go back to San Diego, maybe Mexico. I can straighten this mess out and you can walk away clean if you go now." Os said as he put his own weapon in his holster then raised his arms to show his big, empty hands while he continued to block her most obvious exit from the barn. Volk made her decision as she slid her hand farther under Ella, reaching for her weapon and moving Ella into the path Os would have to fire through if he redrew his own gun. Volk pointed the gun over Ella, still wrapped up in the sleeping bag,

"Help, help, I'm tied up. What's that smell?" Ella yelled coming fully awake.

"Its okay, Ella, you're in the elephant barn." Os offered trying to quiet Ella then he said to Volk, "Don't be a fool Ursula you can leave without my interference if you leave now, but, if you stay, you'll suffer the brunt of this business. You'll be the 'dead scapegoat' I can guarantee it."

Ella turned her head toward the familiar voice, she knew Sheriff Os, and she was certain he must be here to help her get away from her kidnapper, "Sheriff Os, help me! Where's my mom? Where's Stephen?" Ella cried out.

Ella's screaming was upsetting Monica, whose ever-present trunk still protruded into the barn swinging up and down into the empty stall. Monica showed her concern with a large *BELLOW* erupted from Monica's trunk and filled the barn, quickly bringing the other two elephants bunching up behind Monica, shoving her hard against the large sliding door, trying to push their way into the barn.

Volk realized the chaos was beneficial to her and she reached her keys up above her head to activate the OPEN switch that would slide the door fully back and allow the three elephants into the closest stall. As Volk turned her head away to insert the key and find the correct switch, Os stepped from the dim lighting into a totally dark area of the barn and Ella yelled, "Os, Os, don't go, help me Os,"

Volk picked Ella up and began to carry her toward the ladder leading up to the hanging net and as the outside elephant door began to slide open she called, "Monica, move up! Monica, come forward!"

"Don't be stupid, Ursula." Os' warned from the darkness as the sliding door opened and all three elephants, led by Monica, entered the first stall.

"Show your self Os," Volk demanded toward Os' last know position, "Show yourself or I'll toss the girl in with the elephants RIGHT NOW!"

CHAPTER NINETY EIGHT

VIRGINIA ZOO

"STEPHEN IRONS"

As I worked my way into the elephant barn, I heard Ursula Volk threaten Os with harming Ella. I held my breath with fear as I crept closer into the darkened barn with Linda's 38 extended in my right hand then I heard Ella cry out, "Os, Os, help me, Os." and I started to yell back, to warn Volk against hurting Ella and to let Os know I was here to help. But when I saw Volk carrying Ella toward the advancing elephants my heart jumped into my throat and I panicked. Before I could recover or respond, I heard from another dark corner of the barn, Os' unmistakable voice,

"Don't be stupid, Ursula, put the girl back on the table and step away from her. I'll let you leave and no one will know you were here. Be smart Ursula, it's the only way for this to work out for you."

Jesus, I thought, Os is trying to talk Volk out of this, he must have guessed she came back to Norfolk just like I did. But, how could Os guess that? And why would he want to let Volk go? She's responsible for several killings, including one police officer. She's got to be stopped. I finally pumped-up my courage and was about to yell at Os when Volk responded,

"No, way Os, you've screwed me too many times in this operation. You've been getting my instructions and checking on me, and now, you're the asshole that's trying to expose me just to save your own black ass. It's not going to work Os, the girl's going in with the elephants and you'll have to try and save her while I get away."

Volk took several steps toward the stall where one of the elephants had pushed up against the edge of the bars. Using her long trunk the nearest elephant spread her ears wide and grabbed the small metal ladder and hurled it sideways, *SLAM* the ladder crashed loudly against the back wall of the barn and ricocheted off the concrete as the other two elephants pushed into the stall and squeezed up against the bars. I watched frozen to my position when two of the front confinement bars began to bend outward as almost 30,000 pounds of combined elephant weight pushed heavily against the bars.

Volk heard the ladder crash turned and saw the metallic strain on the steel bars and immediately gave the command, "Cita back up, Lisa back up, Monica stay!" Volk shouted, her attention focused on controlling the elephants to her advantage.

Still groping for words to speak I watched as Os stepped out of the darkness and hit Volk a massive punch to her kidneys. Ursula Volk folded up from the force of his strike, released her gun and relaxed her grip on Ella. As the gun CLATTERED to the concrete floor, Ella slid from Volk's grip still wrapped in a protective sleeping bag.

Os looked down at Volk, scooped Ella up in his left arm and retrieved Volk's gun while she remained disabled on the concrete floor. The elephants, now thoroughly agitated began to bellow together,

BRRAAPPT, BRRAAPPT, BRRAAPPT sounded out from the three excited animals.

Ursula Volk still on the floor, stunned by Os' kidney punch, tried in vain to open her mouth to speak. I fought to speak too but my mouth was dry with fear as Os held Ella upright with his left arm and pocketed Volk's gun. I watched stunned as Os pulled his own service revolver from his holster and point it down at Volk. I finally found my voice and began to yell, "NO, Os, don't shoot her, I'm here to help Os,"

Os turned his head toward me momentarily, then, looked back toward Volk. He shook his head in dismay, paused for only a second then he steadied his gun toward Ursula Volk and fired two quick shots into her convulsive body, CRACK, CRACK the rapid reports echoed loud and sharp in the barn and the elephants began to trumpet again,

BRRAAPPT, BRRAAPPT, BRRAAPPT, sounded out again as Volk's extended arm fell lifelessly to the barn floor and Ella screamed,

"Aiiiiiiiiieeeeeee help me Stephen HELP MEEEEEEE!"

CHAPTER NINETY NINE

VIRGINIA ZOO

"STEPHEN IRONS"

As I approached Os and Ella I carried Linda's 38 extended and angled down toward the concrete flooring of the elephant barn. I hoped to appear non-threatening to Os while he held Ella close to his left side. Os' weapon remained in his right hand, pointed down toward Volk's lifeless body as I said, "Os, you should have let her live, she was no threat to you, here let me help you with Ella." I offered my statement calmly as I came out into the dimly lit area and began to move closer to Os and Ella, anxious to have Ella in my own arms.

"Scrap, you're surely a stubborn cuss," Os said as he rotated his body and raised his weapon to point directly at me. "But soon, you'll probably figure all this out. Stop now, one more step and Ella goes in with the elephants. Stop and put the gun on the floor now, then, kick it over to me!"

"No don't do this Os," Is all I could say as I began to kneel down and place Linda's 38 on the concrete floor. I pushed the gun toward Os as he directed then I continued down to the floor finally kneeling on the red-restriction-line about ten feet from Os and Ella maybe four or five feet from Linda's 38. I tried again, "Os, why, are you doing this?"

Ella seemed confused, looking first up at Os, who was still holding her tightly against his huge chest. Then, she looked toward at me, sad like she was pleading to me to help her out of this mess. As Ella continued to wiggle attempting to free her self, she yelled to me confirming my hope that she understood who was really trying to help her,

"Stephen, I'm all tied up, help me Stephen." Os responded to Ella's wriggling by squeezing a little harder and shifting her so he was looking directly at her face. Still pointing his gun at me, Os said,

"Be quiet Ella," He demanded as he moved her body even closer to his face so he could look directly into her eyes. Then, his lips formed a nasty smile and he went on, "If you don't keep quiet I'll kill Stephen before I throw you in the elephant poop."

His statement shut both of us up. Os now took the opportunity to holster his weapon and reach in his uniform pocket for Ursula's gun. Os shifted Ella slightly and pointed Volk's gun at me as he squeezed Ella close to his own chest.

I finally overcame my growing fear and recovered my ability to speak, "Os, what's this about? Are you involved with these killings?"

"Yes and no, Scrap, this mess got bigger than my involvement. It's a Chinese thing Wilber stumbled on, or, maybe he just made it all up, who knows?"

"Wilber, what do you mean?" I asked, stalling, searching for a way out of this mess.

"You knew Wilber. He was always reaching for some startling concept to write a book about. Well, this time he was about to expose some Chinese secret program, but," Os paused to allow the nasty smile to come back over his face, "Then, it all went bad with Volk and Eric. After that, with you checking around for Taylor, it actually turned into a 'Chinese Fire Drill'," Os paused to laugh at his own humor, before he added "Sorry about the poor joke, Scrap, but you know what I mean, their operation was getting out of control. Volk worked for the Chinese and Eric was her muscle, I was meant to be a 'go between' for the Chinese, but you know me, I tried to be more of a 'Controller'. Sadly, I wasn't much good at that." Os paused again seeming to contemplate just how he could have done a better job of controlling Volk, so I said,

"What happened to the Os that got me started as a Deputy Sheriff?" I was trying to stall until some possible solution could present itself.

"I changed some, Scrap, needed more of everything. Then, when it all came available, I just couldn't resist the temptation. But, it started to turn into a real mess right after you signed up. You know, the money and the temptation made the mess for me, but the mess is going to end soon, sadly with you and Ella killed by Volk's gun just before I arrive. Then, I show up and take Volk out, saving what's left of the day. Sounds pretty good, huh?"

"Detective Millers knows about the zoo Os, he's on the way with a bunch of uniforms to catch Volk, I just got here first." Sounded logical to me and I definitely needed more time and a lot more help to stop Os from executing his plan.

"Sorry for your bad luck Scrap, sounds like my plan will still work," Os responded, "you'll surely be a hero again, trying to save Ella, but, you'll be a dead hero this time, like Judge Knutson was supposed to die when you jumped in front of him seven months ago. Its sad Ella has to go too, but those things do happen, even little kids have bad luck sometime. Someone's got to clean up the mess in here Scrap and looks like I'm the one with a big enough shovel to do the job."

"Os, you can't want this to go on, don't you feel bad about the deaths you've been involved with? Judge Knutson was your friend and what about, Peggy Turner, her death has to be sad for you?"

"You're right Scrap, Taylor's wife shot Peggy. Charles was seeing Peggy, my fault there, I introduced them. It's real sad about the Taylor's and Judge Knutson, they were involved in something 'big' I didn't know about. I guess I can understand their guilt pushed them over the edge."

I watched Os' eyes closely now, the light was dim but I thought I had saw a sympathetic reaction so I tried again, "Os you've got to want this to end,"

Os interrupted me immediately, "Scrap, I do believe you're stalling, but we've got to move on, especially if Millers is on the way." Os finalized. My stalling was over and mentioning Millers headed this way had backfired on me. I had to move on now,

"Os, you can stop now, let me have Ella. You can put an end to all this killing."

"I don't think so, Scrap, I've found the thing about doing something really terrible is that in a day or two the terrible stuff is all forgotten and you just move on. Even something as terrible as all this, you and Ella, it's sad, but it'll pass for me Scrap." Os replied thoughtfully.

Still on my knees on the concrete floor in the smelly elephant barn I silently sent a prayer and tried my last chance, "No, Os, not Ella, she's a 'LITTLE PRINCESS'," I shouted hoping Ella would react somehow. But, I wasn't really sure what she could do while I continued to delay and reason, with Os. I was still stalling,   "Ella's confused, Os, she's just an eight year old 'Princess', she'll never convince anyone what she saw here, your word will override her. Please, Os, Ella can't hurt you, let her get through all this."

Os paused again he seemed to be thinking about my request, looking back and forth between Ella and me. As he became occupied with the decision, I tried to scoot forward, toward Linda's 38, but Os recovered and shouted at me, "Stay where you are, Scrap, I'll kill you right now if you move again."

"Os just let Ella go, Please,"

"I don't think so Scrap." Os, now responded, looking directly into Ella's eyes, "Even as much as I like this little gal." Os paused and affectionately pulled Ella closer to him, almost embracing her, "But she's a threat to me Scrap, and you know I don't like threats," As Os spoke, bringing Ella closer to his face, she turned her head toward his exposed neck and thrust her small chin rapidly forward. Then, with all her eight year old strength, Ella opened her mouth wide and bit as hard as she could onto Os' bull-like neck, sinking her white eight year old teeth onto Os' black throat, clamping down onto his neck as tight as she physically could. Ella's attack was fast and unrelenting and she hung on for both our dear lives. Feeling the instant pain, Os reacted,

"Jesus Christ" he yelled, still holding on to Ursula Volk's weapon, but he had to use both hands to try and raise Ella's body high enough above his head to force her attacking teeth out of his neck.

I saw my opportunity and I pulled Linda's GLOCK 26 from behind my back and fired three shots directly into Os' exposed gut, aiming at the center brass button on his uniform jacket, *CRACK, CRACK, CRACK,* the spiked reports from three rapid 9mm rounds reverberated through the elephant barn and the three spent casings *RATTLED AND CLANGED* onto the concrete floor.

Os slumped to his knees with the impacting force of the three shots, shook his head slightly then slowly released his hold on Ella. As Ella slid toward the floor, rolling inside the sleeping bag wrappings, the elephants reacted to the three shots with their ears flapping wildly and their trunks raised-up high in aggression. Their voices joined together, filling my senses with loud trumpeting,

BRRAAPPT, BRRAAPPT, BRRAAPPT, once again echoed throughout the elephant barn.

Os shook off the elephant noise trying to clear his mind as he attempted to recover from my first three shots. He looked directly at me and half smiled as he began to raise Ursula's weapon toward my position, "Good shot Scrap, right on center mass. But sheriff's vests are nylon and titanium these days too damn good for three shots from that little gun. Its tough Scrap but you'll have to look me right in the eyes,"

With the elephant noise echoing in the barn, Os voiced his challenge and made his last smiling effort to bring Ursula Volk's 38 up to finish-off his plan. I took in a short breath let it slide out held and carefully aimed the GLOCK at his massive face. Holding steady with a two-hand grip I squeezed off one last effort, trying to put an end to this whole mess, *CRACK* the fourth shot from Linda's GLOCK erupted without a jitter, blowing the center of Os' large familiar face to oblivion.

As the final brass casing *JANGLED* onto the elephant barn floor and the mass of hamburger meat; now residing where Os' face had last challenged me; slid down and fell away, Os was finally dead on the concrete floor.

I rushed forward and scooped Ella into my arms and moved her away from the bloody mess. She was probably going into shock, now shaking her head from the ringing in her ears, but the sleeping bag had protected her against the fall and hopefully shielded her from witnessing the end. I placed her back on the table and she looked okay, her eyes were slowly coming back into focus. I undid the zipper on the sleeping bag, but kept the bag wrapped loosely around her for warmth as I loosened the ropes binding her small body. Finally I was calm enough to reach in the sleeping bag to untie Ella and hug her close. Tears filled my eyes, as I spoke to her, "Ella, I love you," I said, as I rocked her close in my arms,

"I remembered Stephen, I remembered the 'Problem Princess' and self defense." She whispered, trying to smile up at me, but then, her eyes rolled back and she collapsed.

Detective Sam Millers, Zoo Security and three uniformed Policemen rushed into the elephant barn while I spoke quietly to Ella,

"You saved us both, Ella. You'll always be my Princess." I murmured through my tears of relief. "The police are here now, Ella everything's going to be okay." I whispered to her as Millers and the other officers closed in. I was starting to cry uncontrollably now, I had lied to Ella, everything was not okay, far from it, she had gotten through the kidnapping and threats of ending her young life, but her mother remained critical at DePaul.

"Knowles is going to be okay, Stephen, Dr. Kramer found the problem and stopped the bleeding. They fixed her lung. She's going to be alright."

THE END

EPILOGUE

TUESDAY, OCTOBER 31ST NORFOLK, VIRGINIA

"STEPHEN IRONS"

Ella and I drove to DePaul to see Linda at 10AM, Ella stayed with her mom and Thornton and I headed to Norfolk Sentara to check on Special Agent Davis. Thornton was reluctant to talk in the car but he finally said, "Rusty I think we're done now, you're focused on Ella and Linda now. They'll be better at keeping you straight than I ever was. You've always been my best bud Rusty, but I'm tired, I need a rest. You talk to Ella now, she'll keep you straight. Don't let her down, stay modest but keep a mean streak in reserve. Your time to be okay is here now." Thornton said as he faded to a soft camouflaged pattern then broke into a million pixels dissolving into nothing.

BEIJING, CHINA

Niam Wang listened on the phone to the President of China, and finally answered, "Yes, my President, Iron man Cheng chose to join his ancestors by his own hand, our crisis is past, sir, 'Deep Dragon' is history."

NORFOLK, VIRGINIA, 5:30PM,

"STEPHEN IRONS"

After I checked on Davis at the hospital, Sally called me at home. She had picked up an extra trip and would be back late Thursday evening. I told her about Cooper's package and she allowed me to open the gift. As Wilber wanted, she had deeded the business property to Donald Adams and Lydia Harrington. Emotionally drained I decided to break from everything and handle the Halloween kids coming to our home.

Long after the trick or treat kids departed, I poured my self final glass of gin and went to the den. The presentation clock, a gift from the Betty and Cooper, chimed out twelve distinctive tones as October turned into November and I strained to look through the dim lighting to read the CIA's tribute to Wilber for his service:

PRESENTED TO

COMMANDER WILBER HARRINGTON, USN RETIRED

FOR HONORABLE SERVICE

MAY 3, 2003 TO SEPTEMBER 23, 2006

ABOUT THE AUTHOR

Murder in Mermaid City fictionally occurs in and around Norfolk, Virginia and provides a unique travelogue to inform the reader on local history and the many interesting places and events in and around Hampton Roads. The story's time frame of September/October, 2006 is supported by incorporating quoted articles from the archives of The Virginian-Pilot and the author's candid descriptions of local establishments and events past and present while the story engages the reader.

The unique premise of a weather driven apocalyptic future creates another intriguing page-turner by the local author of "The Methuselah Solution"; (XLIBRIS, COPYRIGHT 2000, ISBN# 0-7388-3216-2); a retired USAF pilot credited with over 700 combat missions in South East Asia and personally awarded: The Silver Star, The Superior Service Medal, 2 Distinguished Flying Crosses, The Bronze Star, and 34 Air Medals in the service of his country.